GHOSTS
OF
GOTHAM

ALSO BY CRAIG SCHAEFER

The Daniel Faust Series

The Long Way Down
Redemption Song
The Living End
A Plain-Dealing Villain
The Killing Floor Blues
The Castle Doctrine
Double or Nothing
The Neon Boneyard

The Revanche Cycle

Winter's Reach
The Instruments of Control
Terms of Surrender
Queen of the Night

The Harmony Black Series

Harmony Black
Red Knight Falling
Glass Predator
Cold Spectrum

The Wisdom's Grave Trilogy

Sworn to the Night
Detonation Boulevard
Bring the Fire

GHOSTS

OF

GOTHAM

CRAIG SCHAEFER

47NORTH

Through a circle that ever returneth in

To the self-same spot,

And much of Madness, and more of Sin,

And Horror the soul of the plot.

—*"The Conqueror Worm," Edgar Allan Poe*

One

With a plastic bud nestled in his ear and a camera concealed in his shirt pocket, Lionel Page had a front-row view at the scene of a crime. Bodies packed into the Union Life Hall, sweating under the hard white lights, stomping their boots on grainy vintage floorboards. Lionel sat sandwiched shoulder to shoulder, and when the entire gallery shot to its feet with a cry of ecstasy, they pulled him up with them. A human tidal wave marinating in the stench of body odor and cheap floral perfume.

"Are you saved?" shrieked the man of the hour. The Reverend Wright dominated the stage, a whirling dervish in a twill suit the color of vanilla ice cream, howling into his microphone. The crowd howled right back at him.

"Are you *redeemed?*" he demanded to know. *Yes,* the devoted roared back. They thrust their hands to the hot lights like they were trying to climb to heaven. The man on Lionel's left rolled his eyes in a fit, showing bloodshot whites as he thrashed his head up and down. When the shouts faded and died, a woman's voice crackled in Lionel's right ear.

"This is the last time I ever doubt you."

Lionel's gaze flicked to the aisle. A long line of parishioners, half of them hobbling ahead on walkers or with canes, waited for their turn in the spotlight. Reverend Wright waved one up to the stage—an elderly woman dragging an oxygen tank behind her like a prisoner with a ball and chain. Lionel casually raised his wrist to his mouth. A tiny gray plastic teardrop dangled in front of his lips, with a wire running deeper up his sleeve. A spreading pool of clammy sweat plastered his shirt to his back.

"You said that last time," he murmured. "Tell me something good."

"The whole operation works just like you thought it did."

Lionel smiled for the first time all day. "We got audio?"

"Enough to crucify him. Get out of there before anybody recognizes you. I've got two more guys hidden in the crowd, one on the balcony shooting B-roll."

The auditorium hall fell into a hush as the reverend laid hands on the elderly woman's tangled cotton hair. He looked to the lights, his sweaty face glowing.

"I'm getting a . . . Oh, Lord, here it comes," he said. "Yes. Mabel. Your name is Mabel, isn't it?"

Her cry of "It *is!*" was almost drowned out under a sea of cheers and applause. She looked at the reverend like he was the second coming while Lionel sank deeper into his stiff wooden chair. He folded his arms across his chest, his thoughts slowly circling like a shark in dark waters as he watched the show.

"Mabel. Beautiful, blessed Mabel." Wright put the heel of his palm to his forehead and squeezed his eyes shut. "The Lord tells me you're struggling. You've got a demon in your lungs, choking out that good, sweet air. It's emphysema, isn't it? They diagnosed you just last year. But the doctors don't know everything—no, ma'am, they do not."

Lionel raised his sleeve to his mouth again.

"You got the Technical Twins in the van with you?"

"Always," the woman's voice replied.

"Can they jack the PA system in here?"

"I assume they already—" She paused. "Wait. Lionel? What are you going to do?"

Onstage, the reverend was anointing Mabel's brow with water from a shiny plastic bottle. Miracle water, free with your prayer gift of twenty dollars or more. The shark in Lionel's mind circled faster, homing in on the scent of blood.

"I'm done watching this," he said. "Back me up. Get the audio ready."

"No." The woman's voice had a knife-edge sound. "*No*. You are surrounded by about eight hundred die-hard believers in the power of Reverend Wright. Now is *not* the time to play Emperor's New Clothes. They can learn the truth the same way as everybody else, on the nine o'clock news. Get out of there."

He was already on his feet, rising with the crowd, a thunderous cheer pushing him forward. Mabel hugged Wright in her frail, birdlike arms as tears streamed down her face.

"These people are being robbed," Lionel breathed into his concealed microphone. "They deserve the truth. Here and now."

"You're going to get yourself killed. *Lionel*—"

Mabel hobbled offstage, and Wright spread his arms like he wanted to embrace the whole room.

"Another miracle in the making! Remember, folks, I'm no healer. No, sir, no, ma'am. Only a vessel for God's divine truth. It's your faith, and the love of the Lord, that will set you free. Can I get a hallelujah?"

Lionel burst into a run. He bounded onto the stage, spinning, and threw his hands high.

"*Hallelujah,*" he shouted as the crowd fell into a confused murmur. Grinning like a madman, he darted over to stand at Wright's side. He did a little foot-shuffling dance and snapped his fingers, pointing to the reverend. "Hallelujah, praise the Lord, and praise the good Reverend Wright. Ladies and gentlemen, my name is Lionel Page. I'm a reporter for Channel Seven News, and I had the honor, the inestimable honor, of sitting down for a rare interview with the reverend and his beautiful wife, Marise, earlier today. It was candid, heartfelt, and I hope you'll all tune in for it."

Wright goggled at him, the showman off-balance and pushed to the edge of the spotlight. "I . . . Well, yes, everyone, that's true, and Mr. Page was a very good interviewer. But I'm not sure this is the right time to—"

"I *would* hope you'd tune in," Lionel said, "but that interview will never air. I don't think the camera was even turned on. No, it was a ruse—a lie, not to put too fine a point on it—to get backstage access. Where, as I took the grand tour, I planted a number of tiny listening devices."

The holy glow faded from Wright's face as his blood drained into his feet. The microphone drooped in his hand, going down in slow motion. "What?" he asked, almost too soft to hear. The crowd murmured and milled, uncertain, casting hard looks at Lionel. They didn't know what was going on, but they all agreed they weren't happy about it.

"See, I'm curious by nature," Lionel told the sea of angry faces. "When I see a magician, I always want to know how the tricks are done. And in this case, well . . . it sure isn't magic."

The PA system popped and squealed. A tinny voice drifted from the speakers: the reverend's wife, secretly recorded from her backstage perch.

"Next up you've got, let's see . . . Mabel Abrom . . . Abromo . . . God, something long and Polish—just call her Mabel. She sent in a prayer card last month asking for help with her emphysema. Oh my God, the dumb bitch hasn't quit smoking. Tell her Jesus says to kick the habit and keep the line moving, or we're gonna be here all night."

Wright took a staggering step back, looking wide-eyed at the speakers. A shadow fell over the crowd, the mood shifting from confusion to slow-brewing anger. High on a spike of adrenaline, Lionel felt their attention swing back and forth across the stage. It was a sniper's scope, zeroing in, Wright's betrayed flock deciding who they wanted to pull the trigger on. The backstage curtains beckoned, offering his last chance of escape. He kept his feet planted.

"His hotline isn't to God, folks." Lionel tapped his earpiece. "It's to the lovely Marise, who uses ringers in the ticket line to spy on you before you come inside, combs through your cards and letters, then feeds all that 'miraculous' information right into his left ear."

The PA system squawked again. Another snatch of stolen audio crackled over the speakers.

"You're doing great tonight, hon," Marise said. "Okay, this is Chester. Chester has an open Facebook account. God, how did we do this before social media? They make it so easy for us. Oh, nice. His ex-wife's a slut, and his nephew is a junkie. Don't mention the wife, just tell him Nephew Billy needs to get right with the Lord and stop running with that gang."

Two years ago, Lionel had reported at ground zero in the middle of a blackout riot. He'd never forgotten the feeling of violent energy, a psychic tornado swirling all around him, hundreds of people turning into one mindless and brutal fist. Here he was all over again, standing in the eye of the storm. He was too exhilarated to be afraid.

"The only true thing he's told you tonight is that he's not a healer. He's not. He's a cheap carny playing cheap carny tricks." Lionel leaned over and snatched the bottle of miracle prayer water from the reverend's shaking hand. He held it up to the stark white lights. "And this? This is tap water, folks. They fill it from a garden hose out back."

He uncapped the bottle and unceremoniously flipped it upside down. A stream of water splashed across the old, scarred floorboards, soaking his sneakers, spattering Reverend Wright's polished white leather wingtips.

"It'll cure your thirst," Lionel said, "but that's about it."

The auditorium hall froze, silent and still. The empty plastic bottle fell from Lionel's fingers. It hit the floorboards, bounced, and rolled to a dead stop at the footlights.

Then the stone-faced audience became an avalanche. The crowd surged as one and rushed the stage, clambering up with an animal roar.

Spontaneous factions turned on each other and shouted as they threw punches and swung chairs, the still-believers and the betrayed clashing like swords against shields. Tiny wildfire melees erupted all over the theater, people hauling on each other's arms to yank their friends back from the fight. Order and pious bliss broke under the pressure of electric, violent chaos.

Lionel had about five seconds to see what he'd done, torn between pride and regret, before a beefy fist coldcocked him. Then he fell. He hit the stage on his back, curled into a fetal ball, and drowned under a tidal wave of bodies and kicking feet.

Two

"You're an asshole," Brianna said.

The voice in his ear, the angel on his shoulder, stood silhouetted in the doorway of Lionel's hospital room. She tossed a wave of kinky black hair and put a dark hand on her hip. He rolled his head back, the mattress feeling like concrete under his aching back, and closed his eyes.

"Love you, too, cupcake."

"You know that crowd could have torn you apart," she told him. "You do understand that, right? You're lucky there were more people angry at Reverend Wright than at you. He says he's suing, by the way."

"He can stand in line and wait his turn. Did we get the story?"

"We got the story," Brianna said. "That footage is ratings gold."

She stepped into the room. The hospital door fell shut at her back. As she stood at his bedside, the antiseptic air took on a whiff of hibiscus perfume.

"But you shouldn't *be* the story," she told him.

"I was angry."

"Yes, you were."

He opened his eyes and squinted at the overhead lights. The fluorescent tubes hummed softly in the stillness. A potted plant sat on his bedside table, some mutant conglomeration of red-and-purple blossoms, with a primly lettered card reading *From Your Friends at Channel Seven Chicago*.

Nobody else had sent flowers. That bothered him, for a heartbeat, until he realized he didn't know anybody outside the newsroom.

"I saw those cheap little con artists," he said, "squeezing pennies out of old people with their 'magic powers.' I couldn't stand by and let it happen."

"Totally understandable. After all, the root verb of the word *reporter* is 'jump in and start a riot.' Oh, wait. No. It's *report*. My bad."

"But I did report," he said, giving her his best look of pure innocence. "I reported from the stage, live and on the scene."

She rubbed his shoulder. Her hand moved in gentle circles, and she gave him a reluctant smile. "Jerk."

"You love me and you know it."

Lionel shifted on the mattress and groaned. His left hip felt like he'd been hit with a steel battering ram. His fingertips probed against the outlines of a spreading bruise.

"So why aren't you happy?" she asked him.

"I am happy. I'm plenty happy. We exposed a fraud, did a public service . . . I'm happy."

"But," she said.

He forced a chuckle and looked up at her, spreading his hands.

"But? There's no but. Just like there's no magic and no miracles."

Lionel's gaze went distant, just for the span of a slow breath. "There never is."

Brianna nodded, to herself as much as to him, and turned to study the plant on his bedside table.

"I don't even know what this is," she said.

"It's pretty." He paused, catching her sideways glance. "Garish. Pretty garish. But thank everybody for me anyway."

"Thank 'em yourself—you're getting discharged in a couple of hours. Apparently there's nothing seriously wrong with you except, you know, that you're an asshole, and they just don't have the technology to fix that yet. We can only stand by and hope for a cure."

Lionel stretched his arms above his head, then suddenly wished he hadn't. His attempted yawn came out as a choking yelp as his back muscles caught fire.

"Yeah, think I'm gonna need a day off and some Tylenol 3. How's my face?"

She studied him, stroking her chin. "You really want to feed me a straight line like that? Pass. Too easy."

"Ha. But really, though."

"You look like you've been in a fight, but like, a 'shoving match in a bar' kind of fight, not a 'first night at Fight Club' kind of fight. Nothing a little concealer and the right lighting can't fix. Also, you've got an interview with the *Chicago Observer* folks at two. They want to talk all about your book, and I already told them you'd be there with bells on."

"What, you're my boss *and* my agent now?"

"Positive press for you means positive press for the news team. You wrote a *book*, Lionel. Milk it. Play the celebrity, just a little bit, okay?"

"I thought I wasn't supposed to be the story," he said.

"Consider it penance for your misdeeds," Brianna told him. "Go and sin no more."

⌒

The hospital kicked Lionel out with his rumpled suit, a prescription for some mild painkillers, and a bill. He called a Lyft and rode across town in the back seat, crawling slug slow through the afternoon traffic. The towers and shopping utopias of Michigan Avenue rose up like canyon walls of white marble. Lionel felt sleepy from the sun, staring at store windows without really seeing what was on sale. It idly occurred to him that he'd been looking at the same scenery day in and day out for so many years, he didn't really see any of it anymore. His mind filled in all the blank spaces with pictures from his memories.

He passed from the air-conditioned car into the breath-stealing summer heat, thankful for the hint of a breeze coming in off the lake. Then he pushed through a revolving door and into an icy tomb; somebody had cranked up the cooling system to museum levels. Lionel couldn't complain. He signed in at the front desk like always, trading everyday nods with the everyday security guards, and rode a stainless-steel cage up to the twenty-third floor. Karen, Brianna's perpetually overworked admin, stopped him at the edge of the newsroom. Lionel reached for the Starbucks cup in her hand, and she yanked it away from him.

"Brianna's," she said, "not yours. Bad reporter."

"I'm the worst. Still, no coffee for me?"

"Interview for you." She jerked her head back, nodding at a polished glass door behind her. "Your two o'clock can't tell time; he's been here for half an hour already. Brianna says remember to smile."

"But, coffee," Lionel said. He stared at her cup, forlorn. "After? I get coffee after?"

"There's a kiosk down in the lobby, and they're open all day long. Knock yourself out."

He came up with a quip, but she was already gone, bustling across the crowded floor and taking the coffee with her. Lionel indulged himself with a deep breath, let it out in a sigh, and set his sights on the interview-room door.

The reporter from the *Observer* could have been Lionel a decade ago. A bushy-haired kid, ink still wet on his college diploma—or more likely, he was interning for credit between classes—wearing his dad's hand-me-down suit. He jumped up from the glass conference table, almost knocking his chair over, and pumped Lionel's hand like a puppy with a new bone.

"Thank you so much for your time today, sir—"

Lionel had to smile. He gestured to the abandoned chair and pulled one back for himself. "Please, call me Lionel, and it's no problem. Happy to talk to you."

The kid fumbled with his notes. He had a voice-activated recorder, a yellow legal pad, a fat envelope, and a hardcover book, all spread out in a jumble. Lionel's face stared out from the cover of the book, under the title *Crackpots, Quacks, and Messiahs: Tales from the Fringes of Journalism.* The photographer had touched him up in post—turning his eyes a deeper shade of blue, banishing any hint of gray in his wispy chestnut hair—and dressed him in a bulky jacket that looked like someone's idea of what an adventurous, globe-trotting reporter should wear.

"Okay, so we're recording—" The kid froze with his finger on a little red button. "Is that okay? That we're recording?"

"Sure. Little tip, though? Always carry a backup, and make notes as if you weren't recording at all. That way—"

"Like your interview with Bill Clinton!" the kid chirped. "I mean, what would have been your interview, if the batteries hadn't died thirty seconds in."

Lionel leaned back in his chair, impressed. The memory was almost too distant to sting. "And I never made that mistake again. You really did your homework, didn't you?"

"Well, like you said in your book, always go in prepared." He rapped his knuckles against the book. "So. You've developed a reputation as a . . . professional debunker, I guess you could say. You've covered faith healers, psychics, art and literary hoaxes. Is it fair to say that most of your professional career is centered around tearing people down?"

Lionel blinked. "I . . . Well, no. I don't know if that's fair. I mean, technically, sure, but exposing criminal acts isn't 'tearing people down,' it's a journalist's job. We investigate and we report the truth."

"But what about objectivity? Aren't we supposed to report both sides of the story?"

"You're assuming there are two valid sides," Lionel told him. "That's just not always true. If somebody is claiming the earth is flat or the moon is made of green cheese, we're under no obligation to provide them with equal time against people who have the facts on their side."

The kid checked his scribbled notes. His fingertip slid down his legal pad, his brow furrowed in concentration, like he was trying to divvy up a restaurant bill.

"So you consider it an undeniable fact that there's no such thing as psychic phenomena, no miracles, nothing that can't be explained by science?"

"Not at all." Lionel rested his hands flat on the table. "It's an undeniable fact that I've never *seen* any. It's also a fact that every single person I've ever met who claims such powers has turned out to be a con artist or self-deluded. Find me an honest-to-goodness miracle, and if it checks out, I promise you, I'll be the first one filing a story on it. I'm just not holding my breath."

"But Mr. Paget—"

"*Page.*" Lionel's voice was a whip crack. He took a slow, deep breath to steady himself, locking eyes with the kid. He felt like a mouse watching the steel lever of a trap thunder toward his neck in slow motion. "My name is Page."

The kid reached for the envelope.

He opened the flap and took out a magazine. A tattered issue of *People* from January 2002, with a candid shot some paparazzo had taken from the safety of his car. Close angle on a stone-faced teenager, trudging down a high school's steps and carrying the weight of the world in his backpack. The cub reporter held it up to give Lionel a good look, pointing to the bright-yellow log line: "Ten years after the Emerald Ranch Massacre: catching up with 'The Real Boy Who Lived.'"

"This *is* you, isn't it?" The kid looked from the picture to the older, tired man sitting across the table. "You're Lionel Paget."

Lionel shoved his chair back and got to his feet. "This interview is over."

The kid followed him to the door, brandishing the magazine like a talisman, and out into the newsroom. "But this is a valid news story. The public has a right to know what happened, how it shaped your life, why you disappeared—"

Lionel spun on the ball of his foot and got right into the kid's face. He dropped his voice to a growl.

"I disappeared because of people like you. And I swear to God, if you follow me onto that elevator, the second the doors close I will knock you the fuck *out*."

The kid stayed put, rooted to the floor, watching Lionel walk away. Lionel waved Karen over as he marched to the elevator bank.

"Tell Brianna I'm taking a couple of days off," he told her.

～

This was going to happen eventually, Lionel told himself. Intellectually, he knew the past wouldn't stay dead and buried forever. It never did. He had just always hoped it would be some far-off and nebulous *later*. It wasn't like he'd been buried in witness protection, and he was surrounded by people who dug up secrets for a living; the only reason they'd never put him under the microscope was because they'd never had a reason to.

He jumped into a yellow taxi at the curb and told the cabbie to take him home. He had some thinking to do.

For the first time in his life, he was grateful for the dawn of the twenty-four-hour news cycle. Let the *Observer* break the story and out him. Lionel could endure his fifteen minutes of unwanted fame, and he'd be forgotten the second some celebrity or politician did something—anything—vaguely interesting. It wouldn't be fun, and his coworkers might not look at him the same way ever again, but he could take it.

I should get ahead of this, he thought. The cab rumbled over a pothole, and he shifted on the patched vinyl seat as he tugged his phone out. *I have to level with Brianna, at least. She should hear it from me and not some dipshit rookie reporter, assuming he hasn't already flashed that magazine at everyone who knows me.*

He didn't have time to dial. His screen lit up as a call came in. A local area code, from a number he didn't recognize. Part of him hoped it was someone from the *Observer*, somebody in charge over there. Lionel still had a full head of steam built up, and he felt like venting it.

"Yeah," he said.

The woman on the other end of the line had an aged and delicate voice, tinged with an accent. *German,* he thought. Something about her made him think of Marlene Dietrich.

"Mr. Page, good afternoon. I apologize for the intrusion; we haven't met. My name is Regina Dunkle, and I would appreciate a few minutes of your time."

He felt off-balance, his anger deflating like a pinpricked balloon. "I . . . don't suppose you're with the *Observer*?"

"I'm afraid not." She chuckled politely. "And I have no intention of exposing your personal secrets, unlike a certain aspiring journalist."

A gust of cold air from the taxi's vents hit Lionel as he hunched forward in his seat. It washed down the neck of his shirt and drew an icy finger along his shoulders.

"How did you—" He paused, catching up with his runaway thoughts. "How could you know about that?"

"Money, Mr. Page, opens all kinds of doors. And I have a good deal of money to throw around. Very little knowledge is denied to me. Yes, I know who you are, and what you endured as a boy. I also don't care. I'm more interested in the man you've become, and your rather unique talents."

"You've got my attention. What's this about, Ms. Dunkle?"

"A story. I have a lead for you. It's either an elaborate hoax—the kind you've spent most of your career debunking—or a window into a historical mystery. Either way, I want the truth, and ferreting out the truth is your specialty. Grant me twenty minutes of your time. I'll pay you for your trouble, and if you choose to pursue the story, you'll have the exclusive rights."

He'd taken calls like this before. People—most of them lonely shut-ins—who wanted to show him the face of Jesus on a piece of burned toast or proof of aliens landing in their backyard. Normally he'd pass it to the newsroom, let some intern waste their time chasing down a lot of nothing. This was . . . different, though. It was something in her voice, something stable as a rock but electric, her cold confidence luring him in.

"I can give you fifteen," he told her.

"Excellent. I'll expect your arrival soon, then." He could almost hear the contented smile on her lips. "And Mr. Page? Please don't keep me waiting."

Three

The address Regina gave Lionel was in Lincoln Park. The cabbie dropped him off at the corner, outside a black wrought-iron fence that curled around a terrace. His mysterious caller hadn't been lying about having money to throw around: she lived in a three-story brownstone at the east end of the neighborhood, poised with a perfect view of the rolling green parkland and, beyond it, the waters of Lake Michigan. Lionel looked up at the venerable mansion and whistled low, while a breeze off the lake ruffled his button-down shirt. A place like this would run three, four million dollars, minimum, and she had intimated it wasn't her only house. "My *Chicago* residence," she had called it on the phone.

He let himself through the unlocked gate, rang the doorbell, and waited.

Eventually the door opened, and Lionel stood face-to-face with Regina Dunkle. She looked the way her voice sounded, like a silent-movie star in her twilight years. He imagined she had aged like a fine wine, her dark eyes sharp and her hair a flowing mane of silver. She stood draped in a satin housecoat the color of a full moon and beckoned him inside. Her every move, even the casual wave of her hand, felt calculated with precision and grace.

"Mr. Page. Please, come in."

He nodded his thanks and stepped across the threshold. She closed the door and led him to a parlor just off the foyer, where scalloped rugs of sea-foam blue decorated a white marble floor. Chairs and a divan, clustered near a cold and silent hearth, were upholstered in the color of freshly fallen snow. The cool, still air carried the faint scent of roses.

"Please, call me Lionel," he said. He glanced around, looking for any hint of a maid or a butler. "Do you live alone, Ms. Dunkle?"

"If I am to call you Lionel, you must call me Regina." She settled into one of the chairs and gestured for him to take the other. A tea service had been set out on a mahogany table between them. A wisp of steam rose from a delicate china teapot. "And yes, I prefer to live alone. It must seem foolish, all this space for one woman, but privacy is something I've always valued."

"Which didn't stop you from digging into my life."

She quirked a tiny smile and picked up the teakettle.

"I believe in keeping secrets, Lionel. You can't *keep* a secret if you don't *know* the secret, now can you? Chamomile?"

"Huh? Oh. Tea. Sure, thank you."

While she poured for both of them, he took another slow look around, studying his surroundings with a reporter's eye. He suddenly realized why the room had felt wrong from the moment he walked in.

No photographs. No artwork. No knickknacks or memories on the fireplace mantel. The parlor was more sterile than an operating room. It didn't seem like anybody really *lived* here, in the way that people clutter and put a personal touch on the places they call home. More like a badly staged set, or a vacant house prepared for sale by a real estate agent.

"Have you lived in Lincoln Park for long?" he asked.

"I summer here, when I can." She finished pouring and met his eyes. "The lake air is good for my respiration. Honey?"

"Little bit."

"I think you'll enjoy this," she said, taking up a spoon. "I'm very particular about my honey. Quality makes all the difference."

"I don't want to rush things along, but this lead on a story—"

"Is best discussed like civilized persons."

She reached out to him, offering a teacup on a delicate saucer. She lifted her own cup in salute, took a sip, and waited in expectant silence until he did the same. The tea was rich, clean, layered in herbs that danced on his tongue with a sinuous, sweet undercurrent.

"And now we can be civilized," she told him. "Do you read for pleasure?"

"Sure. Probably not as much as I should, but I like a good book. Mysteries, mostly."

"I'm not surprised," Regina said. "You strike me as a man irresistibly drawn to mysteries. My personal passion, when it comes to reading, is dark romanticism. It was a movement of the eighteenth and nineteenth centuries. Mary Shelley and Lord Byron . . . dark romantic literature carried a keen, almost obsessive, fascination with the macabre."

"Horror stories."

"Nothing so banal as a hockey-masked killer with a machete, chopping up camp counselors," she said with a wink. "More of a dark celebration. These authors understood that there was beauty to be found in the grotesque. Revelation, in the heart of madness. Have you read Poe?"

Lionel gave a little shrug. "'Quoth the raven, nevermore'? That's about all I remember from high school English, I'm afraid. That and the story about the guy walling up his friend in an alcove."

"'The Cask of Amontillado,'" Regina replied. "You know, Poe drew on real history for that. In Persia, it was once a common punishment for thieves to be sealed into pillars out in the desert. They were walled up in a space so tight they couldn't move a muscle, like a standing coffin. All they could do was wait, and suffer, and *bake*. Dehydration is an exceptionally cruel way to die."

"I . . . was not aware of that," Lionel said.

She set her teacup down.

"Come with me. I want to show you something."

He rose, and she led him down a silent hallway.

"Hopefully not a cask of Amontillado," he said, catching the nervous edge in his own voice.

She glanced over her shoulder and favored him with a faintly impish smile. "To my knowledge, *you* haven't stolen from me."

Wooden doors rolled open, looking in on a library. A capital-*L library*, with artfully rounded floor-to-ceiling shelves that curved like frozen mahogany waves. Spines of pressboard and cloth and old leather packed every shelf. Thousands of books, gilt lettering glistening on the covers like veins of golden ore. Amber lights glittered from a crystal chandelier positioned over a single antique armchair and a side table at the heart of the room.

"My humble collection," Regina said as she ushered Lionel inside.

The air smelled faintly of dried spices and felt a few degrees cooler than the rest of the house. As Lionel strolled the stacks, passing a rolling ladder granting access to the highest shelves, his practiced eye picked out tiny climate-control gauges and the gray plastic eye of a motion-sensor alarm.

"I don't know if *humble* is the word I'd use," he murmured. "You've got some museum-quality stuff here."

"Oh, an abundance. I'm fond of first editions, rare folios, one-of-a-kind pieces. The story is the important thing, of course, but collecting is a pleasurable pastime. To that end, I have dealers in select cities across the world with standing orders to contact me, should they come across something unique that falls under my purview."

Not a spot of dust on the shelves. Lionel turned away from the books.

"I'm assuming that's what you called me about?"

"In 1845," Regina said, "Edgar Allan Poe was in New York City, working as the editor of the *Broadway Journal*. He published a short story in December of that month, 'The Facts in the Case of M. Valdemar.' The titular figure, Ernest Valdemar, agreed to an experiment while on his deathbed. He was mesmerized, placed into a trance. And through that trance—even as his body died, and his heart ceased to beat—he continued to speak and answer questions. This continued until he was released from the trance, at which moment his corpse rotted to nothingness before the horrified onlookers' eyes, including Mr. Poe himself."

"But . . . it was a story, right? Fiction."

There was something cagey in her smile. She held up a finger.

"That's the interesting part. He first published it as a piece of eyewitness journalism. Caused quite the stir back in the day."

"I'm thinking," Lionel said, "people were a little more gullible in 1845 than they are today."

"Oh, quite to the contrary, and *you* of all people should know better. Haven't you spent your entire adult life exposing hoaxes? If nobody believed in charlatans, there'd be no need for you to reveal their tricks, now would there?"

"Gotta admit, you have a point."

"Poe was fond of the occasional hoax, too," she said, "and soon he published a retraction, making it clear the story was merely a piece of speculative fantasy, and that there was no such person as Ernest Valdemar. But that didn't settle things. For years afterward, some people insisted that it was a true account, and that his disclaimer was a cover-up. Then, there's this."

Regina glided across the library floor, the train of her satin housecoat drifting behind her. She slid a black leather binder from a shelf and held it out to Lionel.

"I acquired this at an auction in London last year. It's a letter—authenticated by handwriting experts—from Rufus Griswold. He was a poet of the day, a friend of Poe's, and an investor in the *Broadway Journal*."

Lionel carefully opened the folder. The single page inside—yellowed, tattered, and sealed under vacuum-tight plastic—had only a few terse lines written in a cramped hand.

45/11/02

Edgar—absolutely not. Mad if you do. I say, tell them this beastly piece of fairy-cake is just that, a nightmare you wrote down after eating some bad sausage. You'll cause an uproar if you call this a factual account. For the love of G-d, man, at least change that ending. Some stories shouldn't be told.

—RWG

Lionel looked up from the page. "Sounds like he didn't take his friend's advice."

"He didn't take half of it. My contact in New York reached out to me last night. A manuscript has surfaced on the private art market: the handwritten first draft of 'The Facts in the Case of M. Valdemar.' The very one that Poe likely showed to his friend Rufus." Regina took a step closer to him. Her eyes caught the light from the crystal chandelier, glittering. "I'm told it has a different ending. The *real* ending. I would very much like to read that story, Lionel."

Lionel closed the leather binder and handed it back to Regina. He studied her, feeling uneasy, catching the trail of her floral perfume in the cool library air.

"I'm not sure what that has to do with me," he told her.

"My desires are well-known in collectors' circles, especially after I obtained that letter last year. There's a very good chance that the manuscript is a hoax. A forgery, custom designed to part me from a large amount of my money. You've built your career upon exposing swindlers and thieves; you've got a nose for ferreting out deception, and I don't think you even realize just how good you are at it."

She slid the folder back into its place on the shelf and turned to face him.

"I would like to retain you as my right hand in this matter. Go to New York. If the manuscript is real, I want it. If it's a fraud, I want to know who created it. I'll pay for your transportation, your lodgings, and any and all expenses you might incur. Money is no object. Needless to say, if it is a hoax, you'll have full rights to the story; I only ask that you share the outcome of your investigation with me, privately, before bringing it to the world."

Lionel shook his head. He paced the oaken floor, lacquered boards groaning softly under his footsteps.

"I gotta tell you, Ms. Dunkle—"

"Regina."

"Regina, it's . . . it's an *interesting* story? But that doesn't make it *news*. If it was someone trying to pass off a fake Picasso or a Rembrandt for a few million bucks, that'd be something my boss would put on the air. A short story from the 1800s, fake or not, is a little less of a ratings draw."

"I thought you might need some extra persuasion," she said, "so let me sweeten the pot. As I believe I demonstrated when we spoke on the phone, I have access to considerable resources. Fingers in a myriad of pies."

"Point being?"

She moved closer. Close enough that he felt her warm breath rustling against his cheek as she locked eyes with him.

"You've spent the better part of your life running from your past. Trying desperately to pretend that Lionel Page and Lionel *Paget* are two different men."

He swallowed, hard. He didn't want to meet her gaze, but he couldn't tear himself away. She had pinned him in place, without a touch, like a butterfly on a needle.

"I needed a fresh start."

"No such thing," she said, "but it's a moot point, given that the *Observer* is about to run a story outing you. Or . . . maybe not. I have influence, and I enjoy exerting that influence on behalf of my agents. I would like you to be my agent, Lionel. All I have to do is pick up a telephone. Agree to this errand, and I promise you, that story will not run."

"The kid's a freelancer, I think," he said. "Yeah, you might know somebody at the *Observer*, but he'll just peddle it down the street—"

She cut him off with a word, her voice suddenly whip-crack sharp. "That. Story. Will. Not. Run." She tilted her head, studying him, unblinking. "I believe in keeping secrets. I'll see that yours are kept, too. I also believe that money has two purposes, each equally important: making things happen, and making things *not* happen."

"You never mentioned," he said, "how you made your money."

She favored him with a tiny smile, her dark eyes glittering.

"No. I didn't, did I?"

"I'm naturally curious—"

Regina took hold of his shoulders. Maybe she was stronger than she looked. Maybe he was just off-balance. She turned him around, spinning him in place, facing him toward the open doorway. Her breath was a warm gust against his left ear as she dropped her voice to a whisper.

"I'm not the story. The story is out there, in the wilds of New York City. My resources, your talents. Find the truth and bring it to me, and after that, you're free to do as you please. Are we in agreement? Do we have a pact, you and I?"

He let out a nervous little laugh. "You make it sound like a deal with the devil."

Her hands slid along his breastbone. Her firm grip melted into a tender hug from behind, touching him like a friend who had known him for years. She rested her chin on his shoulder.

"I'm nothing so sinister," she said. "A seeker of truth, just like you. We're two peas in a pod, really. But I'm an old-fashioned woman, and I believe in doing things properly, so I must insist you say the word. Do we have a pact, Lionel? Yes or no?"

Warning bells had chimed in the back of Lionel's mind since Regina's phone call. They'd only grown louder by the minute, and now they were ringing out like a five-alarm fire. He felt like Alice at the edge of the rabbit hole, contemplating a fall.

As strange as the situation was—as strange as his hostess was—he couldn't argue the facts. She needed answers. He needed a patron. If her word was good, a day or two of fieldwork in New York would spare him months of invaded privacy and headaches. His past could stay dead and buried, where it belonged.

So he jumped down the rabbit hole.

"Yes," he said. "You've got a deal."

She gave him a gentle push toward the library doors.

"There's a car waiting for you at the curb outside, and the driver has an envelope of cash for you. That was your payment just for hearing me out, if you declined. Take it as your first-day retainer, and contact me when you need more. Tell the driver to take you to O'Hare. By the time you reach the airport, my assistant will have sent flight data, your e-ticket, and hotel reservations to your phone."

"I can't just go right away. I mean, I need to stop at home, I need to pack a bag, some clothes, my *toothbrush*—"

"That's what the cash is for, Lionel. Buy what you need when you land. Consider it an adventure in the making. *Go.*"

Four

A coal-black Lincoln waited at the curb, sleek and long with livery plates. Regina's hired driver was a tight-lipped woman who passed Lionel an envelope over the seat, gave a curt nod to his request for a ride to the airport, and answered his attempts at small talk with non-committal grunts. When Lionel tried asking her about Regina and her money, she didn't answer at all. The question withered and died in the air between them. In the silence, he opened the envelope and thumbed through a stack of old and rumpled bills. There had to be two thousand dollars in cash, most of it in fifties.

Regina lived up to her end of the bargain. By the time the Lincoln was pulling up to the Delta terminal at O'Hare, a blocked number had texted Lionel with flight information and the address for a hotel in New York. The final message was the last piece of information he'd asked for just before leaving Regina's brownstone: the name of her local contact, the book dealer who'd gotten wind of the Poe manuscript, and where to find him.

An hour later he sat in a window seat overlooking the wing of an eastbound jet. It was an Embraer model, a narrow plane with just two seats on each side of a tight middle aisle, and it felt like they'd barely reached cruising altitude before the captain announced preparations to land. Short flight, just long enough for the whirlwind pace of the day to ebb away and for anxiety to fill the gaps it left behind. Lionel had nothing to do but sit, and think, and take a long walk through his memories.

Regina was right—she wasn't the story here—but he still wanted to know more about the woman who was paying his bills. She had resources she wasn't afraid to use and, if she was telling the truth, enough power to reach into the media and squash a story she didn't want reaching the public. Not necessarily a bad thing; that was powerful clout to have on his side, if he needed it once he touched down in New York. Still, he thought he knew all the power players in Chicago: the industrialists, the aldermen, the lifelong denizens of the political machine. He could walk into any high-society function and identify ninety percent of the guests by name. He'd made enemies out of half of them.

And yet, with all the time he'd spent digging up dirt on the rich and powerful, he'd never heard of Regina Dunkle.

I should call Brianna when I land, ask her to do some digging for me. His thoughts suddenly jarred, jumping across the tracks. *Shit. The kid.*

Regina might be able to get the *Observer* to yank their story, but no amount of money could turn back the clock. If that cub reporter had been smart and left after his disaster of an interview, maybe everything was fine for the moment. If he hadn't—if he'd gone after Lionel's coworkers for info, flashing that magazine around the newsroom— Brianna would have had hours to do some digging of her own. Lionel had always planned to tell her the truth about his childhood—someday. That nebulous sort of *someday* he'd hoped to put off forever. This wasn't how he wanted her to find out.

Lionel sat tight, thirty-two thousand feet in the sky above Pennsylvania, and stared at his worthless phone. He could shell out for Wi-Fi and rattle off a quick email, but that almost felt as bad as her getting the facts from a sixteen-year-old magazine article. He needed to talk to her, voice to voice. Suddenly landing felt hours away.

The kid, and Regina, both coming into his life on the same day. It felt like a fix. For a second, Lionel wondered if they were in it together. United to . . . And that's where his theory fell apart, stalled in a tangle of questions. He looked out the window and had that Alice-down-the-rabbit-hole feeling again.

What happened in that story, anyway? he thought. *Alice went to a weird party, ate some mushrooms, saw some trippy shit, then went home. I've had worse vacations.*

It was eight o'clock Eastern time, summer sun still blazing high in the cloudless sky, when the plane banked hard and flew over the outskirts of New York City. Lionel leaned on his armrest, taking in the endless sprawl of high-rises off the wing, stretching farther than his eye could see. He had never been to New York, and he'd been expecting something like his native home—one tight cluster of downtown corporate towers and then a trackless, endless suburbia. No. This was a *city*, vast, tall as it was wide, filling every last inch of ground and spilling to the edges of every island. Towering cranes dotted the skyline here and there, building ever higher, no place left to go but up. A human hive built for eight million people and still growing, never slowing down. He was suddenly a tiny cog in a vast and uncaring machine.

And somewhere down below, somewhere in the endless streets sprouting long shadows as the sun finally began to set, were the answers he was looking for.

The jet landed with a shuddering jolt. Momentum pushed him against his seat belt as the brakes roared and the narrow craft fought against its own speed. Eventually it slowed to a gentle roll, easing up to the terminal, and announced its final destination with an electronic chime. Lionel joined the line of weary commuters in the halting shuffle-step march off the plane.

Halfway up the boarding ramp, the thinly carpeted metal thrumming under his feet, he dug his phone out and speed-dialed Brianna. He listened to it ring as he emerged into the terminal at LaGuardia, surrounded by a swirl of fast-walking travelers in every direction. It was the city in miniature, a dozen languages filling the air, the aroma from a clutter of food kiosks battling for attention. Barely controlled chaos. Lionel just kept moving, trying to stay out of everyone's way, and followed the signs.

Brianna picked up on the second ring, sounding breathless. "Lionel! I've been calling you for two hours. Where *are* you?"

"New York. It's a long story. Look, before I get to that, I gotta ask—that reporter, the kid from the *Observer*—"

"That's what I've been trying to—"

"Whatever he said to you, don't . . . don't jump to any conclusions, okay? There's more to—"

"Lionel, he's *dead*."

He stopped in his tracks. From full speed to a dead halt, like a car hitting a brick wall. His legs felt like they were made of ice. A traveler in a sharp-cut suit swerved around him, a near miss with his rolling carry-on, and shot him a dirty look as he passed on by.

"What?"

"That's what I've been trying to call you about," she told him. "His boss at the *Observer* called, asking if we knew where he was because he never came back to work after he left your interview. So we both called around, and . . . he's dead. The kid is dead."

Five

Lionel collected angry glares as he stood statue-still, a human obstacle in the flow of traffic. He forced himself to move, to stand over by a news kiosk and out of the way. He kept his back turned to the concourse windows. Heat from the setting sun rippled against his neck.

"What happened?" he asked.

"He left a minute after you did; Karen said you looked angry about something? He was chasing after you, she thinks."

"So he didn't say—" Lionel caught himself. Time for that later. "So then what happened?"

"The police say it looks like a mugging gone wrong. They found his body behind a dumpster, just off North Michigan Avenue."

He shook his head. "Nobody gets *mugged* on the Mag Mile in broad daylight. It's one of the safest places in the city. There are cops every ten goddamn feet because of all the tourists."

"Well . . . he did. I talked to this guy I know, works the Eighteenth District. They took everything he had, not just his wallet. His notes, his recorder, everything. They found him with empty pockets, and . . . he'd been stabbed. A lot."

"A lot?"

"*Butchered* was the word my source used. Lionel, they want to talk to you. You were the last person to see him alive."

"*Karen* was the last person to see him alive."

"Yeah, and she was right here, in front of two dozen witnesses all afternoon. You had an argument, he was chasing after you, and now he's dead and you're . . . in New York, you said? Why are you in New York?"

"They don't think *I* did it." Lionel wasn't sure if he was telling her or asking her.

"No, God, of course not, but you see how it looks. They wouldn't be doing their job if they didn't talk to you. Just call them and set up an interview time. I'll have Morty from Legal meet you at the precinct; just do exactly what he tells you. Don't say a word without him approving it first, and you'll be fine."

"They're gonna have to wait. I'm a little tied up right now."

"Yeah, about that. Why are you in New York?"

The sun against his neck had gone cold, and the phone felt slick against his clammy palm. His thoughts raced too fast to put the words together, because the words he *wanted* to say—the truth, mostly— wouldn't come out. When he'd crashed to a dead stop, they'd crashed along with him, lying in a broken pile at his feet.

The original plan had been to ask Brianna to dig into Regina Dunkle's business. All he could hear right now, though, was Regina's promise.

"I believe in keeping secrets. I'll see that yours are kept, too."

The "pact" they'd struck was simple enough: All he had to do was go to New York, track down this Poe manuscript, and figure out if it was the real deal or if somebody was looking to pull a scam on her. All she had to do was keep the kid's story from seeing the light of day.

Well, now the story was as dead as its reporter. And all the kid's evidence, down to that old and tattered copy of *People* where Lionel was the front-page story, had gone missing. His secrets were safe. Just like she'd promised.

This was paranoid. He knew it was paranoid. Regina was a dotty heiress with a literary obsession and too much time on her hands, not a cold-blooded killer. Sure, the timing was suspicious, but she'd offered to make a few phone calls and throw her influence around, not send a hit man after some dumb, too-eager kid who got in Lionel's way. That wasn't the deal. He never would have agreed to that, and considering the homework she'd done on him, Regina would have known that, too. But.

He couldn't deny the chance, the slimmest chance, that the reclusive Ms. Dunkle wasn't just eccentric. She might be dangerous. And if she was, he couldn't risk sending Brianna into the line of fire.

"I'm following a hot lead," he told her. "Could be nothing, could be a good story in it. I'll be back in a couple of days, okay?"

"What lead? We didn't talk about this. Hey, Lionel? I give you a lot of leeway, but you *do* know you actually work for me, right?"

"I know, I know, just . . . trust me, okay?" Lionel's shoulders thumped against the concourse window. He closed his eyes. "As soon as I get back, we'll sit down, I'll cook dinner at my place, buy a bottle of that Riesling you like for dessert—"

"Don't *even* try to butter me up right now."

"—and we'll have a long talk about it. About a lot of things. There's some stuff that . . . It's overdue, that's all."

The line fell silent. He listened to the faint sound of her breath.

"Yeah," Brianna said. "Okay. Two days. Call me if you need me."

He needed her. He hung up anyway.

He emerged through the sliding concourse doors, out into the sunset. A line of yellow taxis waited at the curb, and he gave the cabbie the address for his hotel. As they swerved into traffic, making their way toward the on-ramp for I-278, Lionel wrote up a mental list. Checking in at the hotel was his first priority; that would give him a foothold, a place to call a home base. Next, he needed to round up some basic toiletries and a change of clothes for tomorrow. Hopefully the hotel concierge could point the way. He'd never traveled without luggage, and it left him feeling weirdly adrift. Nothing but the clothes on his back, not even a . . . phone charger. Right. He glanced at the dwindling bars on the screen and added that to the shopping list.

Manhattan rose in the distance. It wasn't real. Lionel had never been to New York, but he'd spent his entire life watching it on television and movie screens. New York was America's city, the go-to for big stories painted on a big canvas. Cops and robbers, romantics and dreamers—eight million dramas set on location. The taxi eased to one side to let an ambulance in FDNY livery scream past, and for a heartbeat Lionel wondered what show they were filming, until he realized the ambulance wasn't a prop.

Maybe I'm the one who's not real, he thought, *or maybe I fit right in. "Intrepid journalist flies halfway across the country in pursuit of a historical mystery." There's your elevator pitch to the studio right there. If I'm really lucky, I'm about to have a meet-cute with some manic pixie dream girl who'll shake up my world and teach me to appreciate life.*

Romantic comedy was his best-case option. The sun boiled down and the skyline took on the shapes of jagged granite teeth in the dark. It felt like the opening shots of a horror movie. The kind where the hero dies in the end. He considered it a reminder; he might have seen a thousand directors' imaginary takes on New York, but he'd never really been here. He was an outsider, alone on foreign soil.

The cab hit heavy traffic on the Queensboro Bridge, inching across the span of the East River. The gridlock eased up on the far side, and Lionel watched Little Italy roll by outside his window. Then Lower Manhattan, and finally Chelsea, skyscrapers giving way to sedate brownstones and vintage brick warehouses converted into office and theater space. The sky had gone full dark, starless and azure, and the city ignited with a million points of shimmering light. His final destination was on Tenth Avenue, and he double-checked the address as he stepped from the cab: the High Line Hotel looked like a small castle, or maybe a venerable college where everyone wore matching ties. A wall of ornate fencing and shrubbery—like a ceremonial ring of cold iron and earth, interspersed with austere stone posts—encircled an outer garden and a patio bar. Tea lights flickered in glass decanters on a cluster of small, round tables near an outdoor bar. A bellhop ran out and moved to open the taxi's trunk.

"No luggage," Lionel said. He shrugged. "It's a long story."

Inside the double doors, the hotel lobby resembled a coffee shop or a small boutique bar. Travelers and locals mingled, filling a pair of cozy leather sofas and clustering around a table decorated with a vintage typewriter. Dark wood and warm lights, the kind of place Norman Mailer or William S. Burroughs might have haunted in another day. There wasn't a check-in desk; the bellhop led him to a tiny kiosk with a computer on a shelf, where an attendant pulled up his reservation.

"Mr. Page," she said, tapping a few keys. "Excellent, I see you'll be staying with us . . . indefinitely."

"Two days, tops."

She gave him the ghost of a smile. "Of course. We were able to secure the room you requested—third floor, suite three. Paolo will bring your luggage up for you."

"But I didn't—" He paused and let that go. Regina's assistant must have picked out a favorite room and requested it for him. "This was kind of a spur-of-the-moment thing. I don't actually have any luggage."

She gestured to the carry-on bag next to his foot. Gray Samsonite, pristine and factory new.

"Your luggage arrived twenty minutes ago. We were asked to hold it up front until you arrived."

Paolo was a tall, gaunt man, his tanned cheeks darkened by the spread of a five-o'clock shadow. He walked at Lionel's side and escorted him onto the elevator, unlocking it with a wave of a glossy black key card.

"Your first time staying with us, sir?"

"First time in New York," Lionel said as the elevator gave a shudder.

Paolo flashed a yellow-toothed smile. "Welcome! Our hotel was originally a seminary at the end of the 1800s. The brickwork, the molding—all restored to their original vintage design. Of course, the rooms are considerably more comfortable than they used to be. We don't hold our guests to monastic standards of living."

"That's good," Lionel said, watching the lit numbers slowly crawl toward the third floor. He forced a chuckle. "I am definitely not a priest. No, uh, ghostly nuns to worry about, right?"

"This is New York City, sir. *All* the hotels are haunted by someone or other. You just have to pick the one with the ghosts that suit you."

The door chimed and rumbled open. The jet-black door to his suite stood just to the right of the elevator. Lionel took in the art on the wall in passing. Antique prints, wildlife, their colors muted and soft.

As Paolo opened the door to his suite, Lionel did a double take. All the animals were dead.

Nothing gory or shocking about the pictures, not a drop of blood, but the animals were dead. One charcoal sketch depicted a pair of rabbits and some kind of bird on their backs, eyes shut, a hunter's fresh catch. Another captured a single spread-winged pheasant, neck bent in eternal slumber.

"Your room, sir," Paolo said. He beckoned Lionel in with a sweep of his arm.

His suite was a span of warm hardwood, antique Turkish rugs adorning the floor before the dark iron hearth of a fireplace. A twenties-style rotary phone sat upon the bedside table. On the opposite side of the room— under a wall-mounted television, the only concession to the modern world—waited a writing desk with stationery, pencils, and a full-size bronze embosser with a push handle. Books lined the fireplace mantel—an esoteric mix of philosophy, psychology, and astrology. Paolo followed his gaze.

"Every book is from the personal collection of Ingo Swann," he said. "Noted psychic, remote viewer, and UFO investigator."

"Definitely not the Hilton," Lionel muttered to himself, fishing in his wallet for some cash. He sent Paolo on his way with a tip and stood alone in the cool, clean silence of his suite. The luggage waited beside the bed like a jack-in-the-box, just waiting for him to turn the crank— or pull the zipper—and discover what was waiting to burst out at him.

Six

Lionel gently laid the suitcase on the floral bedspread. It was heavy, about the weight he'd expect if he'd packed for a full trip. Holding his breath, he tugged the zipper and peeled back the soft-gray weave of the lid.

Neatly folded clothes in neutral colors waited inside, button-down shirts and slacks in shades of brown and gray, tightly rolled socks, even a brand-new pair of Italian loafers. He was a size nine, and the shoes were a nine and a half, but they were more expensive than anything he'd normally buy on a reporter's salary. A calf-leather toiletry case, soft as butter, unraveled to reveal a full suite of accessories: a travel toothbrush and paste, deodorant, comb, a still-wrapped disposable razor, a tiny bottle of mouthwash. Two phone chargers waited for him in the suitcase's side pocket, one for an iPhone, one for an Android model.

His fingers brushed the fold of a white envelope. It was heavy stock, expensive paper, marked with a prim monogram. *R. D.* He tore it open, and a debit card, a prepaid Visa, dropped into the palm of his hand. A handwritten note accompanied the card.

Dear Lionel,

I hope you'll forgive the presumption of shopping for you; I believe this will save you some time once you're on the ground. I had to guess at your sizes, but I have a fairly good eye for these things. I also hope the suite is to your liking. I'm fond of the High Line, and Chelsea as a whole, but there's also a strategy to my selection: Julian Whitcombe, my New York associate, is in Hell's Kitchen just north of your present lodgings.

Please use the enclosed card for your business expenses. My assistant will monitor the account and top it off as necessary. Your course of action from here is up to you.

With regard,

Your Regina.

"*My* Regina," Lionel murmured with a faint smile. He twirled the debit card in his hand before slipping it into his pocket along with the note. "Well, aren't we familiar."

He checked his phone. The cab ride from LaGuardia had taken nearly an hour, and the clock was closing in on ten. No chance Whitcombe's shop was still open. He'd call it a night and hit the pavement running first thing in the morning. Assuming he could sleep. All his instincts said a story was out there, a juicy one, and he felt like a kid on Christmas Eve: tossing, turning, waiting for the dawn so he could rush to the tree and open his presents.

His stomach grumbled. He eyed the minibar. Well stocked, but while he could make do with a bag of kettle chips and an airplane bottle of gin—he'd had worse dinners on the road, and sometimes at home—his feet were too impatient to be confined. He rode the elevator down, wove through the still-bustling lobby, and headed out onto the streets of New York.

Ten at night and Chelsea was still thrumming, electric as the lights that blazed against the stormy miasma overhead. The air had cooled off, touched with a hint of summer mist, and Lionel watched the endless traffic roll along Tenth Avenue. He didn't have any particular place to go, so he picked a direction at random and started walking, giving himself over to the city.

The city rewarded his trust, offering him pale lights burning behind the windows of an all-night diner. The chrome facade was stylishly retro, a modern idea of a fifties burger joint, and the wafting scents of fried eggs and black pepper pulled him through the front door like a leash. The hostess pointed him to a spot halfway up the bar, the only open stool in a row of late-night diners. Lionel ran his gaze down a laminated menu. The decor was fifties, but the cuisine was hipster modern: omelets made with exotic herbs and Boursin cheese, avocado toast with cilantro and salmon, chilled mint soup, and a dozen uses for quinoa. Lionel ordered a cup of coffee and the soft-shell crab roll.

On the far side of the counter, the waitress set down his cup and saucer to the right of his woven place mat. Lionel reached for it at the same time as his seatmate, a woman in her twenties dressed in a funeral-black pantsuit. Their fingers both curled around the handle from different directions, getting tangled up, and a dollop of steaming coffee sloshed over the rim as they quickly disengaged.

"I'm sorry," Lionel said, feeling blood rush to his cheeks. "Was that your—"

She looked as embarrassed as he felt, wide-eyed with a slow-spreading blush. "Oh, no, I mean, maybe? I don't—"

"Really," he said, "my fault. I thought it was my coffee."

She glanced to the cup, then back to him. She made him think of a classical statue come to life, her cheekbones high and cut from marble, her hair a wave of bright ginger that stood out like a stark flash of color against her pale skin and sharp-cut ebony clothes. She placed her hand on the bar, manicured nails painted the shade of burnt umber, and measured the distance between their place mats with her spread fingers. The coffee sat precisely between them, squatting on the border.

"It's certainly *a* coffee," she said as she leaned in, curious. "I don't know if we can identify it beyond that."

"It's Schrödinger's coffee," Lionel suggested. "Until one of us drinks it, scientifically, it belongs to both of us. But seriously, please, I think you ordered before I did."

The waitress came by to break the deadlock, serving up a second, identical cup, and placing it right next to its companion. Both of them on the border. His seatmate picked one, Lionel dragged over the other, and they raised their mugs in unison.

"And the grim coffee war of 2018 ended at last," the young woman said. "Yay, we're caffeine buddies."

"Here's to newfound caffeine buddies," Lionel said with a smile. "I shouldn't even be doing this, last thing I need is more fuel in my tank, but . . . professional habit."

"You're an out-of-towner," she said, looking him over. "Not a professional driver, not a pilot, but you've got that rumpled-around-the-edges look that says you move around a lot. I'm guessing you're from . . . the Midwest. Chicago, maybe."

Lionel lifted his eyebrows. "And you can tell that how, exactly?"

"Mostly your accent."

"Everybody here sounds like they do back home," Lionel says. "My first visit to New York, and I haven't heard a single person talking like a stereotypical Brooklynite."

"You don't sound like you're about to cheer for da Bears, either. They're called stereotypes for a reason." She tapped her left earlobe. "The average Midwest accent is similar to the average Northeast. They both fall under what's called the general American accent—our ears perceive it as 'neutral'—but there are subtle differences if you learn to listen for them. Vowels are pronounced a little differently, like *cot* as opposed to *caught*."

"Okay," Lionel said, "my turn to guess. You're . . . an actress. And this is New York, so you're a stage actress."

The waitress came over with a pair of dishes. Lionel's fat crab roll snuggled up next to a bed of thick-cut potato chips. His seatmate had ordered a wedge salad, the lettuce adorned with cherry tomatoes and flecks of blue cheese. She batted her eyelashes at him, amused.

"Now why would you guess that?"

"With that kind of linguistics background? You're either an actress or a college professor—"

She brandished her silverware. "If you're about to say something like 'You're too pretty to be an academic,' I'm going to stab you with this fork. Fair warning."

"No, not at all. I mean, no, you *are* pretty, but—" He paused. "I'm just digging myself deeper, aren't I?"

"Please, keep going. I find it highly entertaining."

He shook his head with a tired smile and started over. "What I mean is, acting is a job with odd hours. Academia's a little more structured than that."

"And?"

Lionel nodded at her cup. "And you're sitting in a diner at nearly eleven at night, on a Tuesday, drinking coffee. You're not getting up at five a.m. to prep for class. Then there's your outfit. Tailored, not off the rack. More business meeting than clubwear, but versatile; you're dressed to go anywhere, do anything, and look your best while you're doing it. Which suggests you're either going to, or coming from, a professional engagement."

He wasn't sure if she was impressed, or just putting on a face. "You've got an eye for details."

"That's *my* job."

"I'm taking another bite at that apple," she said. "You're far from home, but you're used to that. You don't work a nine-to-five, either. You care about your appearance, but you wear clothes that let you move, clothes that don't stand out in a crowd. You're aiming to see, not to be seen. A little on the disheveled side—"

"Gee, thanks."

She grinned and held up a finger. "Let me finish. But it's classically disheveled. Like 'Bogie in a fedora before fedoras were for douchebags' kind of disheveled. You've got the PI look going on."

"I'm not a private investigator."

"No. *Public* investigator." She pointed her fork at him before spearing a chunk of lettuce. "You're a writer. Journalist. Some kind of . . . word architect. I'm thinking travel writer, and you're in town on a gig."

He had to smile. "That's pretty damn close. You're good at this."

"That's what everyone tells me."

"I'm Lionel, by the way."

"Maddie."

"Short for Madison?"

She chuckled into her coffee as she took another sip. "Not even my mother calls me that. Names are important, you know. Do you know what Lionel means?"

"I figured I was named after the train sets."

"It means 'young lion.'"

"You're making that up."

Maddie laughed. "No, for real. That's what it means. You should trust me—I read a lot of books."

"I always trust people who read books," Lionel said. "So what does your name mean?"

She twirled a lock of her ginger hair around one finger, gazing up to the heavens.

"Madison is derived from Matthew, which means 'gift of god.'"

"That's a lot to live up to."

"No," Maddie said, "I *am* making that up. It's a total bullshit name. It was super-rare until . . . '83, '84? When *Splash* came out."

"The mermaid movie?"

"The mermaid movie, with Tom Hanks. Remember? Daryl Hannah's wandering around New York, and she sees the sign for

Madison Avenue and decides her name is Madison? After that, boom. A bumper crop of tiny baby Madisons. I am named after a mermaid."

"Do you transform in the water?" he asked.

"I transform in *coffee*." She eyed her phone, slim in a rose-gold case. "And that's my ride. Early. Yay. Or not yay. I gotta go."

He lifted his cup. "Nice meeting you, Maddie."

She slipped off her stool, tossed a few rumpled bills onto the bar, and hustled toward the door. She gave him a fluttery wave. "Nice meeting you, Mr. Word Architect Lion. See you around sometime."

By the time he realized they hadn't traded phone numbers, she was already gone. Lionel shook his head, dug into his crab roll, and sighed. Just one fleeting human connection, there and gone again.

So this isn't going to be a romantic comedy, he thought. *Well, at least it's not a horror movie.*

Seven

Back behind the jet-black door of his suite, in the shadowy gloom and buried under a mountain of covers, Lionel tossed and turned. Unfamiliar street sounds drifted through the windows, and unfamiliar smells—a scent like clean linen and old, faintly musty parchment—surrounded him on both sides of the pillow. He sank into his dreams in slow fits and starts.

When he finally arrived, it was the last place in the world he wanted to be.

He was five years old again, in another strange room, in another unfamiliar bed. An olive army-surplus cot, with too-thin sheets. The autumn night smelled like pine cones and faded, musky incense. He padded across a creaky floor in his *Star Wars* pajamas and socks, a small shadow in the dark, following the sound of voices out on the porch. A plastic lighter clicked, and the acrid smell of cheap tobacco smoke drifted through the ratty screen door.

"—have to send them away," a woman was saying. Her silhouette took a drag from a cigarette's shadow.

"We don't have to do anything of the sort," an older woman replied. "Sheila and her boy need our help—"

"*Boy*, Martha. *Boy.* That's the point. This ranch is a sanctuary for *women.*"

"And their families."

"And their *daughters*."

"You're being dogmatic," Martha snapped. "He's an innocent child. He isn't his father, and he isn't your ex-husband, for that matter—"

"Don't," said the woman with the cigarette. "Don't even go there."

"This is supposed to be a safe place for people who need help. Sheila and Lionel are exactly the kind of people we should be here to support. If we turn them away because Lionel was born with the wrong set of chromosomes, what does that say about us and who *we* are?"

The woman with the cigarette took another drag, breathing a trickle of smoke like an exhausted dragon. "What about Sheila, then?"

"What about her?"

"She isn't one of us."

"Of course she is," Martha countered. "She knows more about the craft than half the so-called elders on this ranch put together."

Lionel crouched in the dark, just inside the screen door, watching and listening. The woman with the cigarette slumped her head against the porch wall.

"If it harms none," she recited, "do as you will. That's our code. That's our law."

"Your point?"

"She went out into the woods this morning. Wren saw her coming back. She had blood on her hands, Martha. And it wasn't hers. Wren asked what she was doing out there. She said, 'Protecting us.' And not another word on the subject."

"I'm sure there's a reasonable explanation."

"Of course there is. Animals. *Blood sacrifice*. She's not one of us. She's some kind of Satanist, maybe, or—"

"You'd better have proof before you start slinging accusations around."

The woman tossed her cigarette to the weathered boards of the porch and ground it out under her heel.

"I believe in the threefold law," she said. "What you put out into the universe always comes back around again, three times as strong. And whatever Sheila is doing, she's inviting darkness to our doorstep. Get rid of her, or we're all going to regret it."

The image lurched and burned away, printed on flash paper and dying in a shower of cinders. Lionel had a sudden sense of dizzying motion, like being blindfolded on a roller coaster and lunging into a corkscrew spiral at a hundred miles an hour. Crackling flames and the rattling of iron chains echoed in his ears. And a chorus of screams. He felt Martha's liver-spotted hands, strong for her age, lifting him and pushing him toward a tiny black hole at the heart of the fire. A chasm untouched by the endless cinder rain.

"—have to run," she whispered. "We'll be right behind you, I promise. Whatever you do, don't look back, and *don't stop running.*"

Then he was charging through a downpour, his pajamas soaked through with ice water, mud and grass caking the bottoms of his bare feet. He lunged out onto a dirt road and jolted to a standstill as headlights bore down on him, and a truck's horn blared, louder than the storm.

Lionel jolted awake. His naked body was tangled and bound, snared in twisted sheets, the fabric drenched in sweat cold as his memory of the rain. He lay there, perfectly still, and stared up at the ceiling. Morning light pushed its way around the corners of the drapes and cast his suite in a foggy amber glow.

He untangled himself and trudged to the bathroom. The floor was a mosaic of white-and-black tiles, smooth and cool under his feet. He turned on the shower, full blast and hot. Lionel stood under the stream for a while, motionless, and let the water do its work. Washing away the sweat and the memories.

⌐

"Poe manuscript investigation," Lionel said to the bathroom mirror. "Background notes."

44

His phone sat on the lip of a forties-style white porcelain sink, voice recorder activated and hanging on his every word as he smoothed a handful of green shaving gel over his morning stubble. He thought out loud while he shaved. Each stroke of the fresh blade carved a clean path along his cheeks, banishing the night.

"Julian Whitcombe is a local rare-book dealer. He has a long-term relationship with the primary source; primary source says she's known him for over twenty years, and he's never proved unreliable. He keeps tabs on the markets in New York, and when something comes along that the primary source might like, he puts out feelers for her. The primary . . ."

He trailed off, lost in thought. He washed his razor under a stream of warm water and tapped it on the porcelain, sending foam and stubble spiraling down the drain. He didn't even want to say Regina Dunkle's name on the recording. No concrete reason, just a vague sense of taboo that had lodged deep in his bones.

"I've run some extremely preliminary background on the primary source." He turned his face in the mirror and slid the razor down his other cheek. "She has no internet footprint whatsoever. Not under the name she gave me. Once I get back to Chicago, I can run the property records for her address in Lincoln Park and see what that turns up. For now, eyes on the prize. Plan of attack: interview Whitcombe, get some good on-the-record quotes for the story—assuming there's going to be a story, call it a coin toss right now—and pin down details on the manuscript. Apparently he doesn't have it, but he knows who does, and they may or may not be willing to talk about having it authenticated; if not, this could get complicated fast. Nothing I can do until I get the facts from Whitcombe, so . . . let's do it. Rock and roll."

He splashed handfuls of water on his cheeks and reached for his toothbrush.

"Memo to myself," he added. "Call Brianna this afternoon, get an update on how things are going back home."

That made him think about the police waiting to interview him. And the dead cub reporter in the alley. The shadow of last night's dream came creeping back in at the edges of his vision, drowning out the morning light.

"Memo to myself." He sighed at his reflection. "Need coffee."

He found it—French roast, black as midnight—at Cookshop, a restaurant just down the block from his hotel. The Cookshop breakfast was a thing of beauty: scrambled eggs, bacon, Italian sausage, a puddle of creamy, meaty grits, and a buttermilk biscuit the size of his fist. The city had already woken up—if it ever slept at all—and Lionel slowly caught up with it. He was fueled and ready for action by the time he hit the sidewalk, stepping to the curb and raising one arm to flag a passing taxi.

He gave the cabbie an address—West Fifty-Fifth Street, just off Ninth Avenue—and didn't get so much as an offhand comment. He was surprised at the driver's lack of reluctance until they got closer, rolling into Hell's Kitchen. The street bustled with life, shaggy slackers walking shoulder to shoulder with corporate suits and fashion plates, rainbow flags dangling from the corner lampposts. Pennants ringed a construction site, advertising a new luxury high-rise on the climb.

"Hollywood totally lied to me," Lionel muttered at the window.

The cabbie gave him a throaty chuckle. "You were expectin' something outta *Daredevil*, right? Muggers and shoot-outs?"

"Pretty much, yeah."

They hovered midway down the block, snared in traffic as a cement mixer blocked the road, inching backward at a snail's pace.

"Nah," the cabbie said. "This ain't the sixties. Or the eighties. My old man, he was a driver, too; back in his day, he wouldn't have taken you here on a bet. These days, it's all primo real estate."

Lionel craned his neck, trying to see past the cement mixer. "Is the construction always this bad?"

"Whole city's under construction. Upward and onward, my friend. That said"—he leaned forward and gave his horn two sharp taps—"don't know what this chucklehead thinks he's doing, and we're only a block away. You might wanna hop out here and walk the rest, save you some time."

Lionel took his advice. He ran Regina's debit card through the back-seat reader, handed over a healthy tip in cash, and joined the pedestrian tide. As different as the city was, at least walking in New York was just like walking in Chicago: all he had to do was stay alert, move at a brisk speed, and dodge the tourists. He turned at the corner and stepped out of the flow of traffic, cupping a hand over his eyes to block the harsh morning light. He spotted his target on the other side of the street, sandwiched between a tattoo parlor and a Verizon Cellular store. Cracked gold paint on a mahogany baseboard read AROUND THE WORLD BOOKS, over a window display of faded hardcovers.

A brass bell jingled as he stepped through the door. The shop was cool and musty, the sounds of the bustling street fading on the other side of the dusty plate-glass window. Eye-height shelves stood at sharp diagonals, drawing chevron aisles along the pale wood floors. The books on display felt like they hadn't been curated so much as grown wild like weeds, taking over without rhyme or reason. First-edition copies of Hemingway stood shoulder to shoulder with '70s dinner-party cookbooks and vintage pulp-crime paperbacks. Lionel crouched down before a shelf, his gaze sliding along mismatched titles and faded dustcovers.

"Not sure how anybody finds anything in here," he muttered to himself.

A response came from the other side of the shelf, a voice like air squeezing through a cracked reed.

"I believe that 'finding the book you're looking for' is an overrated notion," the man replied. "Far better to explore, and let the book you need be the one which finds you."

A scraping sound echoed from behind the shelf, a long slow sandpapery hiss followed by a sharp *thump*. Then another hiss, then a *thump*, as Lionel's host came around to greet him face-to-face.

Eight

Julian Whitcombe's face lay shrouded under three-quarters of a rubber mask. The rubber was almost flesh colored, almost real, adhered tightly to his slightly lopsided skull. One of his eyes, the real one, was brown, set above a sunken cheekbone raked with white scars. The other eye was sky blue, a marble of cheap glass. His dark hair parted to the left, grown long and straight to fall down the rubber-masked side of his face like a bashful waterfall.

He wore a long-sleeve jacket, like an umber lab coat, cut to dangle below his knees and sheathe his body. All the same, there was no concealing the damage done. He leaned on a crutch, body bent, both of his legs replaced by rickety prosthetics. One of his hands was a crablike pincer of black plastic. A leather driving glove concealed the other, and a few of the glove's fingers dangled limp and empty. He greeted Lionel with a pained grimace of a smile, like the simple act of parting his lips took a Herculean effort.

"Mr. Whitcombe?" Lionel asked, not sure what to make of him.

"In the flesh," he replied, and let out a faint, wheezing chortle. "Has your book found you yet?"

"I'm more in the market for a short story. Name's Lionel Page. Regina Dunkle sent me."

Julian gave a twitching nod. "Mmf. Thought as such. You have the look. Glad she sent you, not the . . . the other one."

He turned and shuffle-slid toward the long, low desk at the back of the store. One thumping lurch with his crutch and his left leg, then a slow drag of the right, his empty boot twisted and lagging behind him.

Lionel followed him. "The other one?"

"Oh, yes. Yes. Ms. Dunkle sends any number of different people when she's happy. When she's not happy, she only sends one very specific individual. Not a meeting you want to have, no."

"What do you know about Regina?"

Julian shuffled around the counter. He leaned on it, head bowed for a moment, his good eye closed while the glass eye stayed wide-open and staring. He took a deep breath.

"She's a very loyal customer of mine."

"C'mon," Lionel said. "You obviously know her better than that. What can you tell me?"

Another grimace of a smile. With his teeth clenched, Julian hefted a leather-bound book onto the counter between them. It hit the grainy wood with a puff of dust. He opened it with his gloved hand, paging through the long green sheets of a ledger.

"I've been reading your book, Mr. Page. I'm about halfway through. It's quite interesting so far. You possess a talent for the written word."

Deflection, plus an appeal to my ego, Lionel thought. *Damn, this guy's good.* He let the change of subject slide.

"I suppose Regina told you what I'm looking for?" he asked.

The empty finger of Julian's glove slid down a ledger page, trailing his hand like a dead slug made from glossy black leather.

"She did," Julian replied, "and you have your work cut out for you. The Poe manuscript is in the hands of one Mr. Raymond Barton. I've been unable to find out where he acquired it, but, well, it's an odd place for it to end up. He's not an antiquarian, not active in the book-collector community. He's, ah . . . a *filmmaker*, by trade."

Lionel caught the double-barreled load of venom in the word. "You don't like movies, Mr. Whitcombe?"

"Please, call me Julian. And no, I don't like *his*." His good eye looked up from the ledger. "Mr. Barton would be better served making his sort of movies out west. In the sleazier, smoggier climes of Los Angeles, for instance."

"We're talking about the kind of movies where everybody's naked, I'm assuming."

"That, and the occasional nature film." Julian paused. "Not a euphemism, in this case. He peddles his particular brand of smut to an underground clientele, while his studio and camera equipment—legally and for tax reasons—belong to his humble documentary studio. That, too, is a bit of a lie. His legitimate enterprise exists to launder money for certain track-suited gentlemen residing in Brighton Beach."

"Brighton Beach. What are we talking about here? Russian mob?"

"We aren't," Julian said. "We never had this conversation. I merely offer my off-the-record observations as a polite warning: Ray Barton is a dangerous man with dangerous friends. And he runs with a crowd rather notoriously hostile to truth-seeking journalists such as yourself."

This was sounding more like a scam every minute. If it was common knowledge that Regina Dunkle was loaded, eager to spend her money, and wanted rare books from particular authors, a guy like Barton "mysteriously" finding a lost Poe manuscript—and word getting out to Regina's local go-to guy—was way too convenient. A baited hook, dangling in the water.

"So here are the two big questions," Lionel said. "How much is he asking for the manuscript, and will he let us pick a third-party expert to authenticate the handwriting?"

"That's where the tale twists, I'm afraid. No offer is on the table."

Lionel squinted at him. "Wait. He's not selling it?"

"Not to us, at any rate. I heard about his acquisition through a mutual associate. Per Ms. Dunkle's standing instructions, I sent him a message to express our tentative interest in a buy. He's not deigned to respond."

Still smells like bait, Lionel thought. Playing hard to get was a typical opening move in a smart con—find something the mark wants, dangle it in front of them, then yank it away when they make the first reach. When you do it right, the mark gets so hungry they chase the phony prize and leave their common sense in the dust behind them.

Now he understood exactly why Regina had chosen him for this job. Like he'd told her back in Chicago, the Poe manuscript was interesting, but it wasn't top-of-the-hour news. Lionel didn't have any emotional investment in it, and he wouldn't be swayed by easy tricks. On the other hand, sniffing out frauds was his drug of choice.

"If I'm right," he said to Julian, "and I've got a good nose for these things, he's waiting for the second or third approach. He wants to make sure we're nice and eager before he floats a dollar amount."

"What do you suggest?"

Lionel glanced to the rafters overhead. "I go over there and talk to him face-to-face. I want to look him in the eye. Feel for his pressure points."

"I should call him first."

"Unh-uh." Lionel had to smile. "I'm a big fan of ambush interviews. Never give a con artist time to prepare."

Julian turned slowly, wincing as he shuffle-dragged his way to a second book on the shelf behind him. "I'll get you an address. I think you're being rash, though."

"Nobody ever got a story by playing it safe."

He waited while Julian puttered around, fumbling through the pages and reaching for a pad of scratch paper.

"You're more circumspect than you'd like me to think," Julian said. He opened a ballpoint pen by holding the cap between his teeth. He gave the pen a twist and a yank. The cap, wet with spittle, tumbled to the counter.

"How's that?"

"You look me in the eye. Most people, by now, either can't take their eyes off my . . . various injuries, or are looking for a way to ask me how I acquired them."

"None of my business," Lionel said. "Not saying I'm not curious, but it's none of my business."

Julian ripped the top page off the pad and turned, dragging his way back to Lionel, holding it in his outstretched glove. Lionel took the page. It bore a scrawled address in jagged blue ink.

"People can be cruel, Mr. Page. Very cruel." His marble eye lolled a bit, his good one meeting Lionel's steady gaze. "These days I prefer to interact with humanity through books, as exclusively as possible. The pages, the type, they're like . . . the glass walls of a zoo enclosure. I can watch the wild animals all evening long, safe on my side of the window."

Lionel folded the scrap of paper in half and held it up between his fingertips. "Thanks for this."

"Just be careful."

Julian fell silent, like that was all he had to say; then he bit his bottom lip. The rubber mask flexed, glossy under the overhead lights.

"Mr. Page?" he stammered. "One . . . one last thing."

Lionel's raised eyebrow asked a question.

"If you are very smart," Julian said, "you'll do exactly as Ms. Dunkle tells you. No more. No less. Whatever bargain you struck with her, hold up your end and she'll hold up hers."

"I'm planning on it," Lionel told him.

"Then." Julian's glove twitched, empty fingers flopping as it jerked upward and he forced the words past his fear. "Then, Mr. Page, if you are very smart indeed, you'll run. Run as far and as fast as you can, and pray she doesn't come looking for you."

"Run?"

His head bobbed.

"You see, Ms. Dunkle has a way of drawing people into her world. First it's like . . . it's like you're early man, discovering fire for the first time, marveling at the shadows it casts upon the wall of your cave. Transfixed, as you realize the shadows can tell stories and whisper secrets."

"And then?" Lionel asked.

"And then . . . then, before you know it, you're a shadow, too."

Lionel's brow furrowed, trying to interpret the bookseller's warning. "So you're saying I . . . want to stay out of Regina's world?"

"Oh, no, Mr. Page." His lips curled in that pained rictus. "Oh, no. You're already here, with the rest of us. It's far too late for that. Your only hope now is that when she's finally done with you, she'll allow you to leave."

Ray Barton did his business out of a converted warehouse in Red Hook, a stone's throw from the Brooklyn waterfront. The neighborhood had a small-town feel, old streets and old memories, drenched in the city's seafaring past. Lionel's cabbie took him down a short, curving dead-end road just off Ferris Street. Tapping out notes on his phone, writing down the details of his interview with Julian Whitcombe while it was still fresh, he glanced up to see the sign for Ray's company.

"Barton Educational Pictures," he murmured. "For a certain value of 'educational,' I guess."

Movement on the sidewalk caught his eye. A lone woman, marching fast, and from her direction she could only have been coming from Barton's place.

Maddie. The same woman from the diner last night, same black pantsuit and curly wave of ginger hair, same fast stride. She wore a canvas messenger bag over one shoulder, heavy and fat, and clutched it tight to her side. Her easy smile was gone, lips pursed in a tight and bloodless line. Her eyes were chips of ice.

She glanced over as the taxi rolled past. Her gaze met Lionel's, locking on like a sniper's scope. Then she turned a corner and disappeared.

Eight million people in this city, Lionel thought. *Passing each other by chance twice in two days? Those are some long odds.*

He would have been more suspicious, except she'd been the first one at the diner last night; the hostess had sat him next to her, and only because every other seat at the counter was taken. If anything, it looked like he was the one following her around. Still. Weird. He paid the cabbie and hopped out in the tiny strip of parking lot outside Ray's building.

The front door was a slab coated in reinforced steel. Lionel pushed the buzzer beside the weathered handle and waited. Then he hammered his fist on the door. No answer.

Pacing the parking lot and waiting, deciding on his next move, he glanced to the refurbished warehouse doors. They were tall, double-wide, barn-style, with crisscrossing wood slats for decoration. And one of them was open. Just a crack, just enough to let the shadows inside slip out into the afternoon sunshine.

"This isn't breaking and entering," Lionel said out loud. "I'm just being a good neighbor and letting him know his door's open. After all, *anybody* could walk in."

He grabbed the handle and gave it a tug. The barn door groaned on its rolling tracks. It rattled a couple of feet wider, then stopped, just enough for him to slip inside.

Lionel stood on a concrete slab in a puddle of gloom. A shaft of light came in across his shoulders, pushing back the dark. He watched dust mites dance in the shadows. Wooden partitions separated the warehouse into the suggestion of rooms, and a clutter of tripods and camera equipment stood in a huddle off to his left.

He cupped his hands around his mouth and called out, "Mr. Barton?"

His voice echoed back at him, his question bouncing off the old brick walls.

"Mr. Barton," he tried again, inching deeper into the quiet studio, "my name is Lionel Page. Your . . . your front door was open."

Lionel took out his cell phone, tapped the flashlight icon, and slashed a pale beam across the darkness. He stepped through one of the partitions, easing around a dead standing light and a camcorder on a tripod. The plywood walls were done up in textured wallpaper designed to look like slabs of masoned stone, someone's idea of a medieval dungeon. The camera's silent eye pointed to a butcher-block table, just long enough for someone to lie on. Lionel reached out and picked up a steel manacle with the tip of his finger. A chain, hooked to an eye loop and bolted into the table, rattled and echoed in the silence. Old, rusty stains flecked the table's surface.

"Jesus," he breathed. "What kind of movies are you making in here?"

Around the plywood wall, the next partition was a little more typical. A queen-size bed, point lights covered in sheets of gel for a softer focus. The bubblegum-pink bedspread, trimmed with white lace ruffles, gave Lionel an uneasy pause. The big stuffed teddy bear propped up between the pillows didn't help.

He moved deeper into the studio. He had a coppery taste in his throat, and it spread to the back of his nose. A slow-simmering stench hung in the hot and stagnant air, and his gut muscles squeezed like he was anticipating a punch. He knew that smell from a dozen crime scenes.

The next partition, sporting a high-backed throne fitted with restraining clamps for a victim's wrists and ankles, was another setup for some kind of S&M flick.

Unlike the table in the other room, this one came with its own victim.

Nine

The man in the bondage throne slumped to one side, his jaw slack. His milky eyes caught the light from Lionel's phone, and his lips and chin were matted in layers of dried blood. Lionel moved closer, leaning in for a better look at the dead man's mouth, and suddenly wished he hadn't. He balled up his fist, pressed it to his face, and stepped back, taking deep breaths until his stomach stopped churning.

A folding tray stood next to the chair, with the tools his killer had used on him. A pair of pliers and a cordless drill with a burr-grinder tip. Little chips of jagged ivory lay in a scatter all around them, like a handful of blood-flecked pearls.

The throne faced a standing full-length mirror, carefully positioned a few feet away. It puzzled Lionel for a moment, until he realized what it was there for. *They made him watch,* he thought. *While they were working on him, while they were taking him apart one piece at a time. They made him watch.*

Back in his cub-reporter years, huddling over a police-band radio and hunting for leads, Lionel had bribed his way onto an active crime scene. The victim was a butcher who had squealed on some local wiseguys, and his face met the business end of a machine for slicing lunch meat. After Lionel nearly lost his stomach and contaminated the scene, another journalist—only five years his senior but with an old man's eyes—pulled him aside for a candid chat.

"Head, not heart," the veteran told him. He reached out and tapped Lionel's forehead. "See, right now, you're having a natural human response. Empathy. Fear. You're thinking about that guy's family, right? About his wife and little girl, and how they're gonna feel when they get the news."

Lionel had managed to nod, still pale, wiping the back of his hand across his mouth.

"Kill that shit," the vet said. "When you're on the scene, you need to be a *machine*. You're not here as a human; you're not here as a good neighbor or a nice guy. That's on your own time. Right now, you're a reporter. You're here to get the facts. Record. Document. Objectivity is what counts. Empathy is the enemy."

And now, just like he had ever since that day, Lionel took all his revulsion and distress and shoved it into a closet in the back of his mind. He took out his phone and snapped a string of pictures, capturing the corpse—Ray Barton, he had to presume—from every angle. He didn't know if the murder had anything to do with the Poe manuscript—for all he knew, the guy had ripped off the wrong customer or slept with the wrong spouse—but he didn't know it *wasn't* related, either.

And then there was Maddie. His random encounter from last night, striding away from the scene of the crime.

As he circled the chair, still snapping pictures, his foot hit a chunk of metal. Lionel stumbled and caught himself before he could fall. A floor safe sat open, its iron face built to stay concealed under a square of fake concrete. Lionel crouched down and shone his light inside. Nothing had been left behind, not even a stray moth. As he turned, his beam caught something glittery at the foot of the dead man's chair. Something gold.

He scooped it up. It was a cuff link, fallen from the torn sleeve of Barton's dress shirt. The link sported an oval onyx face inlaid with three golden symbols. Egyptian hieroglyphs. Not the sort of thing Lionel would expect a pornographer and money launderer for the Russian mob to wear. Might have just been a quirky fashion choice, but his intuition told him it was worth checking out.

Lionel pocketed the link.

The contents of the dead man's pockets lay on a second folding table, just beside the mirror. Black leather wallet, watch—a Rolex, and a real one as far as Lionel could tell—and a cell phone in a rigid plastic case. He opened the wallet carefully, touching as few surfaces as he could and remembering the spots so he could wipe them down later. The driver's license inside confirmed his suspicion: Ray Barton had been tortured and killed in his own studio. The phone was locked, but the screen lit up to give a preview of his most recent calls and texts. The two at the top, from just an hour ago, caught Lionel's eye.

Rosa / 1:22PM / Hey babe, Wade says those pages are worth $$$ so you gonna cut me in or . . .

Rosa / 1:47PM / Where u at? Hit me back, we gonna get together 2nite or what?

"That's a definite no," Lionel murmured. He'd gotten all he could from the crime scene, and the clock was ticking. He used his shirtsleeve to wipe down the phone and the wallet, mentally walking backward through everything he'd done since stepping through the warehouse door. Then he got his story straight in his head. That wasn't hard: most of it was true, right up until the moment he started tampering with the evidence.

Lionel called the police and walked out into the sunshine, the summer air suddenly feeling ten degrees colder. He waited there, pacing the narrow lot, until the first squad car arrived.

~

"Good news and bad news," the detective told him.

Her name was Mathers—they weren't on a first-name basis, she made that perfectly clear from the start—and she'd kept Lionel sitting in a tiny white room with a one-way mirror for the better part of two hours. She was a warhorse, a veteran with hard eyes and a chain-smoker's voice, and she ran him through his story over and over until *he* started to wonder if he had murdered Barton. Then she headed out to check his bona fides, leaving him alone with half a cup of ice-cold instant coffee.

It was strangely comforting. After the humid, copper-stench air and darkness of the kill room, bright industrial lights and crisp walls were a return to something resembling a normal world.

"I'll take the bad news first," he said. She pulled back the chair across the table and sat down, locking eyes with him.

"Talked to your boss in Chicago. You aren't here, chasing a story. They didn't send you."

Lionel leaned back and let out a frustrated sigh. "I told you, three times already. *Freelance.* I'm working on a new book. This has nothing to do with my job at the station."

"And the subject of that book is . . . ?"

"The illicit antiquities trade. Counterfeits, stolen art, that kind of thing."

He'd decided a lie would be more believable than the truth, so he hadn't said a word about Regina or the Poe manuscript. Nobody could prove he *wasn't* writing a new book, and the subject wouldn't be too far afield from his debunking work. He left Barton's name out of it.

He also hadn't mentioned Maddie. He wasn't sure why. Lionel only had his gut to go on, and his gut told him she wasn't the killer.

"There aren't any dealers in Chicago you could be investigating?"

"Detective, can I level with you?"

Mathers arched an eyebrow. "Oh, please do."

"I've never been to New York. Always wanted to take a vacation here."

"And?"

"And," Lionel said, "there's this thing called a professional tax deduction. See, if I'm here doing research, I can write off the hotel, the airfare—it's all a business expense. So, yeah, when a source pointed me toward Ray Barton, I jumped at the chance to request a few days off and fly out here. It's dodgy, but it isn't illegal. Call the IRS if you don't believe me."

"And your source is?"

"Confidential. And that confidentiality is protected by law. That information wouldn't help you, anyway. All they knew was that Barton might have been involved in some very nonspecific shady business." He weighed his options, salting the lie with a little truth. "Allegedly, he's got connections to the Russian mob. It was thinner than thin. I just needed the justification to, well . . . visit your lovely city. Didn't plan to spend my trip in an interrogation room."

She set her palms flat on the steel table. Her nostrils flared, just a little, like she could smell the dishonesty on him. His story didn't add up, and they both knew it. She just couldn't find a crack in his armor wide enough to fit a blade through.

"Good news is," she said, grudgingly, "you don't have to. The waitress at Cookshop remembers you from this morning, and so does your cab driver. More importantly, that diner you ate at last night has you on their security camera. The ME estimates that Barton was having his impromptu dentist appointment in Red Hook while you were enjoying your crab roll in Chelsea, so that's a mark in your favor."

Lionel swallowed hard as his stomach knotted up. He tasted bile at the back of his throat. Mathers wore a tiny smirk, watching him.

And Maddie was right next to me, he thought, desperate to think of anything but Barton's mutilated mouth. *That clears her, too. But it doesn't explain what she was doing at his studio, or why she left instead of calling the police.*

His thoughts turned to the open and empty safe. *Or what she was carrying in that messenger bag.*

"So I'm good to go?" he asked.

"I'm not necessarily done with you yet," Mathers said. "Don't leave town until I say otherwise."

He thought about the cops back in Chicago, waiting to interview him about a totally different murder. It felt like a bad idea to bring that up.

"My boss needs me back home."

"Brianna Washington? She didn't tell me that. Maybe I should call her back. Put her on speakerphone, right here and now, so we can all get our stories straight."

Lionel's eyes dropped to the table.

Mathers shoved back her chair. She didn't take her gaze off him as she rose, stepping over to open the interview-room door.

"Something's not right about you, Page. Something just a little off. Don't worry. I'll figure you out. That's my job, and I'm *real* good at it." She nodded to the open door. "Hit the bricks. But don't leave town. And oh . . . right, almost forgot. Welcome to New York. On behalf of the city, we hope you enjoy your stay."

Ten

Out on the street, back in the mix and the crowds and the stark summer sun, Lionel walked. He didn't have a direction in mind, but he always thought better in motion. A light breeze didn't do much to cut the heat beating down from the cloudless sky, and a thin trickle of sweat plastered his shirt to his back. He ducked into a Starbucks, ordering an iced mocha just to have a reason to sit in the air-conditioning for a few minutes, and weighed his options at an empty table.

He called Regina. She picked up on the third ring.

"Lionel, how nice to hear from you. Dare I imagine you've found success this quickly, or is this just a status update?"

"The latter." He pitched his voice low and cupped his hand over the phone. "Whitcombe sent me to the guy with the manuscript, a local named Ray Barton. And Barton is dead. He was murdered last night."

"Oh. Oh, dear. How terrible. Do the police have any leads?"

"Besides me? No, and according to Whitcombe, Barton was mobbed up. That's not exactly a safe lifestyle. Regina . . . that Poe manuscript. Assuming it's real, and I'm not confident it is, how valuable *is* that thing to a collector like you? Is it possible someone might commit murder to get their hands on it?"

She chuckled, her voice dry as a bone. "My dear boy, how charmingly naive. You know perfectly well that murder is humanity's favorite pastime. People will kill each other over a scratched fender or a pool-hall bet. The answer to 'Will someone kill for this,' no matter what 'this' is, is *always* yes."

"What I'm saying is"—Lionel cast a sharp glance over his shoulder, making sure nobody was listening in, and hunched against the table— "what I'm saying is, Barton was . . . questioned. Severely questioned. If your name's been floating around as a potential buyer, and if they *didn't* find it in his safe, they could be looking at going after you next."

"And I'm genuinely touched by your concern. That said, I'm not a public person. I'll relocate to one of my other homes, just to be safe, but you needn't worry. I have very good security. What about you? I hope you're not getting cold feet."

This was the time to walk away and wash his hands. Death had been dogging his heels since the moment he met Regina Dunkle. First the cub reporter, butchered in an alley in one of the safest places in Chicago, and now the man he'd been sent to negotiate with, tortured to death in his own studio the very night Lionel landed in New York. It could all be a coincidence. A cosmic collision of bad luck and bloodshed, nothing to do with him or his mission.

But his intuition said otherwise.

And he knew he couldn't walk away. There was a story here, somewhere between Regina and the manuscript and the dead. Maybe the biggest story of his career. And just like the way he kept the cameras rolling in the middle of a riot, just like he exposed Reverend Wright in front of a packed and angry auditorium, the sense of danger lured him on like the tang of some exotic perfume. He had to follow his nose along the scented trail, wherever it led him, or he'd spend the rest of his life wondering what he'd missed.

"I'm in," he told her. "I'm still in. I'll find the manuscript."

"Good! You have yet to disappoint me. Such a brave young lion you are."

The entire room jarred two inches to the left.

Off-balance, his heart skipping a beat, he was back in the diner last night. Watching Maddie curl a lock of her ginger hair around one pale finger while Barton was being murdered across town. *"Names are important, you know. Do you know what Lionel means?"*

"Regina," he said slowly, "why did you call me that?"

"Oh, just playing with words. Young lion. That's what Lionel means. You did know that, didn't you?"

"Yeah, it's just . . . someone else recently told me the same thing."

"Synchronicity," she said, "I've found, at least, is the universe's way of telling you that you're on the right track. Excuse me, I have another call coming in. Good hunting, Lionel."

She broke the connection. He set his phone down, stared at the screen, and sipped his iced mocha in silence.

All right, he told himself. *Forget the weirdness, the coincidences—all of it. There's a story here, and I've got facts and a lead to chase.*

Time to do some serious journalism.

⌇

Back at the High Line Hotel, in a corner suite one floor directly under Lionel's room, Maddie paced the faded Persian rug in her bare feet. She hated shoes. Feeling the antique weave under her toes, the cool and scuffed hardwood floor, would normally help calm her down.

Right now, nothing could calm her down. She looked at the phone in her shaking hand and started dialing for the twentieth time. Then, just like the nineteen times before, she canceled the call. She tossed the phone onto her rumpled bedspread. She stormed into the bathroom.

A knock sounded at the suite's black door, and a chipper voice called out, "Housekeeping!" Maddie looked at herself in the bathroom mirror. Her cheeks glistened with twin trails of blood, leaking in rivulets from the corners of her eyes. Maddie reflexively wiped her hand against one cheek, leaving her face and palm covered in a sticky scarlet smear.

Another knock. "Housekeeping!"

Maddie's face contorted, and she tore her gaze from the mirror. "I'm—I'm not—" she called out in a hoarse voice, stumbling over her words. "Come back later, please! T-thank you."

The knocking stopped. She leaned on the sink, rested both hands on the pristine white porcelain, and bowed her head. She forced herself to take deep breaths through her mouth, exhaling through her nose, counting to ten in silence. Droplets of crimson drizzled down into the basin and joined the ragged red palm print she'd left on the edge of the sink.

She lifted her head just enough to see the edge of her image in the glass. Wild ginger curls and two scarlet eyes staring back at her, droplets of blood oozing from her tear ducts, like some insane and murderous stranger. "Get it. Under. Control," she told herself.

Her straight razor, folded inside its yellowed deer-bone sheath, sat on the bathtub's rim. As she turned to stare at it, the left sleeve of her blouse pulled back just a little. Just far enough to show the edges of her scars. Thin white lines, ivory on pale skin. She could make a fresh one. Just one slow, shallow slice, something to drown out her fear and her stress with the purity of white-hot pain. She'd feel better if she did. For a little while.

She looked back to the woman in the mirror.

"Not today," she told her reflection.

Not today. Her mantra. She had successfully *not today*'ed for one hundred and eighty-three days. She knew if she gave in and used the razor today, she'd have to start the clock all over again. And it would be that much easier to cut herself tomorrow, and the day after that. No. Not today. Maybe tomorrow, but not today.

She twisted the taps and let the water flow fast and cool. She scrubbed her palm, her face, washing away the tears of blood. There was something calming in cleaning herself up, a quiet ritual, watching the rusty color spiral down the sink and unearthing her freckles from the mess.

"Look at you," she told her clean-faced reflection with a shy smile. "Isn't that better? That's much better."

No more stalling. She walked back out and scooped her phone off the bedspread. The line clicked on the third ring, greeting her with an expectant silence.

"Ray Barton is dead," Maddie said.

"I didn't order you to do that."

"I didn't kill him." She paced the floor again, wriggling her bare toes against the coarse grains of the rug. "He was dead when I got there. Someone took their time with him, tortured him for intel and his safe combination. They left a ledger behind, nothing else. I took it with me."

She strolled over to the heavy book on her writing desk and ran a pale finger down the green lined pages.

"No big chunks of inbound cash," Maddie said, "so it doesn't look like Barton sold it yet. That said, no big chunks of outgoing cash, either. If he paid somebody for the Poe manuscript, he didn't record it here. Still no idea where he got it in the first place. Anyway, we can assume he gave up any info he had. Regina, I told you, I can't operate in New York—"

"You will address me," Regina said, her voice like a razor of ice, "as Ms. Dunkle, *Madison*."

"Why did you tell me to eat at that diner on Tenth Avenue?"

"That's quite the change of subject. And I merely recommended it, no compulsion whatsoever. Did your dinner not agree with you?"

Maddie paced to the closed drapes. She tugged one aside, just a crack, squinting at the sunshine as she peered down to the street below.

"I met a guy. Said his name was Lionel. Some kind of a writer. Allegedly."

"What you do on your own time is none of my concern," Regina replied. "You can take your little animal pleasures with whoever and whatever you please, so long as it doesn't interfere with your work."

"I didn't *sleep* with him." Madison grabbed a fistful of her curls, tugging hard. "When I left Barton's, I saw him again. Rolling by, in a hired car. I think he was following me. I can't operate in New York. This city . . . You know I can't operate here."

"You can conduct my business whenever and wherever I say you can. What are you afraid of, Madison?"

She threw her suitcase, a roll-on with metallic blue sides, onto the mattress and tugged the zipper. It parted with a rustling sound.

"You know what I'm afraid of."

"And I am protecting you," Regina told her. "So long as you stand under my aegis, you'll be invisible to your former sisters. And to *her*."

Her. The word hung in the cedar-scented air. It felt like a threat. Like Regina could simply speak the name aloud and bring Maddie's entire world crashing down. Maddie flipped the suitcase open and ran her fingers along the empty bottom, feeling for a hidden catch in the satin-soft lining.

"Did you send someone to check up on me?" Maddie demanded. "Lionel. Is he one of yours? Because if not, he might be trouble."

"Do you believe he is?"

"I don't know what he is." The catch twisted under Maddie's fingertip. She tugged up the lining, exposing a hidden compartment beneath. "But if he's on your payroll, you need to tell me right now."

"You're being silly," Regina replied. "Why would I dispatch two agents on the same errand and not tell them? That would be counterproductive."

"You do a lot of things I don't understand."

"Your job isn't to understand me," Regina said. "Your job is to serve me."

Maddie's hand dipped into the hidden compartment of her luggage. She tugged at snaps and drew steel, cold to the touch, from custom-sewn pockets.

Her pistol, a storm-gray Sig Sauer with the long, thin tube of a sound suppressor screwed to the barrel, turned in her pale grip. She slapped a fresh magazine into the gun and narrowed one eye as she stared down the iron sights.

"I'm just saying," Maddie told her, "if he's yours, tell me. Because I'm not taking any chances."

"Paranoia is not an attractive quality in a lady of good breeding."

"Cute." Maddie set the pistol down.

"Nor is a rebellious attitude. Do we need to have story time, Madison? Do I need to remind you of how you found yourself in your present circumstances?"

"Please don't."

"Once upon a time," Regina said, "an ungrateful little brat ran away from home—"

"Stop this."

"She found herself lost in the woods, alone, cold, starving, until a kindly old woman opened her hearth and showed her *such* kindness."

"Stop," Maddie said.

"You don't like that story? How about this one, then: once upon a time, a young mother gave birth to two adorable, rosy-cheeked sons—"

Maddie squeezed her eyes shut. They burned behind her eyelids, fresh tears of blood welling up.

"Please," she said, her voice breathy and ragged. *"Don't."*

"If you don't like the terms of your employment," Regina said, "you can walk away from it—and from my protection—anytime you please. Any chains upon you are strictly of your own making. They always have been. Until such time as you care to break them, you are *mine*. Get back to work. Find my manuscript. Report to me once you've succeeded."

Regina hung up on her. Maddie stood still, frozen as a stone, taking slow and deep breaths until the threat of more scarlet tears faded behind her stinging eyelids.

Her fingers dipped into the concealed compartment. She left the pistol alone for now. This time she drew out a purple velvet pouch, plump and heavy in her palm. It rattled softly. She pulled back the

Persian rug, clearing room, and sat cross-legged on the bare and dark-stained floorboards.

Whispers spilled from Maddie's lips, twisting and sinuous and slithering from her tongue. A chant, a tangle of ancient Greek, a prayer without a god to address it to. The world swam in and out of focus as the words embraced her. She poured the contents of the pouch into her open palm as her vision shifted to tones of sepia and scarlet.

She shook her fist like she was rolling dice and let her hand fly. Tiny chunks of faded yellow ivory fell to the floorboards, scattering, bouncing. Maddie watched them land. She tilted her head, deep in concentration as she whispered her chant. The bones told a story. The pattern they fell in, the directions the jagged chunks pointed—it all wove a tapestry of symbols. The last word of the chant faded on the air. She leaned in and studied the fall.

Danger near, she thought as her fingertips traced invisible lines between the bones. *Tell me something I don't know. Unexpected allies? Vague. And . . .*

She paused. The edge of the bone scatter was all wrong. Maddie scooped them up, rattling them with both hands, and threw a second time.

They scattered, bounced, and landed in the exact same pattern. Quietly defying the laws of physics and forcing her to heed their message. One tiny chunk of bone landed just out of position then twisted into place, snapping like a magnet. Maddie stared down in dead silence.

The blood of innocents. And disaster on the horizon, like a gathering hurricane.

Her winding fingertip traced the edge of the pattern. Left to right and back again, sinuous, serpentine.

Shades, drifting, planning. Machinations in the land of the dead.

Maddie's eyes narrowed to slits, glinting in the half light.

No. The dead are here. In New York.

Eleven

Half an hour later Lionel walked into 24 Connect, a round-the-clock PC café. Computers with bulky monitors lined four long rows of tables, tethered to an octopus nest of mismatched cables. Along the walls, under posters for shoot-'em-ups and fantasy role-playing games, a few stragglers sat at small tables and huddled over their battered laptops. Lionel shelled out ten dollars for an hour of computer time and another four for a lukewarm can of Cherry Coke and a plastic cup. Highway robbery, but he didn't have time to shop around for a better deal.

He slipped into an open chair in the back row, opened up a private browsing session, and got to work.

First item on the agenda was a surface-level dossier on Ray Barton. Lionel had learned early on that an investigative journalist's skill set wasn't too different from a private investigator's. Some of the best tips he'd ever gotten came from a PI who specialized in the sleaziest of divorce cases; everyone, he'd said, left footprints. And as technology became a ubiquitous part of everyday life, those prints got easier and easier to follow.

Lionel ran Barton's name through Tracers, IRBsearch, and Transunion's TLOxp database, harvesting the dead man's data with a few clicks of the mouse. It was a torrent of noise with tiny flashes of signal: inconsistent credit reports, a spotty criminal record—all misdemeanors, because felony accusations never quite made it to trial—and multiple registered addresses. If he didn't already know Barton had been a career criminal with mob ties, Lionel would have gotten a pretty solid clue from the pattern.

His real target was Barton's mysterious texting friend, Rosa. The one who knew about Barton planning to sell the Poe manuscript and who wanted a cut of the money. She was the best lead Lionel had, as long as she was still breathing. If Barton's killers hadn't gotten what they wanted from his safe, everybody connected to the man was in danger.

Barton had a Facebook profile. Perfect. He barely used it himself—his last post was from a month ago, giving a birthday shout-out—but he had more than three hundred people on his list of friends. Lionel took a slow walk through the mosaic of faces, names popping up one at a time under his cursor.

Ray had more than three hundred friends, but only one Rosa.

She was in her early twenties, with deep-tan skin, big Disney-princess eyes, and a jet-black tattoo of blooming roses on a gothic vine that ran the length of her left arm. Her feed was an ode to eternal youth, a whirlwind photo gallery of parties, clubs, and high-proof alcohol. Her latest update, just last night, showed Rosa and Ray arm in arm at a house party. They lifted their red plastic cups and flipped off the camera with matching smiles.

OMG, she commented on the picture, was this Lil Bitty's house? Don't even REMEMBER this, LOL.

He could use that. Normally his next step would be a repeat of step one, running Rosa's full name through the database tango. Only problem was, according to her profile, her full name was Rosa Nonyabusiness.

"Presumably," he muttered as he copied the picture and fired up a photo-editing program, "one of the distinguished Nonyabusinesses of the Hamptons."

Time for a little social engineering. In the background of the picture, a sleepy-eyed guy with dreads was sitting back on a couch and puffing a fat joint. Lionel drew a rectangle around the guy's face, snipped it, and saved it as a new picture. Ten minutes later he had a throwaway email address linked to a freshly minted Facebook account featuring the sleepy-eyed smoker as its owner. Rosa had more than a thousand friends linked to her account, so Lionel suspected she wasn't picky. He tossed her an invite.

The ball was in her court. While he waited, Lionel fumbled in his pocket and dug out the cuff link he'd taken from the scene of the crime. The onyx face and tiny gold hieroglyphs were a detail that just didn't fit. He ran a Google search, looking for a website with a list of common glyphs. He didn't have much hope of translating them—ancient near-Eastern languages weren't anywhere near his wheelhouse—but it gave him something to do while he was waiting for Rosa to notice his friend request.

He got lucky. He'd assumed the three glyphs on the link—a bird, an upside-down half circle, and a seated man—were three letters or words. As it turned out, the characters formed the name of a god.

Thoth, he read, *is the Greek derivation of the phonetic* dhwty, *also rendered as Djehuty or Tetu. He was one of the foremost gods of the Egyptian pantheon, usually depicted as a baboon or as a man with the head of an ibis. He was the god of knowledge and learning, associated with magic, the moon, and with the keeping of secrets.*

Lionel sipped his soda and squinted at the screen. Ray Barton was an underground pornographer who laundered money for the Russian mob. Why was he repping the name of an ancient god of knowledge on his cuff links? There was no clear path from point A to point B, and it grated on Lionel like a fly buzzing an inch from his ear. He kept reading, eyes drawn to pictures from faded papyrus, images of judgment and human hearts being weighed on scales while Thoth wrote down the final verdict.

One photo on the sidebar stood out: an image of the bird-headed deity cast as a bronze relief. *Lee Lawrie's* Thoth *(1939), Library of Congress, John Adams Building, Washington, DC.* Curious, Lionel clicked through. The link brought him to a string of photos of the John Adams Building, where the artist had created images of gods from cultures across the world to adorn the eastern and western doors. The Thoth entry, on the list of gods, had a footnote.

Lawrie filed a lawsuit against the architectural firm
of Bruckman & Shale in 1939, alleging they copied
his design for the landmark Blackstone Building in
New York City. Bruckman & Shale countered that
they had drawn the image from original archaeo-
logical sources—

Lionel was running on pure instinct now. He ran a search for the
Blackstone Building, and the breath caught in his throat. The place was
an art deco temple, less an apartment building and more of a set piece
for a Cecil B. DeMille epic. A towering colonnade of white Georgian
marble faced the street, topped with the images of seated Egyptian pha-
raohs. Tall stained-glass arches filled the space between each column, a
riot of color depicting gods with heads of birds, of bulls, of beetles, a
pagan cathedral in the heart of Lincoln Square.

The building had served as a recording studio, a college campus,
a condominium—twice—and closed its doors a decade ago after the
latest owners went bankrupt. Since then the cathedral had stood in
purgatory, doors sealed, frozen halfway through a wall-to-wall renovation. There'd been murmurings about prospective investors ever since,
but nothing had reached the bargaining table.

An exchange in the comments section made Lionel lift his eyebrow.
This place is Illuminati as hell, a writer calling himself ThePythian
commented. Egypt, triangles, pyramids. Do the math, people, it's
right in front of you.

Yeah, another poster shot back, amazing how this all-powerful
secret society leaves clues everywhere, and you're the only one
smart enough to see it. Or maybe it doesn't exist and you're just
an idiot.

That's what they want you to think. Wake up, sheeple!

A third poster chimed in, Half-right. The Blackstone was home to a secret society, but not the Illuminati. Thoth Club. Most of the Vanderbilts were members; so were Henry Ford and Andrew Carnegie. Nothing scary about it, it was just a fraternity for rich guys. It broke up sometime in the sixties.

Obvious disinfo tactic right here, ThePythian replied. Illuminati shill confirmed.

Lionel was about to tap in a search for "Thoth Club" when an open tab on his browser flickered. Rosa Nonyabusiness had accepted his friend request on Facebook.

Now they were connected over the site's messenger chat. She had already sent over a message: Hey, u look familiar. Were u at Lil Bittys the other nite? Party was LIT.

He weighed his response carefully. He'd only get one shot at this; if he scared her off, he could kiss his only solid lead goodbye.

"Sorry," he murmured, typing his response, "just had to get your attention. My name is Lionel Page. I'm a reporter for Channel Seven News in Chicago; if you want, I can provide you with contact information for my boss, and she can verify that everything I'm saying is one hundred percent true. Ray Barton is dead. He was murdered last night; the body was just found a few hours ago, and you may be in danger. We need to meet. Pick any place you want, in public is fine. You can bring friends for backup, whatever makes you feel safe. Please take this very seriously."

He waited. And kept waiting. Either he'd blown it or she was checking up on him. Either way, she hadn't unfriended him, and the messenger window stayed open. Ten minutes later, she replied.

The High Line. 2nite, 8 o'clock.

Lionel tossed back his last swig of Cherry Coke, powered down the PC, and headed for the café door.

Twelve

Maddie took a cab to Brooklyn.

On the south side of the borough, a muggy sunset shimmered down and turned the waters just off the Brighton Beach boardwalk into a sea of molten brass. Across the boardwalk, electric lights ignited under a long money-green awning with the restaurant's name—*Natalya*—spelled out in Gothic gold. Inside, a small sea of round tables clustered before the arc of a stage. The nightingale-blue curtains dangling from the proscenium matched the tablecloths, clashing with the bright-orange napkins at every plate.

On Saturdays, they had a cabaret. Tonight the stage sat empty, and music floated in over an old stereo system. Strings, something listless, something sad, memories of the motherland poisoned by the heartache of nostalgia.

The man of the hour sat at the dead-center table, his orange napkin like a fluttering bull's-eye as he flourished it and spread it across his lap. He wore the color of his age with pride, his hair slicked back and sculpted from silver, formed into a sharp widow's peak. The only things young about him were his eyes. Young and hungry, mostly for the woman sitting across from him. She'd turned heads with her arrival, her body poured into a little black cocktail dress, a slim purse on a silver chain dangling from her shoulder.

The men at the front door, greeting Maddie with polite apprehension and gun bulges under their tailored jackets, had asked her to leave her purse with the hostess. Security. She understood, yes? Yes. She pretended not to notice that the women sitting at the tables all around hers had handbags within easy reach. Just like she politely overlooked their hard-eyed "dates" watching her like hawks as they drank their club sodas and left their wineglasses untouched.

Her dinner companion drank enough for all of them. Burgundy splashed into his bottomless goblet, a silent waiter retreating to fetch a second bottle. The old man lifted his glass and eyed Maddie over the rim.

"You haven't changed a bit, *nocnitsa*. As beautiful as the day we first met."

"You know, Aleksandr," Maddie said, "most women would take issue with being called a night hag."

Their glasses clinked under the sound of his deep-throated laugh.

"You take it in the right spirit, I think. Besides, you inherited the title. How is your mother, by the way?"

"Enjoying her retirement in Spain," Maddie replied.

"You must send her my love." Aleksandr Sokolov sat back in his chair, sipped his wine, and marinated in the violin music. His eyes went distant. "We—I, my entire family—owe so much to that woman."

"She was in the right place at the right time."

"Ah, yes. Right place at the right time to put a bullet through my mad dog of a grandfather's heart." He flashed a grin and winked at her over his glass. "Which normally I'd take exception to, if I hadn't been the one who paid her to do it. You know the funny thing about your mother, *nocnitsa*?"

"There are lots of funny things about my mother."

Aleksandr paused. His smile froze, but the humor left his eyes. He looked like a businessman standing over a contract with a pen in his hand, weighing his options, deciding whether or not to take a massive risk.

His hand emerged from his jacket with a photograph. "She was my family's finest asset. Helped to build us, to make us what we are today. The day she leaves, I all but beg her to stay—and I am not a man who begs, you know this. But she must go. Twenty years later, I learn she has a daughter. Same blood. Same trade. Same . . ." He trailed off, searching for the words in English. ". . . divine prowess. But one thing, I always wonder. One thing keeps me up at night."

He set the faded Polaroid down on the nightingale tablecloth between them. From the bad fashion and the worse hair, it had been shot sometime in the seventies—winter, a light snow falling, and the spires of Red Square in the background. Aleksandr was a much younger man, cold-eyed but smiling, puffed up like a peacock with a woman on his arm. A pale slip of a woman whose curls spilled out from under her knit cap.

"I always wonder," he said, tapping a finger against his temple, "how the daughter looks so *much* like the mother. More like identical twins, somehow. Or . . ."

His voice trailed off, leaving the rest of his thoughts unspoken. His commitment to the question he wanted to ask sputtered and died an inch away from the finish line.

Maddie reached over and placed the tip of one scarlet fingernail on the photo's edge.

"My mother," she said, holding Aleksandr's gaze, "doesn't like photos of herself floating around. I don't like it, either."

The nail hooked the Polaroid's edge and drew it over to her side of the table.

"I'll be taking this with me."

A riot of emotions ran across his face in a heartbeat. He'd broken his own momentum, reaching for answers then pulling his hand away before his fingers could burn, and he couldn't find his balance again. Aleksandr shifted gears, trying to wrest back control of the conversation.

"You haven't been to New York in a very long time."

"I ran into some trouble," Maddie said. "Nothing to do with our business relationship. Different kind of trouble."

"And yet," he said, lifting his wineglass, "here you are. Which makes me wonder what business brings you here."

Again, stopping short of the real question. Maddie knew his real worry, the worry that had made him close the restaurant for the night and stock the tables all around them with his own people.

"*You* aren't the business I'm here on, Aleksandr."

He let out a held breath. His shoulders slacked, just a little.

"Never you," Maddie said. "We go a long way back. Loyalty is important to me, and you have to give loyalty to get it. That said, I've had offers."

His eyes narrowed. "Pietrovich."

"I knew you wouldn't be surprised. He's been waving fistfuls of rubles in my general direction. And if he's courting me for the job—"

"He's courting others," Aleksandr grumbled. "Ones without your loyalty. Thank you for this. But you could have warned me with a phone call. Why the personal visit?"

"The business I *am* here on. You have—had, after last night—a man named Raymond Barton in your employ."

Aleksandr frowned. He waved over the maître d'. The tuxedoed host bent low, and the two of them conversed in soft, rapid-fire Russian. Finally Aleksandr nodded, shooing the man away.

"Yes, yes, Barton. Sorry, not exactly a shining star of my organization. To put it in civilian terms, you are asking the CEO about the boy in the mail room. Were you the one who . . . ?" He pointed a finger to his temple.

"No. I found him like that. I just wanted to talk to him about a manuscript my client is looking for. I don't suppose that rings a bell? An old folio from the mid-1800s. I'm not sure where he got his hands on it, but it wasn't his usual trade."

Aleksandr snapped his fingers, nodding to himself.

"You know, now that you mention this? Yes. I never saw this document, not with my own eyes, but he approached me about it. Raymond was a good money launderer but a terrible salesman. Talked it up too much." He gave her a melodramatic eye roll. "Oh, it's a priceless manuscript, surely worth millions, a lost masterpiece of Edgar . . . Edgar . . ."

"Edgar Allan Poe," Maddie said.

Aleksandr pointed at her. "That's the one. What do I care about horror stories? If it was a lost Dostoyevsky, we might have something to talk about. I told him he was expecting way too much. Take it to a bookseller who specializes in such things—this is New York, we must have a dozen at least—appraise it, sell it, forget about it. Why make such a fuss?"

"So he didn't mention where he found it in the first place?"

"No." Aleksandr sipped his wine, brow furrowed. "He only mentioned the manuscript once more, a few days later. Said he'd found a partner to help him sell the thing."

"He took your advice?" Maddie asked.

"Not a bookstore. No, this man, Raymond's partner, had friends, art collectors, a very private community. They hold auctions among themselves. That's where they were going to sell the pages." Aleksandr waved a dismissive hand. "Call themselves the Thoth Club, name of some god nobody remembers, like it makes them civilized. Bourgeois dilettantes with more money than taste. I wished him good luck, and that was the end of it. Let me ask you, *nocnitsa*: Do you think Raymond's death had anything to do with this folly of his?"

"He was a criminal. Plenty of reasons someone might want him dead," Maddie replied. She contemplated the question as she sipped her wine. The taste was earthy, like peat and musty cherries. "That said, he was part of your family. I assume that wasn't a secret?"

"It was known to the right people."

She took that in. "So anyone on the inside would know: A move against Ray Barton is a move against you. An invitation to retaliation."

Aleksandr's brow scrunched up. "That's right."

A waiter stepped in, summoned by Aleksandr's almost-invisible nod, and set a white paper bag next to Maddie's left hand. A to-go bag for a meal she'd never ordered. She unfolded the top and took a peek. Two stacks of crisp bills nestled inside, fresh from the bank—or what passed for it, in Aleksandr's world—and bound with stiff cardboard bands.

"I really don't have time to deal with Pietrovich right now," she said.

"This isn't dealing-with-Pietrovich money," her host said. "It's more of a . . . token of my family's esteem. A small taste of all you've made possible for us."

So it's not-coming-after-you-next money, she thought. She folded the bag shut and pulled it half an inch closer to her side of the table, a quiet acknowledgment.

"May our friendship be a long and healthy one," she said.

A flicker of relief showed on his face. Then he got back to business. "So . . . Raymond's death. A message to me? A deliberate affront?"

"Nobody looking to start a gang war is going to pick a bottom-feeder like Ray for their opening salvo," Maddie said. "No, this wasn't Pietrovich or any of your other rivals. Doesn't make sense. It had to be an outsider, someone who didn't know or didn't care what kind of trouble they were inviting to their doorstep by killing a man under your protection."

"Which is it?" Aleksandr asked. "Didn't know, or didn't care?"

A waiter swooped in. They fell silent as the man refilled their glasses. Maddie switched from wine to sparkling water. She wanted a perfectly clear head right now.

"They tortured him, killed him, ransacked his safe, didn't even try to hide the body or cover up the crime," she said. "My intuition says, didn't care. They think they're untouchable. My intuition also says they're expecting you to come looking for them. But they're not expecting me."

"Your intuition," he echoed.

"My intuition is rarely wrong." She offered a faint smile and lifted her glass of water. "My mother taught me that."

Thirteen

The High Line—sharing a name and part of an address with Lionel's hotel—swept along the west side of Manhattan. It was an elevated train track, rolling from Hell's Kitchen down to the Meatpacking District, until a demolished spur cut it off from the West Side Line. The city found new uses for things. Struts became sturdy walkways, railings bloomed with stainless-steel planters, and the planters—lined with rich dark soil, fed with cold New York rain—bloomed wild and green. The dead and severed limb of the transit system found new life as a mile-and-a-half ribbon of public park.

On one side, the last glimmering rays of sunlight glittered off the Hudson River. On the other, Lionel leaned against the polished rail and looked down a city canyon, streetlights dangling pennants for the Whitney Museum of American Art. He hadn't realized how long the High Line was or how even at eight in the evening, the park would still be thronged with tourists, couples, and power walkers, all competing for space on the twisting lane between the trees and wildflowers. He shot Rosa a follow-up message, asking for a more specific spot to meet.

Just off 27th st stairs, she replied. He made his way there and kept an eye out.

She wasn't hard to spot. She looked just like her picture, wearing a neon-purple halter top and yoga pants, eyes shrouded behind chunky plastic sunglasses. She kept her back to the railing and her arms crossed tight over her belly. She looked like a scared deer about to bolt. Lionel moved in, keeping his pace casual, his hands open and easy at his sides.

"I'm Lionel," he said. "Can we talk here?"

She didn't look at him. She talked perpendicular to him, keeping him in the corner of her eye.

"I called the cops. They said you were right. Ray's dead. No details, though."

"You don't want the details," he told her.

"They fucked him up good, huh?"

"You know who 'they' is?" he asked.

"His business was none of my business," Rosa said. "That's what he always told me. I knew he was into all kinds of shady shit. Just didn't think it'd ever come home to roost. Why you think *I* got anything to do with it?"

"You texted him about some 'pages' that were worth a lot of money."

She pulled down her glasses and stared at him over the rims.

"Is *that* what this is about?" She slid them back up on her nose. "Damn. What I get for trying to help. Yeah, Ray got his hands on this, I don't know, binder of old sheets of paper. All old-school, handwritten and shit, some kind of short story."

"Do you know where he got it?"

"Didn't know, didn't care," she told him. "Like I said, his business wasn't my business. I was in some of his films, okay? I am an *actress*. Other than that, we'd party together now and then. Or I'd party with friends of his. He'd set up the date, take a commission, you understand what I'm saying?"

Lionel nodded. "So how did you help? With the pages, I mean."

She put her arms behind her on the railing, stretched her shoulders back, and rolled her neck with a tired sigh.

"This other guy I party with sometimes. Guy's *loaded*. Pure Wall Street. Anyway, he's into collecting all kinds of weird historical stuff. Once, when he was all coked up, he started bragging about it, said he's tight with this crew of art collectors. Called 'em the, uh . . ." She snapped her fingers, trying to remember. "Tooth something."

"Thoth Club?" Lionel asked.

"Yeah, sounds about right. Whatever. Sounded like weird, rich white people doing weird, rich white-people shit. So I played matchmaker. Hooked up my man Wade with Ray, thinking they could do some business, and I'd get a little something off the top. Way I heard it, they were gonna cook a deal with Wade's buddies and sell it at their next get-together. So, tell me something: That why Ray had to die? Did he steal those papers from somebody?"

"That's what I'm thinking," Lionel said. "So, who actually had the manuscript? Was it in Ray's safe?"

"Nah, Wade took it off him a few days ago. Said he had to get it authenticated, you know, get some college professors or whoever to say it ain't a fake. Otherwise nobody would buy it."

Ray would have talked before he died. If Lionel knew anything, after seeing the condition Ray's body was in, he knew that much. He moved a little closer to Rosa, freezing in place when she started to bristle. Her bubble of personal space was a finely tuned instrument.

"There's a very good chance that the killer was after that manuscript," he told her. "I need to know how to get in touch with this Wade guy."

"Dawson. Wade Dawson, with Stamford and Cross Investment Partners. Hey, what about *me*? Do I need to worry about this coming back on me?"

Lionel thought about it, doubling back and checking every angle just to be safe, before he shook his head.

"I don't think so, no. They're after the manuscript. You don't have it, and Ray would have told them you don't have it, so they've got no reason to go after you."

"He mighta lied. Ray lied out his ass on the daily."

Lionel saw a flicker-fast vision of the death room. The slumped body in the bondage throne. The tray with the pliers and the cordless drill.

"He didn't lie," Lionel said.

Whatever Rosa saw in his eyes, it made her take an inching step away from him.

"Yeah," she said, "all right."

"All the same," he said, "just to be safe, lie low for a little while. What else can you tell me about Wade Dawson?"

"Only that he's a freak behind closed doors. Got a wife at home, and he's out getting strange at all hours of the night. Sometimes I party with him and this girl I see around, Chantille? Girl's barely older than sixteen, and he knows it. He likes 'em young, especially after he's had a couple of bumps." Rosa stuck out her finger and wriggled it, making it flop like a dead fish. "Can't always *do* anything after he's had a couple of bumps, but he tries real hard. Look, isn't this a job for the cops? And what's your deal? You aren't even *from* here."

He wished he had an answer to give her, one that made sense, one that wouldn't sound like a lie even as he spoke the words. He'd come to New York on what was supposed to be an open-and-shut job, a day or two of fieldwork and a quick case closed, all to keep a cub reporter off his back. Now the reporter was dead, the last man to hold the Poe manuscript was dead, and the cops in two cities were giving him the side-eye for it.

That strange falling sensation, from when he'd contemplated Regina's offer and made his pact, washed over him all over again. Lionel felt like he was being drawn down a tight spiral staircase, built inside a shaft of midnight-black stone, with nothing but a dying candle to light his way. He couldn't go back up. Couldn't even look up. The dark below had a magnetic pull, and the farther he walked, the harder it was to stop.

And Lionel didn't want to stop. His nose told him there was a story here, something bigger than the Poe manuscript and bigger than Ray Barton's murder. He wasn't leaving without it.

"It could be more dangerous if the police get involved," he told her, though he hoped she didn't ask him to explain his logic. He was making it up as he went along. "Better if I warn Wade directly, myself."

"You gonna leave my name out of it? I don't need Wade mad at me."

"You're a confidential source," Lionel said. "Your name never passes my lips."

It was getting dark on the High Line. Rosa didn't take her sunglasses off. He couldn't see her eyes, but he could feel her studying him, weighing his words, deciding if they were made of cotton candy or stone. She gave him a tiny nod.

"Just watch yourself. Wade is . . . He's got some issues."

"Issues?"

"He's not, like, violent," Rosa said. "He's never hurt me or any of the other girls he parties with, not that I know of. But there's always this . . . edge, talking to him. Like he won't hurt you, but he really kinda *wants* to. Never seen him really angry, and I'm not looking to, either."

"I'll be careful. Thanks, Rosa."

He turned to go. She lifted her chin, eyeing him. "Hey. Reporter man."

Lionel glanced back at her.

"Confidential source. That job pay anything?"

He reached into his wallet and folded a pair of twenties around his fingertips, passing them over to her. She made the twenties disappear.

⌒

Tea lights danced in the dark outside Lionel's hotel, casting shifting shadows across intimate tables and an open-air bar. The floating party filled the space between the former monastery's Gothic facade and the shrub-lined iron fence that drew a protective circle around the property. There wasn't much Lionel could do tonight—catching up with Rosa's "friend" Wade would have to wait until morning—but a drink or two was definitely on the agenda. The menu offered a curated list of frozen cocktails, antidotes for the muggy summer night's heat. He found an open spot at the bar and ordered a mojito.

The clear rum drink came in a frosted glass, a sprig of mint leaning to one side like the feather in a cap. The gentle din of conversation and the first cool sip of his drink wove a fog around Lionel. It was a muddle of voices but no words, no context. Background music for his thoughts. He set his glass down and put together a battle plan for the morning. Dropping in on Wade Dawson was his best move, but there were a few ways he could play it—

An identical glass clinked against his. He looked up, jolted from his reverie.

"Look at that," Maddie said. "We've gone from caffeine buddies to mojito buddies."

He hadn't seen her sidle up beside him at the bar, but there she was, with a gleam in her eye and a smile that said *I dare you*. He wasn't sure what she was daring him to do. He wasn't sure if it mattered.

"Too hot for coffee," he said. "Hate to do it, but if you'll forgive a cliché . . . Do you come here often?"

"When I'm in town." She nodded past the bar's awning, to the soft glow behind the hotel's front doors. "I like the vibe here. Beats staying at a chain hotel any day of the week."

"Staying . . ." Lionel paused, taking her in. A tea light on the bar, caged in a bubble of glass, cast a pale glow across her high cheekbones. "I thought you were a local."

A warm breeze gusted across the courtyard. Maddie's tiny smile, and the challenge in her eyes, grew with the flicker of the tea light.

"And an actress. Yes, you *thought* these things. I never said you were right. Travel writers should pay more attention to detail."

"Never said I was a travel writer." He sipped his mojito. "Just said you were close."

She put one hand on her hip and affected a halfhearted pout. "Lionel, I'm starting to think our entire relationship is built on a foundation of lies and treachery. Now how am I supposed to bring you home to my parents for Thanksgiving dinner? 'Mom, Dad, this is Lionel. I really don't know what he does for a living.' Flatly unacceptable."

He tried to keep a straight face. It lasted all of three seconds.

"Oh?" he shot back. "And how do you think I feel? 'Everybody, this is Maddie. I dreamed of watching her from backstage, bringing her a bouquet of roses as she made her triumphant debut on Broadway. Then I found out she's neither an actress nor a New Yorker.'"

"Would you really bring me roses?"

"Of course I'd bring roses," Lionel said. "We do have culture in Chicago. Despite what people on the coasts think of flyover country, we aren't total barbarians."

"A-*ha*," she said, pointing a finger at him over her glass. "Chicago confirmed. A clue. A solid clue. And I was right about your vocal inflection, so that's a tick in the win column for me."

"You're good," he said.

She arched an eyebrow. "You have *no* idea. So what part was I wrong about? The travel part or the writer part?"

"Oh, no," he said with a chuckle. "There's a distinct lack of back-scratching going on here. I gave you something solid about me; now you have to return the favor."

Maddie took a deep breath and let it out as a melodramatic sigh. She pressed the back of her hand to her brow, defeated.

"Fine, fine, fair's fair. I'm from a small town called Athens, originally."

"And there's an Athens in . . ." Lionel racked his brain. "Illinois, Michigan, New York, Pennsylvania—"

"Don't forget Georgia, Ohio, Alabama, and Maine. Probably a few others I'm forgetting. It's a popular name."

"Not much help pinning you down," he said. "Though I don't think you're a southern girl."

"Well, *ah declare*," she replied, fanning herself as she drank her mojito. "Mah papa'll get his shotgun if he finds out ah'm datin' a northern boy. All the same . . . might be worth the risk."

Outside the hotel fence, the pavement was rigid and firm under Lionel's feet. Everything was material, real, predictable. Stepping inside the courtyard, past the ring of cold iron and earth, it was like he'd breached some ancient and magical ward. He was on sacred ground now. There were fairies flitting in the tea lights, glinting in Maddie's eyes and her perpetually amused smile.

He was a long way from home. There were no maps for this part of New York City. Only a guide. He wasn't sure if he could trust her. He wasn't sure if he cared.

"Dating?" he replied. "Oh, is that what we're doing?"

She gave a nonchalant shrug. "I don't know. Two travelers, ships passing in the night—who knows what might happen? Could be nothing. Could turn into one of those life-changing, passionate, heartbreaking flings that people write bestselling books about. Ever had a fling like that?"

"Can't say I have. My exes mostly report feelings of overwhelming disappointment. It's the only thing they have in common."

She reached over. Her fingertip touched the side of his glass, tracing lazy circles in the frosty condensation.

"If you could, would you like one?"

"Passion and heartbreak? Can't I just have the passion part?"

"No," she said. "Pleasure without pain is a waste of time; nobody ever wrote an epic poem about happy people who get everything they want. Besides, scars build character. So, would you? Would you throw yourself into a hurricane, just to have the experience?"

He thought about it, brushing past his knee-jerk denial before it even reached his lips. He thought about standing on the stage after exposing Reverend Wright and seeing the crowd surge toward him like a tidal wave, feeling the adrenaline rush hit his veins like a heroin spike.

He thought about reporting from the heart of a riot, surrounded by a furious mob. His entire career had been about pushing limits, taking risks, flying at the edge of a candle's flame and trying to flit away before his wings could burn. He'd claim that was just his job, not his life, but that would mean pretending he had any kind of a life outside his job.

Lionel was a storm chaser. Maddie was a storm.

"Sure," he told her. "If I could."

"I promise nothing," Maddie said. "But I want to know more about you, Lionel. Tell you what: let's make a trade."

"Shoot."

"Tell me who you work for," she offered, "and I'll give you my phone number. We'll see how the night goes from there."

Fourteen

Lionel looked to Maddie, and she watched him with quiet expectation. Her offer dangled in the air like bait. Normally he was open about his work; just being on the air made him a C-list celebrity back in Chicago, and he had nothing to be ashamed about. That said, he wasn't here on official business. And somehow, though she hadn't forbidden it, he had a feeling Regina Dunkle wouldn't appreciate her business being made public.

Then there was the cub reporter. Dead in an alley, half an hour after Regina promised Lionel he'd be silenced.

That had been enough to get him to keep his mouth shut when he had the chance to ask Brianna for research help, and doubly so when the local cops hauled him in. He could lay all his cards on the bar—all except that one.

"I'm a reporter," he told her. "So you were close."

"I was *sure* you were a writer."

"I wrote a book," Lionel said. "*A* book. It just came out."

Maddie plucked a napkin from a stack on the bar, produced a pen, and jotted something down.

"I'm always looking for new reading material. Fiction?"

"Getting a head start on my memoirs," he told her. "I made a name for myself digging into hoaxes, frauds, con artists. Investigative reporting. It's sort of a greatest-hits compilation."

She slid the napkin over to him. Seven digits and an area code, in prim, tight letters.

"Oh, look, it's my phone number," she said. "So, you must be in town on business. What are you investigating?"

He folded the napkin carefully, rubbing a finger across the ink to make sure it was dry, and slipped it into his pocket. "What, don't I get something?"

"You just did. As promised."

Lionel shook his head. "I mean, don't I get to know something about you now?"

"Maybe I like being an international woman of mystery."

"C'mon. Give me something. What do you do?"

"*Ugh.*" She rolled her eyes. "Ever wonder why that's the conversational default? People always want to know your job. Not what you love, what you hate, but what you do to earn money. What does that say about us as a society?"

"Didn't you just ask me the same question?"

"I asked who you work for," Maddie replied. "Not exactly the same as what you do for a living. Subtle semantic differences."

"Okay," Lionel said. "Who do you work for?"

The curve of her smile didn't droop a bit, but some of the amused glint faded from her eyes. A breeze wafted through the courtyard, pushing the muggy air around, making the tea light between them flicker and bow in its glass-bubble prison.

"I'm in insurance," she said.

He tilted his head at her and lifted his drink. It had sounded, the way the words tumbled off her tongue, like "I'm *an* insurance." The ice in his mojito had melted to jagged little shards, and the glass was slick against his hand. He felt the ghost of her fingertips from when she'd traced idle little designs in the condensation.

"Like a claims adjuster, or—"

"Something like that." The light returned to her eyes, her smile offering a fresh challenge. "How long are you in town for?"

Lionel pinched the bridge of his nose. He normally didn't have a problem holding his liquor—it was basically a job requirement for any veteran reporter—but the frosty drink had crept up on him like a mugger with a roll of quarters in its beefy fist. The booze struck from behind and left his senses reeling. *It's the heat,* he thought. *Stealth dehydration plus liquor equals one hell of a hangover tomorrow morning if I don't cut myself off.*

"Couple of days, I think. Listen, I hate to cut this short, but I've got to get some shut-eye." He paused, eyeing her. "You want to . . . I don't know, grab lunch tomorrow, maybe?"

She tossed back one last swig of her drink and set her glass beside his. "I think we might just be able to arrange that. Call me. C'mon, I'll walk in with you."

They crossed the lobby—quiet now, this late—and waited for the elevator to creep its way down. They got on together. He hit the button for three; she hit the button for two. When they reached her floor, Maddie stood on the elevator threshold, keeping the door from closing with the heel of her glossy black pump. Their eyes met. For a moment, Lionel thought she might invite him to her room. Instead, she flashed a grin and pulled her foot back.

"Sweet dreams, young lion," she said as the door rumbled shut between them.

～

Back in his suite, Lionel filled a glass with water from the bathroom sink and pounded it down. Then another. Then a third. When it came to drinking, chasing booze with water was the only reliable hangover preventative he'd ever found, and he'd tried them all. He was hunting big game come sunrise, and he'd need all his senses in working order to get the job done.

He fell into the unfamiliar bed, under unfamiliar blankets, and drifted into a turbulent sleep.

He wasn't sure when he woke up. No light glowed around the edges of the drapes, no sound from the street. Only the rustle of footsteps.

Someone was in his room.

His sleep-fogged brain tried to process that. He'd latched the door and fixed the dead bolt; nobody should have been able to get in . . . but there it was, a shadow on the edge of his bedroom, hunched over his writing desk. He thought about throwing back the covers, jumping up, taking them by surprise with a shout—then the shadow turned, and he saw the outline of a gun in the figure's hand. A slim pistol with the telltale snout of a sound-suppressor tube screwed to the barrel.

Lionel had worked mob stories and reported on contract killings. He knew there was only one reason someone carried a silenced weapon on a break-in: to kill someone and get away clean.

His muscles turned to taut stone. He fought the sudden fight-or-flight impulse, every nerve screaming for him to go on the attack. He did the smartest thing he could do: he lay perfectly still, eyes half-lidded, watching the intruder through his eyelashes and pretending to be asleep. Making a move, any move, would just get him shot. He resolved to maintain the charade for now. If they just searched his room, they could have whatever they were looking for; the cash in his wallet wasn't worth his life.

If they approached his bed, gun in hand, that was a different situation.

There were times when Lionel, a skeptic to the bone, halfheartedly wished he could believe in God. Praying might not help, but it would give his fevered mind something to do. Instead, he swallowed his fear, focusing on staying perfectly limp, his breath steady, and reassessed his options with every move the shadow made. It turned its back to him, and he heard the sound of his suitcase's zipper tugging down.

Now, he thought. It might be his best chance. His only chance. Jump up, three quick steps to cross the room, hit him from behind—

A wet, rattling sound jarred his thoughts. He slowly turned his gaze, following the sound to his left.

He wasn't alone in bed.

A second shadow crouched on all fours at his side, staring right at him. It was a woman, long limbed and gangly, a curtain of stringy hair shrouding her tilted face. In a heartbeat, he knew one thing for certain.

She knew he was awake.

The mattress sank under her gnarled hands as she crawled toward him. Her throat made that wet, rattling sound, and her shoulder bones creaked. Lionel was frozen now, not by choice: his muscles seized, rebelling against his brain, locking him into a wooden puppet of a body.

She climbed on top of him. Her hands pressed against his ribs and squeezed the air from his lungs. Brittle nails dug into his skin, one bending and snapping over his heart. One bony knee sank into his belly, heavy as a lead weight, starving him of air. His last gasp wheezed from his lips, and when he tried to inhale, her weight kept his lungs as empty as a balloon in a clenched fist.

His heart pounded in his ears, blood surging, and his arms still refused to move. The shadow across the room kept rummaging through his luggage, oblivious. Lionel tried to cry out to him—pistol or not, he needed help and he'd take his chances—but he couldn't make a sound. He couldn't breathe. She wouldn't let him breathe. His vision went gray around the edges, burst-vessel splotches littering his sight, and the woman stroked his cheek like a lover.

She turned her head. The curtain of hair fell to one side, baring half a face—an impossibly old face, almost mummified, leathery skin lined with canyon-deep veins. One mad, bloodshot eye stared at him, unblinking. Then she licked her cracked, desiccated lips, and leaned in for a kiss.

⌒

"Fuck!"

Lionel threw punches at his bedsheets—twisting, turning, throwing himself from the mattress and landing on the hardwood floor with a jolting thump as his shoulder smacked against the bare planks. He jumped to his feet, wincing, still flailing at phantoms.

He caught himself and froze. Morning light pushed against the edges of the drapes. Nobody was in his bed. His luggage was exactly where he'd left it, zipped and pristine. The dead bolt held fast, his silent sentinel.

He pumped his arms, bouncing on his feet, just to reassure himself that he could move again.

"Nightmare," he said out loud, pacing to the bathroom. "Lionel, you are officially getting old. That was one drink. One. A *mojito*, for crying out loud."

The black-and-white bathroom tiles were cool under his bare feet. They felt real, polished smooth and hard, drawing a line between the waking world and the slippery, fast-fading memory of his night terrors. He looked himself in the mirror, bleary-eyed, and ran a hand along his sandpapery cheek stubble. His phone balanced on the edge of the sink. He tapped the screen and scrolled down his list of contacts. A good fifty names flickered past in alphabetical order before he hit the *B*s. The phone rang twice; then the clamor of the newsroom echoed over the phone's tinny speaker.

"Tell me you're on a plane," Brianna said. "Specifically, a plane coming home."

"I would, but you hate it when I lie."

"What are you *doing*? First I get a call from the Chicago police, asking why you haven't shown up for an interview yet. Then I get a call from the NYPD, asking me to 'substantiate your whereabouts' and whether you were in town on official business."

"I noticed you didn't cover for me."

"I can't cover for you if I have no idea what you're doing," she said. "I need you to fill me in."

Lionel turned on the tap and splashed cold water on his face.

"Hello?" Brianna said. "You still there?"

"Yeah, I just . . . I'm sorry, you need me to fill you in? You fed me a line like that, and I couldn't decide on a snarky comeback. So many to choose from. Do I go for the subtle flirt, the full-bore James Bond innuendo—"

"Hey, Lionel? I'm officially taking off my ex-girlfriend hat and putting on my boss hat. You can't see it over the phone, but it's happening. Three, two, one, there. Hat changed. Talk."

He caught the edge in her voice, drawing a line he knew better than to dance over. He reached for the shaving cream as he weighed his response.

"Following a lead about a possible literary hoax," he said. "I'm still working the story, but it might have legs."

"You traveled a long way for 'might.' And why did the NYPD ask me if I sent you there?"

He lathered on the shaving gel, drawing a beard on his cheeks in lime-green foam. He took a deep breath.

"Because one source sent me to a second source, who had met a bad end, and I was the schmuck who found the body."

Brianna paused. Her voice, when she spoke again, held a cagey edge to it. "How bad are we talking?"

Lionel smiled at his reflection as he put the razor to his face and drew a long, slow line down his cheek. Frothy cream and stubble spattered the porcelain basin.

"How does 'underground pornographer with Russian mob ties found tortured to death' sound? And yes, I took photos of the crime scene."

Brianna was like Lionel in all the ways that mattered to him. She believed in investigative journalism, *good* reporting, the power of a free press to expose evil deeds and make the world a better place. That said, she was still beholden to her own bosses, and everybody knew the credo that drove network news: if it bleeds, it leads.

"How much longer do you need?" she asked him.

"Couple of days," he said.

"I'll talk to Legal. They can keep the cops on this end busy for a little bit, but they *do* need to see you. This isn't going away until you make it go away."

"I hear you. Hey, can I ask you a favor?"

"A favor," Brianna said. "Right now? After the headaches you've been giving me? You really think that's a wise idea?"

"Not remotely, but I'm asking anyway. I'm looking for background on a group called the Thoth Club." He spelled it out for her and waited while she took it down. "Sounds like it was a semisecret fraternity for the city's moneyed elite. It supposedly broke up in the '60s, but it's looking like maybe it's still around, or maybe a new group started up under the same name."

"I'll get an intern on it. Hey, Lionel? Remember something for me?"

"Name it."

"You are not the story," Brianna told him. "You're a reporter. Get in, get out, then report. That's your job. That is the extent of your job."

"You say that as if I have a history of reckless behavior."

Her sigh drifted over the phone line. "Just . . . be careful, okay?"

She hung up on him. The razor made its final clean stroke, leaving his face bare and glistening. He glanced to the phone, the screen showing a closed connection.

"Love you, too," he said.

Fifteen

The morning light and a taxicab carried Lionel to Lower Manhattan. He stood on the corner a stone's throw from the stock exchange, gazing up at granite-and-glass monuments. Everyone had phones to their ears or cups of coffee in their fists or both, power walking to their offices to start the morning grind. Human gears in a vast, invisible machine designed to shuffle money around.

Stamford and Cross Investment Partners kept their offices on the forty-fifth floor of one of those human beehives. One wall of the lobby was floor-to-ceiling glass, looking out over the city skyline. Lionel imagined they must have paid for that view by the square inch. The rest of the lobby was furnished in soft wood the color of brown sugar and butter, and the perfectly climate-controlled air carried the faint scent of potpourri. He expected he'd have to fast-talk his way past the receptionist, but once he mentioned he was a reporter, she nodded sagely and invited him to take a seat before he could go into detail.

He figured Wade Dawson had an interviewer coming to see him. He also figured he should probably correct her misunderstanding and let her know he wasn't the reporter in question. Instead, he sat patiently, flipped through a fresh copy of *Bloomberg Businessweek*, and kept his mouth shut.

"Mr. Dawson will see you now," she said. A door to her left clicked open, the lock flipping as if she'd just said *Open sesame*.

Lionel wasn't sure what to expect from Dawson's office, but a museum wasn't anywhere near the top of the list. The office was longer than it was wide, a short gallery leading up to a rounded desk with polished windows and the entire city at its back. Along the way, six podiums—three on each side, spaced perfectly, glowing in soft LED underlights—displayed history sheathed under glass. A shard of Egyptian pottery, paint still clinging to the faded clay; a dramatist's mask, neutral face under sculpted curls of ivory hair like something from ancient Greece or Rome; a faded metal badge bearing crossed rifles, evoking images of the Civil War. Lionel tore his gaze from the displays and looked to the man in the high-backed leather chair.

Wade Dawson rose to greet him. From the moment their eyes met, Lionel understood what Rosa's warning had meant.

He was a predator in his element, the kind of man who made a dozen million-dollar deals before lunch and thrived on every second of pressure. Every successful gladiator on Wall Street had his own pressure valve. For some, it was booze. Some preferred blow. He knew one of Wade's vices, besides the occasional line of coke—the man liked escorts, and he liked them young—but he could tell that wasn't the only skeleton in his closet. With his hair in a slicked-back two-hundred-dollar cut and his suit tailored within a millimeter of his athletic frame, Wade shook Lionel's hand like he wanted to crush it. The idea of violence clung to the investment guru's skin like a musk cologne.

Lionel wondered if he'd deliberately cultivated it, some alpha-wolf air to deter his rivals, or if he just couldn't help himself.

"Peter," Wade barked, dropping back into his chair, "great to finally meet in person. Take a seat. I can give you fifteen minutes."

"Afraid I'm not Peter," Lionel said, "but on the bright side, hopefully I won't need all fifteen."

Wade's brow crinkled as much as the taut skin would allow. *Botox,* Lionel thought. *Lots of it.*

"I'm sorry, you are . . . ?"

"The name's Lionel Page, and I *am* a reporter, but I'm here strictly off the record. I'd like to talk to you about Ray Barton."

Wade shut down like the jaws of a steel trap. His shoulders hunched in, arms tight to his sides, head ducking on his neck like a turtle trying to escape inside his shell.

"I don't know who that is."

"You know, Mr. Dawson," Lionel said in a gentle voice, "a man in your position should be aware that journalists are a lot like police detectives. If we ask you a question, generally speaking we already know at least part of the answer. For instance, I know about the Poe manuscript. I know you and Barton entered an agreement to auction it off and split the proceeds."

"You need to leave. Now."

Lionel didn't move from his chair. He fixed Wade with a steady gaze.

"Mr. Dawson, Ray Barton is dead. There's a very good chance he was killed for that manuscript. And if he was, then I guarantee he gave his killer your name before died. I didn't come here to make trouble for you; I came to warn you."

Wade swallowed, hard, and snatched the phone off his desk. It rattled in his hand.

"You've got five seconds to get the hell out of my office, or I'm calling security to *make* you leave. Then I'm calling the police."

Lionel rose, showing his open hands as he pushed his chair back.

"Fine, fine, I'm going. But listen . . . I can help you, all right? I'm not your enemy. All I want—"

Wade's voice rose an octave. "I don't give a damn what you want. I don't—I don't know what you're talking about or who Ray Barton is. You've got the wrong person. Now *get out*."

His shaking fingers punched the numbers for security. Lionel made his exit before Wade could finish.

That could have gone better, Lionel thought. On the other hand, it had gone about as well as he could expect. He'd landed a direct hit: Wade's reaction told him that Rosa's story was legit, and that he was sitting on the Poe manuscript. He couldn't exactly expect the man to suddenly unburden himself to a stranger, much less a reporter.

For that, he'd need a little extra motivation.

Rosa had kept their connection open on Facebook, possibly hoping for another confidential-source bonus. Lionel stepped to one side, out of the flow of pedestrian traffic, and tapped out a quick message on his phone.

Need a little local help, he wrote. Two hundred in it for you. Cash. Hit me up if you're free.

For two hundred, she was free. Twenty minutes later, as he rode uptown in the back of another cab, Lionel hammered out the finer details of the plan.

Then he went shopping. He kept one eye on the clock. It was around eleven when he emerged from a shoebox of a store with a fat paper sack tucked under his arm. He had copied Maddie's number from the napkin to his phone earlier that morning, debating over when he should dial the digits.

Too soon could look too eager. Too late could look like he was blowing her off. He shook his head at his own waffling. *I'm in my thirties,* he thought. *That is way, way too old to be acting like an infatuated teenager. C'mon, just call her. Two adults having lunch together. You've done it a million times.*

This felt different, though. There was something special about Maddie. Something unique, like a perfume he'd never smelled before or a spice he'd never tasted. He'd had just enough to whet his appetite and leave him wanting more. If anything, he wanted to peel back the careful veils she wrapped around herself and get a look at the real woman beneath. If only she'd let him.

"Hey there," he said when she picked up. "It's me. Just wondering if you were still up for that lunch date?"

"Hey, it's me," she said playfully. She let out a frustrated sigh. "I'd love to, I'm just—"

He jumped at the sound of a sharp metallic *crack* on the other end of the line and an echoing cascade, like a shelf of piled cans spilling free and scattering in all directions.

"Maddie? You okay?"

"Yeah," she said, sounding breathless. "Sorry, it's . . . My boss has me doing some follow-up work for her. Probably going to be stuck here for a few more hours. Dinner?"

He winced at the time. Rosa was expecting him around sunset.

"I can't, duty calls. I'm following up on a lead," he said. "Shit. I was hoping . . . Anyway, maybe tomorrow?"

"Let's try for tomorrow. Maybe we'll both catch a break." She paused. "Hey, Lionel?"

"Yeah?"

"I *like* you."

He had to smile. "I like you, too."

Sunset found Lionel on a fifth-floor fire escape down in Brooklyn, skulking like a thief.

Or maybe like the private investigator who had taught Lionel all his best tricks. Lionel camped out on the rough metal grating, the tools of his trade set out beside him on the fold of the rumpled shopping bag. He'd picked up an energy bar at a bodega on the corner to quiet the rumbling in his stomach. He'd reluctantly passed on the fresh-ground coffee, as good as it smelled: he didn't know how long he'd be perched up here, stalking his prey, and bathroom breaks weren't an option.

The fire escape faced a second apartment building, fifteen feet across an alley. Pigeons clustered on the sagging, white-spattered eaves, staring down at him, cooing and shoving. Lionel's sights were set on one particular window. Five floors up, three from the right, with a cheap polyester curtain blocking the view. He held his focus, like a sniper in the bush, and waited.

A gauzy shadow moved behind the curtain. A hand tugged the fabric back, tying it off to one side, and cracked the window to let a little air in. Rosa. She glanced across the alley at Lionel, fast and smooth, and gave the tiniest nod before turning her back to the window.

Lionel scooped up his new purchase, a Canon Rebel digital camera with a high-powered zoom lens. He focused the camera's eye on the window, took careful aim, and opened fire.

Sixteen

"Check your email," Lionel said. It was morning. He'd slept just fine. No nightmares, for once.

"How did you get in here?" Wade Dawson leaned sideways in his chair, shouting past Lionel's shoulder. *"Marcie!"*

"You can throw me out again if you want." Lionel nodded toward the monitor on the desk between them. "But you should check your email first."

Wade slouched in his high-backed leather chair like a sullen king. A few mouse clicks later, his confidence quietly shattered. His receptionist loomed in the doorway.

"Mr. Dawson?"

Wade didn't look away from the screen. He fluttered his free hand at her. "That's . . . Sorry, nothing. Nothing."

She vanished, and the door drifted shut.

"You son of a bitch," Wade said.

Lionel had snapped a good two dozen pictures out on the fire escape. He'd cherry-picked the best ones to share. The ones that clearly showed Wade's face through the window, the naked meat in a sandwich between Rosa and her friend Chantille.

"I had to get your email address off Stamford and Cross's website," Lionel said. "Good thing I was paying attention. If I'd sent these to your bosses by accident . . . Hey, you know that girl's only sixteen, right?"

"You son of a bitch," he said again.

"So. *Now* can we have a conversation?"

If looks could kill, Lionel would be as dead as Ray Barton. Wade fixed him with a burning glare and squeezed the armrest of his chair like it was Lionel's throat.

"What do you want?" Wade asked him, spitting the words. "Money?"

"Nope. I'm not blackmailing you, Mr. Dawson. Well, I mean, technically I am, but I'm real easy to get rid of, and it won't cost you a dime. As to what I want, for starters, honesty would be nice. And it's not mandatory, but a tiny amount of gratitude for trying to save your life wouldn't be remiss."

"Ray was sloppy," Wade said, "and he was careless. I'm neither."

"Those photographs say otherwise."

Wade clicked his mouse, banishing the pictures. "Those photos don't show the two hired gorillas I had stationed down in the lobby. Or the security watching my house and my car, twenty-four-seven. Ray was a soft target. I'm not. And you're assuming his business with me was the reason he died. Trust me, lots of people in this town had lots of reasons to want Ray Barton dead. Guy was a scumbag."

"And yet, you did business with him."

"Once." Wade held up a finger. The sleeve of his tailored jacket slid back, baring the onyx-and-gold link on his ivory shirt cuff. Hieroglyphs spelling the name of Thoth, just like Ray wore. "One time, only because Rosa played matchmaker. He had a product; I had access to interested buyers. After that we would have gone our separate ways."

"I hear you're members of the same club," Lionel said.

Wade curled his lips in a sneer. "You heard wrong, then. I got him provisional membership—*provisional*—so that he could come to the auction. He didn't trust me to tell him how much money we made and secure his cut. He wanted to see for himself. Ray Barton wasn't club material."

"Bank account too small?"

"It's not just about money. It's about good breeding. A pedigree. It's about having a stake in this city. *Roots.* Things Ray didn't understand. Look behind you. What do you see?"

Lionel turned his head, taking in the display cases that lined the walls of Wade's office. Soft LEDs glowed beneath a scattering of artifacts, pirated remnants of history.

"It's a tiny museum," Lionel said.

"Museum, from the Greek *mouseion*, which means 'Seat of the Muses.' The Muses were goddesses. The unearthly forces that inspire men to create and build and make art. See, that's what a museum *is*. It's where you go to commune with the Muses." Wade tapped his thumb against his middle finger, twice, and pointed to the ceiling. "To find inspiration. Anyone can make money. To build *wealth*, the kind of wealth that lasts for generations, you have to be connected to something bigger than yourself."

"And Ray didn't get that?"

"Ray couldn't see past his own nose." Wade tapped his cuff link. "People are vetted for years before they get a full invitation, and a single nay vote is enough to blackball you."

Lionel gestured toward Wade's monitor, evoking the memory of the photographs.

"They let *you* in," he said.

Wade barked out a laugh. "Seriously? Ten seconds before you walked in here, I brokered a twenty-million-dollar deal. Three guys on the line with me. One had septum surgery to repair the damage from the heroic quantities of blow he does on a daily basis, one pays street bums to let him beat the shit out of them, and the third, I'm pretty sure, collects honest-to-God snuff movies. I'm just an ephebophile. For a man in my position, my sins are positively vanilla. And you're nobody to be throwing shade. You said you were a reporter. That true?"

"That's right."

"I thought 'journalistic ethics' was still a thing. Do you always blackmail your interview subjects, or am I just that special?"

Lionel had had a long conversation with himself, out on that apartment fire escape. The plan had been easy to go along with in the heat of the moment; he had all the tools he needed and the drive to make it happen. It wasn't until he was all alone and waiting, nothing but time on his hands and no company but his own thoughts, that the reality of what he was doing sank in.

There was Ethics 101, and then there was the real world. He'd learned on day one that crossing lines was part of a reporter's job; nobody ever broke a big story by following the rules. Misrepresenting himself or lying to the target of an investigation? Sure. Slipping somebody a folded twenty to open a closed door or two? All the time. Social engineering, bribery, deceit—they were just tools in the toolbox. Necessary evils in the service of a greater good.

Actual, literal blackmail, though . . . that was one line he'd never crossed. Part of him thought he'd finally gone too far. The rest of him just saw it as a natural progression. One more step on the spiraling staircase down. It was easy as walking. *I guess it comes down to one question,* he had asked himself, raising the camera to his eye and taking aim across the alley. *How much do you want the truth?*

This much, he thought. The shutter snap felt like the trigger of a gun.

"I'm not looking to hurt you or cause you any trouble," Lionel said. The deflection felt weak, even as he offered it up. A shield made of soggy cardboard.

"Yet here we are." Wade drummed his perfect manicure on the desk. "So if it's not money, what are you after? I assume you're writing a piece on the Thoth Club. Hate to disappoint you, but it's been done. Nobody talks about it, because truth is more boring than fiction. There's no *Eyes Wide Shut* business going on behind closed doors—no orgies, no virgin sacrifices."

"What's with all the secrecy?"

"Well, for starters, know what happens when you put some of the richest men and women in New York in the same room together?"

Lionel guessed with a shrug. "You trade insider stock tips?"

"Even if we don't, the SEC sure as hell takes notice. Keeping our membership under wraps is less of a headache for everybody. Besides, the secret-society vibe, the pomp and circumstance"—Wade spread his open hands—"it's *fun*. Strip all that away, what you're left with is a group of like-minded, upwardly mobile citizens with a shared love of history."

"I'm actually here about your deal with Ray Barton," Lionel said. "The Poe manuscript. Is it real?"

"Real as anything in the Met. I had a handwriting expert compare it to old Edgar's penmanship. Outside freelancer, no connection to the club, just to make sure the auction couldn't be tampered with. Didn't want someone calling it fake, then telling a buddy to buy it on the cheap, you know? Anyway, she gave it a ninety-seven percent chance of being legit, which is more than the expected standard for authentication."

"So you told Ray you'd auction it off to your buddies at the Thoth Club and split the proceeds."

"That was the plan." Wade leaned back in his chair and fixed Lionel with a steady gaze. "Now I guess I get *all* the money."

He didn't have to spell it out. Lionel didn't see why the lost manuscript would be worth killing over. Maybe it wasn't. Maybe the money was. He thought it over and met the challenge in Wade's eyes.

"You didn't kill him," Lionel said.

"How do you know?"

"Because you had to jump through hoops to get him those cuff links," Lionel said with a nod at Wade's sleeve, "and it was a onetime deal for a man you and your buddies had no intention of welcoming into the fold. He'd already given you the manuscript. You telling me you couldn't just break your word and have him turned away at the door? Ray probably stole those pages in the first place; he wasn't going to run to the cops. You could have ripped him off easy, no murder required, and you didn't do it."

Wade held his gaze steady, cold as ice, trying to cow Lionel from across the desk. Lionel imagined he used that look at a lot of board-room meetings, and it probably worked on most people. That "three seconds from getting violent" face that Rosa had warned him about. All the same, even knowing it was probably an act, Lionel shifted closer to the edge of his chair so he could get up fast if he needed to. Faster than Wade.

"Who do you think killed him, then?" Wade asked.

"Like I said, he probably stole the manuscript. We both know the kinds of circles he moved in. These *Bratva* guys, the Russian mob—they've got this whole culture. They idolize thieves and bandits. But steal *from* one of them?" Lionel blew air between his lips and shook his head. "You don't just die. You die badly. Like Ray did. Which is a problem for you, since you're holding the goods."

"Like I said, I'm protected. And Ray wasn't the only person in this town with powerful friends." Wade leaned forward in his chair, getting a little closer. "Something you probably should have thought about before you played shutterbug."

Lionel squared his shoulders. He mirrored Wade's moves, leaning in, and his voice went deadly soft.

"I'll tell you a secret," Lionel said. "I've spent my entire career pissing off people with powerful friends. I'm still standing. Most of them aren't. So you've got a choice to make: you can keep slapping your dick on the desk, trying to intimidate me, or you can do me one little favor and I go away forever. The photographs disappear, and so do I."

Wade chewed that over. His eyes narrowed, just a hair.

"What's the favor?"

"The auction," Lionel said. "I want to be there. You got Ray in, you can get me in."

"No, I can't. For one thing, it's going down tonight. For another, you're a reporter. No chance they let you through the front door. Not for one night, not ever."

Lionel rubbed his chin, thinking it through.

"You said they vetted Ray? His background, his financials and such?"

"As much as they needed to," Wade said. "Since he wasn't a prospect for real membership, most of it was on my say-so. They understood this was a onetime deal, and more importantly, they understood what he was bringing to the table. We're collectors. We look for the unique, the unobtainable, pieces of history you can't find in any *public* museum. A one-of-a-kind first draft by Edgar Allan Poe? Let's just say some of my colleagues were too busy wiping up their own drool to think straight."

"So they didn't interview him in person?" Lionel asked.

"No, just me."

"Have you told them he's dead?"

Wade stared at Lionel like he was trying to read his mind. "Where are you going with this?"

Lionel smiled and set his hands on the desk, sealing the deal.

"I'm going to that auction, tonight, with you," he said. "As your very good friend Ray Barton."

Seventeen

Warm water spun a slow circle down the bathtub drain, leaving traces of suds on pristine white porcelain. Maddie's straight razor still sat on the tub's rim, untouched in favor of the disposable safety razor in her steady grip. She ran a hand along one freshly shaved leg, fingertips on silky skin, and half smiled at the blade. *One hundred and eighty-five days without an incident,* she thought.

Today had been easy. Today she'd been busy. Work crowded out the bad thoughts in her head and made it harder for them to get a handhold. She had to admit, she'd been thinking about Lionel, too. That wasn't bad, either.

Her smile faded as she looked to the long padded bench across from the tub. Her clothes lay scattered where she'd shed them on the way in. Blood—none of it hers—drew Jackson Pollock spatters across her favorite tunic top and dotted the hip of her jeans. "That's not coming out," she said to the empty room.

She'd mourn her casual clothes later. Tonight called for a more upscale look. She stepped out of the tub, toweled off, and opened her suite's closet. She eyed the black cocktail dress she'd worn to her dinner with Aleksandr, wrinkled her nose, and reached for her second choice: a backless number in elegant plum. She was getting dressed when her phone, abandoned on the bedspread, started to chime.

"Status report," Regina Dunkle said, her voice as dry as a mummified body.

"On my way to a party," Maddie replied. "I asked around town and got a few answers. Ray Barton had a deal to auction the manuscript at a private lodge called the Thoth Club. That's where it is now."

"Excellent. Get eyes on and verify its authenticity."

Maddie set the phone on speaker and carried it into the bathroom, resting it on the edge of the sink. She tilted her head, putting on a delicate pair of pearl earrings. Vintage, expensive without being loud about it—exactly the look she was going for tonight.

"And the retrieval?" she asked. "Do you want me to bid on it, or just take it from them?"

"Neither," Regina replied. "Don't interfere. Watch the auction, identify the high bidder, and contact me for further instructions. I'll have you reach out to them afterward with a private offer to take it off their hands."

Maddie frowned at her reflection. Didn't make sense. Sitting the auction out, then going to the highest bidder with an even higher offer was a waste of money. She almost said so, then she remembered who she was dealing with. She changed the subject.

"Crossed paths with Lionel again," she said. "Turns out he's a journalist. I checked into him. Still not convinced he's as innocent as he looks. He's somebody's pawn; I'm just not sure who's playing him."

"Everybody is somebody's pawn, dear girl. You should know. I assume he recently suffered from a terrible nightmare?"

"Like I said, I checked into him," Maddie replied. She unzipped her clear plastic makeup bag and unfurled a kabuki brush as she studied her cheeks in the mirror.

"Deeper than you needed to, perhaps?"

"Meaning?"

"A certain lightness in your tone," Regina told her, "most distinctive for how long it's been absent. Are you sweet on the boy?"

Maddie thought about that. The feather-soft brush whisked against her cheekbones, layering soft color over her pale skin and highlighting the contours of her face. The question sounded like a trap, half-hidden in a patch of rough ground. She pitched her voice carefully, office neutral.

"I thought you preferred to keep our conversations on the professional level, Ms. Dunkle."

Regina's chuckle was a scaly, reptilian thing.

"I like to take a personal interest in the lives of my operatives from time to time. So what's your strategy? Will you do something horrible to deliberately drive him away from you, or will you simply vanish and leave him wondering about what might have been?"

Maddie's composure frayed at the edges. "Why do you do this?"

"I'm just wondering how you're going to sabotage things. It sounds like something good might have come into your life, and we can't have that, now can we? Self-destruction is your most reliable, consistent trait."

"Why do you do this? I do everything you tell me to. Everything. You've even admitted I'm the best asset you have. Why are you so"— Maddie gritted her teeth, as if she could cap the frustration welling up in her throat—"*horrible*?"

"Because I *can* be," Regina said lightly. "And you're free to walk away anytime you like. You always have been. *I* certainly would, if I were in your shoes. I can only surmise the obvious: that despite your whining to the contrary, this is exactly how you want it. Much like a sinner in purgatory. Mmm. Wait, I have another call coming in. Hold that thought, I'll be right back."

The line clicked and went silent. Maddie held that thought.

⌒

When he made his pitch to Wade—the idea to take Ray's place at the auction—Lionel saw something entirely new creep over the man's face. Fear. Just a flash of it, a hint of something cornered and desperate, before he buried it under a blank mask.

"That wouldn't be a good idea," he said.

"Why not? Nobody knows Ray's dead, nobody's met him. Who's to say I'm not him? The invitation's already set up, and he's expected to be there."

"You're asking me to lie to the club. If they found out . . ." Wade bit his bottom lip. His gaze darted away. "These aren't good people to lie to, okay?"

Lionel eased closer to the edge of his seat. He turned a shoulder to Wade, leaning in with his voice nice and easy, pitching the sale.

"They'll never know," he said. "You're a confidential source. Wade, I swear to you on my mother's grave: I have never, in my entire life, burned a source. Not for anything."

Wade snorted at him. "You'll commit blackmail, but you won't do that."

"That's right. I've got rules. If you don't believe me, look me up: I spent thirty-three days in county once on contempt-of-court charges because I wouldn't give up a source. I would have done a year if I'd had to. You will be protected."

"And what happens when you break your 'big story'?" Wade asked him, hooking his fingers to make air quotes. "What happens then? What if somebody recognizes you after the fact?"

"I'm not doing a story on the club. I'm just here for the manuscript."

And frankly, Lionel didn't know if there was a story to break. Just the maddening scent of one. He was like a starving man in a labyrinth, catching the tantalizing aroma of a steak on the grill just around the next corner. Or the corner after that. Or the one after that. Almost close enough to taste, and leading him deeper into the maze.

"What *if*?" Wade demanded.

"Nothing goes on the air with my name or my face attached to it," Lionel said. "I'll cut the evidence trail. I'll even let somebody else take the credit for the story. You've got my word on it. All you have to do is get me into that auction, and I'm out of your life forever. That's all I'm asking."

Wade fell into a sullen silence and weighed his options.

"Well?" Lionel asked. "What do you say?"

Come sunset, Lionel was back in his room at the High Line Hotel, with a rented tuxedo hanging from the back of the bathroom door. He shaved, checking his face in the mirror, sending foam and stubble sluicing down the drain. He made a phone call while he worked.

"Lionel," Regina said. Her voice was a gust of refined warmth, like an elderly aunt greeting her favorite nephew. "I'm glad you checked in. I almost started to worry about you."

"I've been hunting, and I'm about to bring home the bacon. I found the manuscript. Ray Barton made a deal with this guy, a money mover with a mutual friend, to auction it off. It took some doing, but I wrangled myself an invitation."

"You don't say. Fascinating! And how did you manage that?"

"Like I said," Lionel replied, "it took some doing."

"Well, I'm certain it wasn't easy. I do hope you're feeling proud of your accomplishments."

Lionel tore his gaze from the mirror. He pretended it was to wash his razor, tapping it against the white porcelain, not because he suddenly didn't feel like looking himself in the eye.

"I'm getting the job done."

"Indeed you are. And you're one step closer to that pesky story about your childhood going away forever."

"About that," he said. He'd wavered on whether or not to confront her, but with his task almost at an end, this felt like the time. "That kid, the cub reporter who was doing the story on me. I heard from my boss at the station. He's dead."

"Really," she said, as casually as if she were discussing her shopping list. "Well. No matter. My promise still holds: help me to acquire that manuscript, and I will protect your past from any and all attempts to expose it. I mean, really, come now: he was *a* problem, but he wasn't the only potential problem. You've lived a charmed life, keeping the truth concealed this long without my help."

"He was murdered. Someone jumped him in an alley and took everything he had on him. Including his notes about me."

"Is that what you're worried about? I doubt any mugger is going to even understand what they took," Regina said. "I suspect his little dossier on you is currently composting at the bottom of a dumpster somewhere. In fact, I guarantee it."

That was what he was afraid of. That she could, in fact, guarantee it. Because she'd made it happen that way. He didn't—couldn't—ask her head-on. He fumbled for something to say, trying to skirt the obvious question, and sideswiped his own emotions.

"I feel like I'm responsible," he blurted out.

"Responsible?"

"Like it's on my shoulders," Lionel told her. "I'm not . . . I'm not saying that his death had anything to do with me, or the story he was working on, understand. I'm not saying that—"

"But if he hadn't been trying to expose you, he wouldn't have been at your newsroom that day. And if that was true, he wouldn't have been on that street, walking back to his office, afterward. And if that was true, he wouldn't have been waylaid in an alley, robbed, and stabbed to death."

Lionel looked up again. The man in the mirror looked ten years older, haunted, standing on the wrong end of all his bad decisions.

"Regina," he said.

"Yes, Lionel?"

"I said he was murdered. I never said he was stabbed."

Eighteen

Regina didn't reply.

Lionel counted the seconds as they fell in the silence between them. *One. Two. Three. Four.*

"I'm certain you did," she said. Breezy, quick, as if there hadn't just been a chasm in the conversation.

"I'm pretty sure I didn't."

"Then where would I have gotten such a horrid notion?"

She lobbed the challenge into his court and left it there. He left it there, too.

"I just feel like whatever happened to the kid, it's on me."

"It never fails to amaze me," Regina said, "how people will pile guilt upon their own shoulders until it crushes them under the weight, especially when they could free themselves with little more than a carefree shrug. Nothing is on *your* shoulders save for what you choose to carry. You made a choice to run from your past, Lionel. You've been choosing to run for years."

"I'm not running," he said. "I'm just . . . not that person."

"The nice thing about running is, you can stop doing it anytime you want. But let's turn to more important matters, shall we? The manuscript. Has it been authenticated?"

"According to Ray Barton's partner, yes." Lionel splashed handfuls of cold water on his face and patted his cheeks. "They tested the handwriting and the paper itself. It's the real thing. So what's the call? Want me to stand in for you and try to bid on it?"

"No. Don't interfere. Watch the auction, identify the high bidder, and contact me for further instructions. I'll reach out to them afterward with a private offer to take it off their hands."

Lionel glanced to the phone, lifting an eyebrow. "Um, wouldn't it make more sense for me to just bid on it? I mean, no matter what it ends up selling for, you're going to have to pay even more money to get it from the person who—"

"Listen carefully," she said, cutting him off. "Identify the bidder. Tell me all about the person who buys that manuscript. I want to know who they are, how much they pay for it, and where they rest their head at night."

"Why do I get the feeling there's something you're not telling me?"

"When we entered this partnership, I told you to consider it an adventure in the making." He could hear the sly smile in her voice. "What's fun about an adventure with a clearly marked map? Oh, and while you're at the auction, get me some photographs of the manuscript. I need clear, legible shots so I can have my own expert look at the handwriting. The final page in particular, please."

"I'm not going to be able to get a camera in there," Lionel said. "My contact says they're really gun-shy about surveillance."

"Then it's a good thing that I recruited such a clever young man to help me, isn't it? I'm sure you'll have no problem coming up with a solution. Now if you'll excuse me, I have a call waiting on the other line." A faint, almost-inaudible chuckle rasped over the line. "Be brave and resourceful, Lionel, as I know you can be. And rejoice; I'm *almost* finished with you. It's all downhill from here."

"And then?" he asked.

"And then you get everything you have coming to you. All the rewards I promised, and then some."

Maddie had put her clothes on, put her face on, all while the screen of her phone mutely counted up the minutes. Regina hadn't come back after putting her on hold. She didn't dare hang up. Maddie had done that once before—*once*—and regretted it for a month. Instead, she paced and watched the clock and waited, the carpets rough and cool under her bare feet. She had a pair of kitten heels picked out, the same plum shade as her dress, but shoes were always the last thing she put on before leaving and the first thing she took off after coming home.

It struck her that she had no problem thinking of her suite as home. Maddie lived out of hotels. Berlin to Milan, Los Angeles to Albuquerque—she hadn't had a stable address in years. Home was just the place where she felt safe sleeping at any given moment. Or just the place where she slept. There should have been something weird about that—she knew most people had a different relationship to the word—but she'd been doing it for so long it just felt normal to her.

A permanent home was a kind of attachment. Maddie didn't do attachments.

Her phone flickered. Regina's voice washed over the speaker. "Are you still there?"

"I think you know that I am," Maddie said, about as arch as she dared to get with her.

"The person on the other line was a researcher in my employ," Regina said, "an expert on the local power structure. I wanted more information on this Thoth Club organization, since I'd never heard of it myself."

"Yeah? What do they know? I mostly gathered it's a social club for the moneyed and the weird. Anything I can use?"

"Nothing concrete," Regina said, "but from the scraps and rumors they've accumulated? You should carry a weapon tonight."

Maddie paused in midpace, stopping dead in the middle of the Persian rug.

"What do they know?" she asked again.

"Only that the club is keeping secrets. Secrets rather more sordid than their members' bank balances. And some of those secrets may *bite*. Hopefully it's not a worry, but all the same, arm yourself before you go."

"I always do," Maddie replied.

"Good girl. Off with you, then."

~

Lionel stepped onto the elevator and eyed himself in the mirrored walls of the cage. He punched the button for the lobby. Then he checked himself again and fidgeted with his black bow tie. Given he was about to embark on an undercover mission, he hoped he'd see James Bond reflected in the glass. Reality fell short of expectations.

"Good evening, monsieur," he said to his reflection, draping an imaginary towel over one arm. "Welcome to Chez Snootee. My name is Lionel, and I'll be showering you with disdain tonight. Would you care to see our wine list? No, sir, *none* of the prices are marked—"

The elevator stopped on two. The door rattled open, and Maddie stepped into the cage with him. He stared just long enough to realize he was staring.

"Maddie," he said, "uh . . . hi. You look . . ."

He took her in—the pinned-up hair, the dangling pearls accenting the curves of her face, the plum dress that clung to her body like water on a leaf. She tilted her head and arched a sculpted eyebrow.

"Yes?" she asked.

"Amazing. You look amazing."

"Eh." She shrugged. "Practice. And look at you, rocking the penguin suit. You clean up nicely."

"I'd say it's practice, but that'd be a damn lie. The bow tie took me half an hour and three YouTube tutorials to get right."

"But you got there." She looked him up and down. "Here, you're wearing the cummerbund a little too high."

She stepped up to him, toe to toe, and took hold of the sash around his waist. Tugging it down, her fingers were snug against his hips. She looked up at him, their noses almost bumping, and the musk of her perfume danced a slow tango around his head.

She blinked. Then she shifted gears.

"The cummerbund was developed in the 1850s by British officers serving in India," she told him. "They needed a dinner-dress alternative to the full waistcoat. Because of the heat."

He gazed into her eyes. "You don't say."

"The pleats are always supposed to be worn facing upward. Gentlemen would often keep their opera tickets tucked in the pleats so they wouldn't have to dig through their pockets. Yours are facing upward. So that's good."

"Maddie?"

She didn't move. Her hands stayed curled around the sash, holding his body just a breath away from hers.

"Yes?" she asked.

"Do you . . . routinely launch into lectures about the history of odd pieces of menswear?"

"Not just menswear," she said. "Do you know why so few pieces of women's clothing have pockets? I do."

The elevator rumbled to a stop. The door chimed and slid open. Neither of them moved.

"Maddie?"

"Yes?" she asked.

"We should probably get off the elevator."

She let go of him. They walked together, side by side, hands almost close enough to touch, through the lobby and out into the gathering dark.

"So where are you headed?" he asked her. "Someplace fun?"

"One can always hope. How about you?"

121

"It's a work thing." He stepped out from the curb, arm raised to hail a cab. The taxi swung in, and he opened the back door, waving Maddie inside. "This one's yours, I'll get the next one."

She smiled and stepped past him. "Such a gentleman. It must be the tux."

"It's the only explanation."

He closed the door after she got in. She said something to the driver, then rolled the window down a couple of inches.

"Have fun tonight, and don't do anything I wouldn't do," she said.

"I have no idea what you wouldn't do. Oh, hey! So . . . why, anyway?"

"Why what?"

"Why don't women's clothes have pockets?"

She called out to him as the taxi pulled away, fluttering her fingers through the window in a goodbye wave.

"Oh, because fashion designers are assholes. See you later, Lionel."

He watched the taillights of her taxi fade into the night. Lionel had a hard time pulling his gaze away; it felt like two magnets breaking apart. Wherever Maddie was going, he wished he was going with her.

The woman was a mystery. No. Mysteries were made to be solved. She didn't want any part of that. Maddie was a palace of locked doors. Lionel had been invited into her halls, permitted to walk through her world and get the barest sense of her design, but the actual rooms—the places where Maddie actually lived, where her heart and her memories held sway—were denied to him.

He knew he could do a deep dive on her background, take the trace details—her picture, her phone number, her first name—and dig for information. It was part of his job; he did it all the time. But it didn't feel right. He wanted to know more about her, to get closer to her, but he wasn't going to barge into the mansion of her heart and kick the doors down.

He'd wait for her permission, if it ever came. And if it didn't, well . . . she'd be the mystery he never solved, and live in his memories.

He finally caught a second taxi and made his way to the Upper West Side of Manhattan. The cab rolled past the opulent, darkened facade of the Blackstone Building. Lionel had seen the pictures, but it was grander in person. The Ionic columns of white marble were Olympian, towering, seeming to lean forward as if the building were looming over the street like a waiting vulture. Stained glass filled the arched windows between each pillar, art deco murals of Egyptian gods painted in triangles of gemstone color. High in the eaves, nine stories up, a clock stood with its granite hands frozen at 3:33.

Wade Dawson was waiting for him on the corner.

His tux was silver, tailored, not a rental. He wore it like he'd been born in it. His polished Oxfords paced a trench in the pavement. He had two curved bits of ivory cupped in his hands, and as Lionel walked up to him, he realized what they were: masks. Wade handed him one; it was a white domino mask, scalloped on the sides with stylized Greco-Roman wings.

"I figured you didn't have one. Don't put it on yet."

Lionel gave the mask a dubious look. "Why am I putting it on at all?"

"It's a *masquerade*," Wade told him, like it was the most obvious thing in the world. "Hey, you can walk away. I wish you would—I've been sick to my stomach all afternoon about this."

"Relax. Hey." Lionel waved a hand in front of Wade's face, stopping him from pacing. "Listen to me. Nobody is going to know a thing; nobody's even going to suspect. All you have to do is introduce me as Ray Barton, and I'll make like a bunny: quick, quiet, and gone before you know it."

"Don't talk to *anybody*."

"I won't. I'm not looking for interviews."

"Who knows you're here?" Wade's eyes widened with fresh paranoia. "I mean, if you're five minutes late getting home, is somebody from your newsroom going to come looking for you? Are they gonna call the cops? Swear to God, if the cops bust up this party and it lands on me—"

"Nobody knows I'm here. Okay? Nobody. I work alone."

Wade leaned in. He jabbed his finger into Lionel's chest. "You swear? You swear to God nobody knows about this?"

"I promise, okay? I'll pinkie swear on it if you want, but we're two grown men standing on a street corner in tuxedos, so it'd look *real* weird."

That calmed him down a little. He held his hands up, head bowed, relenting.

"Okay. Cool. Cool. Let's just get this over with."

He led the way—not to the Blackstone's front door, barred behind steel shutters, but to an alley that snaked around the side of the building. Away from the streetlights, with only a sliver of bone-white moon in the overcast Manhattan sky to guide their footsteps.

Nineteen

Wade led Lionel to an old service entrance and produced a key on a fine silver chain. The lock turned with a dull metallic *clunk*, old hinges groaning as the door yawned open. A cold hallway waited beyond, with walls of exposed drywall and wooden struts. A paint bucket and a leaning stepladder cluttered the bare concrete floor just beside the doorway. Lionel imagined they'd been abandoned by the last worker to leave, back when the Blackstone's owners went bankrupt and the last of the renovation money dried up. A masterpiece in the making, never to be completed.

"Mask up," Wade told him. "From here on in, you follow my lead, don't speak unless spoken to, and don't touch *anything*."

The ivory domino mask fit snug over Lionel's eyes, tightening behind his head with a simple clasp. Wade's was more elaborate, the upper half of a Greek-tragedy mask, adorned with sculpted curls and laurels. He nodded up the hallway. The door swung shut at their backs as he steered them toward an open stairwell.

Near the top of the stairs, Lionel heard the first faint strains of music. Something classical, like a string quartet, but too distant to make out the tune. Faint emergency lights shone in recessed alcoves and painted the concrete box in velvet shadow. They rounded the landings, the black steel handrail cold and smooth under Lionel's hand, and emerged on the third floor.

Electric sconces glowed along a corridor paneled in rich mahogany. The lights, tinted candle-flame yellow, shifted and danced to mimic open flames. The men's silhouettes shivered on the walls. Tall double doors stood at the hallway's end, barred by a pair of men in masks and suits. One mask resembled a goat, complete with ivory horns and a sculpted tuft of beard. The other was abstract, all art deco zigzags.

The goat moved to stand before Wade and held up his right hand.

"*Konx om pax,*" he said.

Wade held his left arm before him, level like a bar across his chest, and angled the other like the rising slope of a pyramid. His palm, flat, rose up to point fingers at the ceiling.

"*Khabs am pekht,*" Wade replied.

The man in the goat mask pressed his hands together, fist to open palm.

"Light in extension. Welcome, brother. I see you've brought a potential initiate."

"This gentleman is Ray Barton," Wade said. "He's been approved."

The silent man in the corner by the door had a list of names on a clipboard. He checked it, eyes narrow, and carved a red-marker line through two entries. He gave the goat a nod of approval. The goat turned behind him, reached into a low cabinet on the wall, and produced a tray lined in black velvet.

"Your cell phones, please, gentlemen." He looked to Lionel. "They aren't allowed on club grounds, for the security of our members. You understand."

Lionel had already been stewing over how he was going to get surreptitious shots of the Poe manuscript. A task they'd just made a dozen times harder. *I'll figure it out,* he thought as he dropped his phone onto the tray. Wade did the same. The man in the goat mask slid the tray back into the cabinet, out of sight and stowed away safe.

The goat locked eyes with Lionel, as if he could see right through his mask, right through his flesh and bones.

"I realize you're an outsider, so our manners may be strange to you, but I must ask you to indulge me in a question before I allow you inside. Please answer with absolute honesty."

"What's the question?" Lionel asked.

"You stand at the threshold of a museum. Illumination waits within. Do you enter of your own free will, without any outside compulsion? And do you accept the consequences of your actions, whatever may transpire within, as entirely yours and yours alone?"

"Yes, and yes," Lionel said.

"Then, welcome, friend," the goat replied, approval in his voice. "Welcome, and may you find the truth you seek."

Wade took a step forward. The goat stopped him with a raised finger.

"You must *also* answer the question."

Wade's eyes squinted behind his mask, thrown off by a beat. Lionel gathered this wasn't the usual script.

"Yes. And yes," Wade said.

The guardians of the threshold pushed the double doors open wide and welcomed them inside with a sweep of their tailored sleeves.

Sudden sharp lights jabbed at Lionel's eyes, flickering amber giving way to strident beams of icy blue. Chamber music drifted from the open doors, and as he stepped across the threshold, the air suddenly cold enough to prickle the skin on his arms, he smelled mint and fragrant berries. The party was in full swing. The chamber beyond the doors was a ballroom, fully renovated from the black-and-white marble checkerboard floor to the gold gilt adorning the Roman-styled crown molding, and couples in formal regalia and baroque masks swept across the floor in time to the violins. The overhead lights subtly shifted in regular intervals, the electric-blue beams changing direction and obscuring themselves like a dozen slow-motion eclipses. They painted the ballroom in bands of lunar light and darkness.

"One last hurdle," Wade said in his ear. "The Heirophant is expecting an introduction. Once again—"

"Follow your lead, don't talk, and don't touch?" Lionel asked.

"And don't make me regret this any more than I already do."

Wade led Lionel along the edges of the dance floor. Museum cases lined the walls at regular intervals, underlit glass cubes upon pylons of green-veined marble. The Thoth Club's collection put Wade's office gallery to shame. Lionel's gaze drifted over stone tablets chiseled in hieroglyphs, faded Roman tapestries, a box of luminous jade marked with the chop of a Chinese artisan. Relics from around the world and back again. He wondered what this room was worth—not just the artifacts but the people. He figured there were about forty guests, and while they shrouded their faces under a myriad of masks—bone and brass and silver, evoking animals and gods—he noticed the familiar curve of a chin here, and a snatch of a familiar voice there. He was almost certain he recognized an A-list celebrity or two, and one dead ringer for a Fortune 500 CEO he'd interviewed last year. He was suddenly grateful for his own mask.

In the far corner of the room, a rail-thin woman in a sweeping black gown was holding court, cradling a glass of white wine while she conversed with a trio of hangers-on in low tones. As Wade and Lionel approached, her eyes widened behind her mask. Hers was silver, scalloped, with a round and swirling symbol emblazoned between her sharp blue eyes. She flicked her fingers, and her friends disappeared into the crowd.

"Wade," she said. Her voice dripped with cold condescension. "You've brought us such a . . . treat."

"I brought the star of the evening," he replied.

"I wouldn't call myself the *star*—" Lionel started to say. Both of them hit him with an ice-cold stare.

"I *meant*," Wade said through gritted teeth, "the *manuscript*. Dolores, allow me to introduce Ray Barton. Ray, this is our kind hostess, Dolores Croft."

The name rang a bell. He'd seen her on a society page or two, and her family name on the side of a hospital. Philanthropist, made her money in pharmaceuticals. Her hand was emaciated, bird bones under parchment-tight skin, and she shook like he was the last person on earth she wanted to touch.

"Thanks for having me," Lionel said. "Quite the place you've got here."

Dolores's eyes narrowed to serpentine slits.

"'Quite the place,' he says. Mr. Barton, do you even know where you are?"

Lionel raised a sleeve and tapped his borrowed cuff link. "The Thoth Club."

"That's just a name. We are seekers of the blessings of the Muses. The art all around you, these fragments of history, aren't just a vulgar collection of eccentricities. They're a font of prayer."

His reporter instincts took over. He cast out a line, but not too deep.

"You've got quite the following here, I understand. Some big names. Deep pockets."

"The elite," she replied. "But what you must grasp is the order of events. We are the elite of this city *because* we sought the blessings of the Muses. We made sacrifices to advance our standing. Piety and devotion are what elevate us above the hoi polloi. It's not about inherited wealth or political power—it's about character."

"So," he said, "if somebody like me wanted to . . . join the elite?"

"I'd tell you to find a less repulsive line of work, for starters." Her disposition softened, just a bit. "But while we wait for the auction, I'd invite you to tour the outer gallery here. Study our collection. See if anything speaks to your heart. As Socrates taught us, wisdom begins in wonder."

"When is the auction, exactly?"

"Oh, not much longer—" Dolores paused. One of the men from the door, the one with the art deco zigzag mask, stepped close and whispered in her ear. Lionel could only catch the word *hotel*, nothing more. She gave him a discreet nod, and he vanished. "That is, it may be just a bit while we set up. Twenty minutes? Half an hour, at the most."

"Great," Lionel said. "And where's the manuscript now? I'm just a little antsy, you know—"

"Safe." She favored him with a thin and humorless smile, her lips a tight line beneath the curve of her mask. "Very safe. Go, Mr. Barton. Observe our collection, and listen for the voice of your Muse. Wade, stay here with me. We have more to discuss."

He knew when he was being dismissed. Lionel stepped away, slowly skirting the edge of the room and getting some distance. The less time he spent under Dolores's eagle eye, the less of a chance she'd have of finding him out. He pretended to study the museum cases. His real quarry was the room itself. He passed the double doors they'd entered through, sealed again, and made a slow circuit. There was a single door with a punch-key panel beside the lock—no getting through that without help—and a short, stubby hallway that looked like a utility corridor. That had potential, if he could slip down there without anyone noticing. Even if he found where they'd stashed the manuscript, he still needed to get hold of a camera. He felt naked without his cell phone, untethered to the world. Or maybe that was just the general vibe under the shifting ice-blue lights.

He was so lost in his schemes that he didn't notice the woman at his side, not until she hooked her arm around his and drew him onto the marble floor. The pale curve of her chin, beneath her mask, offered a clue to her identity. Then her voice gave the secret away.

"Dance with me," Maddie told him. The skirt of her plum dress swayed, and her eyes were glittering diamonds behind her mask: contoured bone shot through with sculpted cracks, resembling the upper half of a bared human skull.

"Funny meeting you here," he said. He flowed into the dance, taking her hand and taking the lead, old lessons coming back to him.

"And you. Didn't know you were a member."

"I'm not," he said. "And you?"

"Not remotely supposed to be here. You know, you're causing a serious problem for me."

"Why's that?"

"Because I meant what I said," she told him. "I like you."

"Why is that a problem?"

She turned her body, pressing herself to him, a pair of magnets pulling close. They stepped across the floor hand in hand.

"Because you might be after the same thing I am. And if you are, that means I might have to hurt you." Her cheek nuzzled affectionately against his, her voice light. "I might have to hurt you really, really badly. And I don't want that. So let's play a game."

His stomach clenched. She wasn't joking. And despite being in the middle of a crowded dance floor, he had a suspicion it somehow wasn't an empty threat. He forced an anxious chuckle.

"You're making me a little nervous, Maddie."

"I'm supposed to be making you a lot nervous, Lionel. Ready to play?"

"What's the game?"

"Truth or dare," she said.

Twenty

Lionel and Maddie turned at the edge of the dance floor, reversing course. She took the lead now, her hand firmly upon his.

"Truth," Lionel said.

"How did you get in here?"

He took a deep breath and weighed his options.

"I'm pretending to be a dead man," he told her. "I blackmailed a member into passing me off as his recently deceased guest."

"That's good, Lionel," she purred in his ear. "That's really good. Not just the technique, though I do admire your moves. What I mean is, I've been shadowing you since you walked in the door, and that answer lines up with what I overheard. That means you're telling me the truth, and *that* means you're in the proper spirit of the game."

"Your turn?" he asked.

"My turn. Truth."

"How'd *you* get in?"

"Upstairs window."

He gave her the side-eye. "The ground-floor windows are stained glass, and they don't open. Next windows are three stories up."

"I'm a good climber. Your turn."

"Truth," he said.

The last strains of the waltz faded under the shifting lunar lights. Lionel and Maddie turned face-to-face within a crawling band of darkness, the eclipse falling across their gazes, as the next song began. Something slow, mournful, a sad memory set to violin. They slow-danced, his hands on the small of her back, her arms holding him close. She whispered her question in his ear, carried on a puff of warm breath.

"What are you really here for?"

"The Edgar Allan Poe manuscript," he whispered back. "The one they're auctioning off tonight."

Her arms tightened around him.

"You're bidding on it?"

"That's two questions," he said.

"No. Play right. You didn't completely answer me."

He almost argued, but seeing as she was answering a question for every one of his, Lionel decided to keep it candid.

"No," he whispered. "I was hired to authenticate it. There's a potential buyer—not here, out of state—and they're in the market for that kind of stuff. Figured it was either legit or a hoax custom-tailored to scam 'em out of a bundle of cash. So far, it looks legit. I'm supposed to watch the show, find out who the lucky winner is, and report back."

Maddie's lips pursed in an angry bow.

"My turn," she said. "Truth."

"Same question."

"Same answer. Your turn."

"Truth," he said.

"This one's important." Her words were slow, as sinuous as the turn of her hips. Her body fit against his like two pieces of a puzzle. "This one's for all the marbles. Ready?"

"Go for it."

"Lionel, who hired you?"

"That's confidential."

"Then you should have asked for a dare instead." She shook her head. "I'll tell you what. You trust me, and I'll trust you. On the count of three, we'll answer the question together. Same time. All right?"

He trusted her, too, though he wasn't sure why. She was a spark of the familiar in dark, unfriendly territory, a guide in the maze of ice-blue lights. He swallowed, hard, and nodded.

"Okay. On three."

They counted down in silence, staring into each other's eyes.

"Regina Dunkle," they both said at once.

"Bitch," Maddie hissed, her eyes blazing behind her skull mask.

"What?"

"I almost—" She shook her head. "Never mind what I almost did, what she almost *let* me do. That . . . *damn* her."

"Wait," Lionel said. "She hired both of us to do the exact same job?"

"You're not supposed to bid, right? Report and observe? Did she ask you to get pictures of the manuscript?"

"Especially the last page," he said, "but they took my phone at the door, and I couldn't sneak a camera in. Why would she hire both of us and not just, you know, *tell* us? What's the point? We could have gotten more done if we were working together from the start."

Maddie snickered, but there wasn't any humor in it.

"It's your first time, isn't it? She swooped into your life out of the blue and offered you something shiny. Something you couldn't say no to. She's good at that. Finding people's levers. It's what she does."

"It's . . . not your first time, I take it?"

"I work for her," Maddie said. "I'm on the permanent payroll."

"Doing what?"

"Whatever she wants, anywhere she wants, anytime she wants. Okay, let's focus. For now, the mission is still the mission. We're going to split up, canvass the room, and try to get eyes on the manuscript before the auction starts. Then we watch the auction and leave. Separately. Don't even make eye contact with me if you don't have to. We'll rendezvous at the hotel bar."

"And then?"

"And then we have a conversation. And I have to figure out what I need to do to get you out from under her thumb before you end up like me."

"I'm not under her thumb," he said.

The look in her eyes turned tender, almost pitying.

"Oh, Lionel. You don't get it. This isn't your world. You left your world the second you walked through Regina Dunkle's door. We've got to find a way to get you back home."

The final note of the song faded into silence. Her hands slid along his shoulders as she took a step back.

"Worry about that later," she said. "For now, eyes open, mouth closed, and keep a low profile. Regina doesn't do anything without a reason, and that means something's seriously fishy here. I'll see you back at the bar."

She drifted into the crowd and left him standing alone.

Now he wanted his phone for two reasons: to get his connection to the outside world back, and to call up Regina and get to the bottom of this. It would have to wait. *We'll call her together,* he thought. He resumed his circuit of the room, mapping exits, hunting any clue as to where they might be holding the manuscript.

Time went on. The dances went on. The ballroom was built like a casino: no windows, no clocks, no connection to reality. He was sure more than half an hour had passed, though, with no signs of anything getting started. The organizers were dragging their heels.

He rounded the edge of the room. A warm glow caught the corner of his eye. One of the partygoers leaned casually against the wall, phone in hand, shooting off a quick text before he pocketed it and went back to the dance floor.

Lionel's brow furrowed. On a hunch, he slipped into a knot of conversation. "Excuse me," he said. "Does anyone know what time it is?"

A man in a swan mask pulled out his phone and checked the screen. "Quarter to ten," he replied.

Lionel thanked him and kept walking.

There was no rule against cell phones. Not for the rest of the club's members, anyway. Just for him and Wade. The guardians at the door had cut Lionel off from the outside, and they'd done it on purpose. He thought to the man in the zigzag mask—how he'd whispered in Dolores Croft's ear, and she'd revised her estimate of the schedule on the spot.

He said the word hotel, Lionel thought. *She said half an hour. About as long as it might take to send somebody to toss my room.*

Lionel had run enough undercover stings to know when his cover was blown. And he'd been blown before he walked in the door. He scanned the crowd, hunting for Maddie's mask. Every instinct screamed at him to get the hell out of there, just make for the closest exit and disappear, but if they'd been watching him, they'd have noticed his conversation with Maddie. He had to warn her.

A hard metal tube jammed against the small of his back. A hand clamped down on his shoulder.

"Yes," said man in the goat mask, standing behind him, "that's a loaded pistol. Yes, I'll pull the trigger if I have to. No, not a single person in this room will call the police. If I've answered all your questions to your satisfaction, please start walking."

He jabbed Lionel with the muzzle of the gun. Lionel started walking.

The zigzag mask joined him, along with two more heavies in black suits: one wearing a golden cherub mask, the other fashioned like a Dalmatian, complete with painted spots. All of them had bulges under their coats. Dolores and Wade joined the party. Wade gave Lionel a sidelong glance and a smirk.

"Couldn't have asked for a better outcome," Wade said.

Lionel arched an eyebrow. "What happened to all that hand-wringing and all the trouble you'd be in if I got found out?"

"*Got* found out? I'm the one who set this up." Wade wriggled jazz hands, mocking him. *"Acting."*

"What about Ray Barton? I thought your hands were clean on that. So, what, your buddies here killed him?"

"Nope," Wade said. "That I told you the truth about. We honestly have no idea who did the guy. But it was a pain, seeing as we really did want him to come tonight."

"He had a purpose," Dolores added. "A purpose that you, Mr. Page, will now fulfill in his stead. Anton, how did things go?"

The big guy in the Dalmatian mask bounced behind her, puppyish. "His room was clean—just some luggage, nothing to find."

"We haven't cracked his phone yet," Zigzag added, "but we will. Unless Mr. Page would like to give us the pass code?"

Lionel shot him a look. "Mr. Page would like you to go screw yourself."

Goat mask cuffed him upside the head. He winced, stumbled, and kept walking.

They passed through the keypad-locked door and down a narrow, tall corridor lit by electric sconces. The LED bulbs blazed from ice blue to molten gold and flooded the frigid hall with jeweled light. The air grew colder. Lionel watched his breath turn to a puff of curlicue mist, and a sudden shiver jolted down his spine. The ballroom music faded away at their backs. In its place, a low and steady thrumming seemed to rise up from the marble beneath their feet, as if the building itself was shuddering in hungry anticipation.

"You should be happy about this," Dolores told Lionel. "I've read up on you. You're a self-styled crusader, a seeker of truth. You're about to get all the truth you can handle. Just remember, you agreed to this before you stepped through the door: your choice, and on your head the consequences."

"I don't think that's legally binding," Lionel said.

Her droll laughter echoed down the icy hall. "Oh, I assure you, it is. Not by *man's* law, I suppose, but we don't live by man's law. That's for the little people. Like you."

"You apparently didn't read that much about me," Lionel told her, "because that's just about the dumbest thing you possibly could have said."

"Why?" Her lips curled in an indulgent smile. "Am I on your list now? Are you going to do a tell-all story on me? Bring me down, topple my throne? Ridiculous. Do you know what your problem is? You think your job is speaking truth to power."

"I'm a reporter. That's exactly what my job is."

"You have never *seen* real power," Dolores said. "Allow me the honor of making a proper introduction."

The procession filed under an open archway, the white marble shot through with veins of gold. They emerged into a frozen chamber. The breath caught in Lionel's throat. He stared dead ahead, eyes wide and unblinking.

"What . . . ," he whispered. "What the hell *is* that thing?"

Dolores folded her arms and raised her chin high.

"The secret to our success, Mr. Page. As I told you, we've all made sacrifices to get to the top."

Twenty-One

The gathered party—Lionel, Wade, Dolores, and her four masked thugs—stood on the lip of an octagonal chamber. Bronze sconces along the walls crackled with naked flame, wreathing the high, vaulted ceiling in coils of gray smoke. The air smelled of stale incense and half-forgotten dreams.

At the heart of the chamber, mosaic tiles drew a circle upon the floor in a riot of colors. Rust red, midnight black, bilious green. Greek letters drawn in tile ringed the outer rim of the circle, along with symbols Lionel didn't recognize. One of them, prominent and laid in amethyst purple, matched the symbol on Dolores's mask.

That wasn't what drew his attention, though. His gaze was fixed on the air *inside* the circle.

Black smoke swirled like a cyclone, rising a head taller than he was, spinning as it drifted back and forth within the circle's confines. Sometimes it took a sharper form, just for a second, before dissolving once more. Something like a floating serpent, flashing impressions of hooked teeth and baleful eyes. Too many eyes.

"What is this?" Lionel said. "It's . . . it's a hologram, right? Some kind of optical illusion." He craned his neck, looking to the ceiling and squinting through the haze of smoke. "Where's the projector?"

Zigzag and goat mask flanked him, grabbing him by the forearms and holding him in place. Dolores let out a heavy sigh. She strode to the circle's edge, holding out her hands, her open palms to the heavens.

"Not this time, Mr. Page. No hidden projectors, no technological trickery, no clever hoaxes. I'm afraid you've reached the end of your crusade." She glanced back at him over her shoulder. Her eyes caught the light, reflecting pinpricks of dancing fire. "For the first time in your entire pointless life, you are an eyewitness to the truth. Behold her. Behold *Melpomene*. Behold her, and worship her."

The smoke held its form longer, now. An alligator head gnashed its teeth. A rattlesnake's tail cracked like a whip. An echoing voice emerged from the chaos, a young woman's, sonorous and cold.

"You speak words to honor me, little priestess, but I crave more than words. Come inside this circle. Kneel down before me. Let me reward you for your kind service."

Dolores's lips curled into a smirk. "I think I'm best able to serve you exactly where I am."

"You should free me. I've foreseen your fate, if you do not. It is not a kind one."

"My beautiful lady," Dolores said, "kind lady, generous lady—"

"Flatter me not, witch."

"Why do you scorn our company? Am I not a gracious host? Do I not give you fine lodgings, abundant food, the best of all things?"

"A jailer," the smoke seethed, "should not pretend to be her prisoner's friend."

Dolores touched her hands to her chest, her mouth falling open in mock dismay. "Prisoner? Why, how could mere mortals take Melpomene, Muse of Tragedy, Mother of Sirens, as a prisoner? The daughter of Zeus himself, cast in chains? Unthinkable. No, no, I won't believe it. We must agree that you are an esteemed guest."

It's an illusion. Lionel's thoughts raced in time with his pounding heartbeat. His eyes were lying to him—it was the only rational explanation. He couldn't figure out the trick, but it had to *be* a trick. *Dolores. Her family is in pharmaceuticals. She must have drugged me somehow, slipped acid into my—*

He froze as the presence in the circle turned its full attention upon him. He felt it like a lead weight pressing down on his heart, his stomach, squeezing all the air out of his body. Fingers of icy marble sifted through his mind, flipping through his thoughts as if they were written on index cards.

"You haven't been drugged," Melpomene told him.

Dolores blinked. "I—What?"

"I am thinking," the voice in the chaos said to Lionel, "of scribing a new tragedy. You're going to be the hero of the play."

Still thinking the presence was talking to her, Dolores lifted her chin higher. "I realize you mean that as a threat, great Muse, but I choose to accept it as a token of your esteem—"

"Or maybe your woman would be a better choice," the voice echoed. "There's more than a little of Macbeth in that one's heart. You would be best suited for the part of Macduff. You were, after all, untimely ripped from your mother's womb."

Dolores peered at the smoke. "My . . . woman? Who are you talking about?"

"Self-obsessed dullard," Melpomene snapped at her. "Not everything is about you. Ask me for stock tips or something, like usual. Let me help you make more *money*. You'll soon learn just how well it spends in Hades."

Dolores took a step back. She bit down on her offended snarl and took a deep breath.

"Gratitude would not be remiss, my Muse. I've brought you a pair of fine offerings."

Wade cocked his head, his own tragedy mask slightly askew on his face. "A pair? What—"

That's when the two other bruisers, the Dalmatian mask and the cherub, grabbed him by the arms.

"A pair," Dolores told him. "That means two."

Wade shook wildly in their grip. His mask came free and clattered to the mosaic tile, baring his reddened face. Droplets of sweat plastered a tangled lock of hair to his forehead.

"What the *hell*, Dolores? What do you think you're doing?"

"When Raymond Barton was killed, you should have gone dark until this entire mess blew over," she told him. "Protecting our club and its members is our first and foremost responsibility. Instead, what did you do? You brought a *reporter* in here."

"I told you what I was doing—"

"After you made the arrangement."

"I checked, okay? Nobody knows he's here. Nobody's coming to save him. I *checked*."

Dolores circled him like a shark. Her heels clicked on the icy tile floor. "You're a buffoon. What did you do, ask him nicely? Barton was an ideal sacrifice. Him? Once he disappears, we're going to be cleaning this up for months. Looking over our shoulders, wondering if we left a loose end anywhere. Unforgivable."

She stepped close to him, eye to eye.

"You're not worthy of our company any longer. And you know as well as anyone that there are only two roles in this world. You're either eating the steak, or you *are* the steak. Now if you'll excuse me, I have an auction to run. Goodbye, Wade."

She started to leave, then paused, looking back at Lionel.

"As for you? I mean you no malice, Mr. Page. I pray that your death is swift and merciful. I very much doubt it will be, but I pray for it regardless. More importantly, I hope your final moments bring you a measure of enlightenment. And perhaps, peace. As I said, I read up on you. Whether you realize it or not, you've spent your entire life looking for real magic."

Dolores raised her hand. She languidly gestured to the cyclone of smoke.

"There you are. And there you go."

She turned her back and walked through the open arch, up the corridor of golden lights.

Wade kicked, flailing in his keeper's arms, face glistening with sweat. "Dolores," he shouted, twisting his shoulders as he squirmed. "Don't *do* this! *Dolores!*"

She never looked back.

Three of Dolores's men looked to the one in the goat mask, silently showing Lionel the pecking order. Goat mask looked between him and Wade, head tilted, considering.

"Wade goes first," he said. "Y'know why, Wade? Because you're a dick, and I never liked you. Bye-bye."

"C'mon, don't do this." One of Wade's sleeves ripped as he struggled, stitches tearing, but the Dalmatian and cherub held him fast. "For the love of God, not like this! *Please!*"

Goat mask rolled his eyes. "I'm not sure what part of 'Bye-bye' was hard to understand. Gentlemen? Dinner is served."

They took a running start and heaved, throwing Wade across the scarlet-and-black mosaic tiles and into the circle. Into the cyclone of smoke.

He stumbled, falling to his hands and knees, and Lionel had just enough time to register the horror on Wade's face before the smoke engulfed him. Then he started to scream.

Gashes opened in his upraised hands. His clothes tore, long and thin cuts, as if the smoke had become a whirlwind of scalpels. His blood joined the cyclone and spiraled through the air in red ribbons. Lionel's feet turned to ice. The surge of cold spread upward through his body, freezing him in place, while he watched the smoke tear Wade apart.

Wade kept screaming. One long, endless shriek, going on longer than he should have had breath for. An invisible mouth met his in a blood-smeared kiss, and invisible teeth tore his bottom lip away. His eyes were next.

My whole life, Lionel thought, his mind as turbulent as the churning, hungry smoke. He'd spent his life on this hunt. Psychics, faith healers, miracle men—he'd busted them all, exposed their powers for nothing but parlor tricks, proved time and time again that magic didn't exist. And every time, some tiny part of him had slumped its shoulders in quiet disappointment. Some tiny part of him, deep down inside, had always ached to see something wondrous. Something science and logic couldn't explain away.

One of Wade's arms snapped, flesh ripping, a shard of bone jutting free. Scarlet rivers flowed from the gaping tear, joining the wet streamers that encircled his shrinking body like a DNA helix. He was still screaming.

As if reading his mind, goat mask leaned in close behind Lionel. His hot breath, stinking of wine and stale cigarettes, washed over Lionel's neck.

"So," he asked, "was it worth it?"

Lionel felt his lips contorting in a rictus. He couldn't help it. Wade's big toe, exposed under the leather scraps of his shredded shoe, disappeared. An invisible mouth closed over it and gnawed it to the ragged bone. One detail out of a hundred at once as the creature in the circle mutilated and devoured its victim, still alive, still shrieking. *This is what going insane feels like,* Lionel thought. It was too much. It was just too much.

Wade's spine went *snap* with a thundercrack of bone. The screaming stopped. The room went silent.

The ribbons of blood, swirling in an elegant dance, tumbled to the floor. It was as if someone had just flicked an *off* switch. They'd been floating, defying gravity, churning around the smoke cyclone; then they suddenly plummeted and splashed in a rust-red wave across the mosaic tile.

The man in the goat mask patted Lionel's shoulder.

"Your turn," he said.

Twenty-Two

The heavy in the golden cherub mask took over for the goat, grabbing hold of Lionel's left arm. Lionel didn't even struggle. He was still frozen, his muscles turned to icy stone, as he stared at the smoky wraith and the pile of soggy, shredded meat that used to be Wade Dawson.

Goat mask stepped in front of him. He held up two objects, waving them in front of Lionel's face to get his attention. In his left hand, he had Lionel's cell phone. In his right, a gun.

"I know it doesn't seem like it," he said, "but this is your lucky day."

Lionel couldn't stop his trembling lips from curling back. The lunatic, terrified smile stayed plastered to his bloodless face.

"See," goat mask said, "cleanup's gonna be a bitch tonight, and I'm not talking about the literal viscera. We usually offer up people who nobody's gonna miss. Folks like the late, unlamented Ray Barton—criminals, y'know? People who are more or less *expected* to go missing or meet a bad end. You? You're a solid citizen and a public figure. That's a big problem. Key to solving that problem is to find out exactly who you've been talking to and what you've been saying, and for that, I gotta get this phone unlocked."

Lionel found his voice again, but he had to force the words past his convulsive shivers. The room was an icebox now, his breath trailing white, misty tongues in the air.

"Screw you," he stammered. "I'm not going to help you murder me."

"Sure y'are," goat mask said. "Not only are you going to help, you're going to thank me for it."

Lionel squinted at him. "How do you figure that?"

"You're going in there, just like Wade. You saw what happened, right? That's your future. Everything that just happened to him is going to happen to you. *But*"—he wriggled the cell phone—"there's an escape clause. All you have to do is give me your unlock code, and I'll put a bullet in your head before we toss your body in. Quick and painless. You *are* gonna die tonight, pal. I'm not going to lie to you, there's no getting around that. But you don't have to suffer like Wade did."

Lionel was out of denials. They'd been torn from him, one by one, like the ragged pieces of Wade's flesh. The thing in the mosaic circle wasn't an illusion, wasn't a trick, wasn't a man in a rubber mask. He'd just uncovered the biggest story of his life. Maybe the biggest story of anyone's life.

And he was about to be eaten alive by it.

But maybe, he thought. His mind raced, a drowning man snatching at life preservers as the icy waters pulled him under. Maybe there wasn't a way out, but that didn't mean he couldn't file his final report. Brianna would come looking for him when he didn't check in, maybe as soon as tomorrow. The Chicago cops were still eager to talk to him, too. Goat mask was right: nobody was going to sweep his disappearance under the rug.

Others would come, if he gave them the time they needed. If he made it harder for Dolores and her cult to lay a false trail and throw his rescuers off the scent. Others would come, they'd find this place, and they'd find the truth.

"C'mon," the man in the goat mask said. He showed Lionel the phone and the gun. "Make it easy on yourself. Make the right choice."

Lionel looked past him, to the hungry and expectant darkness.

It was a simple binary. Give them the unlock code, die by a bullet, and they'd cover it all up. Or walk into the arms of Melpomene. He'd die like Wade did—slow, in unimaginable agony—but he'd give

Brianna and his friends time to follow his trail. He'd give them a chance to reveal the truth to the entire world and finish the job he'd started.

In the end, it really wasn't hard to choose.

"This is Lionel Page," he said softly, "live from New York, signing off for his final broadcast. Good night, ladies and gentlemen."

The goat's eyes narrowed behind his mask. "What are you talking about?"

Lionel turned to regard him. He felt strangely calm now. It was okay.

"I've never met a goddess before," he said. "I'd like a closer look, please. You can save the bullet."

The other three men—cherub, Dalmatian, and the man in the zigzag mask—looked to the goat for his final verdict. He scowled and cocked back the hammer on his pistol.

"You stupid, arrogant son of a—"

Through the open arch, up the hallway of golden light, heels clattered on the marble floor. Running, coming in hard and fast. The men turned as one. Maddie sprinted toward them, eyes burning behind her skull mask, copper glinting in her left hand as she raised it high.

Her hand swooped down. Her knife, a thin copper blade with a hilt wrapped in leather cord, whistled through the air. It punched through the goat's throat and speared out the back of his neck.

The goat collapsed to his knees and spat a gout of blood onto Lionel's shoes. Ten feet away and coming fast, Maddie twisted and yanked her empty hand. The knife tore from the dying man's throat, dancing in the open air as if she were holding it herself. Her empty hand swung left. The blade did, too. Zigzag shrieked and staggered back, letting go of Lionel's arm, as it slashed him across the eyes. Lionel's paralysis shattered. He curled up a fist and drove his knuckles into cherub's fat chin, bone cracking against bone. Zigzag, blind, had his hands clamped over his torn face. He stumbled across the room—and over the edge of the mosaic circle. The cyclone of smoke engulfed him, and his screams rose four octaves.

Dalmatian had his revolver out, the tail of his jacket swinging back as he ripped it from a shoulder holster. Maddie was on him. She slapped his gun hand, grabbed his wrist, twisted, and drove the heel of her other hand against his elbow. He howled as his arm shattered. She wrestled the gun from his grip, spun it around, and pulled the trigger. The shot echoed off the chamber walls like a cannon, and the bullet blew the back of Dalmatian's skull across the mosaic floor in a fine red mist.

Cherub grappled with Lionel, crushing his wrists in a vise grip, trying to wrestle him toward the circle. He shoved him across the tiles one rough foot at a time. Behind Lionel's back, zigzag's screams suddenly went silent. Lionel felt the smoke hovering by the circle's edge, close, still hungry. Two more steps and—

Maddie popped up behind cherub, the knife back in her hand, and slit his throat from ear to ear. The big man's eyes went wide. Then he crashed to the floor. His blood drained between the mosaic tiles, painting a serpentine river along the grout.

Lionel stood in the sudden silence, stunned, the aftermath of the gunshot still thrumming in his ears. Maddie grabbed a sleeve of the Dalmatian's jacket and wiped the blood from her blade. She hiked up her plum dress, baring a sheath—slim black leather on a buckled garter—on her inner thigh. Her next priority, after hiding her dagger, was to take off her heels and kick them across the room.

"You know what sucks worse than shoes in general, Lionel? *Heels.* Oh, they make your calves look great! Well, my feet want a word with my calves. Screw this, I'm officially done with shoes tonight."

"You—" Lionel said, realizing he was surrounded by the corpses of men who had been alive less than a minute ago. "You just—"

She shook her head at him. "What? Killed four dirtbags who had it coming, before they could murder you? You're welcome."

The air shook with a dry chuckle. Melpomene's voice rustled from the eager cyclone of smoke.

"*Maddie.* It's been years. Come close, let me get a good look at you."

"You two know each other?" Lionel said. "And how did you do that thing with your knife? It—it *moved*, on its own—"

Maddie shut her eyes. She took a deep breath and pinched the bridge of her nose.

"Okay," she said. "Lionel, we do *not* have a lot of time here. There's another thirty or so where these guys came from, plus Dolores Croft, who—from the glow she's giving off—is a witch of *stunning* power, and we've gotta slip past all of them before they figure out you're still alive. The auction just started, and they're all distracted; that's our window of opportunity, and it's closing fast. So let's get out of here, and you can ask me all the questions you want once we're back at the hotel bar. Deal?"

"A witch," Lionel echoed. "An actual witch. And . . . and you did that thing, with the knife. Wait. You're . . . Wait."

"Oh my God, you're adorable. It's like a little lightbulb just went on over your head. Yes. I'm a witch, that's a demigoddess, it's all true, and we are leaving. *Now*, okay?"

She snatched his fallen phone off the floor and shoved it into his pocket. Then she grabbed him by the hand and yanked him toward the archway. Melpomene's voice reverberated against the stone, hitting their backs like a blast of arctic air.

"You aren't leaving me here, prodigal. Even if you refuse to honor your mother, you will *not* turn your back on the pacts of old."

"I don't have time to bargain with you right now," Maddie snapped, looking back over her shoulder. "I'll come back for you, okay? My word on it."

The cyclone of smoke grumbled, then fell silent.

Lionel wanted to ask what she meant. He wanted to ask a million questions at once. Instead, he gritted his teeth and ran at Maddie's side, sprinting up the molten-gold corridor toward the only way out. Back through the ballroom, right past Dolores and her entire cult.

Twenty-Three

"You got it together now?" Maddie whispered.

They stood at the back edge of the gathered crowd in the ballroom, easing their way across the shifting bands of ice-blue light and shadow. The entire Thoth Club was there, gathered with their backs turned, all eyes and masks facing the other side of the room. Dolores held court, standing behind a mahogany lectern with a gavel in her hand. On her left was a polished plinth bearing a purple velvet pillow—and upon the pillow, a small stack of yellowed pages secured in a thin sleeve of glass.

"I'm good," Lionel whispered back. "Just . . . took me a second."

She squeezed his shoulder and gave him a tiny smile.

"Under the circumstances, you're doing great. Here. Here's a good place to wait."

He looked from Maddie to the double doors, twenty feet to their right.

"Wait?" he said. "Wait for what?"

Maddie nodded to the prize at Dolores's side. "We still have a job to do."

"Worthy souls," Dolores called out, raising a hand to the crowd. "Seekers of truth. As we speak, the Muse is receiving her sacrifice. As always, we will draw lots: three of you will accompany me into the sanctum, to receive Melpomene's oracle—and the blessings of good fortune that accompany it. But first, a special treat. We've come into a special acquisition tonight, suitable for any collection of rarities—"

"Are you *nuts*?" Lionel hissed in Maddie's ear. "The door's right there. Let's get out of here before these freaks notice us."

"Regina wants to know who the winning bidder is. We already didn't get the pictures she wanted, and I'm not going back empty-handed. Besides."

She took hold of his wrist, curling her fingertips over his pulse, feeling the beat of his veins. She nodded to herself, as if confirming a suspicion.

"Besides?"

"Besides," she said, turning her head to meet his eyes, "don't lie. You're more excited than scared. You're just like me. You *enjoy* this."

Lionel's mouth tightened. He glanced away, toward the plinth, toward the case of glass that held Poe's lost story. *The* story.

He was still processing everything he'd just seen, the revelations that had thrust themselves into his life, twisting and tearing his perceptions like a serrated knife. He was still the same man, though, deep down inside. Still willing to charge into a downtown riot or take the stage in front of a hostile crowd. Still chasing the truth along the razor's edge of adrenaline.

"Yeah," he whispered back, "maybe just a little."

Her fingertips slid down his palm, twining with his as she held his hand. She wore a simple, thin chain of silver around her wrist, one tail dangling loose, and it tingled against Lionel's skin like an electric wire.

"—and of course," Dolores was saying, "authentication papers will be provided to our lucky winner. With that, shall we begin? I'd like to open the bidding at twenty thousand dollars."

The double doors swung open wide.

Two men in domino masks—they must have taken over bouncer duties for the dead men in the inner sanctum—came in with nervous, drawn expressions and took up stations beside the doors. Lionel ducked his head. He turned his face as his heart kicked up a staccato beat. A final guest strode into the ballroom, passing between the doormen, the crowd parting like the sea as he made his grand entrance.

No tailored suit for him. The final guest wore rags of gray and black, torn and tattered, caked with dirt as if he'd just clawed his way from a wet grave. Under a peaked hood, he wore a full-face rubber mask: the face of an old man, old enough to be ancient, his white skin spattered with scarlet ink. His cloak was pinned with a faded brooch, its hammered-copper face encircled with mismatched gemstones in a chaotic jumble of color.

He whistled as he walked, a perky melody. Lionel's guts twisted into knots. He froze, suddenly petrified, every muscle in his body going rigid as stone. His hand clenched tight around Maddie's.

"What is it?" she whispered.

"That . . . that song. I know that song."

He struggled to explain it. He didn't understand it himself. Only that he knew that song. And it scared him more than anything in the entire world.

Dolores gave a giddy laugh and clapped her hands as the ragged man approached the podium. "Ah, now *this* is getting into the spirit of things, people. I told you we'd be celebrating the works of Edgar Allan Poe tonight, and it appears we've been graced with a visit from the Red Death himself. Well done, and with perfect timing, no less."

He stopped whistling.

The man in the mask moved to stand beside the lectern and turned to face the room. Behind his mask, his eyes were a piercing blue, almost too bright to be real. He raised his gloved hand in a casual wave. The crowd offered up a round of polite applause, following Dolores's lead.

"Really," she said, smacking her palms together. "Who is that, under the mask? Jackson? West? It's you, isn't it, Jackson? Always the showman. I should have expected this."

The blue-eyed man spoke with the voice of a storyteller. Weathered, older but not old, the voice of a man who had seen the world and could describe it all beside a crackling campfire.

"I'm afraid I'm not a member of your club," he said. "But when I heard about tonight's festivities, well, I just couldn't stay away."

"Not a . . ." Dolores furrowed her brow, studying the man beside her. She pitched her voice a little lower, no longer playing to the crowd. "I'm assuming this is part of the game, but under the circumstances, I'm going to have to insist that you unmask."

"Unmask?" he replied. "I wear no mask."

He chuckled, a pleased rumble that washed over the crowd's growing uncertainty, and held his hands aloft in mock defeat.

"Sorry," he said, "I'm mixing my literary references. That's actually Robert Chambers, not Poe. *The King in Yellow*? Are you familiar with it?"

"I am," Dolores said, her frown deepening by the second.

"It's an apt comparison, though. Both Chambers's fictional play within a story and Poe's 'Masque of the Red Death' share some striking parallels. Both feature a party, gathered aristocracy, and a decadent fool of a ruler who thinks herself untouchable."

"I insist," Dolores said, "that you unmask."

The man's blue eyes seemed to flare as he turned his head, the corners crinkling with a smile. He stripped off his gloves, one by one, and tossed them to the floor at his feet. His hands were broad and strong, with a ruddy tan.

"Another important parallel," he said. "At the end of both stories, everybody at the party dies."

He slapped his palm against his brooch and bellowed a word, something grating and grinding in his throat, like the sound of a garbage disposal made of human flesh. The gemstones flared brighter than the ice-blue lights. Every door in the ballroom burst open, and Lionel reeled, buffeted by a desert-hot wind that hit him from every direction at once. Tossing him, turning him, staggering his senses. All he could hear was the screaming of the wind and the screaming of the guests as the party became a living nightmare. Shapes circled the room, translucent gray and muddy brown, flitting through the air over their heads. Shapes with elongated arms and clawed hands and distended, hungry jaws. Lionel watched, shell-shocked, as one of the phantasms descended on a club member and hauled him to the marble floor. It ripped the man's chest open with savage rakes of its claws, like a dog digging for a bone, then buried its head in the gaping wound to feast.

Maddie grabbed Lionel's shirt collar and yanked him backward, toward the far corner of the room. The silver chain around her wrist fell loose into her hand. She hissed something, swift and sibilant in words that sounded like ancient Greek, and turquoise sparks flared along the chain.

"Stay next to me!" she shouted over the howling din. "Keep your head down!"

Lionel crouched low and watched the world go mad. People were running, falling, trampling over each other in their rush to escape, and the throng of misshapen phantoms picked them off like lions chasing a herd of confused gazelles. A woman in a gown—he thought it was colored burgundy until he realized it was white, drenched in blood—staggered past with her jaw shattered and her gums raw and empty. A spectre mockingly danced along behind her, a court jester in funeral gray, juggling the teeth it had ripped from her mouth. One by one, it tried to shove the jagged ivory chunks into its own toothless maw, the teeth falling through its translucent face and plinking onto the gore-stained marble floor.

Maddie spun her chain, drawing a sparking violet figure eight in the air while she whispered a rhythmic chant. One of her bare feet slapped the floor in time, drawing a steady drumbeat. The rhythm was a bulwark against the chaos, a small bastion of order that shoved back the winds. A dome rippled like a heat mirage, just big enough for the two of them. One of the phantoms screamed toward them, shooting across the ballroom like a bottle rocket, claws grasping for Lionel's face. It struck the dome, bounced off, and reeled away. Its shape frayed at the edges, fuzzed like static on an out-of-tune television channel.

The blue-eyed man was on the move. He casually strolled through the carnage, whistling again, the slim glass case with the Poe manuscript tucked under his arm. He paused at the door. Then he glanced over, looking from Lionel to Maddie and back again, and tilted his head.

"Huh," he said. Then he walked out, taking his trophy with him.

The last body hit the floor. All five pieces of it. One by one, the phantoms departed. They flitted through the floor, through puddles that glowed purple-black under the colored ballroom lights, or drifted through the walls, their groans and the howling wind dying, fading, gone.

The rippling dome melted away as the chain slowed in Maddie's hand. She twirled it slower and slower, then finally let it fall limp. She snaked it back around her wrist, wearing it as a dangling bracelet again.

Lionel swallowed. His mouth was bone-dry. He could barely inhale without gagging, the air thick with the stench of copper and rotten meat. He and Maddie were the sole survivors. The members of the Thoth Club littered the floor all the way to the lectern. Dolores Croft was only recognizable by the gown she'd been wearing; she had aged a hundred years in an instant, reduced to a desiccated, emaciated mummy sprawled dead on the floor.

Silence fell over the room like a burial shroud. Only Maddie's voice dared disturb it.

"Come on," she said. "We're leaving."

It was past late when they got back to the High Line Hotel. The court-yard bar was closed, the tea lights doused. The lobby, still dimly lit, stood empty. Maddie and Lionel trudged onto the elevator, only inertia keeping their exhausted bodies in motion. He took a look in the elevator's mirrored cage and wished he hadn't. He was a mess, his rented tuxedo dusty and torn, both of them painted with dried spatters of other people's blood and looking like they'd just run a marathon.

Maddie didn't get off on the second floor. By silent, mutual consent, she followed him up to his suite.

The place had been turned upside down—his luggage dumped out on the floor, the drawers ransacked, even the contents of the minibar fridge tossed and plundered for secrets that were never there to find. Lionel took a deep breath, bent over, and started to pick things up. Maddie stopped him with a hand on his shoulder.

"In the morning," she said.

She guided him to the bed. He kicked off his shoes, peeled off his jacket, and lay down in the remnants of his rumpled tux. She pulled him down onto the mattress and turned him onto his side. He lay still while she climbed onto the bed, slipped in behind him, and spooned against his back. One arm curled around his side. Her breath was a puff of warm air on the back of his neck as she held him close.

"Sleep, young lion," she whispered. "Everything else can wait until morning."

Twenty-Four

Sunlight crept in around the corners of the blinds and poked Lionel's eyelids until he stirred. He rolled onto his back, stretching out in an empty bed, still wearing last night's clothes. He forced his eyes open and squinted until he could see. His shower was running behind the closed bathroom door.

"Maddie?" he called out.

"Out in a minute," she shouted back.

He forced himself up, groaning as a muscle in the small of his back twinged like a piano wire strung too tight. He looked around the murkily lit bedroom and the mess the searchers from the Thoth Club had left in their wake.

"Take your time," he said. He picked up his clothes, repacked his suitcase, salvaged what he could from the minibar fridge. The bedside clock said it was almost ten in the morning. His phone had four calls, no voice mails—one call from Brianna and three from Regina Dunkle.

Seeing Regina's name brought last night back to him in a sudden, screaming torrent. The entire nightmare flashed behind his squeezed-shut eyes, and he had to grab hold of the nightstand to steady himself.

The shower died. The bathroom door cracked open, and Maddie—a towel wrapped like a turban around her shiny curls—poked her head out. "Regina's burning up both of our phones," she said. "Don't call her back. I'll be out in a minute."

"I don't . . ." He flailed his hand, the disheveled bedroom feeling like a map of his life. Everything out of place and wrong. "I don't know where to start with any of this."

She gave him a wink. "That's my job. Wait for me."

She must have grabbed clothes from her room while he was still sleeping. She emerged in black jeans and a concert T-shirt for a band he'd never heard of, toting a pair of beat-up sneakers but not wearing them, and steered him into the bathroom.

"Clean up and get changed," she told him. "You'll feel better. I'll finish tidying up out here. Then you and me are going to have a talk."

She wasn't wrong. The hot water washed away some of the night, clearing his head as he scrubbed his body clean, and he shaved in the fogged-up mirror. He buttoned up a dress shirt, stepped into clean khakis, feeling ready for the world. The world he used to know, anyway. The rest, he'd figure out along the way.

Light flooded the suite's bedroom. Maddie had opened all the curtains, letting the sun in, and cleaned up the last of the damage. She pirouetted to greet Lionel as he stepped out of the bathroom.

"Ta-da," she sang. "All better now."

"I've got one question. And it's a stupid question."

"I'd say there's no such thing as a stupid question, but we both know that's a dirty lie."

"Am I crazy?"

She shook her head, offering him a soft, almost-wistful smile.

"No," she said, "you're not. God, I almost remember what this feels like. You're not the first person to see the real world for the first time and wonder if you're losing your marbles. We all go through it. Let me put it this way: If you saw what you saw last night, and it seemed perfectly rational? *That* would mean you're crazy."

"That guy, who *was* he?"

"You tell me," Maddie said. "You froze up like a deer in the headlights when he started whistling."

He shook his head and frowned at the floor.

"I don't know. I feel like I *should* know. I just . . . don't."

"Don't sweat it," she told him. "So, we've got a lot to do today, and daylight's burning. I think we should handle the unpleasant part first."

"What's that?"

She held up her phone.

They sat on the bed together, side by side. She set the phone between them, switched it to speaker mode, and hit the speed dial. They waited in silence as it rang.

"Madison," Regina said, "I've been waiting for your report all morning. Where have you been?"

"Oh, *hi*, Ms. Dunkle. I've just been spending quality time with a new friend. Say hello, Lionel."

"Hello, Lionel," he replied.

Maddie smirked and gave him a thumbs-up. Regina's heavy sigh slithered over the speaker.

"Well," Regina said, "you've made contact. Good. I assume at least one of you succeeded in getting the information I wanted?"

"*Good?*" Lionel stared at the phone. "That's . . . that's all you have to say? Regina, I almost died last night. *Twice.* If Maddie hadn't been there—"

"But she was," Regina said.

"I point-blank asked you if Lionel was working for you," Madison said. "If you'd just been honest with me from the beginning, this could have gone a lot smoother."

"I never explicitly said he wasn't one of mine. My dear, for a woman of your cunning, you shouldn't need to be schooled on the power of words. I also told you that your job isn't to understand me, it's to obey me. In the end, everything came together just as I designed it to. Just as it always does."

"Except it didn't," Lionel said. "The manuscript is gone. This guy in a Red Death costume showed up and—"

He trailed off, giving Maddie a questioning glance. She shook her head at him, not following, and he leaned close.

"Does she know," he whispered, "about the witch thing, and, you know, all that stuff?"

"Ooh," Maddie said. She looked to the phone. "Lionel lost his virginity last night. He wasn't sure if you were in on the big secret."

"Maddie," he said.

"Hey, there are more vulgar terms I could have used. I modulated my language for the sake of your sensitive disposition."

"That's unfortunate," Regina said. "I take it, then, the esteemed members of the Thoth Club are . . ."

"Splattered all over some prime Manhattan real estate," Maddie replied. "Game's over, okay? Whatever you promised Lionel, he lived up to his end of the bargain and then some. I can take things from here. Give him his prize and send him home."

"Nonsense," Regina said. "Lionel is done when I *say* he's done, and I want both of you working on my behalf."

"He's not equipped for—"

"Then *equip* him, Madison. I want that manuscript found, and I want it in my hands as soon as possible. Given the circumstances, we've clearly gone past the stage of peaceful negotiation. Find this 'costumed man,' and kill him for me."

Lionel stared at the phone. A slow, cold finger trailed along his spine. He thought of the cub reporter back in Chicago, stabbed dead in an alley. He had wondered if Regina Dunkle was capable of having someone murdered.

Now he knew for certain.

"Whoa," he said. "I didn't sign up for that."

"Lionel." Her voice was a sheet of ice over a bottomless lake. Cool and smooth as glass, only hinting at the dark killing waters below. "We have an agreement. Serve me, and I protect your good name. That arrangement can go the other way, too, you know."

"Meaning?"

"Meaning, if you walk away from this, I'll see to it that the story you're so keen on burying ends up on every television station in America."

"Maybe I can live with that."

"Can you?" she asked. "Journalism—your particular brand of journalism—is your life and your passion. How will you go under-cover when everyone in America knows your face and your name? How will you expose the wicked and bring down the mighty when they see you coming from a mile away? Yes, you'll survive the story. Your career won't, and you can say goodbye to everything you love, everything that matters to you. I'll make certain of that."

"You're blackmailing me," he said, his voice flat. Maddie squinted at him, as if trying to read the truth on his face.

"I'm motivating you," Regina said. "You have your orders. I'll expect to hear an update on your progress shortly."

She hung up on them. The phone, nestled between their laps, went dark. Maddie reached over. The tips of her fingers played across the back of Lionel's hand as she deliberated something in silence.

"Lionel, what did she offer you? What's this story she's talking about?"

He kept his gaze fixed on the rug at their feet.

"It's not important."

"It's important to you."

"It's really—" He shook his head. "I don't want to get into it."

"You should go home," she told him.

"I can't. You heard her."

"Lionel."

Maddie reached up. She took gentle hold of his chin, lifted his head, and made him face her. She met his gaze with soft compassion and the faintest twinge of worry.

"You aren't ready for this," she told him. "What you saw last night . . . that's just the tip of the iceberg. Now, you had an experience, okay? But that's all it was. You can still walk away. You can go back to Chicago, back to your old life, back to the way things were before you met Regina Dunkle. I know her, how she operates. She probably won't even follow through on her threat. Don't take this the wrong way, but you're just not that important to her. If you leave, right now, first plane out, you can still *have* your old life. Years from now, you'll probably rationalize this all away. You'll tell yourself it was a hallucination, or a trick, or you'll just chalk this entire trip up to a vivid bad dream. People do it all the time."

When he weighed his options, oddly enough, Regina's threat didn't even come into the picture. He'd survive the exposure. He understood what Maddie was really offering him: the chance to live in a world where goddesses didn't eat men alive inside mosaic-tile circles, a world where ghosts didn't lay siege to Manhattan ballrooms. The sweet bliss of ignorance, where all the monsters were only make-believe.

"What if I stay?" he asked her.

"Then this"—she twirled her hand, taking in the room, the city, the whole wide world—"this is your home now. What you saw last night? That's what *every* night is like for me. I mean, not that violent—usually—but the point is, you don't ever get to shut it off. You don't get to stop seeing the truth, no matter how bad it gets. You don't ever get to live a normal life again. That's the price of admission. That's the sacrifice."

He bowed his head, falling silent. When he raised it again, he felt something new in his eyes. Something like quiet resolve, and new determination.

"Okay," he said.

"Okay?"

"I've spent my entire life hunting for the truth. That's who I am. That's what I do." He looked to the open windows and listened to the sounds of traffic on the sun-drenched street below. "When I met Regina, I felt like I was falling down a rabbit hole. Like Alice in Wonderland."

"This isn't Wonderland," she told him.

"No. But it's real. And I can't turn back now."

Maddie took a deep breath. She puffed out her lips as she let it go and drummed her fingers on her legs.

"Okay," she said. "We need to get you some basic skills first. And fast."

"Skills?"

She wriggled her fingers at him. "Witch skills."

"You're going to teach me how to be a witch?"

Maddie blurted out a laugh. "Oh, *hell* no. We're kind of on a tight schedule here, in case you haven't noticed. No, I'd need a year and a day just to teach you the foundations. Then another year and a day to put your brain back together so you could start learning the *useful* stuff. No, this situation calls for a quick-and-dirty initiation, something to crack your brain open a little so you won't get blindsided out there."

"What . . . kind of initiation?" he asked.

She patted his knee and rose from the mattress.

"The kind that sucks and hurts a lot, like all good initiations. I have to grab some stuff from my room. I'll be right back. Take your shirt off."

Twenty-Five

The curtains were down again, drawn tight, plunging the room into shadow. Lionel and Maddie sat facing each other on the floor with their knees touching. The rough fibers of the Persian rug scraped against Lionel's fingertips. Per her instructions, he'd taken his shirt off. So had she, casually stripping down to her purple cotton bra. She shrugged a bare, freckled shoulder at his raised eyebrow as she dug around in a canvas tote bag.

"This isn't a sex thing," she told him. "Sex magic can be super-potent, but that's like, grad school–level witchcraft, and you're a high school freshman. Also, it's not as much fun as you might think. Lots of concentration involved. And math."

"Sex math?"

"The *Kama Sutra* ain't got nothing on the *Litanies of Aphrodite*." She held up a small plastic jar with a screw-on lid and opened it to show Lionel the bed of rich snow-colored cream inside. The scent of wintergreen mint and some faint, peppery spice filled the darkened room. "Flying ointment."

"We're not . . . literally going to go flying," Lionel said. He paused. "Right?"

"Not *literally*, no. My broomstick's in the shop."

She set down the open jar and picked up a pouch of purple velvet. As she did, Lionel's gaze drifted to her left arm. Thin scars marred the length of her pale skin from the wrist to the bend of her elbow, like tick marks on the wall of a prison cell, puckered white and faded with time.

She caught him staring, frowned, and pointedly turned her arm, pointing the scars toward the floor. He didn't ask. She opened the pouch and dropped a deck of cards, the backs midnight blue and adorned with pinpoint golden stars, into her open palm.

"What do you know about the tarot?" she asked.

"I played poker with tarot cards once," Lionel deadpanned. "Five people died."

Maddie scrunched her face at him. "Very cute. You're not far off the mark, though, just not in the way you think. There are a lot of stories about the origin of the tarot; some people say they originated in ancient Egypt, as tools of divination. Others claim the symbolism in the cards is tied to the Hebrew kabbalah, the 'Tree of Life' that forms the foundations of the universe."

"Which one is true?" he asked.

"Neither. Both stories are total bullshit. The tarot was invented in Italy in the 1400s, for playing a card game called *tarocchi*. The tarot was intended for gambling; the idea of using the cards to read fortunes came after the fact—like, a hundred *years* after the fact."

She shuffled the deck in a lazy, easy overhand, snaking cards from the bottom of the pack and bringing them up, murky light glinting off the gold-foil stars.

"Doesn't sound very mystical," Lionel said.

She gave him a coy smile. "Lesson one: Witches use what works. It doesn't have to have a grand lineage, doesn't need to be part of a secret mystical tradition handed down from secret mentors. What matters is that it works. And the tarot works."

"But if the stories aren't true—"

"Lesson two," she said. "Factually true and mythically true aren't the same thing. This, I can predict, is going to be hard for you to wrap your brain around."

"Because it's not so," he replied. "True is true. Facts are facts."

"Factually, there's nothing supernatural about a tarot deck. But let's check in with your initiator, the high priestess."

Maddie stopped shuffling. She rapped her knuckles on the top of the deck and flipped over the top card. The card depicted a woman in soft blues and whites and an ivory crown, a fallen crescent moon at her feet, sitting between a pair of pillars: one black, one white. The base of the card read *II: The High Priestess*.

Lionel's first impulse was to make a comment about card tricks. Maddie met his eyes, one eyebrow slightly lifted, silently daring him to do it. He kept his mouth shut.

"The original name of this card was the Papess," she said. "It's been said to represent any number of people over the years, including Maifreda Visconti. She made a bid to become the Catholic pope back in 1300. Didn't work. They burned her at the stake. It's also been attributed to the cross-dressing Pope Joan from the thirteenth century, who may or may not have actually existed, or to a generalized, metaphorical female embodiment of the Church's spiritual essence."

"Which do you think it is?" Lionel asked.

"Doesn't matter. The facts aren't important, for our purposes; what it represents is important. And symbols call to symbols. Look closer."

She trailed her fingernail along the face of the card. Lionel squinted, picking out details he hadn't noticed at first glance. Objects hidden in swirls of paint. Tiny letters scattered along the hem of the priestess's robe.

"This scroll, this veil, this pomegranate—every single detail on this card has historical resonance. It's a catalog of symbols, all bound together to express a unified idea: the idea of the high priestess. Think of it as a new language: the more words you learn, the more clearly you can read the message."

She set the rest of the deck aside. Then she took Lionel's hand, turned his palm upward, and gave him the card.

"Study the card."

"But," he said, "I don't know the language. I see the stuff you pointed out, but I don't know what it all means."

"This is part of the lesson. Don't go with your head. Go with your heart. Witchcraft isn't about facts and figures, and that's going to be the hardest thing for you to unlearn: it's about impulse, emotion, intuition. Study the card and explore how you feel about it. See what stands out, what details pull you in."

He stared at the card in his hand. "How do I know when I'm doing it right?"

"You start by letting go of that question. Magic is best performed without expectations, of success or otherwise. Don't look for a goal or a finish line. Just be in this moment."

Lionel let out a halfhearted chuckle. "I'm really, really not good at being in the moment."

"Nooo." Maddie put a hand to her mouth, her eyes going wide. "*Really?* I never would have guessed."

"Ha ha."

"Just study the card. Feel. Flow."

She picked up the open jar, dipped her curled fingers inside, and scooped out a glob of frost-white ointment. She chanted under her breath, a sibilant whisper too soft for Lionel to make out the words, as she smeared it along her arms, her upper chest, her belly, leaving glistening trails and arcs.

His turn was next. Her fingers ran along his bare chest, slowly, tracing just below his collarbone. The ointment tingled against his skin, hot at first, then turning wintry cold. She scooped out another handful and anointed his arm, from the curve of his shoulder down to his wrist.

"I want you," she whispered, breaking her chant midstream, "to be here with me. In the moment. Okay? Just you and me and the card. There's no outside world, there's nothing outside this room. Nothing matters but you and me and the card, and right now."

He tried to respond, but his voice fled from him, carried on a frosty stream as Maddie's slow, soft touch slid down his other arm. She was close, leaning in, her breath puffing along his chest and making the patch of drying salve on his chest tingle. Then she circled him, easing around behind Lionel on the Persian rug. She did his back, hands rubbing the cream into his muscles, kneading as the scent—tantalizing and peppery—did cartwheels inside his brain. He felt like he'd downed a magnum of golden champagne. He felt like he was floating, the lights going from dim to dark, the ceiling of the room cracking and opening wide. All of space was above him, a starless void waiting and calling, but he didn't look up. His eyes were locked on the tarot card.

The woman in the portrait lifted her chin. She met his gaze with a gentle smile. He didn't think this was strange at all.

And it wasn't strange when the card began to grow, its borders rippling as they stretched, the painted details becoming crisp and clear as a photograph. Or when Maddie, her hands firmly on his shoulders, shoved him inside.

Bright lights behind Lionel's eyelids roused him. He wasn't sure how long he'd been unconscious. He squinted, cupping a hand over his brow to block out the harsh and sudden sunlight. He was lying on dew-damp grass, and a gentle breeze ruffled his hair.

He sat up. He was on a hill somewhere, no signs of the city—or any city—in any direction. Just a small pavilion, where the high priestess sat in contemplative silence upon her throne.

He jumped to his feet. It was real. The card had come to life, the painted image taking on three-dimensional form five feet in front of him. The woman in her blue-and-white robes, the standing pillars rooted in the wind-kissed grass, the cornucopia of symbols. A crescent moon made of buttery gold lay at the foot of the woman's chair, mirroring part of her ivory crown. She watched him without saying a word, as if waiting for him to make the first move.

Maddie stood at his side. She wore a flowing white robe, almost like a toga, belted with a scarlet sash. A woven headband pulled her ginger curls back, and she held the corded hilt of her copper-bladed knife in a casual grip.

"Where the hell are we?" he asked, looking between her and the priestess. "Are we . . . *inside* the card?"

"More like . . . we're inside the card, inside of you. Don't overthink it. Don't think it at all. The lesson hasn't changed." Maddie gestured to the scene before them. "Study her. This is a rare situation where it's perfectly all right to stare. She doesn't mind."

Lionel looked to the high priestess. He realized, now, that she didn't match the painted portrait. Not at all. How hadn't he noticed that before? Her hair was different, long and blonde. The curve of her chin, the soft glint in her big hazel eyes, it was all so familiar. Where had he . . . ?

"Oh my God," he breathed. *"Mom?"*

"No," the priestess said. "I'm sorry, Lionel, but your mother is dead. You know that."

"But . . . but you . . ." He felt his eyes going wet, felt whatever tenuous grasp he had on reality slipping out from under his fingers. Maddie took his hand and gave it a squeeze.

"I am the nexus," the priestess explained, "where a universal symbol manifests in your internal landscape. To put it more simply, I am *every* high priestess, and I am *your* high priestess. Your subconscious mind has painted a face for me. Something that resonates deeply inside of you."

"She looks totally different to me," Maddie added. "To everyone, really."

He took a deep breath and bit his bottom lip until he felt steady again.

"What are we doing here?" he asked.

Maddie lightly rapped her knuckles on the side of his head. "We've got to open you up a little. There's a lot of dangerous critters out in the big, bad world. Like last night, except they aren't always so easy to see with the naked eye. I don't have time to teach you a witch's skills, but we can at least give you a proper witch's senses."

The priestess folded her arms. "Are you sure you want to do this? This process wasn't meant to be rushed."

Maddie's hand rested on Lionel's shoulder.

"We can get him through it," she said. "Just the three of us."

Except there were four people on the grassy hill.

The third woman was just *there*, as if she had been the entire time and Lionel somehow hadn't noticed her. She was tall, willowy, pale, standing behind the high priestess's shoulder and off to her left. Her hair fell in a raven-black wave of curls, down past the shoulder of her dress—a flame-red gown, like a torch singer from the '20s might have worn. Around her neck, on a silver chain, dangled an antique key.

"Wait," Lionel said. "Who is—"

The woman in red put one finger to her burgundy lips. She flashed a mischievous smile as she whispered, *"Shhh."*

Twenty-Six

"Who is what?" Maddie asked.

Lionel looked from her to the woman in red and back again. Before he could raise his hand, pointing out the intruder in their midst, the woman's voice echoed in his mind.

"This secret is for you alone," she said, her voice tinged with dark amusement. "If you care for Maddie, hold your tongue."

"I'm just . . . a little off-balance," Lionel said.

"Then let us address that," the high priestess replied. "Come before me."

His legs moved on their own, drawing him toward the tableau. The priestess sat on her simple throne, elegant and graceful, and raised her chin to study him. Behind her, the woman in red watched in eager silence. Neither Maddie nor the priestess seemed to know she was there.

The priestess cradled a silver goblet in her hand now. A deep amber fluid swirled in its depths. A fresh breeze ruffled the dewy grass, carrying the faint scent of fresh berries.

"Knowledge," the priestess said, "can be sweet ambrosia or bitter as ashes. A true seeker of wisdom must always be willing to drink, regardless of the flavor."

"I always have been," he told her.

Sadness touched her gaze. She shook her head.

"That isn't true, Lionel. Part of your heart is missing. You've sealed it up behind a wall. But that's like ignoring a leak in your basement: it may only be a trickle, but eventually that trickle will swell and erode the very foundations your house is built upon. You can't escape your past by running from it."

"Maddie knows *all* about that," said the woman in red. Lionel looked to Maddie. She stood impassive, eyes fixed on the high priestess, like she hadn't heard a word.

"I'm not here to give you a gift," the priestess said to Lionel. "I'm here to challenge you. To show you the flaws that need repair before you're ready for true power."

"I'm not looking for power," he said. "I'm just looking for the truth."

"And without power, that truth will be the death of you."

"Listen to her," Maddie told Lionel. "We're playing by big-girl rules now, okay? Last night wasn't remotely as bad as it can get out there. And it's going to get a lot worse before we're done."

"Now that's an understatement," said the woman in red.

She sat on a stool now, still perched behind the priestess's shoulder. An easel stood beside her. Lionel took in the painting on display, cast in rich, dark oils. A burning chariot hovered in a starry night sky above a thatch-roofed house. The vague figure of a man knelt on the ground below the chariot, clutching his bowed head, his posture radiating abject misery and despair.

The woman in red twirled a wooden paintbrush in her fingertips. "What do you think, Lionel? I'm fond of this one myself. Don't answer that out loud. But do remember the painting. There'll be a quiz later."

He wavered on his feet, attention torn in three directions at once. He looked to the priestess. "What do I have to do?"

"I am a symbol, and yet, I am as real as you. I embody the bridge between the feminine and the divine. The flows of the moon. The currents of magic. Do you understand?"

"I . . . think so," he said. "I mean, I'm starting to get it."

"I cannot point the way to your transformation unless you choose to open the door."

"It's that free-will thing, right?" He shot a sidelong glance at Maddie. "First Regina, then the bouncers at the Thoth Club. People keep asking me to do things 'of my own free will.' And I keep getting screwed right after I say yes."

"Words have power," Maddie told him.

"They do." The priestess sat back upon her throne. She cradled her chalice in both hands. "As do bargains. You are free to walk away, Lionel."

He cast a look over his shoulder, at the vast and flowing grassy plain and the crisp blue sky.

"I'm still here," he said.

"Then answer with your heart. Will you accept my authority as your initiatrix? Will you follow where I lead you, no matter where the trail goes?"

"In other words," the woman in red added, "fasten your seat belt and prepare for turbulence. Also, no guarantees that you won't crash and burn. Think you can handle that?"

When he replied, he spoke to them both at the same time.

"If I have to," he said, "if that's what it's going to take to get through this . . . then, yeah. I accept."

The priestess swept a languid hand toward the grass at her feet.

"Kneel before me," she said.

He knelt down. He bowed his head, an inch from her lap, the silver chalice centered in his sight.

She offered him the chalice. "Drink. Every drop. He who hesitates is lost."

He glanced to his side as he took the cup. The woman in red loomed over him, wearing an expression of cold, almost malicious, glee.

"Courage, young lion," the woman in red told him. "You're going to need it."

He closed his eyes, pitched his head back, put the chalice to his lips, and drank. Rich amber wine splashed across his tongue—tart, peppery, suddenly turning acrid and vile as it touched the back of his throat. He choked it all down as the world spun around him, fading to serpentine bands of scarlet and black.

"I'll tell you a secret," the high priestess whispered in his ear. "You've already been initiated. *Remember.*"

⁓

Lionel was five years old.

He lay awake in bed, eyes open and fixed on the rustic, splintery rafters of the old farmhouse, listening to the crickets trill outside the screen window. It was early autumn, the weather starting to shift toward harvesttime, and a cool night breeze was rolling in off the trees. It smelled like pine cones.

Someone was outside his window.

He'd had this nightmare before. He knew how it would go. The man would stand there in silhouette—showing the bend of his broad shoulders, the low, slouching brim of his Stetson hat, so motionless that Lionel could almost convince himself it was a trick of the light.

Then the whistling began.

He knew the tune now, the one that had eluded him at the Thoth Club's ballroom. He knew it once the man broke into a low, eager song, his voice drifting on a gust of forest wind.

> Oh Buffalo gals, won't you come out tonight?
> Come out tonight, come out tonight?
> Buffalo gals, won't you come out tonight?
> And dance by the light of the moon.

Then the man would turn his face, staring through the screen at Lionel in his bed. Still cloaked in shadow, except for his piercing blue eyes.

~

Lionel wasn't dreaming.

He stood, rooted to the floor of his childhood bedroom in his bare feet and pajamas, watching the woods encircling the Emerald Ranch burn under a bone-white moon. Flames roared up to lick the sky and cast plumes of roiling black smoke to blot out the stars. People were screaming, running. A horse galloped past. It was burning, too, blazing like a Roman candle as it thrashed its head and raced into the forest to die.

"Get everyone out the back," he heard his mother shout. "I'll slow him down."

"Janet went to get the shotgun—" another woman called back. A dresser scraped on the bare-plank floors, rattling against a door, an impromptu barricade.

"That won't stop him! Where's Lionel? Martha! Find Lionel!"

Strong arms swept him up. Holding him close. The kind of love that could move worlds. He looked up into his mother's face as she forced a smile to keep the fear from showing, and brushed the unruly curls from his forehead. She kissed him and whispered in his ear.

"Listen to me—" she said.

But the image skipped and lurched and fast-forwarded like film rattling in a broken projector. The old woman holding him—Martha—shoved him toward the open hatch of a crawl space. Forest air, kissed by pine trees and smoke, gusted across his face.

"We'll be right behind you, I promise," she whispered. "Whatever you do, don't look back, and *don't stop running*."

The sky opened up and drowned the world. Lionel charged through the downpour as fast as his tiny legs could carry him, all alone now. He

175

broke through the tree line, out in an open field now, all alone. The icy rain soaked through his pajamas, and his bare feet squelched into the mud and grass, splashing through puddles. He stumbled and fell. He landed on his belly in the mud, shoved himself back to his feet, and kept running. His heart pounded, ready to burst, every breath burning in his lungs. Then he lunged out onto a dirt country road and skidded to a dead stop as amber headlights pinned him in place like a panicked deer. A car's horn blared, louder than the storm.

The Persian rug over the smooth hardwood floor came back. His suite came back. New York and the world came back.

Lionel jolted from the vision and landed flat on the floor. He yanked his body into a fetal position, rolling on his side, clutching himself as he shook like a leaf in a thunderstorm. Someone was hammering on the door. He was vaguely aware of Maddie on her feet, tugging on her T-shirt and moving fast.

"We heard screaming—"

"It's okay. My boyfriend had a nightmare, he's fine."

"Are you sure? We can get someone—"

"He's fine, really, thanks."

He had never been further from fine in his entire life.

She latched the door and then she pulled him up, into her arms, holding him close against her body. Her fingertips ran through his hair.

"Shh," she whispered. "It's okay. You're on the other side. You got through it."

"No," he stammered. "N-no, it's not, it's—"

She kissed his cheek and nuzzled him. She gave him a soft, affectionate chuckle. "It will be, I promise. I'm sorry. Like I said, initiations suck. We've gotta ground you, get some water and some protein in your body."

Then the dam inside his heart—the wall he'd built with stubbornness and fear and anger—burst wide-open. And the tears he'd been holding back for decades came out as floodwater. He curled his chin to his chest and wailed for all that he'd lost and all that had been taken from him, and she held him, rocking him against her shoulder without a word, until his sobbing faded to a quivering, broken tremor.

He pulled back, just far enough to look her in the eye. He knew he was a mess. She didn't seem to care.

"I know why I'm here now," he said. "I . . . I mean, I don't, I don't know if it's fate, or chance, or some one-in-a-billion—"

"It doesn't matter." She reached into her tote bag and took out a plastic packet of tissues. She plucked one from the pack and dabbed at his cheeks. "What did you see in there?"

He ran through it one last time, before he gave it voice. The answer threatened to bring the tears back all over again, but he got through it, one word at a time.

"The man with the blue eyes," he said. "Maddie . . . he killed my mom."

Twenty-Seven

"I don't remember much," Lionel said. "But I remember more, now."

He sat on the floor, back to the edge of his bed, with Maddie's tissues in one hand and a glass of water from the bathroom tap in the other. She'd produced a box of saltines from her tote bag and made him eat three before letting him say another word.

"For grounding," she explained. "I realize it doesn't seem super witchy, but crackers and tissues are essential post-ritual supplies."

"My name wasn't always Lionel Page," he said. "It was Paget, originally."

She rose, walked past him, and opened one of the blinds. Fresh sunlight flooded the murky room, chasing away the shadows.

"I was five. Back in the early '90s, my mom took me to live on this . . . Well, it was a commune, basically. This ranch out in Michigan. My dad was never in the picture. I got the idea that he might have been abusive, that we were running from him. That's what these people helped with."

"Sheltering abuse victims?"

Lionel nodded. He sipped his water.

"Women and kids. I was the only boy on the ranch. They had this whole neo-pagan thing going on. Witches, not like—" He waved a tissue, trying to find the words. "Not like *you* kind of witches, more like . . . New Agers? Dream catchers and tie-dye shirts and prayers to the great moon goddess. That kind of thing. Hippie stuff. They were good people. I remember, more than anything . . . it was a feeling."

"A feeling?"

"They didn't know me or my mom. No reason to care, no reason to take us in. But I felt . . . loved. The commune was a place for women to heal. I wasn't supposed to be there. I knew a couple of them weren't happy about it, but even them, maybe especially them, they tried real hard to make sure I still *felt* wanted. I never felt wrong or out of place."

He slumped his head back against the foot of the bed.

"Sometimes," he said, "I think that's the last time I ever knew what that felt like. And then, one night, everything went wrong."

Maddie sat down beside him on the rug. She gently nudged his hand, the one cradling the water glass, encouraging him to take another swallow. He drank, steeling himself for the story to come.

"Ever hear about the Emerald Ranch Massacre?" he asked her.

Her eyes widened, lips parting as she put the pieces together.

"I remember," she said. "Wasn't that some kind of Manson family—"

"That was the popular theory. That a quote, unquote, 'rival cult' had attacked the ranch in retaliation for some slight. A war between 'satanic witches.'" Lionel's lips twisted into a bitter grimace. "The media went nuts. Nobody could find any living kin, so I went into foster care, the sole survivor of the massacre. I took my foster parents' name, but that wasn't enough to keep me hidden, not when child protective services was willing to take a bribe from any tabloid hack who waved money in their general direction. I was six years old, and reporters were camped out on the steps at my elementary school, shoving cameras in my face and asking me how I *felt*."

"Jesus," Maddie said. "No wonder you blocked it out."

"Yeah, well, eventually the press lost interest, like they do. I had just enough time to build something like a normal childhood. Then the ten-year anniversary hit, and this bloodhound from *People* tracked me down."

"You had ten years to get past it," Maddie said. "Then he brought it all back again."

"Oh, with accumulated interest. See, this was January 2002. The first Harry Potter flick had come out in November, and between that and the books, the whole planet was going nuts for orphaned wizards. So this . . . this absolute bastard not only writes an article about me, complete with outing the town I lived in and the school I was going to, but he pitches it as 'The *Real* Boy Who Lived.' At least he stuck to the facts. Once the tabloids jumped into the feeding frenzy, that was when the real fun started."

His hand shook as he raised the glass to his lips. Maddie cupped her fingers over his, holding the glass steady as he drank, and eased it back to his lap.

"They *made shit up*, Maddie. Both times. But it was even worse with ten years gone and no suspects in custody. These women were good people. They helped people, *saved* people. And I had to hear about how the police found slaughtered goats and upside-down pentagrams at the scene of the crime. How the detectives who investigated the ranch were haunted by a 'sinister curse' that touched anyone who set foot on the property. See, it couldn't just be a crime. It couldn't just be evil people doing evil shit. They wanted to believe in curses. They wanted to believe in *magic*."

He took a deep breath and stared at the open window. Motes of dust danced silently on bolts of sunlight.

"So I'm the school freak, I've got people spray-painting upside-down crosses on my locker, my life is more or less ruined, and the media just packs up their gear and moves to the next story as soon as the ratings die down. On to the next sensation. And there's me, standing in the wreckage."

"When did you become Lionel Page?" Maddie asked.

"The day I turned eighteen. Changed my name, changed my address, cut my hair. Martha, one of the women at the ranch, she'd read books to me and the other kids every afternoon. She always told us 'there's a world of possibility on every new page.' So Lionel Page was born. A man on a mission. I was going to show the world the price of superstition. I was going to prove that there were no miracles, no magic, no monsters going bump in the night . . ."

He closed his eyes and sagged against the mattress.

"Wow. Guess I'm a big dumb asshole, huh?"

"No." Maddie's hand closed over his. "*No.* Because you weren't wrong. You set out to reveal hoaxes, Lionel. To expose people *pretending* to have real powers, and exploiting the believers. You've done that. It's good work, important work. The fact that magic is real doesn't change one jot of that. You think I'm any less of a skeptic just because I'm a witch? If anything, it's the other way around. I question everything and test it twice. Just like you. Is that what Regina offered you? That she'd keep your past in the dark?"

"This cub reporter dug it all up, tracked me down, threatened to expose me. It'd all come back, all over again. A fresh walk through hell, and this time I can't just disappear. Last time, I lost my privacy, my name, I was hounded until I wanted to crawl under a rock and die. This time . . . well, it's like Regina said. I'm an investigative journalist. My work depends on being able to go undercover, incognito, keep the bad guys guessing. Want to imagine how well I'd do once I'm the center-ring attraction of the circus again?"

"You could find another line of work."

"Sure. Give up the only thing that's ever meant anything to me. The only job that makes me feel like I'm doing any good in the world, like I'm *worth* anything." He glanced sidelong at her. "That reporter . . . he's dead now."

"I'm sure he is," Maddie said, as matter-of-fact as talking about the weather outside.

"It worries me that you're not surprised."

"Lionel," she said, "I told you. I work for the woman. I'm on the full-time payroll. Can you talk about the other thing? What you saw?"

The other thing. He gave her an uneasy nod.

"I have these gaps in my memory," Lionel said. "I know my mother said something to me, something important. I know I saw more than I remember, the night it all happened. There's something else, too. Something *after* the massacre. Martha slipped me out through a crawl space. I ran out into the road as a car was coming around the bend. Except sometimes I remember it as a semi. And sometimes I remember it as a pickup."

"Did they stop?" Maddie asked.

"I think so, but . . ." He shook his head. "It's gone. The cops said I showed up at the door of the nearest neighbor, a farmhouse about eight miles up the road. I was alone, soaking wet, in a state of shock. No sign of who gave me a ride, and I can't . . . I can't remember one second of that drive. *Something* happened to me out on that road, but it's gone now."

Her fingertips brushed his leg. "You've spent your entire life running from what happened that night. Lionel, these gaps . . . Do you think maybe you don't *want* to remember?"

"No. Maybe. I don't know."

He dug into the box of saltines, chewed on a cracker, and washed it down with a swig of lukewarm water.

"Tonight, though," he said, "I got more back. It was him, Maddie. From the Blackstone. The same man."

"So the alleged 'cult'—"

"No. *Just* him. He killed them all. The women, the children. He burned the place to the ground. And there are two things I . . ." He looked to Maddie. "This is just my gut, okay? I can't back this up, I don't have any proof—"

"Lionel." She held up a finger. "Intuition. Trust it. Speak."

"I think my mother was a witch," he said. "A real one. Like you."

"And the other thing?"

He took a deep breath. "I think she was the reason he was there. The blue-eyed man followed her from . . . from wherever we came from originally. *He* was the man she was hiding from. Everyone else, the two dozen people he murdered that night, they were just collateral damage. He came for her."

Maddie took that in. She chewed it over in thoughtful silence. The saltine wrapper rustled under her fingers as she dug for a cracker.

"You can't go home now," she said.

"I know," he told her. "Don't want to."

His thoughts drifted to the initiation, and his walk inside the tarot card. Everything seemed a little more vivid than it had before that moment. The colors a little sharper, every shadow more defined, as if someone had tuned his eyes like a television set to bring in a better picture. Even his sense of smell seemed sharper: he could pick up traces of old paper on the air, of bathroom soap, of the salt on the crackers. Not superhuman, just . . . more.

He thought about the woman in the red dress, standing at the high priestess's shoulder.

"I'm not sure we saw the same thing, inside the card," he said.

"We didn't," Maddie replied. "That's normal. We weren't in the same place, so much as our brains sort of intersected at a right angle."

He thought about mentioning the woman and immediately remembered her cold smile, the finger pressed to her lips. *Shhh.*

He also remembered her warning. That if he cared for Maddie, to hold his tongue.

"I saw . . . a painting," he said, stepping around the subject.

"A painting? Interesting. Probably some kind of personal symbol, something you haven't uncorked yet. Keep an eye out, in case you see it again." Maddie craned her neck, glancing back at the clock on the bedside table. "Time for your second lesson, and this one's going to be a doozy."

"Yeah? What are we going to do, jump off a cliff?"

She pushed herself to her feet and held out her hand.

"Close enough," she said. "We're going back to the Blackstone Building."

He took her hand. He followed her to the door.

"Listen," she said, "we'll scout this trail together, but once we get to the end, and what needs to be done . . . I'm just saying, regardless of what *Regina* thinks, you don't have to do anything you don't feel ready for. You don't have any blood on your hands. It's okay if you want to keep it that way."

She reached for the dead bolt. He stopped her with a hand on her arm. She turned to face him.

"Maddie, I've spent my entire life trying to come to terms with what happened the night my mother died. The night I lost the only real family I ever had. I've been running toward, running away, just *running* since I was five. I'm done running."

He flipped the dead bolt. It landed open with a deep metallic *clunk*.

"This has nothing to do with Regina or what she offered me," he said, "not anymore. I'm going to find this evil son of a bitch, and I'm going to make him answer for what he did. Not for Regina. For *me*."

Maddie looked him up and down. She nodded to herself, coming to some quiet decision.

"Cool," she said. "All right, then. Saddle up and hold on tight. Shit's about to get real."

Twenty-Eight

The first time Lionel laid eyes upon the Blackstone Building, it had looked like a temple. The second time around, as the granite tower's Ionic columns painted prison bars of shadow across the street, it felt more like a mausoleum. The sun hid behind the clouds over Manhattan, denying its warmth to the city below, and a cold breeze whistled through the concrete canyons. The animal-headed gods in the stained-glass arches stared down at Lionel like judges in some infernal court, their dark, jeweled eyes contemplating his eternal punishment. He and Maddie rounded the corner and ducked into the side alley.

"No police tape, no signs anybody's come this way," she said. "Good."

He glanced back over his shoulder, expecting a squad car to roll up at any moment. "How could nobody have shown up yet? That was like a who's who of high society in that ballroom. There's gotta be people wondering where they are right now."

"The thing about a secret society, Lionel, is that its members tend to keep their meetings secret. Sure, the missing-persons reports will go out in a couple of days, and eventually someone will trace *somebody* back to the Blackstone, but until then? They're pretty much just going to rot in there. Which reminds me, two advance warnings. Number one, those bodies have had about a day to percolate, and . . . well, just prepare yourself. This won't be pretty."

"It wasn't pretty when we left," he said.

"The flies hadn't shown up yet when we left." She stopped at the side door and tugged a slim leather sheath from the hip pocket of her jeans. She folded it back to expose a neatly nestled row of lock picks. "Second, you've just had your third eye chiseled open. Sometimes you get remnants lingering at the scene of a violent death. Most people can't see them, but you? You bought the ticket, so get ready for the ride. *Usually* they can't hurt you."

"Usually?"

She crouched down and slipped a pair of picks into the lock, clenching a third between her teeth like a toothpick as she worked the tumblers.

"Usually." She swapped one of the picks with the one between her teeth and squinted. She tilted her head as if she could hear the inner workings of the lock.

"Can't you just . . . use a magic spell for that?"

She paused, plucked the pick from between her teeth, and wriggled it at him.

"This," she said, "is an excellent learning moment. Okay, yes. Theoretically. I could reach out to some gnomes—"

"Gnomes? Like, little guys with pointy hats?"

"Not like lawn gnomes. More like primal spirits of elemental earth. I could reach out, offer a pact and a favor in return for their aid, and they could make the steel in this lock turn brittle as balsa wood."

"That sounds like a lot of work," Lionel said.

"Bingo. Plus, I'd owe them a favor. Here's the bottom line, and it's probably the most important thing I'll teach you today: being a witch is about knowing things. I know magic. I also know how to pick a lock, handle a gun, change a car battery, speak fluent French, and find the best pizza in Brooklyn at two in the morning. All of these skills have saved my life at one time or another, including the pizza—remind me to tell you that story later. And when a witch faces a problem, she uses the best tool for the job."

"Hence the picks." Lionel nodded, taking that in. "Before last night, I felt like I knew everything."

"You knew everything you needed to know, for the world you lived in. Now you're living someplace new. There's no shame in being a student, Lionel, and there's no shame in ignorance. There's only shame in *staying* ignorant when you have the opportunity to learn. Your ambition didn't go anywhere. It'll serve you now, just like it always has before. Just keep your eyes and ears open. Your heart, too. That's the most important part."

"I'll give it a shot. So . . . what's waiting for us in there?"

"Do you like horror movies with lots of jump scares?"

"Not even a little bit."

The lock let out an audible click as the tumblers rolled over. She stood up, stepped back, and put her picks away.

"Huh. Well, I was gonna do a 'but the *good* news is' bit, you know, about how much money you'll save on movie tickets, but you just ruined that."

"I'm a jerk," Lionel said. "What can I tell you?"

She hauled the door open and gestured with a bow.

"After you, my fledgling apprentice."

He cracked a smile as he stepped across the threshold. "I'm your apprentice now?"

The door fell shut at their backs. An oppressive silence hung in the dusty hall. Maddie walked to the foot of the stairwell and leaned in, staring upward.

"Well," she said, "I initiated you, as quick and dirty as it was. That makes you my responsibility until you can stand on your own feet."

That jogged his memory. "There was something else. Just before I went back, back to that night—the priestess told me I was already initiated. What does that mean?"

Maddie shrugged and led the way up the concrete steps.

"Living symbols have a habit of talking in riddles. They love that fortune-cookie stuff—it's kinda baked into the cosmic process. We'll figure it out. One mystery at a time."

They smelled the ballroom before they saw it. The stench set in just one flight up the stairs, slapping Lionel in the face as he rounded the iron rail. When he was fifteen, he'd gone on a camping trip with his foster family; they'd returned to find that a blown fuse had cut the house's power for nearly a week. He remembered opening the refrigerator, a full-face blast of rotten hamburger and curdled milk washing over him.

This was worse. Close—that rotten-meat smell—mingled with the excrement stench of an open sewer on a hot summer day. He tried to breathe through his mouth. Mistake. He grabbed the handrail and squeezed it until the bile at the back of his throat settled back down again. From the strained look on her face, Maddie wasn't taking it much better.

"On the plus side," she told him, "in about ten minutes you won't even notice it. It's a neat mental trick: your brain just gradually adapts."

"I don't think I could ever get used to this."

She rounded the stairs and led the way into the ballroom's vestibule.

"You'd be surprised," she said. "The number one defining trait of humanity, beyond our predilection for violence, is our ability to get used to anything."

The vestibule was abandoned. Lionel took in the sight—the bouncer's stool, the little cabinet where they'd stashed his cell phone before letting him in—and tried to put on his professional face. Studying the scene of the crime, focusing on the facts and details—it was all part of the coping mechanisms he'd learned as a reporter. They made it easier to prepare for what was waiting beyond those double doors.

"Something's missing," he said.

Maddie paused with one hand on the door. "Huh?"

Lionel frowned at the stool in the corner as he mentally retraced the steps of his arrival.

"When I got here with Wade, there were two guys working the door. One took our phones. The other had a guest list; he was checking people off as they came through." Lionel pointed to the stool, then pulled open the cabinet to peek inside. "It's gone. Wade's phone is gone, too."

"Who would steal them? The guy in the Red Death costume obviously came here intent on killing everybody in the room; he didn't really need a list."

Lionel's brow scrunched a little, and he joined Maddie at the double doors.

"Don't know. Just seems odd. So . . . we gonna do this?"

They shoved open the doors. The stench shoved back, the odor of thirty murder victims left to rot in a sealed ballroom. They littered the marble floor, corpses and pieces of corpses—an arm here, a scattering of teeth there, dried streaks of viscera as if the green-veined stone had been painted with human brushes. The party lights were still on, the overhead track lighting striping the room in bands of ice blue and shadow. Fat black flies buzzed in the silence. Lionel swatted one away as it dive-bombed his ear. At his side, Maddie wore a curious frown.

"What is it?" he asked her.

"Remember what I said about remnants?"

He eyed the stray corpses, bracing himself. "Yeah?"

"There *aren't* any." She squinted, taking in the room. "That's not normal. If you want to leave a place good and haunted, a violent death or two—or thirty at once—is the best way to make it happen. This room is just . . . *empty.*"

"Is that good or bad?"

"It's not normal. There's no value attached to that observation. It's just . . . C'mon, we need to talk to an eyewitness."

He followed her to the keypad-locked door. She punched in five quick digits, and the light above the lock flashed from red to green.

"How do you know the code?"

"I was watching when they brought you and Wade through the door," she said. "People are always careless about keypads. Doesn't matter how long the code is if you type in the password right in front of everybody."

The door swung wide. The corridor beyond, lit in flowing golden LEDs, waited for them. Lionel's shoulders tensed. The skin prickled on the back of his neck, like a teasing fingertip luring him closer to the grave.

"She can't get out of that circle, right?"

"Not yet," Maddie replied. "Not until I let her out."

"Are you . . . going to?"

"Unless she gives me a good reason not to."

Lionel walked at her side, the open archway looming ahead.

"She tore two people to tiny pieces and ate them," Lionel said. "I was almost the main course."

Maddie shrugged. "And?"

"I'm just saying, that seems like a good reason not to let her out."

"Well, that's why I'm the teacher and you're the student," she said. "Brace yourself, by the way. Last time you were here, it was before you had your eyes opened."

Lionel stood at the chamber's edge and froze. The cyclone of smoke, straining to take on form, was gone.

In its place, a woman stood in serene silence. She was at least nine feet tall, with skin, eyes, and hair as ivory as her robes, like a marble statue brought to life. In her left hand, she loosely held a long, thin-bladed knife.

In her right, she held a human face.

The skin had been sliced neatly from the skull, with a few stray locks of curly hair clinging to the scalp. Gravity pulled the corners of his lipless mouth downward, in gruesome mimicry of a tragedy mask. Lionel's stomach tightened as he realized the lips were moving. Without a voice, without a body, the eyeless face was trying to speak.

"Didn't anyone ever tell you not to play with your food?" Maddie asked. She stepped over a fallen corpse—the man in the goat mask, eyes still wide, his throat a crusted river of rust—and up to the mosaic circle's edge.

"Ah, the prodigal," the giantess replied in a dulcet voice. "With all of the insolence I've come to expect from you. They stole my mask. I felt improper without one. Besides, I had to keep myself busy while I was waiting for you to uphold your obligations. Now free me. At once."

Maddie held up her hand. "Not just yet. Introductions, first. Lionel?"

He stood where he was, rooted to the floor under the open arch, until she waved him up. He took a few steps closer, skirting the fallen bodies, as the giant woman scrutinized him.

"It appears," she said, "that someone has grown eyes to see with. Hello again."

Lionel didn't reply. He wasn't sure what to say, and that feeling was back again—of cold, marble hands riffling through his thoughts, seeing inside his mind. Her unblinking stare trapped him like an ant under an overturned glass.

"Well, little witch?" she asked, an edge of annoyance in her voice. "Did you sacrifice your tongue for power?"

Lionel looked to Maddie, uncertain.

"Introduce yourself," she told him.

It seemed pointless—he was pretty sure the towering woman could read his mind and knew exactly who he was—but he gave it a shot anyway.

"Uh . . . hi? I'm Lionel. Lionel Page. Nice to . . . meet you?"

The woman looked to Maddie, scowling. "Not even past introductions and he lies to me already? Truly, he's one of yours."

"I'm not lying," Lionel said. "That's my name."

"We both know that isn't so. And the rest?"

He shook his head. "The rest of what?"

Maddie folded her arms and sighed. "Lionel *Paget* is of my lineage, and of no coven. He bears no debts that demand disclosure, and he will enter into no pacts without my leave."

She jabbed a marble finger at Lionel. "*He* should have said those words. You haven't even taught him the basic etiquette, yet you bring him into my presence?"

"He was just initiated an hour ago. He's new, okay? Also"—Maddie nodded down at the symbol-ringed circle on the floor, drawn in scarlet, green, and black—"considering you're trapped and we're not, maybe you should be a little less of a raging bitch right now."

Lionel swallowed, hard. "Uh, Maddie?"

The giantess loomed over her. She seemed to grow even taller at the circle's edge. "Mind your words, child. Trapped or not, you stand in the presence of a goddess."

"*Demi*goddess," Maddie snorted. She put her hands on her hips and dropped her voice to a mutter. "*Semi*goddess, maybe."

"*Maddie,*" Lionel rasped. He grabbed her by the sleeve of her T-shirt, tugging until she stepped back a few feet with him.

"What?" she whispered.

"I don't want to tell you how to do your thing—"

"And yet," she replied, "I'm looking forward to hearing you apprentice-splain it to me."

"Maybe you shouldn't insult the literal divine being?"

She cracked a smile, turning so the giantess couldn't see her face.

"It's just warm-up banter, Lionel. There are traditions for this sort of thing. I'm supposed to push her a little so she can push back harder and list her bona fides; then I act contrite and fluff her ego, and she goes to the bargaining table feeling respected."

"How do you know you're not, you know, pushing a little too much?"

"A lot of study and a lot of mistakes. Like I told you outside: Being a witch is about knowing things. We deal with all kinds of beings, creatures you can't imagine—yet—and each one has their own specific rituals, their own customs." Maddie stroked his collarbone through the fabric of his shirt. "The most important thing to remember: A witch always bargains from a position of power. Even when she isn't in one. *Especially* when she isn't in one. Am I your teacher?"

"Well, yeah—"

"Then I need you to do two things. One, I need you to trust me. Will you trust me?"

"I trust you," he said.

"Good. Two, I need you to watch what I do, and learn. This could save your life someday. In fact, it's going to, right now."

"How do you figure that?"

"Because I'm about to set her loose," Maddie said with a wink. "And if I don't handle this perfectly, she's going to kill us both."

Twenty-Nine

Maddie and Lionel stepped up to the mosaic circle's edge, standing side by side.

"I was going to turn around and walk out of here," Maddie told the giantess, "but my apprentice seems to think you might be entitled to some modicum of respect."

The giantess tilted her marble face, staring down upon them.

"The apprentice is more intelligent than his mistress. Perhaps I misjudged him." She swung her gaze toward Lionel. "You stand before Melpomene, little witch. Muse of Tragedy, first of her sisters."

"Eight of the nine all say they're 'first of her sisters,'" Maddie muttered to Lionel. "Polyhymnia, now she's easier to get along with. Real salt-of-the-earth type."

"You haven't seen her lately," Melpomene told her. "Polyhymnia has nurtured an unhealthy obsession with machines. The industrial revolution did not treat her kindly. And now the introductions are satisfied. Why do you delay? Strike the stone. Free me."

Maddie leaned back and cast a dubious eye at the tile circle. "It seems such a small task for one of my powers. Would I not be lowering myself by aiding you?"

"*Lowering* yourself?" Melpomene seethed. "I gave humanity a voice. I gave you art. I taught your storytellers how to compose line and verse, to depict the full spectrum of tragedy upon the stage."

Maddie rubbed her chin. She nodded slowly, as if coming to some realization. "True, true."

"Your greatest authors and playwrights have labored under the heels of my sandals. Did I not inspire Sophocles? Euripides? Did Shakespeare, in his darkest hour, not offer me gifts of milk and honey? And did I not reward him with inspiration?"

"I've heard that he did," Maddie replied.

The lights from the sconces ringing the room flickered and faded. Maddie and Lionel stood in the giantess's shadow as it lengthened over them, enveloping them in darkness.

"And am I not the mother of sirens?" the Muse demanded. "When Thamyris challenged my sisters and me to a singing contest, was he not blinded and tongue-cut for his arrogance? Were the daughters of the fool King Pierus not transformed to magpies when they challenged our prowess?"

Maddie raised both her hands, sharp and swift, high above her head. She bent both hands, cupping her fingers in a ritual gesture.

"All true!" Maddie proclaimed. "You are Melpomene, greatest of Muses, bringer of terror and beauty."

She dropped her arms and bowed her head, pressing one hand to her heart.

"I stand before you chastened. It would be my greatest honor to serve you by securing your freedom."

The Muse raised a graceful hand, a gesture of absolution. Lionel watched, looking between the two women, and finally grasped what Maddie had meant. It was a dance. Supplication, forgiveness, and then—

"But you are so powerful," Maddie added, "and we are but ants in your presence, as you have made so perfectly clear. As such, before I strike your bonds, it would surely be of no difficulty for you to give your bond of peace. It's such a trifle I'm embarrassed to ask for, but we humans are fearful in the presence of divinity."

Did she—did she just smile? Lionel thought as he studied Melpomene's face. Just a tiny twitch of her marble lips, the faintest trace of amusement in her eyes. Enjoying the game. The Muse let out a snort of calculated disdain, back to stoic and cold in a heartbeat.

"Of course. By my father, by his throne upon Olympus, I give you my word. You and your apprentice will come to no harm at my hands, lest you strike first."

"And your word is true," Maddie said. "Just . . . one other thing. This is my apprentice's first brush with a goddess. He will remember this moment until the end of his days."

She wasn't wrong, but Lionel still gave her a nervous look, finding himself the unexpected center of attention. The Muse stared down at him, contemplative.

"As he should," Melpomene replied. "What of it?"

"If you would grant him your blessing, I would consider it a boon to me, personally."

"Oh," Lionel said, "that's okay, you don't have to—"

The Muse did smile then. A cold and terrible smile. She gestured to the floor before her, still glistening with the shredded remains of the men she'd devoured.

"Very well," she said. "I can be generous. Lionel . . . come here. Stand before me."

Inside the circle.

He didn't know if Melpomene's promise would hold. He didn't know if he'd survive two seconds after crossing the curve of blood-flecked tile. He didn't know if Maddie had any power to pull him out if things went wrong.

Catching the measured look in Maddie's eyes, he realized that was the point. She'd asked for his trust. He'd said he would give it to her, but those were just empty words. Now he had to prove it.

He took a deep breath, faced the Muse, and stepped over the scarlet line. He held her gaze as she crouched down before him so their heads were almost level.

"I am . . . embarrassed," she said, "by how you first saw me. I was kept in a state of unnatural hunger by that *foul* little magician."

"Dolores Croft?" he asked.

"Her. Is she dead?"

He thought back to seeing Dolores's corpse in the ballroom. Aged a century, shriveled to nothing, her thousand-dollar gown caked in dust. A witch powerful enough to make a goddess her captive, and the blue-eyed man had destroyed her on a whim.

"She's dead," he told her. "They're all dead."

Melpomene took the news impassively. One of her hands, cold and hard as stone, cupped the back of Lionel's head. She looked to Maddie.

"And as I grant you a boon so kindly, you will surely grant me one now. Your oath of silence, so that none will know of my predicament here. You will take it to your graves and beyond."

Maddie clasped her hands before her. "I do swear it, as will my student."

The giantess could crush his skull as easily as swatting a fly. In a heartbeat, Lionel grasped the next layer of the dance. Melpomene needed to save face. By sending Lionel into her clutches, and asking for the gift of a blessing, Maddie had set the stage for the Muse to demand the gift of their silence in exchange. One oath for another, so that when all was said and done, everyone got what they wanted, and no debts remained outstanding. The elegance of the ritual almost distracted him from the danger. Almost. Jarred from his thoughts, he realized Melpomene was staring at him.

"I swear, too," he told her. "I won't say a word."

"So be it. Has your teacher told you what happens when you break an oath to a goddess, little witch?"

He tried to shake his head. Her marble fingers held him fast.

"Furies," she replied. "If you're lucky."

Her grip softened. She patted his head, like he was a particularly awkward puppy, and pulled her hand away. Then she leaned in close. The giantess put her lips to his ear.

"Remember what I told you, Lionel. Your teacher has more than a little of Macbeth in her heart. She's determined to hunt her own ruin. Guard yourself close, that she doesn't pull you down into the grave alongside her when she finally succeeds. And that is a blessing of wisdom, from me to you. Mark it well."

She rose to her full height, towering over him, and turned to Maddie. "You may proceed."

Maddie knelt down on the mosaic floor. She brandished her copper dagger high above her head, point downward, and her eyes squeezed tight in concentration. Her lips moved, a nearly silent litany carried on a gust of breath. Then she struck. She brought the knife downward, braced in both hands, and drove it point first into the tile with a resounding *clang*.

Any other blade would have snapped under the impact. Hers held strong as the mosaic ruptured beneath its tip, one square piece of tile sprouting hairline cracks like a road map of a foreign kingdom. A sudden jolt shot up Lionel's legs, like a shock of static electricity. Then . . . nothing.

"Is that it?" he asked, disturbing the silence.

Maddie held out a hand, palm down over the tile circle, and waved it from side to side as if testing the air. She pushed herself to her feet. "It's done."

Melpomene walked past Lionel, drifting over the circle's edge. She stopped in the open archway.

"My lady," Maddie said.

The Muse glanced back at her. "I'm not your lady, prodigal. *Your* lady is waiting for you to come home, where you belong."

Maddie flinched as if the giantess had just slapped her across the face. She took a deep breath, face red, and steadied herself. "We're seeking a man, a magician with bright-blue eyes. He was the one who laid waste to Dolores and her followers—"

"Convey him my thanks, then," Melpomene said.

"—and he did it with the aid of mad spirits. He stole a manuscript, a work of Edgar Allan Poe—"

"I visited Poe's bedside once or twice in his day, to whisper in his sleeping ear. He had a talent for darkness. The rest of your story means nothing to me. I came to this city two years ago to answer a prayer for aid. One of my daughters." She glanced to Lionel. "I *do* still have worshippers in this day and age, those who respect the Muses and our gifts, and make the proper devotionals. She was a playwright. Chandra Nagarkar."

"I know her," Lionel said. "I mean, I never *met* her, but I know her work. She wrote that musical about the Kennedys; I caught it when the touring company came through Chicago a while back."

"I like to think it was a collaboration," Melpomene replied.

"Didn't she commit suicide?"

"No." Melpomene's marble eyes narrowed at him. "She did *not*. Not unless one prefaces a 'suicide' by crying to your goddess for salvation from harm. Whatever your mortal doctors decided, she didn't take her own life. Worse, I felt her pulled from my grasp. Her soul is mine by right, and her weary spirit did not find its way to my household. Or *any* household."

"Someone took her soul?" Maddie asked.

"Yes. Though I might have reclaimed it if I hadn't been interfered with. Dolores Croft had a nose for power and sniffed my presence out when I entered the city. She set a lure, and, well . . ." The Muse cast a baleful glance at the circle, then turned her back. "I have spent the last two years trapped in this chamber. My knowledge of the outer world is understandably limited at the moment. I have much work to do. Best of fortune on your search, but I know nothing that can help you."

Melpomene strode down the molten-gold hallway, her marble skin cast in the shifting electric light. Then she vanished from sight, and the last of her stone footsteps echoed into silence.

Maddie grabbed Lionel and hauled him into a hug, almost yanking him off his feet. He blurted out a surprised laugh as she planted a kiss on his cheek.

"What was that for?"

She beamed at him like he'd done the impossible and made it look easy.

"Trusting me," she said.

"I told you I would."

"There's a difference between saying and doing. And I kinda put you in the hot seat back there."

"I think I get what you were doing, though," he said. "There was a kind of rhythm to it, a . . ."

"Reciprocity," Maddie said. "It's dangerous to owe favors. It can be even more dangerous to be *owed*, sometimes. Depends on who you're bargaining with."

"I just wish we got something out of it. I mean, we did our good deed for the day. I . . . I *think* it was our good deed, anyway. But we're not any closer to figuring out what happened last night."

Maddie looked to the open archway. Her gaze stretched farther than that.

"Maybe we are."

"What do you mean?"

"The blue-eyed man had a company of spirits at his beck and call," Maddie said. "Not the normal kind. They'd been twisted. Empowered."

Lionel thought back to the assault. How he'd stripped off his gloves, tossed them to the floor, then—

"That brooch, on his costume. It flared up just before everything hit the fan."

Maddie tapped her chin. "No remnants left behind. No wandering souls, not even an echo."

"So you think he . . . what? Took everybody with him when he left?"

"He's clearly a necromancer, and one on a level I haven't seen in a long, long time. I can't rule it out. And if he did it here, he can do it elsewhere. That might explain what happened to Melpomene's playwright two years ago. Human shades don't just disappear, especially not when they've been marked and promised to a goddess. Not like that."

"Sounds pretty thin to me." Lionel glanced from her to the archway. "Could be a coincidence. That said, beyond the missing guest list—and I can't figure out *why* it's missing—the playwright lead is all we've got to work with. What's our next move?"

Maddie took his hand and gave it a tug, leading him to the door.

"We find out where Chandra Nagarkar's body is buried," she said. "I think we should do a little necromancy of our own."

Thirty

A crosstown train brought Lionel and Maddie to Chandra Nagarkar's final destination: Woodside, in the borough of Queens. It was a working-class neighborhood, old Irish with a growing Asian bubble, cultures grinding and pushing together. Like the neighborhood itself, old towers of mismatched brick were flush against new construction, but somehow it all fit.

They got off the train at the Sixty-First Street station and started walking, keeping their eyes open for a taxi. Maddie glanced at her phone, double-checking the map.

"Chandra was buried at Calvary Cemetery," she told Lionel, "which, for purposes of your education, is actually a lucky break."

"How so?"

She turned her face to the sun, slowly starting to sink as the clock hit four, and preened in the summer heat.

"Well," she said, "it's one of the biggest, oldest cemeteries in the country. Over three hundred acres, over three million corpses."

"And that's good . . . why, exactly?"

"Because now that you've got a witch's eyes, I can show you what you've been missing all these years. I was hoping we'd see a remnant soul or two back at the ballroom, and I could teach you how to deal with them. A graveyard the size of Calvary, though? There's bound to be a few angry dead people floating around."

"Wait," Lionel said. "Are you *trying* to get me into a fight?"

They stopped at a street corner, waiting for the light to change. "Yep. That's exactly what I'm doing. Number-one rule of dealing with the dead: If you can see them, they can see you. And if they're strong enough, they can do a lot more than look. Would you rather learn to protect yourself now, while I'm here and can jump in if things get dicey, or just take your chances and hope for the best?"

"When you put it that way . . . ," he said.

"Right? The more you listen to me, the less it'll hurt."

The *walk* light flickered on. Maddie stood in Lionel's path, put her palm on his chest, and leaned in close. Her face was grave, her voice firm, as if delivering a message of dire importance.

"Lionel . . . the first rule of witch club is that you don't talk about witch club. The second rule of witch club is, if it's your first night, you have to do witch stuff."

She grabbed his hand and tugged him across the street.

Inside the gates of Calvary, they stood surrounded by silence and stone. From the moment he'd arrived in New York, Lionel had been struck by how *busy* it all was. In constant movement, night or day, the sidewalks and streets teeming with life in motion. By contrast, these manicured lawns, the groomed paths, the endless rows of monuments and markers, stood like a frozen bulwark at the end of the line. He imagined generations of people rising like a tide, filling the streets and cascading down through the boroughs, crashing into Calvary. Flooding open graves, fresh markers counting off another span of years as the water levels fell. Then another generational wave swelling up upon the last, and another after that. Endlessly rising higher, building higher, reaching for the stars. And the graves of Calvary waited in gentle anticipation, ready to catch them when they crashed to earth.

"Penny for your thoughts," Maddie told him. He realized they'd been walking in silence for a while.

"I met a goddess this afternoon," he said.

"*Demi*goddess."

"My entire cosmology has just been thrown into a state of . . . doubt?"

She hooked her arm around his. "Aw. Are you having an existential crisis?"

"I was pretty happy being an atheist."

Maddie cupped her free hand over her eyes and scanned the horizon. More rows of the silent dead, as far as they could see in every direction.

"That technically doesn't have to change," she said. "The thing about gods is, they usually won't bother you if you don't get in their way."

"Yeah, but like . . . where do people *go* when they die? Under normal circumstances, I mean."

"That is a question best discussed over drinks. But for the time being, just understand that you have options. A few good ones, and a whole lot of bad ones. Make the right deals and you can improve your prospects considerably."

"Like with Regina Dunkle?"

She shot a sidelong glance at him. Her eyes narrowed.

"Regina isn't a goddess. She's a witch. Just a very old, very dangerous one, and you've made your *last* deal with her. As soon as I figure out how to get you clear, anyway."

"So why do *you* work for her?"

She pursed her lips and turned away. Then she changed the subject.

"Chandra should be buried up this way. It's a long shot, but I'm hoping there's something, some trace of energy, still clinging to the burial site. If there is, we can use it to track where her soul went—sort of like giving a scrap of clothing to a bloodhound."

Lionel didn't want to ask, but he forced himself to do it anyway.

"We don't have to . . . dig her up, do we?"

Maddie's eyes went wide. She stopped in her tracks and turned toward him.

"*Shit*, Lionel. We have to go back. We forgot the shovels."

"Wait, are you . . ." He squinted at her. "Are you serious, or . . . ?"

She broke into a grin and slapped the back of her hand against his arm.

"No, silly, we don't have to dig her up." She paused, a wicked glint in her eye. "Probably. Besides, you don't use shovels to dig up a body. You steal a backhoe for that kind of work—it's *way* easier."

Maddie took a long look around. Orienting herself, Lionel guessed, but her smile slowly faded.

"This isn't right. It's too quiet."

"It's a graveyard," he said. "Not known for being party central."

"No, this is wrong. Look around. Look *hard*. What do you see?"

He followed her lead and turned slowly, taking in the scene. A thousand monuments to a thousand forgotten lives. A finch landed on the tip of a concrete cross, twitched its wings, then flew off again, winging toward the boughs of a shady oak.

"Graves," he said. "Grass, a few birds, just . . . what I'd expect to see, I guess."

"That's the problem."

Maddie broke into a sudden sprint, dashing between the rows. He scrambled to keep up with her, trailing in her wake.

"Maddie," he called out, "what are you—"

She jolted to a stop and held up one hand, the other cupped to her ear.

"Three hundred acres," she said. "Three million burial plots."

"Yeah, so you told me when we got here. What about it?"

She hunched her shoulders a little, eyes hard and darting from side to side, like a soldier in a war zone—scouting for danger, and not finding it.

"I've never, in my life, been to a graveyard that didn't have some kind of residual energy floating around. Memories, echoes, a few lost and confused souls drifting around. This . . ." She took her hand from her ear and fluttered it all around them. "It's *empty*. Like the ballroom. You're not seeing anything because there's nothing to see. And there should be."

"What, like somebody hoovered up all the ghosts?"

"For lack of a better way to put it," she said, "yeah, pretty much. I did a reading after we met. Sort of an oracular thing. The message I got was 'The dead are here.' Here, as in, in New York. But they're not here. They're not *anywhere*."

"So . . . what do we do about it? Is that a thing we do something about? I mean, how concerned should I be right now?"

"I don't know," Maddie said, "and that's what bothers me most. C'mon, let's find Chandra's grave. Now I *really* doubt we'll find anything, but as long as we're here, we might as well give it a look."

The fallen scribe had been laid to rest alone at the top of a small, lonely hillock, beneath a black obsidian stone. Simple, stark block letters had been carved upon her marker:

CHANDRA NAGARKAR

1992–2016

"MORTAL FATE IS HARD. YOU'D BEST GET USED TO IT." —EURIPIDES

They stood before the gravestone. A hot breeze swept across the cemetery and ruffled the grass at their feet.

"Anything?" Lionel asked.

Maddie responded with a tiny shake of her head. She stared at the marker like it had personally offended her.

An elderly woman in a flowered frock hobbled up from their left, cradling a bouquet of flowers in her thin, bony arms. She had a beak of a nose and small, bright magpie eyes, and stray tufts of cotton-white hair peeked out from under her bonnet.

"I thought I knew all of Chandra's friends," she said.

Lionel's reporter instincts kicked in. He still suspected they were following the wrong horse on the wrong track, but *something* had happened to Melpomene's pet playwright, and he knew a good source when he saw one. He scrambled to remember the play he'd seen and craft a story that would hold up. The lies rolled effortlessly off his tongue.

"Oh, we weren't close," he said, "not as close as I would have liked, anyway. A few years back, I was part of the stage crew for the touring company of *Fall of the House of Kennedy*, on the Midwest leg. Are you family?"

He stepped back as the woman approached. She crouched, slowly, wincing a little, and set her bouquets down at the foot of the obsidian stone.

"Family? Not by blood, but in the ways that matter. Helen Grimble. I met Chandra when I was the dean of the theater program at Columbia University. Championed her from the start. Oh, that girl was a rare gem."

Maddie wasn't done being angry at the gravestone. She thrust a finger at it. "Who chose that?"

"The quotation?" Helen said. "She did, before she passed. It was one of her favorites. Chandra was in love with Greek tragedy; if you've seen her work, you recognize the influence, I'm sure. Euripides—"

"I'm familiar," she said, "with Euripides."

Lionel cleared his throat. "We're in town on vacation and thought it'd be good to honor her memory. She really was something special."

Helen slipped a pamphlet of folded paper from her purse, a too-light photocopy on green stock, and pressed it into Lionel's hand.

"If you want to honor her memory, you can join the fight. Next meeting's on Monday night."

He glanced down at the pamphlet. **SAVE OUR CITY'S HERITAGE!** it shouted in bold capitals. **A MEETING OF THE COMMITTEE TO PRESERVE THE PARTHENON THEATER.**

"Her most passionate cause before she left us," Helen said. "I've taken up the torch ever since."

"The Parthenon?" Lionel asked.

"One of the oldest theaters in New York. It's been shuttered since the late '90s, and a sword's been dangling over its head ever since. Land disputes, people fighting over ownership, restoration attempts that never quite happen. Frankly, it's a mess. Chandra wanted to see it designated as a historical landmark. I think the stress of the fight . . . that's what triggered her decline, in the end."

"Who was she fighting, exactly? The city?"

Helen looked to the gravestone, a trace of bitterness in her eyes.

"Money, mostly. This pack of paper shufflers called Corbin Investment Partners. They wanted to buy up a block for 'redevelopment,' and the Parthenon is smack-dab in the middle of it. Eventually they got their land, but we've been holding off the wrecking ball with injunction after injunction." She gave Lionel a wry look. "Donations *are* appreciated, I should add. Every little bit helps."

While Lionel dug out his wallet, Maddie tore her gaze from the stone.

"She was only twenty-four," she said to Helen. "So young when she passed."

"And she wrote the first draft of *Kennedy* when she was seventeen," Helen replied. "An absolute prodigy. But with her gift came tragedy. I like to think she'd have found that amusingly ironic, if she'd been capable of it in the end. By the sheer bad luck of the dice, she was born with immense natural talent and a serious genetic defect in her brain."

Maddie tilted her head. "She was mentally ill?"

"Haunted," Helen replied. "I would say that Chandra was haunted."

Thirty-One

Helen stood before her friend's gravestone. Lionel watched as she bowed her head, just a bit, her flowered bonnet shading her eyes as her thin, frail hands clasped tight.

"She'd always had her quirks, but in the last month or so before Chandra took her own life, that was when the delusions really set in. She was convinced she was being followed by the restless dead. She'd call me and talk about how she could hear them hammering from the walls, pleading for help."

Maddie's lips tightened. Lionel tried to read her face, to discern some meaning from the storm clouds in her eyes.

"I'm sorry," he said. "Did anyone try to get help for her?"

Helen didn't look at him. She gave her answer to the stone.

"Not as much as any of us should have. She'd had fits and obsessions in the past, plenty of times, and she'd always just . . . snapped out of it. A couple of odd weeks and she'd be right as rain again. We never thought . . . Well, we never thought this would happen, not until it was too late."

"I'm sure you did your best," he told her.

"There was a moment when I knew. I knew it wasn't going to be all right. She was a fixture at this coffee shop in the East Village, Spence's Beans. I mean, every day, nine to five, same table. That's where Chandra wrote, you see. Said she couldn't make art without her favorite chair and

Spence's coffee. The last time we ever spoke, she told me she could never go back there again. She said there was a coffin in the alley, stuffed with dead people—she said she'd *seen* it—and she couldn't think because they wouldn't stop screaming to be let out."

Helen squeezed her eyes shut.

"I *tried*. Do you know how hard it is to have someone committed, especially if you aren't related by blood? If they haven't actually made a suicide attempt, or hurt someone else, forget about it. I called hospitals, doctors, lawyers—I wasn't going to give up. Six hours after I started, someone called me. That's when they said she was gone. And I suspect I'm going to spend the rest of my life wondering what might have become of her, if I'd just been a little faster."

Maddie shook her head slowly. She held out a hand, almost close enough to touch Helen's shoulder. Then she let it drift back down to her side.

"Guilt is a millstone around your neck," Maddie said. "It'll drown you if you let it. I don't think that's what Chandra would have wanted for you."

Helen opened her eyes, wiped away a smear of moisture with the flat of her hand, and forced a smile.

"Me either. Yet here I am." She sighed. "It's good of you to remember her. Please, do something for me: Put this out of your heads. When you think of Chandra, remember her work. Her art. That's the best tribute you can give her."

"We will," Lionel said. "Thank you."

Helen went one way, hobbling between the graves alone. Lionel and Maddie walked side by side in the opposite direction, in contemplative silence, toward the distant cemetery gates.

"That penny you gave me for my thoughts when we got here," Lionel said. "Want to buy it back?"

"I'm processing," Maddie replied.

"You seemed . . . kind of upset about her gravestone? What was that about?"

"I just thought 'mortal fate is hard' was a shitty thing to write on a suicide's grave." She paused. "When I still thought she might be a suicide, anyway."

"You think Melpomene was right?"

She took a deep breath and tilted her head back, exhaling at the overcast sky. The sun still hid behind the clouds, refusing to show its face.

"When a person has a natural gift for magic and no teacher, no one to help them understand and focus it, their grasp on reality often becomes dangerously tenuous. To the rest of the world, it can look a lot like unmedicated schizophrenia."

"Wait," Lionel said, "so you're saying she really *was* being chased by dead people?"

"I'm saying that she witnessed something, something other people couldn't perceive, and that's how her mind interpreted it." Maddie frowned at the horizon. "I want to see what she saw. What was the name of that coffeehouse where she did all her writing?"

"Spence's."

"Last place she went, six hours before she died. I'm suddenly in the mood for a cup of coffee—how about you?"

⌒⌒

Given that it had been two years since the playwright had died, Lionel wasn't sure if Spence's would even still be standing. The life span of an independent coffeehouse back in Chicago could usually be measured in weeks, and he suspected the competition in New York was even tougher.

Maybe it was the location, maybe the coffee was just that good, but the place was open for business. A cab let them out on a narrow, stubby little street in the Village, under a long vinyl awning the color of espresso. A hipster with a man bun and a lumberjack beard strolled out the front door, and the aroma of freshly ground beans wafted out with him.

"I know we're looking for clues," Lionel said, "but now I really do want coffee."

Maddie nodded, her eyes going wide. "Right? There are worse places this job could take us. Trust me, I speak from experience."

He stepped over to hold the door for her, glanced across the street, and froze.

A sign above a long glass window—silver stenciled in midnight blue—said **L. JACKSON FINE ARTS**. A boutique art gallery two doors down from a wine salon called Corkshop. Normally he'd crack a joke about needing a cheese store on the same street to complete the trifecta, but the display in the gallery window stole his full attention and ran away with his voice.

It was an oil painting, and he'd seen it before. A burning chariot in a midnight sky, an anguished and defeated man crumpled upon the grass below.

His initiation. The woman in red—the woman neither Maddie nor the high priestess could see—had shown it to him. Her sardonic voice drifted back to him. *"But do remember the painting. There'll be a quiz later."*

"Uh, Maddie? Remember I said I saw some stuff in the tarot card that you didn't?"

"Sure." She paused in the doorway. "Did something just jiggle your brain?"

"Oh, yeah. Big-time. It's—"

He pointed. Inside the gallery window, a dark-skinned woman in a flowing turquoise gown was rearranging the display. She took the painting and lifted it from its easel, moving it out of sight just as Maddie turned around.

"It *was* right there," he said.

"Remember what I said about intuition? Trust it and get over there. Keep your eyes and your mind open."

"You're not coming with me?"

"The symbol was for you," she told him, "not me, and the high priestess isn't going to lead you into any trouble you can't handle. Might help unlock some of those missing memories of yours, if we're lucky."

But she wasn't the one who—he wanted to tell her. He heard the woman in red's voice again, clear as day, like a serpentine hiss in his left ear. *Shhh.*

Maddie gave his shoulder a squeeze. "Go on. I'll check out Spence's, and we'll meet up in ten minutes, okay? I might even save some coffee for you."

A metallic chime sounded as Lionel stepped into the gallery. The walls were frosted white, the pale mint of Maddie's flying ointment, and lined with portraits in a dark rainbow palette: the blues of night, the reds and oranges of fire, careful smears of royal purple and envy green. A warm, clean scent, like the smoke from a pine-scented candle, lingered in traces in the cool air. The woman he'd seen in the window gave him a confident smile. Jewelry draped the neck of her gown, strands of copper and turquoise and glass, even a necklace of tiny seashells, and her wrist dripped with heavy bangles as she raised a hand to welcome him.

"Good afternoon," she said, standing behind the curve of a buttery-pale wooden desk. "If you have any questions about the art, please let me know."

He thanked her and turned his attention to the wall. Searching for what he'd seen among distorted faces and jarring abstracts, the image locked in his mind's eye. It wasn't there.

"Um, I had seen—I thought I saw—a portrait here. It was a chariot." He posed his hands, trying to capture the picture. "A flying chariot, sort of, on fire. And a man and a hut on the ground underneath?"

"Mmm," the clerk said. She swept her gaze across the gallery wall and shook her head. "Doesn't ring a bell. Are you sure it was this gallery?"

I just saw you take it from the window, he wanted to say. He also had just enough presence of mind to realize how crazy he'd sound.

"Maybe not," he told her. "Thanks, though."

He pretended to study the art while he put his thoughts together. He *had* seen the painting. Or at least, someone had wanted him to think he had. It was a custom trail of bread crumbs designed to lure him to this exact spot.

So now what? he thought. He felt like he was standing outside the door to enlightenment, and he couldn't find the knob. He realized he only had one real card to play.

"Out of curiosity," he said, "do you know if a woman named Chandra Nagarkar ever shopped here? It would have been a couple of years ago."

Her soft, dimpled smile rose a notch. She inclined her head.

"Oh, I knew Chandra. She'd pop in once or twice a week after spending all day at Spence's. We weren't good friends, but she'd ask me about the art, and sometimes she'd show me what she was working on." The clerk's gaze drifted sideways, as she thought back. "*Sad* girl. Even when she was happy. You know how some people are just kinda born sad?"

"Sure," Lionel said.

"One week she just stopped coming around, and well, I knew."

"I heard she was under a lot of stress."

"That theater-landmark project." The clerk waved a dismissive hand. "You ask me, she was just trying to distract herself. Real problem was, she wrote a Broadway musical when she was a teenager. She was too young for that kind of success. Then the run ended, and everyone wanted to know what she was going to do *next*. She was just a kid. You don't put that kind of pressure on a kid's shoulders."

Lionel leaned on the other side of the desk, dropping his voice as he looked to the gallery door.

"Weird question," he said, "but did she ever talk to you about . . . ghosts?"

The smile flipped off like a light switch. The woman's eyes went hard, studying him like a textbook.

"And you are . . . who, exactly?" she asked.

"Well, it's kind of embarrassing," he said, his words wriggling as he tried to bait his hook with a believable story, "but I'm a playwright, too. Not anywhere near Chandra's level, I mean. But, well, I really want to write a play about her life. A respectful one. One that tells the real story and gets at the real person behind the work."

The clerk took that in. Her eyes softened a little. "You don't say."

"I've been researching her life, talking to friends of hers—like Helen Grimble? I don't know if you know her, but she was Chandra's professor at Columbia. Anyway, this idea that she thought she was literally being haunted keeps coming up, and I realized it might be the perfect imagery to work into the play. Like, the external idea of ghosts is a metaphor for the mental trauma she was wrestling with."

She was nodding now, right in the groove alongside him.

"I just want to do it the right way," he told her. "Not sensational-ized or cheap. So I'm trying to find out all I can about her last couple of weeks, to get the details right."

The clerk's necklaces jangled in a tuneless melody, like wind chimes, as she leaned to one side and reached under the desk. She came up with a fat plastic binder. She laid it out flat and opened it, flipping through page after page of rumpled, faded business cards.

"All I know is what you've already heard," she told him. "That said, about a month before she passed, I told Chandra about somebody she ought to talk to. She'd tried a shrink, tried meds—none of it was helping."

Five pages in, she found what she was looking for. She slipped out a card—pale-violet stock, with reddish-brown type like terra-cotta ink—and offered it to Lionel. He turned it in his fingers. WEN XIULANG, HERBALIST. Chinese characters shadowed an address in English.

"Xiulang *knows* things," the clerk told him. "My cousin Letisha was having migraines, like, five-alarm, all-day-long migraines, damn near lost her job from missing so much work. Hospital couldn't do a thing for her. Xiulang mixed up this special tea for her, and before you know it—no more headaches. Totally gone. I told Chandra, if anybody can help, she's the woman for the job. I don't know if she actually made the appointment, though."

"Thanks," Lionel said. He held up the card. "Can I hang on to this?"

Thirty-Two

"I found something," Maddie said. From the look on her face, it might have been one of Chandra's ghosts. She had met Lionel on the sidewalk as he emerged from the gallery, coming at him as fast as she could without breaking into a sprint.

"So did I." He showed her the pale-violet business card. "There's a chance Chandra talked to this Wen Xiulang a little before she died. It might be worth checking out."

Her hand clamped on his wrist, harder than it needed to, and she tugged him across the street toward the coffeehouse.

"Oh, fuck no," she said with a humorless laugh. "We are *not* going to see Wen Xiulang."

"Wait, you know her?"

"And she knows me. No, that's not happening."

He waited for an explanation. She didn't offer him one. Maddie led him past the espresso-brown awning of Spence's, around a crumbling brick corner. Lionel jarred to a dead stop at the mouth of the alley.

"Whoa. What was that?"

Maddie's eyes widened. "You saw it?"

He wasn't sure. He'd seen the alley, a gaping mouth of oil-stained concrete and bare red brick. An overstuffed dumpster stood shoved to one side, rusting away with a couple of trash bags tossed at its feet like offerings to a second-rate god. Across the concrete span, graffiti

grill trap after a big barbecue: it was technically part of the food, but you wouldn't want to eat it."

"So why is it *here*?"

"Excellent question," she murmured, moving a little closer. "Even better question: What the hell is in that box? First thing we've got to do is clear it out; residual or not, concentrated death energy is—predictably enough—toxic to living things."

"What happens if you get some on you?" he asked.

"In small, natural doses? Not much. This kind of concentration? Oh, blisters, burns, tumors—maybe all your hair falls out. Probably die in slow agony."

He gave her the side-eye and took a step back from the box.

"Sounds like radiation poisoning," he said.

"You're not far off. Occult radiation. Different source, same great taste. Okay, lesson time. This gunk needs to be banished, and you're going to do it. Stand beside me. Hook your fingers, like this."

It took him a minute, and a few tries, to mirror her gestures while they stood shoulder to shoulder. Left index finger curling around right pinkie, wrists tilted, some fingers linking and others touching. She exhaled, swift and sharp, and twisted her hands into an entirely new configuration. It was like the world's most complicated game of cat's cradle.

"This is a warding gesture," she told him. "The first pose is a declaration of intent. The second is the strike. Inhale on the first; exhale on the second. And *focus*. Keep your goal in mind; push everything else away."

"Declaration of intent?" He tried again. First pose, then the second. His fingers moved like a classroom full of gangly third graders trying to learn how to ballroom dance.

"You're telling the universe who you are and what you're capable of. Then, with the strike, you prove it. Exerting your will upon the world."

She walked him through it again. Her fingers fluttered like a ballerina's pirouette.

"You make this look easy," he said.

"I've been doing it for a long time. Now we add the words. The *voces mysticae*. It's a language no human culture ever spoke. Spirits know it, though. And when you use it correctly, they have no choice but to listen. There are seven thousand words that I know of. For this, we only need three."

"So who taught you all this stuff, anyway?"

Her gaze flicked to one side. She took a second, deliberating over her answer. She forced a smile that didn't entirely reach her eyes.

"I learned from the best. Which means you're *technically* learning from the best, so pay attention." She brought her hands up. "Declaration. *Akhas.*"

"How important is pronunciation? Like, will I turn into a fish if I get a syllable wrong?"

"Maybe a pig or a goat." She winked at him. "The words themselves aren't magic the way you think. They don't have objective power in and of themselves. They're a command. A command that certain natural forces are bound, by the rules of their existence, to follow. Your focus and intent are the key: you project your energy, and the words and the gestures channel it along the proper paths. Picture a circuit board. It can't do anything on its own, but once you add a source of electricity, suddenly it fulfills whatever purpose it was built for."

"I think I'm starting to get it," he said.

"Good. Then second step." She held the first pose, fingers tight, and lifted her hands a couple of inches as she squared her shoulders. "*Dromenei.* Assert yourself here. Your magic is only as strong as your confidence."

He mirrored her pose, feeling like an awkward duckling next to a bright-winged swan. It had been a long time since Lionel had learned anything new, let alone a skill he hadn't believed existed before

220

yesterday. He had gotten used to being the resident expert in any given room, a pro at the top of his field. Coming back down to earth wasn't easy. All the same, he swallowed his pride and lifted his hands, following Maddie's lead.

She seemed to read his mind. "Like I told you: you don't have the knowledge—yet—but you have the ambition, and you have the smarts. You can do this. I wouldn't be wasting my time trying to teach you if I didn't believe you were capable. Will you give it your best try?"

"Yeah." He nodded, feeling a little more ready. "Let's do this."

"Now." She switched to the second pose, shoved her hands forward in a slow-motion punch, and brought her left foot forward, all in one motion. "*Keh.* You exhale on the word. This is the strike: you put all your focus into it, all your energy."

"But faster," he said.

"The whole thing, right. All three steps should flow into one smooth motion."

She took a step back and gestured to the box. A dark ripple shot through the black-violet glow in an agitated wave, as if the toxic energy somehow knew what was going to happen. Just like Lionel, as he took a deep breath and squared his footing, it was bracing for a fight.

"Go for it," Maddie told him. "Take a shot."

He made the hand gestures in silence a few more times as he stepped up to the plate, a quick warm-up. Then he hooked his fingers, raised his hands, and fixed his gaze on the box.

"*Akhas. Dromenei.*" He lunged forward, off the beat by a second, knowing he'd screwed up the timing even as he did it. "*Keh.*"

The glow flickered like a torch in a mild breeze.

"Good," Maddie said. "Again."

"It didn't work."

"You're *learning*. Failure is part of learning. Do it again."

He took a step back, nodded, and prepared himself. The declaration, the assertion, and as he prepared for the strike, he realized he hadn't lifted his hooked fingers the way Maddie had on the second step, and then he stumbled into the third—

The glow didn't even flicker this time.

"You're second-guessing yourself," she told him.

"I feel like I've got two left feet." He paused. "Hands. Whatever. I'm trying to get the gestures perfect and get my posture right *and* time the words to the movements—"

"You're overthinking it. The craft isn't about thinking, Lionel. It's about knowing, and feeling. Remember how we danced, at the Blackstone?"

"I'm never going to forget anything about that night."

She strode over to him, moving to stand just behind his back. Her hands closed over his shoulders.

"When you dance, are you calculating your trajectory? Figuring out the angles of the room?"

"No," he said, "I just . . . I don't know, I don't think about it, I just dance."

"Witchcraft is a dance."

Her lips brushed the nape of his neck. The warm, fleeting kiss sent a tingling surge down his spine.

"Dance with me," she whispered. Then she stepped back, pulling her hands away. "Try again."

He fixed his gaze on the glowing box. He sidestepped his fears, his insecurity, himself. *The only person throwing bricks in my path is me,* he told himself. *I know the words, I know the moves. All I have to do is—*

He didn't even finish the thought. Something, some sweep of an invisible hand on the cosmic clock, told him that now was the moment.

"Akhas. Dromenei." His fingers danced as he lunged forward, left foot stomping down, leaning in and thrusting his clasped hands. *"Keh."*

The air rippled with a lance of boiling heat as it surged along his arms and burst from his hands. The shimmering mirage tore through the stagnant air, splashing over the box with a sudden flash of light that left angry orange splotches printed behind Lionel's eyelids. The black-violet glow withered, shrinking, but what was left of it still clung to the corroded metal box like a jealous lover's grip.

His muscles ached. His breath had gone somewhere and not bothered to come back. Maddie caught him before he could fall, and he leaned into her, stunned.

"Easy, easy," she said. "Takes a lot out of you when you're not used to it."

"What just—" He blinked. "What happened?"

She turned him around and pulled him into a hug.

"What happened is, you just cast your first actual, honest-to-goodness spell. A banishment, no less."

"This stuff looks easy when you do it. I can barely stand up right now."

"I've had years to practice. Everything looks easy when an expert does it, but don't confuse *looking* easy with *being* easy. What matters is getting the job done, and you did it."

He looked to the box. "But it didn't work."

"Sure it did. Look at the glow; you see the difference from before? You cleared away about half of that gunk. You don't have a frame of reference for this yet, but trust me, that was pretty impressive for a first-time effort. You relax; I'll clear out the rest. Pop quiz: What do you need now?"

He thought back to his initiation, the aftermath of his voyage into the tarot card.

"Grounding," he said. "Um . . . water and crackers?"

She laughed and let go of him, once she was sure his feet were steady.

"Water and carbohydrates, in general. Protein helps, too. Let's finish this up and find some dinner."

Her fingers hooked and flicked faster than Lionel's eye could follow, the three words of the spell—her *voces mysticae*—flowing as if they were

one word with three sharp beats. Her power surged against the junction box with the force of a sandblaster, scouring the glow away until
nothing was left but bare, crusted steel held shut with a heavy padlock.

"There we go," Maddie said. She fished out her sheath of picks and
studied the lock, turning it in her hand. "Huh. Heavy-duty."

"Can you open it?"

She looked over her shoulder at him and arched an eyebrow. "I said
heavy-duty. I didn't say difficult."

She had it open in five minutes. The lock clattered to the pavement
at her feet. The lid of the box groaned on warped hinges as she gave it
a yank and forced it open.

"That's . . . not normal," Lionel said.

A rat's nest of electrical wiring, copper coils, and vacuum tubes
filled the steel box. His eyes were locked on the upper left corner and
the sapphire-blue glow that washed across their faces. A steel disk, about
two inches across and half an inch thick, had been fitted into a custom socket like a battery. The disk had been engineered with a pair of
swirling tadpole-shaped windows, like the swirls on a yin-yang symbol,
showing the surging, crackling power within.

Lionel leaned closer and stared into the pocket of blue mist beyond
the windows. Lightning flickered under the tempered glass, a hurricane-
force storm trapped within a pocket-size miracle, and shapes floated in
the tempest.

"Are those—" he started to ask.

A distinct shadow, tinier than a thumbnail, drifted past one of the
windows. He couldn't deny the silhouette: arms, legs, a distended and
silently screaming mouth, clinging to the glass before the tempest tossed
it away and sucked it back into the maelstrom.

"People," he said, answering his own question. "There are people
inside that thing."

Thirty-Three

"What was it Chandra told Helen?" Maddie asked. "A coffin in the alley, stuffed with dead people, screaming to be let out? This is what she was actually seeing."

"Those silver darts we both saw on our way in." Lionel pointed to the alley at their backs. "So those were . . . ?"

He didn't want to finish the sentence. She did it for him.

"Human souls. Freshly deceased human souls." Maddie reared her head back, her cheeks contorting in sudden revulsion. "This thing is a trap for dead people."

"So, the ballroom, the empty cemetery—"

She shook her head, brows furrowed. "I don't know. Not certain. This—this shouldn't be possible, not by any principles of magic I've ever learned. This literally should not exist."

"Well," Lionel said, "we're looking right at it. So what now?"

Maddie stared at the open box. The blue light from the soul trap washed over her face, lighting crackle reflecting in her furious gaze.

"First things first, we shut this shit down. *Now.*"

She dug in, got her fingers around the edges of the disk, and yanked it out.

Lionel's shoulders tensed as he braced for an explosion, some kind of blowback, but nothing happened. The box just sat there, letting out a faint electrical hum. The disk glowed between Maddie's fingers.

"Can you break it open?" Lionel asked. "We've gotta get those people out of there, don't we? I mean, dead or not, that doesn't look like a good place to be."

"Not without knowing more. No telling how many souls are squeezed inside this thing or what's keeping them trapped. We get this wrong, they could be destroyed when we open it. Or worse."

Another question Lionel didn't want to ask, but he did anyway. "What's *worse* than literally having your soul destroyed?"

She grabbed hold of the rat's nest of electrical wires and yanked them loose. She left the vandalized cords dangling from the lip of the open box, copper ends stripped and torn.

"There," she said. "It'll take them a while to fix this, if and when they figure out we stole their little battery. And to answer your question, lots and lots of things, but you've had a long day, and we don't need to get into that right now."

She slipped the disk into her hip pocket and gave the denim a pat.

"Let's find some dinner," she said.

⁓

Maddie knew a good Greek place in Midtown. She hailed a cab. There were low lights, white candles on every table, walls adorned with murals of the old country; and slow, sonorous strings piped in over the speakers. The hostess put them at a two-seater by the far wall, in the shadow of painted farmers tending an olive grove. The restaurant smelled like fresh bread and peppery wine.

Lionel had drifted through the afternoon in a state of self-induced shock. Nothing seemed quite real anymore. *I cast a spell,* he thought, *which I think makes me a witch now, to banish some congealed toxic death energy because somebody built a machine to trap human souls and hid it in a junction box in an alley in Manhattan.*

So that happened.

His fingers brushed the thick linen napkin spread across his lap. Textures, weight. Real things.

"The *dolmadakia*," Maddie said, "is excellent. It's grape leaves stuffed with rice, dill, and herbs and served with a yogurt sauce. *So* yummy."

"I was thinking about the chicken kebabs." He stared at his menu like it was written in a foreign language. His mind was anywhere but the chicken kebabs, his thoughts still rooted in the alley behind Spence's, but those were words he understood and could latch on to.

"I don't want to be *that* friend," Maddie started to say.

"I have very few real friends, and you are like absolutely none of them."

"I'd like you to consider trying vegetarianism. You don't have to commit—just try it for a week and see if you like it."

That broke his trance. He lifted an eyebrow at her. Then he cast a glance across the half-empty restaurant, making sure nobody was in earshot. Couples were all around them, clinking glasses, making bedroom eyes over their roasted lamb. Normal people on normal dates.

"Maddie," he said, "back at the Blackstone, I literally watched you kill four people right in front of me."

"Three," she replied. "Melpomene ate one. I just blinded him."

"I'm not ungrateful, seeing as you saved my life in the process, but . . . really? After that, you can't honestly tell me you're concerned about the plight of the cows."

She laughed. The waitress came by.

"Two glasses of the 2006 Pavlidis Thema Red, please. Actually, bring the bottle." Once she left, Maddie looked back to Lionel. "Greek wines are so underrated, it's criminal. And no, this isn't an ethical qualm. It's practical."

"How so?"

She held out her open hands, palms up, imitating a scale.

"Life, death, nature—these aren't just metaphorical concepts. They're genuine forces, energies that we can, and do, work with on a regular basis. The more you practice and learn, the better you'll perceive them."

Craig Schaefer

"Not seeing why that should stop me from enjoying a good porterhouse," Lionel said.

"Because, while you couldn't see it before today, remember that glowing gunk on the junction box? Next time you order up a juicy hamburger, take a close look at what's between the buns before you pop it into your mouth. Don't think you're going to like what you see."

"That . . . doesn't sound appetizing."

"Nope. We are what we take into our bodies. Food, words, thoughts, attitudes. The world shapes us, and we in turn shape the world. *Killing* doesn't bother me; witches are stewards of nature, and there's nothing more natural than violence when it's necessary."

"Nature, red in tooth and claw," Lionel said.

"You've read your Tennyson. I approve. And very true. But by keeping my body as free of contaminants as possible, calling upon and manipulating the natural forces around me is a smoother process all around. It's not a moral stance; it just makes my job easier. It also makes my food choices a little harder."

"Harder is a good thing? I thought easier was a good thing."

"In this case, harder is good. You've already seen what magic does to your body and how you need to take care of yourself afterward."

"Crackers and water," Lionel said.

"Well, that was the starter pack, yeah. The more you practice, the more you'll get in tune with how different foods balance you out differently. Or imbalance you, for that matter. Being vegetarian means you have to take a few extra seconds to really think about what you're putting in your body and make certain you're getting all the nutrients you need. For people like us, living more deliberately is *always* a good thing. Y'know, considering magic is a little like juggling dynamite with a blindfold on. Plus, there's another important aspect to a vegetarian lifestyle I don't think you've fully considered."

"Which is?"

"That veggies are delicious," she told him. "Try the *dolmadakia*."

228

As he dipped his second rice-stuffed leaf into the cool, minty yogurt sauce, Lionel had to admit that she wasn't wrong. The wine, a heady red with peppery traces of blackberries, didn't hurt, either. He tried to listen to his body. It was a new sensation. Beyond the basics—hungry or full, sleepy or awake, properly caffeinated or not—it wasn't something he usually paid much attention to.

"Nature," he said. He stared down at the bone-white tablecloth as if he could see right through it, to the hip pocket of Maddie's blue jeans and the glowing disk inside. "But there's nothing natural about that thing."

She curled her lips like she'd bitten down on something sour. "No. And mixing magic with machinery is rarely a good idea."

"Violation of some cosmic law?"

"*Unaesthetic.* And it usually doesn't work. When it does, it tends to be a cheap substitute for real prowess."

"Looks like that disk works pretty well."

She reached for the bottle and poured a fresh dollop of wine into each of their glasses.

"And it shouldn't. Look, I learned about necromancy from—" She paused. She tossed back a swig of wine. "Like I said, I learned from the best. Right now I just want to know two things: who built it, and if there are any more of them out there."

"Do you think it has anything to do with us? I mean, this whole—" He paused, not even sure how to word it at this point. Job? Quest? Regina had called it an adventure, back when he was a hardheaded journalist who had no idea what kind of nightmare he was walking into.

Amazing to think that was just four days ago. Four days was all it took to flip a life upside down and inside out. And he knew, no matter what was waiting at the end of this road, he'd never be the same man again.

"I think it does," Maddie told him. "Melpomene and her playwright, the soul trap, you and your mother, the Poe manuscript, the blue-eyed man . . . my intuition says it's all connected somehow. And my intuition's saved my life more times than I can count, so when it talks, I listen. I just don't know which strand of the web to start plucking at. I guess we can try some divinations—I need to teach you how to do that anyway—but bones and cards aren't always a great substitute for real clues. They're mostly good for vague and ominous portents that only make sense in hindsight."

Lionel sipped his wine, took a few slow breaths to steady his racing thoughts, and worked the problem. He'd chased a hundred stories with less to go on, building a narrative from scraps and rumors; witchcraft or not, this was no different. He wrote a mental list of loose ends and red flags—everything that stood out. Two stray pieces from opposite ends of the jigsaw clicked together perfectly.

"Two things have been bugging me," he said. "First, that guest list."

"The missing list from the ballroom?"

"Right. The blue-eyed man must have taken it, but why? Doesn't make sense: he killed everyone in the room but us."

"Maybe he wanted to double-check," Maddie said. "Make sure he got everybody."

"Very possible, but why bother? He came to steal the manuscript. This guy's not worried about someone coming after him. I mean, with power like that, would you? So he's not going to be looking over his shoulder, afraid some straggler from the Thoth Club's gonna be out for revenge."

"Maybe he just wants to scrub his trail." Maddie contemplated her glass. She turned it, catching candlelight in the burgundy depths of her wine. "Maybe he doesn't just want the manuscript, he wants to get rid of anybody who knows about it."

"Or anybody who might have read it," Lionel said. "Okay, so somebody killed Ray Barton at his studio. They tortured him, searched his safe, wrung him empty, and finished him off. I don't know how much digging you did, but I found out Barton had organized-crime connections. Russian mob."

Maddie lifted her eyebrows in mild surprise. Not convincingly. "You don't say."

"Again, same MO: whoever killed him didn't care about Ray's bosses being out for payback. And massive, overkill levels of payback are something the *Bratva* is known for. Tells me the blue-eyed man did it. Mobsters, magicians—he just doesn't give a damn."

"Sure." Maddie nodded, following along. "He killed Barton, found out about Barton's partnership with Wade Dawson and the plan to auction the manuscript off; then he showed up at the ballroom to grab it. It all holds together."

Lionel couldn't keep the smile off his face. This was the part of his job that he loved more than anything. That moment when the bits and pieces, all the stray facts and research, came together to draw a picture.

"But it doesn't," he said. "If he only wanted the manuscript, he would have gone straight to Wade's office and taken it from him. Instead, he waited a few extra days and went to *way* more trouble than he needed to. What would he have gotten out of Ray? The deal with Wade, the time and place of the auction . . . and the fact that Wade had taken the manuscript to be authenticated."

"So if he's looking to bury this thing," Maddie said, "to make sure that anybody who laid eyes on the manuscript ends up dead . . ."

"He'd be hunting the expert Wade hired. And if he assumed that expert was one of his buddies in the Thoth Club—a perfectly reasonable assumption—he'd want to take the guest list when he left, to see who didn't show up to the party and make sure every last name was crossed off."

Lionel rested his palms on the table and grinned like a wolf.

"A reasonable assumption, but *wrong*. Wade told me he hired an outside freelancer with no connection to the club. The blue-eyed man is looking for the wrong person."

"Then we need to find the right one," Maddie replied.

Thirty-Four

They polished off the bottle of wine and made plans by candlelight. Then they finished their meal and emerged—just full enough, just drunk enough—onto streets cast in an electric glow. Lionel couldn't stop looking up. On his first ride into Manhattan, the skyscrapers had looked like granite teeth, the jaws of some misshapen beast. Now they looked like the castle spires in a fairy tale. Maybe it was the magic. Maybe it was the company. Maddie walked with her arm hooked in his, following the edge of Central Park, taking a walk together by some silent mutual accord. A night breeze ruffled their hair, carrying the scent of oak trees and wildflowers.

He couldn't help stealing little glances at her as they walked. Out of the corner of his eye, he caught her doing the same. Her arm felt right, cradled in his; it fit perfectly, snug, like two pieces of a jigsaw puzzle. Maddie was still a house of mysteries, but she'd unlocked a few more of her doors, just for him.

"So . . . what now?" he asked.

"Nothing productive we can do until morning," she replied. "You're not one of those travelers who looks down on doing anything touristy, are you?"

"Not in the slightest. I actually kind of want to see Times Square."

She scrunched up her face. "No, you don't. Well, maybe once. Just once. Anyway, I've got a better idea."

Horse-drawn carriages trotted down Fifth Avenue, escorting lovers around the outskirts of the park. Maddie flagged down an empty one, passed the driver a couple of folded bills, and off they went; she and Lionel sat nestled side by side on the back perch, watching the city roll by. The carriage was a dirty off-ivory with a wobbling wheel, and the shaggy, mismatched horses were on their last legs, but Lionel kept thinking about fairy tales.

"Figured you could use a little downtime," Maddie told him. She snuggled against his arm. Her touch left a faint tingle along his skin, electric. "We both could, but mostly you. Don't want to make your head explode on your first day or freak you out too much."

"Too late."

"We have not begun to get freaky." She gave him a sidelong glance. "Seriously, though. You coping okay? Is it too much?"

He thought about it. Then he shook his head.

"Nah. I can handle it. Today's been a lot to process, and I've probably got about a hundred questions and a hundred more I haven't thought of yet, but I'm . . ." He searched for a word. "Floating."

"Welcome to New York," she told him.

The wail of a siren up the street, faint and fading, sparked a memory.

"It's funny," he said. "My entire life, I've only seen this city on screens. When I first landed, I saw an ambulance with the FDNY logo, and for just a second, I wondered what show they were filming. I thought that feeling would pass, you know? Like, I'd forget all that and it'd just be another city, like back home."

"But," Maddie said. She wore a knowing look in her eyes.

"But with all that's happened since I got here . . . I'm not sure what's real anymore. Hell, I'm not sure if *I'm* real. Maybe I'm just a character in somebody else's story."

"Your mistake," she said, "is thinking that stories and reality aren't the same thing. Do you know why New York is in so many movies and shows?"

He shrugged. "Crossroads of the world, right? It's big, it's iconic—"

"Iconic. Mythic. That's not by accident. There was magic in the soil here, in the water, before there were people. The first ship crewed by merchants from the Dutch West India Company—they had a magician on board. He knew. He wrote about it, and others came. *Strega* came from Italy, the wives and daughters of landless farmers searching for a new beginning. The *bandraoi* from Ireland. From Poland, the wise women they called *czarownice*. When the slave trade was finally abolished in New York, some of the victims stayed behind and fought to build pockets of freedom here; among them, they had *mambos* and *maes-de-santo*."

"Sort of a . . . magical melting pot," Lionel said.

Maddie drew her hand across the overcast sky. He thought he could see the weave of history, trailing along her fingers, like strands of gossamer web.

"They came to Five Points and they came to Harlem, spreading out through the boroughs, bringing their gods and their secrets with them." Maddie turned on the padded bench, meeting Lionel's gaze. "This city is *steeped* in gods and secrets. And magic. Passed down through generations, built into the foundations and carved into the brickwork. It's in the air. So tell me this: What's a story?"

"It's . . . an accounting of events, usually but not always told in linear order."

She gave his forehead a gentle poke. "Stop being analytical. What's a story?"

He looked to the sky, to the city, to the shadowed forest of Central Park on one side and the granite high-rises on the other, and took it all in with a deep breath. He'd been holding himself apart from the city since he landed, a stranger in a strange land, but a new understanding sparked in his mind like flint striking an ancient stone.

"It's . . . this. It's us. It's everything around us."

"We are all a story," she told him. "I'm a character in your story; you're a character in mine. And we're both part of the story of New York, along with eight million other people. It's all fiction, it's all true, and just like you were taught as child, there's a world of possibility on every new page. Once you accept that, there's only one question worth asking."

"What's that?" he said.

"What kind of story do you want to live in?"

Maybe it was the wine. Maybe it was the way Maddie's eyes caught the lamplight as the carriage rattled past. The words flowed off his tongue before Lionel thought to stop them.

"What was it you suggested back at the hotel bar? A life-changing, passionate romance?"

A hurricane of emotions flickered across her face. She raised her hand a little, reaching toward his, then hesitated. Not pulling it back, not touching him, just floating in uncertainty.

"I believe," she said, forcing a breezy tone into her voice, "I actually said 'a passionate, heartbreaking fling.'"

"I remember. You were adamant about the heartbreak."

She pulled her hand away and faced the avenue ahead, leaning back on the bench. Her shoulder still rested against his.

"I don't like to disappoint people," she said. "So I try to warn them up front."

"Sounds like self-sabotage."

"Sounds like real life. I know what I am, Lionel."

He tilted his head, studying her. The sharp curve of her cheek, the trace of bitterness in her eyes.

"Honestly," he said, "I'm not convinced you do."

"I'm Regina Dunkle's errand girl. And once we're done here, she's going to give me another job, and send me somewhere far from here, and you'll never see me again." She bit her bottom lip until it turned white. "Can we just ride for a while? And not talk?"

He nodded, didn't answer, and listened to the plodding, uneven hoofbeats as he tried to figure out where the night had gone off the rails. She hadn't pulled away from him. Not her body, anyway, her shoulder still pressed to his, leaning close. He'd felt her bottle herself up, though. She'd almost reached to him. Then she'd reached for fresh bricks and mortar instead.

Lionel looked up to the buildings, into the lit windows that dotted the darkened Gothic facades. He caught snatches of other people's stories, here and there: portraits from lands he'd never been to, the flicker of a television tuned to a show he'd never seen. Eight million lives.

Someone was looking back at him.

A woman stood dead center in a long, horizontal window, three floors up. Even if he didn't remember her clothes—the deep-red torch singer's gown, the antique key dangling from a silver chain around her pale throat—he would have recognized her cold, triumphant smile in a heartbeat. It was the woman from his tarot vision, as real as he was, looking down as his carriage rolled by. She slowly raised one hand and curled her fingers in a mocking wave.

He must have jolted when he saw her. Maddie looked his way, brow faintly lined. "Lionel? What is it?"

He fumbled for something to say. He hadn't mentioned what he'd seen in the vision, for no better reason than the woman in red had signaled for his silence, and his gut told him to listen. Especially considering the way this night had gone—the sudden wall between him and Maddie—he could hardly come clean now. On the other hand, he couldn't *not* say something.

"Just, uh, someone watching us from a window," he told her. "She looked . . . different."

The lines on Maddie's brow got a little deeper. "Different how?"

"Pale, curly black hair; she was wearing this vintage red dress like something from the '20s—"

Maddie's eyes went wide. She grabbed his wrist. Hard.

"Keep going."

"Um, she had this"—he gestured at his collarbone—"this old-fashioned key . . ."

Her gaze whipped to the driver, and she hammered her palm against the back of his seat. "Stop the carriage. *Stop the damn carriage!*"

The carriage was still rolling when she jumped out. She hit the sidewalk and broke into a sprint.

Lionel tossed some crumpled bills to the driver and offered half an apology, clambered down from the perch, and ran after her. Maddie was up ahead, a shadow on the edge of the park and racing like the devil was on her heels.

"Maddie," he called out. "Maddie, *wait!*"

She stopped long enough to lunge off the curb and shoot her arm up, flagging a taxi. Lionel caught up with her as she was climbing in back. He panted out his words, trying to catch his breath.

"What is it? What's wrong?"

"Get in," she hissed, then looked to the driver. "High Line. Tenth Avenue and West Twentieth. Fifty bucks, cash, if you can get us there in fifteen minutes."

The cabbie hit the gas, jumping into a break in the traffic, and Lionel fell back against the vinyl seat. A loose spring prodded him in the small of the back.

"Maddie, you're kinda scaring me right now."

She folded her arms tight across her chest and clenched her jaw so tight he could see it trembling. She almost said something. Then she bit down on the first word before it could escape her mouth. Just like before, he could feel her reaching for him. Wanting to reach for him, and fighting herself tooth and nail.

"Who was that woman?" Lionel asked.

"There are things—" She shook her head. "Don't ask me that."

She fumbled with her phone and squeezed it in a shaky hand. Sitting beside her, he could hear Regina's voice on the other end of the line.

"I presume you have my manuscript?"

"*She's* here," Maddie said.

"Of course she is." Regina's voice carried a tinge of annoyance. "It's her city."

"She *saw* us, Regina. Lionel saw her, she looked right at us—"

"You called me for this? You stupid, insolent little girl. If he actually had, and you weren't under my protection, do you really think we'd be speaking on the phone right now? *She wouldn't have let you go.*"

Maddie didn't have an answer for that. Just a hard swallow as her head sagged.

"You're invisible to her as long as you're useful to me," Lionel heard Regina snap, "which won't be much longer at this rate. Do you hear me? Or you can do us both a favor and hand in your resignation. You can quit anytime you like."

Maddie's voice was soft now, broken at the edges.

"Yes, Ms. Dunkle."

"I don't know what I'm more tired of, your whining or your blistering incompetence. I do have other operatives in New York, you know. You can be replaced."

Her head drooped lower. Her eyes closed. "I'm . . . I'm sorry, Ms. Dunkle."

"Get back to work."

Regina hung up. The phone dropped into Maddie's lap, dangling limp in her hand. She kept her eyes shut.

Lionel didn't ask about the woman in red. He knew she wouldn't answer. He had a more pressing question on his mind, anyway.

"Why do you let her treat you like that?" he asked her.

The cab pulled up to the curb outside the protective wall of their hotel. She paid the driver, shoved the door open, and gave her answer to the night air as she turned her back on Lionel.

"Because I deserve it."

They didn't speak in the lobby, or on the elevator. He felt like he should, like she was waiting for him to find a path through the mine-field between them, but he didn't know how. The elevator stopped on the second floor, and she got out.

She stood there, not moving, staring at something he couldn't see. The door started to glide shut, and he blocked it with his foot. Then he poked his head out.

The landing was just like his, one floor up. Taxidermy prints, black doors, the former monastery turned into a travelers' retreat. He followed Maddie's gaze to her door.

Her fingertips traced the door, right next to the lock. Scuffs marred the wood, thin rents in the onyx paint. Her depression and anxiety melted while he watched, transforming into sharp, keen eyes and a hunter's grace.

"Maddie?"

She held up a finger. She hunched toward the door, turning one shoulder, ears perked.

"Stay behind me," she said.

Thirty-Five

Maddie slid her key card over the lock. It beeped and strobed green. Then she swept into the room, Lionel on her heels, and froze.

She had a visitor. He sat in the armchair by the window, one leg crossed over the other, almost casual in the way he held the snub-nose revolver in one liver-spotted hand. Light from a single bedside lamp cast his long jaw and sallow cheeks in a sickly yellow glow. He looked like a silver-haired cadaver in a thousand-dollar suit.

"Please shut the door, and kindly do not raise your voices." His pistol waggled at them. "If you raise your voices, I will have to raise mine."

"Pietrovich," Maddie said. She kept her hands open at her sides, limber and ready. Lionel shut the door and did the same, looking between them.

"You know this guy?" Lionel asked.

"The *nocnitsa* and I used to be friends," he said.

"Who said we aren't still friends?" Maddie asked. Her voice was level, cool, as if she were sitting at a business meeting instead of staring down the barrel of a gun.

"A little bird told Aleksandr about my ambitions. There are two things we cannot abide in the *Bratva*, Madison. Cops . . . and snitches."

"Three things," she said. "Cops, snitches, and fools. You've been recruiting muscle all over town, trying to find someone crazy enough to take Aleksandr out. Run your mouth long enough, word does get around. I'm insulted you assume I'm the one who warned him."

He gave a little giggle, high-pitched, like a violin string taut enough to snap. Lionel got a better look at him now that the shock had worn off. There was something desperate in his eyes, like a starving rat in a maze, scrabbling for an exit that didn't exist.

"Who says I did? You're my third visit tonight, on a list of five. I have to flee. Fly, like a birdie, into the wind. But I'm cleaning up before I go."

"First things first." Maddie nodded toward Lionel. "Let my friend walk. He's got nothing to do with this."

Lionel swallowed a lump in his throat as the fat muzzle swung his way. Pietrovich's finger was too tight on the trigger, too twitchy. From ten feet away, with the barrel aimed straight at Lionel's face, he wouldn't miss.

"I do not know this," Pietrovich said. "Perhaps the *nocnitsa* no longer works alone."

"He's my companion for the evening. My *hired* companion. He doesn't know anything about this business of ours. Let him walk."

Pietrovich arched a sparse eyebrow at Lionel. "This true? You a gigolo?"

"It's an honest line of work," Lionel said with a shrug he hoped looked nonchalant enough to be real.

"More honest than most, but you made a poor choice in clients. Bad luck, my friend."

Pietrovich rose from the armchair. He shifted his aim, covering Maddie now.

"I won't beg for my life," Maddie said, "but I'm willing to buy it."

He tilted his head. "I'm listening."

"You need to do more than skip town. You need to vanish off the face of the earth. That takes cash. Not investments, not abstracts—liquid, hard cash. You know how Aleksandr deals with turncoats. He's got a meat hook and a blowtorch with your name on it, and if you don't have the green to turn invisible, he'll snatch you up before you reach the Jersey turnpike."

Lionel watched one of Pietrovich's eyelids twitch, a spasmodic fear dance that ran all the way down his arm to the tip of his trigger finger. Most people would be trying to calm a gunman down, but Lionel caught on to Maddie's strategy, every word chosen for maximum impact. She wanted him scared. Scared enough that he'd reach for any hope she offered him.

"You think I don't have resources?" he said.

"I think you had to run away from home with five minutes' warning. Ten, if he felt like giving you a head start, just for kicks. You didn't even pack a bag, let alone clean out your safe, and you can't hit any of your stashes in New York, because Aleksandr already has eyes on every single one of them. You remember Valeriy Utkin?"

The only response he gave her was another eyelid twitch. His knuckles went white around the grip of his gun.

"I was there. He only *stole* from Aleksandr. They took him to that place up in Asbury Park—you know the one. Six days." Maddie's eyes were cold iron, fixed, unblinking. "They kept him alive for six days. Would you like to know what was left of him when Aleksandr finally allowed him to die? There wasn't much."

His finger tightened one fraction of an inch. "What are you offering me?"

"Like everyone else in town, Aleksandr hired me to hunt you down. Unlike everyone else, he paid me in advance. Let's trade. My cash for your word of honor that you'll let us go."

"You're trusting a great deal to my word of honor."

"You aren't giving me much of a choice." Maddie's voice turned conciliatory now, soothing. "You're in control here, Pietrovich. You're holding all the cards. Make the smart choice and give yourself a fighting chance."

He thought about it. The barrel of his gun bobbed along with his head.

"The money," he said.

She pointed to her suitcase on the writing desk. "May I?"

He didn't stop her. She took two steps and unzipped the case. Lionel watched her fingers twist on a hidden catch. A second lid pulled up, revealing the tiny hidden space beneath and the treasures it hid: two crisp stacks of cash, wrapped in cardboard bands around the middle, and her backup piece, a storm-gray Sig Sauer with a sound suppressor screwed to the barrel.

Her hand dipped into the case. Pietrovich raised his gun, taking careful aim.

"Easy now," he said. "When I see your hand again, there'd best be nothing but money between your fingers."

"Relax." She gave him a sidelong glance. "I'll bring it over to you."

"No. I know you, *nocnitsa*. Close enough to kiss is close enough to kill." He nodded at Lionel. "Have the fuck-boy do it."

Maddie put the stacks of cash into Lionel's open palms. Her every movement was slow, deliberate, and she locked eyes with him as she dropped her voice low.

"Do exactly what he says. No funny business."

She punctuated her words with a flick of her eyes, down to the pistol in her suitcase.

It would take her one, maybe two seconds to draw and fire. Even if he wasn't twitchier than a jackrabbit on crystal meth, Pietrovich could empty his gun faster than that. Lionel knew what Maddie needed from him: a distraction.

Hopefully one that wouldn't get them both killed.

His heartbeat lurched to a crawl, booming in his ears as he walked toward Pietrovich. Every footfall, the weathered floorboards groaning under his shoes, echoed in time with his pulse. The entire world slowed to a molasses drip. The room, Pietrovich, Maddie . . . everything but Lionel's thumbs.

He tilted the stacks of cash upward in his hands like a magician manipulating cards for a magic trick. His thumbs slid under the cardboard bands, out of Pietrovich's sight, and snapped the brittle glue. The tips of his index fingers held the bands firmly in place on the other side.

Pietrovich was watching Maddie, his gun level and his other hand held out to Lionel. "Give it to me," he said.

Lionel flung both stacks in his face. The unbound bills fluttered free, a sudden storm of green that kicked Pietrovich's anxiety into flat-out panic. He staggered back, eyes wide, and the muzzle of his gun swung toward Lionel.

Maddie shot him in the face.

Lionel barely saw her move. One moment her hand was in the suitcase, the next it was bristling with cold gray steel. The suppressor barked like the sound of a slamming door. Pietrovich fell to his knees, his eyes wide-open as the ruptured crater in his forehead flowed like leaky plumbing. A scarlet line drooled along one side of his nose and pooled in the cleft of his chin. Cash fluttered to the floor all around him, some of it flecked with wet stains.

Maddie rushed over, grabbed him by the front of his shirt, and kept him hoisted upright. *"Towel,"* she snapped. "If any of this gets on the floor, we're going to be scrubbing all night."

The gunshot still echoed in his ears, or maybe it was just his imagination. Lionel didn't have time to think about it. He dashed into the bathroom, ripped a damp towel from the shower rod, and ran back to her. Maddie had him hold Pietrovich by the shoulders while she turned the towel into a turban that covered half the dead man's face.

"You did good," she said. "You okay?"

Lionel looked to her pistol, abandoned on the writing desk, while he tried to put his thoughts in order and breathe around the stone in his chest.

"Louder than they are in the movies," he said.

"Oh, yeah, that *pfft* sound is pure Hollywood. Still, it makes a gunshot sound like a dozen other totally normal noises, which is exactly what you want when you're shooting somebody in a crowded place. Help me get him into the bathtub."

He got his hands under Pietrovich's shoulders, the dead man's head pressed to his belly as Maddie hoisted his legs. They lugged him into the bathroom and laid him down in the tub. The slow-spreading stain of the bullet turned the twisted towel into a cherry-vanilla ice-cream cone. The stone in Lionel's stomach got a little bigger.

Maddie put her hand on his shoulder. "Seriously. You okay?"

"You want to tell me what that was about?"

"In a second. Need to make a phone call."

She left him alone with the body. The killing didn't bother him as much as he knew it should have. He'd cut his teeth working a crime blotter, and he'd spent more time at murder scenes than some actual cops. As for Maddie, she'd killed three men right in front of him just last night; one more didn't change things. It was more the suddenness of it—a carriage ride and a cool summer night punctuated by the sudden raw threat of violent death.

This was the world Maddie lived in. She'd warned him, but he was just starting to understand.

She came back, tapping the screen of her phone. "I've got a cleaner on the way. We just have to hold down the fort until he gets here."

"So you've got time for an explanation," Lionel said. His tone didn't offer any other options.

Maddie put her hands on her hips. She sighed at the body in the tub.

"Long story short, a while back, Regina wanted a regime change in the New York underworld. Certain people in, certain people out. Things have been more or less stable since then, but somebody's always got to try and upset the apple cart."

"You're telling me," Lionel said, "that Regina Dunkle orchestrated a mob war? Why?"

"That's the wrong question."

"How far does her reach *go*?"

"That's the right one," Maddie said. "And the answer is, as far up and as far down as she wants it to go. She points, I shoot . . . and occasionally deal with the fallout."

A knock sounded at the door. Lionel followed her out of the bathroom.

"What was that name he called you? *Nocnitsa?*"

"I have a lot of names," she said. "Stick around long enough, you'll have a lot of names, too."

She paused with her hand on the doorknob.

"This is my life," she told him. "This is my normal."

An earnest and smiling young man stood on the threshold, looking like an artifact of another time in a bright-red sweater and a polka-dot bow tie.

"Eugene," Maddie asked, "how's the family?"

"Mom sends her regards. You really need to come over for dinner some night."

"Next time I'm in town."

"Next time," he said. "Where's the client?"

She led him into the bathroom. Lionel watched as he huddled over the tub, *hmm*ing and *ahh*ing at the body. Eugene tugged at the lapels of Pietrovich's jacket.

"This is nice. Tailored." He asked Maddie a question with his eyes.

"Knock yourself out," she said. "I just need you to pull a Houdini with the body. Everything must go."

He stood up and stepped back, rubbing his chin. "Let me get the tools from my van. I'm going to need some private time with the client, please."

Maddie hooked her arm around Lionel's.

"I'll be in the suite just above this one if you need me," she said.

Thirty-Six

The adrenaline hit Lionel in the elevator. He'd interviewed combat vets who talked about staying frosty in a firefight, cold and professional until the shooting was over, then found themselves laughing or sobbing as soon as the dust settled. Suddenly he wanted to do both at once. He wanted to start screaming. He wanted the fist-size stone in his stomach to let him breathe again.

Maddie seemed to sense it. She put her arms around him, pulling him tight against her body, rocking him gently as the elevator shuddered its way up to the third floor.

"I know," she said. "I know."

Skin to skin, cheek to cheek, the stone in his chest melted into a molten spear. It surged up, something animal, primal under his skin. He turned his head. Their mouths met, drawn like hungry magnets.

"I know," she murmured between kisses.

They pushed through the door to Lionel's suite together. He shut the door and flipped the latch, and then she was on him. They kissed again, slow, wet, as her fingers clawed at the top button of his shirt. He didn't know how badly he wanted her until he had her in his arms. His hands slid along the curve of her back, her hips, slipping under her cotton T-shirt and tracing warm, smooth skin.

He forced himself to pull away. Not far, their foreheads touching while their lips parted, just far enough for him to speak.

"We don't have to do this," he said. "If you just want to share a bed, sleep, we can do that, too."

"I know we can. This is what I want."

She bent her head and kissed his neck. The tip of her tongue flicked across his skin, leaving a tingle in its wake. They stumbled to the bed together and fell onto the mattress. She pulled her shirt over her head and tossed it aside, and then he kissed his way down her throat, down between the valley of her breasts. Their shoes clattered to the rug. She'd given up trying to get his shirt off, one of his buttons hanging torn on a loose thread. Her fingers scrabbled at his belt.

Blood rushed through his body, pounding in his ears, drowning out his thoughts. She grinned at him, feral, and bit his lip between kisses. He felt his belt slither off, his zipper jolting down.

"I should"—he managed to say—"get some protection."

"It's fine." Her hand slipped into his slacks and closed around him. Her thumb rubbed in firm, slow circles.

"Yeah, but—"

"I'm on things. Herbs. Shut up."

Maddie shoved him back on the mattress and straddled him. Her tangled hair fell around his face, like an intimate curtain around them.

"Herbs?" he gasped. "You mean the pill, or—"

"*Lionel.*" She loomed over him, her eyes bright in the darkened room, sharp and hungry and fierce. "Do you want me?"

His hands closed over her hips. "Since the moment I laid eyes on you."

"Then, please," she breathed, "stop worrying, shut up, and *fuck* me."

He reached for the button of her jeans. The denim shrugged down a tug at a time, and he hooked his fingers in the waistband of her panties as she kicked her pants off. She took hold of him again, confident, like they'd been lovers for years and she already knew every inch of his body. Then she guided him inside her.

They made love like they were trying to devour each other. Maddie's emotions seemed to wash over Lionel like he was standing in the path of a burst dam, all of her pent-up fear and misery coming out as raw animal aggression. They rocked together until he couldn't hold back any longer, and he came, back arched and groaning out as she bit into his shoulder.

The pace slowed, and they kissed, and he gently rolled her onto her back while he caught his breath. Her curls shimmered on the pillow. He made his way down her body, exploring with his lips. Past her stomach, down between her thighs, inhaling her musk. The tip of his tongue traced slow, featherlight circles, offering a wordless promise. Her fingers curled in his hair and gripped tight.

—

Afterward, cradling Maddie in his arms, the sweat-damp bedsheets made Lionel think of canvas sails after a hurricane. He'd been storm-tossed and caught up in the maelstrom, drawn into the thunder behind Maddie's eyes. Now she was at rest, her waters tranquil. Her chest slowly rose and fell under his curled arm like slow, rhythmic waves.

He fell asleep holding her.

The bedside clock read 2:14 a.m. when he woke up alone. A thin blade of light glowed against the Persian rugs, slipping out from under the bathroom door. He smiled to himself, rolled onto his back, and waited for her to return.

A sound broke the stillness. Like a sob, choked off in the pit of her throat. He pulled the covers back and swung his legs over the edge of the bed, the rug scratchy and warm under his bare feet.

"Maddie?" he whispered.

He heard fervent whispers behind the bathroom door, open just a crack. Maddie's voice, talking to herself. Something like, *"Never should have, never should have."*

"Maddie?" he asked, his voice a little louder. He touched his fingers to the smooth wood of the door.

The whispering stopped.

"Don't," she said. One jagged little word.

Lionel had reluctantly accepted her code of silence. Her refusal to talk about her past, her twisted relationship with Regina Dunkle, why she was terrified of the woman in red; he took it all in stride as best he could. Maddie was a book of secrets, and while he wanted to read every page, to *know* her, he hadn't been invited. She could keep her secrets, and he'd enjoy the company of whatever face she decided to show him.

That was then. This had gone too far. He'd heard her weeping, whispering, raving, eight feet and a cracked door away from him, and walking away now wouldn't do her any favors. He'd be complicit in her pain, like a bystander leaving the scene of an accident and abandoning the wounded. And that wasn't who he was.

He gave the door a push.

Maddie was perched on the closed lid of the toilet, knees to her chest. She cradled a bone-handled straight razor. In a heartbeat he understood the rows of faded scars along her left arm. She hadn't cut herself tonight, not yet. There was blood, though: twin trails of scarlet on her face, leaking from the corners of her eyes. She looked to him, her face contorted with humiliation and anguish, and her hand squeezed the hilt of the razor until her fingertips turned white.

"I said don't," she told him.

He held up his open hands, gentle, slow.

"Maddie. It's okay."

"It's *not*"—she squeezed her eyes shut—"it is not *okay*. What I did to you is not okay. I was selfish, I was lonely, I—"

"Hey, wait, are we talking about tonight?" Lionel nodded back over his shoulder, toward the empty and rumpled bed. "Because that was pretty incredible."

She took a deep breath and opened her eyes, fixing him in her blood-flecked stare.

"You don't get it. I'm setting you up. I warned you. You're feeling all lovey-dovey right now, sure, and we can play boyfriend and girlfriend and go on our little fairy-tale adventure. And you know what happens next, Lionel?" She pointed the razor at him. "You know what happens next?"

"What happens next?" he asked.

"You wake up one morning, and I'm gone. I'm just . . . I'm just gone. Because I always leave, because I'm a colossal piece of shit, and because hurting people is the only thing I'm good at."

She took a deep, wet breath through her nose and rubbed the back of her hand against her cheek. The blood smeared, painting her sharp cheekbones in a rust-red crescent. She stared at her hand and flopped it around.

"Birth defect," she said, sniffling again. "My tear ducts are fucked up. It's not magic. There's no magic. It's all bullshit. You should leave, Lionel. You should get on the next flight out and never look back. Because if you don't, I swear to god I'm going to mess you up for the rest of your life. It's going to happen. Just a question of when."

"I'm not leaving," he said.

He crossed the tile floor, carefully, approaching her from the side like she was a cornered animal with a razor-toothed bite. He swallowed, steadying himself, and reached toward the blade in her hand.

"I'm going to take this from you now, okay? You don't need this tonight."

She didn't answer, but she let her fingers go limp as he pried the razor from her grip. He set it on the far rim of the bathroom sink, just outside her reach.

"You know, I get it," he said. "You think you're damaged. Think you're toxic. I am on the tail end of . . . *so* many bad relationships. I mean, time after time, everything starts out strong and passionate, then the next thing I know, we're plowing into the rocks at full speed. Got to the point where I started to think, you know, the one common element in every one of these shipwrecks isn't the woman. It's me. Then I realized the truth."

Her bloody eyes squinted at him. "What's that?"

"That I was right," he said with a wistful smile. "I'm the king of taking a good thing and wrecking it. Every one of my exes has a different reason to blame me for the breakup, and every one of them is right. I'm a workaholic, I'm caustic, self-righteous, I use people to get what I want, I need to hire a moving van to handle all this baggage I carry around . . . and that's me. That's who I am. And I'm okay with that."

He reached out to her. His hand cradled her chin, fingers stroking her cheek, brushing away a crimson trickle under his thumb.

"And I'm not going anywhere," he said. "Because I'm thinking maybe, just maybe, you and me are broken in all the right places. Like maybe our sharp edges and our cracks just . . . fit together. I'd like to give it a try and find out."

"Even if I end up hurting you," Maddie said.

"I've got a long list of regrets. Know what the worst ones of all are? The times I look back and wonder what might have happened if I'd had the courage to reach for what I wanted." He crouched beside her, eye to eye. "And I want you. If you want me, too, then, well . . . let's give it a shot."

She turned her face away, pulling her chin from his fingers.

"It's not that easy," she said. "When we're done here, when the blue-eyed man is dead and I get that manuscript back, Regina's going to send me on my next job. I could end up on the other side of the world. Probably will."

"She said you could quit. It sounded like she almost wanted you to."

"It's not that easy. It's not that simple."

"So I'll come with you," Lionel told her.

She met his gaze. Her eyes widened.

"You can't . . . Lionel, you don't know what you're offering. What happened in my room tonight wasn't an aberration, okay? Dealing with pissed-off gangsters is a light evening where I come from. I'm *lucky* if that's the worst thing I have to deal with."

"And we dealt with it. Together. He's dead, and we're still standing. That means something, doesn't it?"

"You have a home, a job, you've got a *life*—"

"Sometimes you need a change of perspective," he said. "I'm thinking you're worth it."

Maddie tugged a tissue from a box on the floor, blew her nose, and tossed it into the wastebasket at her side. "You're different. You know that?"

"Tell you what: Let's not make any plans right now. We'll just take it day by day and do what we came here for. When we're done, then we'll decide our next move. Together. Deal?"

Her head bobbed. He reached for a washcloth and ran it under the tap, drenching it in warm water.

"Let's get you cleaned up," Lionel said. "Few hours left before sunup, and I think we both need a little more sleep. Besides, you can't stay in here much longer."

"Why?" she asked him. He leaned in and dabbed at her face with the washcloth, scrubbing gently at the trails of blood.

"Because," he said with a nod to the toilet, "I've *really* gotta pee."

She blurted out a laugh and leaned into his arms. He held her close, tight, pressing his lips against her shoulder. It was all right. For the moment, everything was all right.

Thirty-Seven

The next time Lionel woke up, Maddie was still there. She curled against him like a cat, her curls against his chest, and she gave a little kick as the alarm clock trilled.

"Nooo." She rolled over and slapped the clock until the noise stopped. Then she lay flat on her belly, pressing her face into the pillow. "I was having such a nice dream."

He stroked her back, kneading in soft circles, a half-awake massage. "Yeah? What about?"

"I dreamed we were sleeping in."

Neither of them moved. Lionel dug deep for a Herculean burst of willpower and forced himself to sit up.

"I'll take the bathroom first. Enjoy another fifteen minutes."

"Wonderful apprentice is wonderful," she murmured into the pillow.

By eight, they'd both showered, cleaned up, and made themselves presentable. Professional, even. They were going corporate today. First, though, they got on the elevator, and Maddie hit the button for the second floor.

Eugene had hung out the **Do Not Disturb** sign. Maddie waved her key card at the lock and poked her head inside. Standing at her shoulder, Lionel scrunched up his face; the stench of chemicals wafting from the suite was strong enough to singe his nose hairs.

"We good?" Maddie called out.

Eugene poked his head from the bathroom door, goggles over his eyes, and flashed a thumbs-up with a hand sheathed in an industrial-strength rubber glove.

"Eight more hours," he said. "Twelve, tops."

"We'll leave you to it," she told him.

Lionel was quiet until they got on the elevator.

"So that's . . . what he does?"

"Make bodies disappear? Mm-hmm. Eugene is responsible for over a hundred unsolved homicides in New York alone. And as far as I know, he only killed six of those people himself."

"Another one of Regina's people?"

Maddie looked up to the glowing numbers over the elevator door, watching the lights blink one by one.

"We're all Regina's people down here," she said.

They made camp down the block in Cookshop, making plans over breakfast. Lionel fidgeted with the knot of his copper-brown tie as he looked over the menu, saying goodbye—for now, at least—to the bacon and sausage. The sun came out at last, casting the city streets in a warm, dusty glow.

"Mmm, frittata," Maddie said. "Roasted squash, spring onions, fresh mozzarella . . ."

"I really liked the chicken sausage," he said into his cup of coffee.

"Power demands sacrifices. Hey, some people pluck out an eye for mystical enlightenment. You just need to eat a little healthier. If you put it in perspective, it's kind of a small ask."

They had their target in sight, their one advantage over the blue-eyed man; Wade Dawson had hired an outside consultant to authenticate the Poe manuscript. They knew it; their enemy didn't. For now, anyway. Eventually he'd figure it out, which meant they needed to find Wade's accomplice first.

The massacre at the Blackstone Building still hadn't been discovered. No doubt by now people were starting to get worried, and the nightly news would have something to say about so many of New York's elite disappearing at the same time. For now, though, Wade wasn't officially dead or missing, which meant nobody had searched his office for clues.

After breakfast, Lionel set up back at the hotel room and got to work while Maddie went on a supply run. She came back with bags from three different craft-supply stores. While she was out, she'd given him a challenge: they had to get past Wade's receptionist, and for that, she needed the woman's full birth name.

Stamford and Cross had an official website, but they didn't include the support staff with the roster of executive biographies. A little digging brought Lionel to a photo gallery for their last company picnic, and a softball-team lineup gave him one Ms. Marcie Nowak-Connors. He stated a social media trawl to figure out which of those two hyphenated names was originally hers and track down a middle name to go with it. Over at the writing desk, Maddie was creating a tiny poppet from a gray lump of modeling clay. She smoothed out the rough impression of stubby arms and legs, her lips pursed in concentration.

"What is that, like, a voodoo doll?" he asked.

"Fun fact: voodoo dolls were an invention of Hollywood. Voodoo's one of the only magical traditions that *doesn't* use this kind of substitutional iconography. Pass me the scissors? And the packet of paper from the bag on the bed."

The doll spouted a head. Maddie cut thin strips of parchment as Lionel ran down the last piece of the receptionist's birth name. She scribed the name again and again in tiny black letters along the paper strips, then wrapped them around the doll's body like the shroud of an Egyptian mummy.

"This would be much, much more effective if we had something of hers," Maddie said, "like a nail clipping or some of her bodily fluids. As it is, the poppet will buy us five minutes. Maybe."

"I've gone digging with less." He darted in and pecked her on the cheek. "And without a witch on my side, so that's a big plus."

She snagged him by the tie and yanked him close. Their lips pressed together, fast, fervent, hungry. She inhaled his breath and let him go.

"If you're going to kiss me," she told him, "do it right."

The Stamford and Cross office looked just like it had on Lionel's last visit, from the cool, potpourri-scented air to the brown-sugar wood and the wall of windows that looked out over the Financial District's skyline from forty-five stories above the street. They'd arrived together, but Lionel waited down in the lobby, giving Maddie five minutes to establish the story he'd crafted for her.

He made a string of phone calls on the way over, posing as a salesman, until he social-engineered his way into a piece of info he could use: that Jordan Cross was going to be in an important teleconference for another hour or so, with no way to reach him. Maddie's job was to pose as his ten o'clock meeting. What? She wasn't on his calendar? Of course, it must be an oversight of some kind, and she'd be happy to sit in the lobby and wait. It was a scheme he'd used plenty of times on the job, staking out ambush spots for an interview.

"The two keys are to be firm, and to be nice," he told her. "Firm makes you hard to get rid of. Nice makes it easy for them to cooperate. The idea is to turn what you want into their path of least resistance."

"What do you do when that doesn't work?" she asked.

"Be firm, nice, and run away before the cops show up."

Maddie sat midway along a row of chairs on the left-hand side of the lobby, reading an unfurled copy of the *Wall Street Journal*.

Pretending to, anyway. From his angle, he saw the clay mummy doll on her lap. She turned her cupped hand as he passed, flashing the tiny spear of a toothpick painted black. He made his way to the reception desk with a smile.

"Hi," he said. "Not sure if you remember me, but I'm that reporter who stopped in to interview Mr. Dawson the other day? I had some follow-up questions, and I was hoping he could spare a couple of minutes for me. Literally, just a couple of minutes."

The receptionist wore a pained look on her face. "I'm sorry, um . . . no, he's . . . he's out today."

Either the firm hadn't decided on a story to explain his disappearance, or they hadn't even gotten to the point of filing a report. Perfect. He reached one arm behind him and scratched the small of his back, signaling to Maddie.

"Oh, I'm sorry," he said. "Do you know when he'll be back? I'd like to make an appointment, if that's okay."

"Well, he's—he's out sick, so I'm not really sure. What I can do is take your number, and once he's back—"

She paused. The blood drained from her cheeks like someone had pulled a plug in the bottom of her foot. Dots of sweat freckled her forehead.

"Are you okay?" Lionel asked, leaning in.

She clutched her stomach and winced. Then she kicked her chair back, standing up so fast it rattled against the wall behind her.

"No, I mean, yes, I—I think I ate something, I— Excuse me."

The receptionist clamped her lips shut and barreled out of the lobby, heading for the ladies' room around the corner. Maddie tossed her newspaper aside, pocketed the doll—the black toothpick jutting from its clay gut—and stalked behind her. Her job was simple: comfort the woman as the wave of sickness passed, stall her, and buy as much time as she could.

Lionel's was a little harder. He ducked into Wade's office.

He punched the power button on the desktop PC, searching through the dead man's desk as Windows booted up. Stock reports, printed memos, everything organized in labeled folders. "Thank God for neat freaks," Lionel muttered. He didn't see what he was looking for, but at least he felt confident there wasn't a clue hidden on a stray, crumpled scrap of paper just under his nose.

"Speaking of noses," he added as he scooped up a small glass vial from the top drawer. A few grams of white powder nestled inside. He set it back where he found it. The computer was live and asking for a password.

Most people were careless with their computer security, more than they would be with a website password: after all, nobody expected hackers to walk into their home or office. Good chance it was something easy to remember. A name, a birthday . . . He looked over the glass cases along the office walls, Wade's tiny museum.

Museum. No access. *Muse.* No. *Melpomene.* Nope. Lionel took a closer look at the artifacts on display. They came from a scattering of places and times, but half were clearly Egyptian; Wade had a fondness for the period.

Thoth, he typed. No dice. He dug out his phone, typing fast, and pulled up a list of Egyptian deities in the web browser. He plowed through *Isis, Horus*, feeling his choices running out. Good chance Wade's computer would lock him out after too many misfires, and this entire trip would be for nothing.

Sekhmet. The screen flickered and unlocked, displaying a row of neatly spaced icons, as clean as his physical desk. He'd used up two minutes, and Maddie had warned him to get out in five. He double-clicked on Wade's appointment calendar.

Most of the crammed calendar tied to Stamford and Cross email addresses or to financial firms Lionel recognized by name. A couple stood out, no description or email chain, just a time and *"R. B."* *Ray Barton,* he thought. Just after his second meeting with Ray, Wade had scheduled an off-site appointment with someone named Lana Taylor. He'd noted a phone number, an address, and a single word: *Valdemar*.

As in the name of the Poe story. "Gotcha," Lionel said. He jotted down the name and number, shut off the computer, and darted out of Wade's office.

The door had just swung shut at his back when the receptionist returned, her face still pale and her lips wet, rounding the corner in the other direction with Maddie on her heels. He struck a pose against the reception desk and tried to look innocent.

"Really," Maddie said, "I can call someone—"

"No, it's okay, really, I feel fine now," she replied. She looked more puzzled than anything as she took her chair behind the desk. "Better than fine. I guess I just needed to get something out of my system. Weird."

"I'll call back tomorrow," Lionel told her. "With any luck, you and Mr. Dawson will both be feeling a lot better."

Maddie lingered behind for a few minutes, a ruse to keep her cover intact. They'd agreed that three minutes after Lionel's departure, she'd get an "emergency text" on her phone and have to take off in a hurry, promising to catch up with Mr. Cross next week. If everything went just right, the receptionist would forget about both of them by lunchtime— and when the cops inevitably came around, checking up on Wade's disappearance, they wouldn't even rate an offhand mention.

Maddie got off the elevator on the first floor, walking fast. Lionel fell in alongside her. He matched her stride all the way to the revolving doors and the waiting city beyond.

"Catch any fish?" she asked him.

"I did, indeed, and her name is Lana Taylor. I looked her up while I was waiting for you. She's an associate professor at New York University, and her specialty is handwriting identification and document forensics. Looks like she picks up some extra bucks here and there, consulting freelance on the side."

"We're going to school?"

"Her place. The address in Wade's calendar is an apartment building in Brooklyn, just off Seventh Street." They emerged onto the sun-drenched sidewalk. Traffic was a tangled snarl, horns blaring, a truck jammed halfway into the intersection under a red light. Lionel glanced behind them, back at the glass-walled tower. "Is she gonna be okay?"

"The receptionist? Oh, she'll be fine. I slipped a fifty into her purse while she was tossing her breakfast. She won't know where it came from, but hopefully she'll treat herself."

"That was nice of you."

"Not really," Maddie said. "It's Regina's money."

Thirty-Eight

Lana Taylor's street had frozen sometime in the 1950s. A jumble of beige brick apartment buildings and shops had sprouted along the broken asphalt like weeds, offering dusty windows, OPEN signs, and empty doorways. A retro-handwriting sign in yellow advertised LEMMON'S SHOE AND BOOT REPAIR. Or maybe it hadn't been retro, back when the sign went up. Lionel and Maddie stood in the foyer of Lana's building, where last names printed out on uneven red punch tape lined a row of door buzzers.

Lana was in 302. Lionel hit her buzzer and waited. No reply.

"Think she's out?" Maddie asked.

"Best-case scenario."

From the tight look on her face, she was thinking the same thing he was. They were racing the blue-eyed man. He might have been farther ahead than they thought.

"I can try to get it open," Maddie said. She eyed the thick metal plate on the vestibule door. On the other side, behind a thin rectangle of mesh-reinforced glass, a wooden staircase with a dirty olive-colored runner wound upward.

"I've got a faster solution," Lionel said.

He punched every single button on the grille, one after the other. A medley of voices erupted from the tinny speaker at once, drowned out and talking over each other. He tapped the call button and replied, "Delivery from UPS."

The door buzzed—a single harsh, grating blast—and Lionel pulled it open before it could lock again.

"Old reporter trick. Works every time," he said. He held the door for Maddie and waved her in with a flourish.

They rounded the stairs. A door rattled open beneath them, a confused resident looking for a package that wasn't coming. They kept quiet and made their way to the third-floor landing.

The door to 302 hung wide-open.

No damage to the lock. It looked like someone inside had opened up for a visitor. The shards of broken glass strewn across the hardwood floor, the overturned credenza, and the scattered flowers dying in a puddle of spilled water told more of the story.

The limp curl of an elderly woman's hand, at the edge of the living room arch, told the rest.

Lionel started to move. Maddie held him back, pressing her hand to his chest, and went in first. They moved fast, as soft as they could, every groan of the floorboards sounding loud as a gunshot in the stillness. Lionel had seen Lana's picture on the web: she was in her thirties, maybe pushing forty. The corpse might be her grandmother, an elderly guest . . .

He rounded the corner, and the breath choked in his throat. It was Lana, all right. The prune-skinned corpse on the floor, swallowed by a sweater and skirt suddenly too big for her shriveled body, looked just like Dolores Croft had at the Blackstone. Prematurely aged beyond any mortal life span, *drained*, sucked dry of everything that made her human.

Rustling from the room up the hall. Someone pulling out drawers, searching for something.

The blue-eyed man was here.

Craig Schaefer

Lionel's hands curled into fists. Maddie must have seen something, the murderous edge in his eyes, and touched his chest again. She shook her head, and pointed at Lana's body. A reminder of what the man was capable of. He understood. They needed a plan, and "run in and start swinging" didn't count.

The rustling stopped.

He felt something at the edge of his senses. A probing, sharp-edged stick along the ridges of his brain, like when Melpomene had sifted through his mind. This was cruder, not as thorough, not as deep. As soon as it touched him, the hard tendril of thought yanked away.

The man's voice drifted from the room up the hall, as rustic and folksy as he was back at the ballroom.

"I was in a hurry that night," he said. "Figured you two were just putting off the inevitable with that fancy warding spell, so I didn't stick around to finish things up. Most people, surviving a situation like that, they'd take it as a sign of a charmed life and mosey off to greener pastures. Last thing they'd do is poke around for more trouble."

"Do you know who I am?" Lionel asked.

"I do now. Checked you two out when I crossed every last name off the club's guest list and you weren't on it." He laughed, low and rich. "Lionel! Little Lionel Paget, as I live and breathe."

Lionel's fists tightened at his sides.

"You killed my mother."

"Sure did," the voice replied. "Would have done you, too, just to close out my books, but your mother, damn, she was a *smart* one. I knew she had a kid about your age, but I hadn't seen her in years, so that was all I knew. Not even a name. When I came for her, she had a little girl with her. Musta been one of the other kids at the ranch, somebody's daughter. Anyway, she kept the girl behind her, all protective-like. So I made a natural assumption that it was her own flesh and blood. I was tearing that little girl to pieces while they were slipping you out the back

264

door. Like the old saying goes: when you assume, you make an ass out of you and me. Mostly me, in this particular case."

A million questions boiled up inside Lionel's chest, swelling until he thought he would burst, and they all came out in one strangled *"Why?"*

The blue-eyed man responded with a long, slow chuckle.

"Your mother was a whore, Lionel."

He started toward the hallway. Maddie held him back, firm, getting in his way.

"Don't," she hissed through gritted teeth. "That's what he *wants* you to do. Don't let him bait you."

Lionel stood his ground. He took a deep breath to steady himself.

"You owe me answers," he said.

"You already have 'em," replied the voice. "C'mon, son. How many years have you been chasing my tracks? Don't tell me you haven't figured it all out by now. You never would've gotten this far if you hadn't."

"I haven't been chasing you at all," Lionel said. "I didn't even know you existed until I saw you in the ballroom. I . . . I blocked out my memories of that night."

"*Horsefeathers.* You mean to tell me that Sheila Paget's baby boy *just happens* to be at the Blackstone the night I drop by to run a little errand? All these years, a whole wide world between us, and we cross paths by *accident*? You're a man out for vengeance if I've ever seen one."

"I wasn't, not before that night." Lionel fixed his gaze on the back hallway, upon the faint, barely moving shadow of a man cast along the wooden floorboards. "But you'd better believe I am now."

That invisible stick poked at his brain again. Lionel swatted at it with his mind, acting on instinct, like slapping a mosquito with his palm. He felt a little satisfaction as it bounced away. The blue-eyed man fell silent for a moment. Then he spoke, his voice echoing up the hall with an edge of fascination.

"You ain't lying. She didn't mark you. Didn't claim you for her own."

"Who?" Lionel asked.

"You really don't know." His voice tumbled into a wry chuckle. "Well, I suppose you can't lose what you never had. Your mama was a witch. You *do* know that much, right? Not like those airy-fairy crystal wavers she was using for camouflage. She was the real deal."

"I know."

"She also had the hand of a goddess on her shoulder. Your mother was bought and paid for, branded and soul sworn. Now I was thinking, maybe, just maybe, you got the mark, too. Maybe that goddess sent you after me for a little payback. They go for that kinda deal. Grand schemes of vengeance, warring bloodlines, the sort of epic that keeps the poets in business." He chuckled again. "But you ain't got it. Son, you been kicked to the curb. Your mama's goddess straight up *abandoned* your sorry ass."

Lionel wasn't sure how he should feel about that. Like the man said, you couldn't lose something you never had. Could you miss it, though? If he was telling the truth, his mother had had a brush with the divine, something bigger than this world.

Something that didn't think Lionel was good enough to stick around for.

"I don't need a goddess to take you on," he said. He knew it was bravado, but his anger was in control now, and the only thing keeping him from charging up that stubby hallway was the cool, calm press of Maddie's fingers against his chest.

"Hey, mystery girl," the blue-eyed man called out. "You, I can't get a fix on, but I'm gathering little Lionel here is under your wing. That right?"

"That's right," Maddie said.

"You gonna let him commit suicide? Or are you going to take that boy's hand and walk out of here the way you came in?"

Her eyebrows tightened, and Lionel didn't need words to follow her train of thought. They knew he was powerful: he'd proved that with a storm of ghosts at the Blackstone, and the shriveled corpse at their feet was a second helping of evidence. Why wouldn't he come out and fight?

"Lionel says you owe him answers," Maddie said. "I disagree. You owe him a lot more than that. I'm here to help him collect. Do I need to make this a formal challenge?"

"Do I strike you as a man who follows tradition? No. Something's wrong here, *something's* hinky about this whole deal, and I'm not letting you blindside me into making a bad move. You can challenge all you want, but we're not scrappin' today. Not until I get to the bottom of this."

A rattling echo, rough wood sliding on wood, sounded from the back room.

"You want answers, Lionel? Here's one for free: I killed your mother in self-defense, to stop her from coming after *me*. That's all it was, nothing personal about it. Nothing personal between you and me, neither, not if you don't insist on it. Go home. Go back to Chicago, get married, pop out a couple of kids, and be a family man. This world isn't for you. Go home."

Lionel thought about the other morning, sitting at Maddie's side, feeling like Alice at the edge of the rabbit hole and deciding whether or not to make that final jump. A normal life, or initiation. He'd made his choice.

"This world *is* my home now," he said.

"Then dig your grave, son," said the blue-eyed man. "Dig it long, and dig it deep. I'll see you real soon."

Shoes clattered on metal. Lionel realized what the sliding sound had been.

"Window," he said to Maddie. "He's going out the fire escape!"

They scrambled up the hall and burst through the open doorway. The blue-eyed man had been lurking in a tiny office, barely bigger than a walk-in closet, with a low, overstuffed bookshelf and a computer table. The computer looked like it had gone twelve rounds with a heavyweight boxer. A long, narrow window gaped open on the opposite wall.

Lionel jumped out onto the fire escape, landing on both feet with a *clang*. His quarry was two flights down, rounding the bend, one hand clutching a tan Stetson against his head so it wouldn't fly off. Between the metal slats, Lionel caught flashes of ruddy skin, a beige suit coat, polished spats. He chased him down, Maddie on his heels.

The figure below jumped from the bottom ladder, down onto the back-alley pavement, and kept running. He paused at the next corner. He whirled around and looked back as Lionel dropped down in his wake.

It was him. A fragment of memory tore open inside Lionel's mind as if it had been sealed under plastic. He smelled the thick woodsmoke of the burning ranch, heard the crackling of the flames and the screams. And he saw the blue-eyed man, striding unscathed through the fire.

He wasn't a monster. Without his mask, he was just a man: forty-something, a little puffy cheeked, his nose a little sharp, his chin a little long. Forgettable. Beyond his eyes, too blue to be real, he could have vanished on any crowded street in America.

He cracked a grin, tipped the brim of his hat to Lionel, and winked. Then he vanished around the corner.

"Lionel!" Maddie shouted as Lionel sprinted after him. "Be careful! It might be a—"

The word froze on her lips as they rounded the bend. Nothing ahead but an empty stretch between brick walls, a rare spot too small to squeeze another chunk of real estate onto the map.

That, and a manhole, its dirt-caked steel cover lying discarded beside it. The hole stood dark and wide-open, an invitation to the dance.

"Trap," Maddie said.

Lionel gave the cover an experimental tug. It barely budged under his curled fingers, and his back twinged in protest. No chance the blue-eyed man had gotten it open, not this fast, not without a pry bar to help. Which meant it had already been open before their chase began.

"This is where he came from," Lionel said. He crouched and peered down into the shadows. "It's how he got here. Hell, he might be *living* down there. And he wasn't expecting us to show up."

"Doesn't mean it isn't a trap."

Lionel dug out his phone. He flipped on the flashlight mode and cast a pale beam down into the depths. Nothing moved down there. No sound.

"Why did he run, Maddie? We've seen what he's capable of. So why wouldn't he face us?"

"He's afraid of something," she said.

Crouched at the manhole's edge, Lionel looked up and locked eyes with her.

"I want to know what he's afraid of."

Thirty-Nine

Two beams strobed across dank concrete walls. The light from Maddie's phone caught stencils on the wall, stark yellow in block letters: **ACCESS JUNCTION 23-B-1**. The air was stagnant down here, hotter than the summer streets above, choked with a stench like rotting garbage mixed with wet dog fur. At least it wasn't the sewer main: the stone under their feet was mostly dry, stained with faded moisture. They walked slowly down the maintenance tunnel side by side, ears perked for movement, hearing nothing but the lonely sound of their own footsteps echoing back at them.

"He's right," Lionel mused, his voice a whisper. "What are the odds?"

"Of?"

"That I'd end up in the same room with the guy who killed my mother? Maybe a goddess didn't send me here, but somebody sure as hell did."

"Regina," Maddie said.

"Do you think she knew? About him?"

"It's Regina," she said. "I learned a long time ago that trying to second-guess what she knows and why she does things is a waste of time. She'll show her cards when she feels like it."

They froze. Something slithered in the darkness ahead, where the gallery widened and dropped. Thick metal pipes lined one side of the wall. They rumbled softly, collecting wet condensation on their steel faces.

Maddie raised her phone's beam. It captured a glimmer of motion, quick and low to the ground.

"What is that?" Lionel asked, squinting. "A rat?"

The answer shambled from the darkness. All eight feet of it, its scaly armor glistening in their lights as it dragged itself forward on four clawed, stubby legs. The alligator let out a rattling hiss, one bright brown eye glaring back at them.

"An alligator," Lionel said, "in the sewers. Maddie, that's—that's an urban legend. They aren't real."

"That looks pretty damn real to me," Maddie replied. "Remember what I taught you: just because something is a story doesn't mean it isn't true."

The alligator turned its head. Its other eye was milky white, bulging from a skull stripped of flesh. Half of its body was a mass of rotted scales and exposed bone, its internal organs shriveled with decay. In his freshly awakened sight, Lionel couldn't miss the thick black-violet mist clinging to its undead guts like a coat of toxic moss.

"An alligator with a serious skin condition," he said.

"It's dead, Lionel. The alligator is dead."

Its tail thrashed, thumping the damp concrete.

"And yet," Lionel said.

"We should back away very slowly now."

No time. It let out a strangled, wheezing growl, like someone forcing air through a rusted and broken bellows, and charged.

Dead or not, the thing was fast. It barreled straight ahead, roaring toward Lionel like a runaway train. He threw himself to one side, hit the concrete on his shoulder, and rolled hard. Maddie was fast on the draw. She spun, brought her hands up, hooked her fingers, and hissed ritual words. The banishment thrummed through the dirty air, a heat mirage in motion, and splashed across the alligator's rotten hide. The death energy stubbornly clung to its ribs like rust on steel. The gator jolted for a second, startled by the hit. Then it scampered, slow to turn, and set its sights on Maddie.

She waited until the last second as it bore down on her. Rotten teeth snapped at her heel, just missing, gnashing like the jaws of a bear trap. The alligator's tail thrashed against the concrete floor in hungry frustration.

"Too strong to banish," Maddie gasped, breathless. "That death energy is animating it. Gonna try to siphon it off. I need a few seconds; keep it distracted while I work."

He looked at her like she'd sprouted a second head. No time to argue, not with the alligator chasing its tail and spinning around to make another run. Lionel stomped his feet and wriggled the light on his phone, shining it into the creature's good eye. That got its attention. He just wasn't sure what to do with it. He braced himself, squaring his footing, a matador without a cape as the dead thing came for him.

Instinct took over. He squared his footing, hooked his fingers, and projected the *voces mysticae*.

"*Akhas. Dromenei.*" The gator closed the gap, jaw wide and rotten teeth ready to chomp, as Lionel's fingers curled and he thrust his hands outward. "*Keh.*"

In the parking lot, he'd had time to second-guess himself. Time to worry, time to *think*. Now he was running on intuition, emotions, and his terror fueled the spark in his belly into a roaring blaze. He felt the heat surge down his arms and cascade loose in a billowing torrent. The banishing spell hit the creature in the skull with the force of a lead-packed boxing glove, knocking it senseless. It yowled, a guttural garbage-disposal roar, and careened off course.

Maddie had been preparing her own retort, chanting under her breath as she darted around the beast. Now she struck. She dropped to one knee and thrust her open palms against the alligator's side. Her fingers dug into rotten meat and seething death energy, clutching exposed rib bones and hanging on tight. The cloud of violet mist pulsed and surged, fleeing the animated corpse on her command. It slipped under Maddie's skin and billowed into her body.

The alligator thrashed one last time, braying, and fell silent.

"Maddie," Lionel said, "are you—"

She collapsed onto all fours. Her back made crackling sounds as it arched, brutally hard. Then her jaw wrenched open, and she vomited a torrent of black smoke. It gushed from her lips and dissipated on the air, leaving behind the stench of sour milk. The last wisps came out on the tail of a wet coughing fit. Lionel rushed over, holding her shoulders, not sure how to help.

"S'okay," she rasped. "Internal alchemy. Drew the energy off, passed it through my own body, harmless when I spit it out again. Just smells bad."

Her skin was clammy, hot to the touch. He pressed his hand to her forehead, and it came away slicked with sweat.

"You don't look good," he said. "Jesus, you're burning up."

She managed to raise her head. She gave him a pained smile. "It's death energy, Lionel. Know what's not supposed to be inside a living body, ever? That. The name is kind of a giveaway. It's okay, I just need rest. Get me home?"

He managed to get her up the ladder, back to the street, half holding and half pushing her up a rung at a time. She leaned against the alley wall while he ran to the curb and hailed a cab. By the time he found one and eased her into the back seat, she was hovering on the border of delirium.

"Don't ever let me catch you trying that," she murmured, barely loud enough to hear. "Seriously advanced technique. Need at least a hundred years practice 'fore you even think about it."

He assumed she meant that metaphorically. He wasn't going to ask. Not the time for it. He leaned her back in the seat and buckled her in as the cab took off, then mopped a fresh crop of sweat beads from her forehead with his sleeve. A blister had broken out on her cheek, and he remembered her admonishment from before.

"Sounds like radiation poisoning," he had said.

"You're not far off. Occult radiation. Different source, same great taste."

"I'm going to take care of you," he told her. "Everything's going to be okay."

He felt like a liar. He hoped she was right—that all she needed was a little bed rest and this would pass like a flu bug—but she looked worse now than she did in the tunnel. Her color was gone, her face pallid and glistening, and a fresh blister had sprouted on her bottom lip.

"Been a long time since I had to do that," she breathed, her voice a hundred miles away. "Think I might have made a mistake. Don't tell my mother, okay? Promise me you're not going to tell my mother, Lionel. You promise me. I'll never live it down."

The cabbie glanced in the rearview mirror, his beetle brows furrowed. "Hey, buddy. Your lady okay? You need a doctor? Hospital?"

No hospital in the world could fix this. Lionel tried to force a carefree smile. It turned into a grimace.

"We're good," he said. "Just the hotel. Please."

"She ain't contagious, is she? I can't have no contagious people in my cab. I don't get paid for no sick days."

"No." He mopped at her brow again. "She . . . she ate some bad seafood, that's all."

The thick brows got tighter. "You let me know if she's gonna puke, okay? I'll pull over. Not in my cab."

At least he had an incentive to drive faster. Fifteen minutes later, Maddie leaned against Lionel as he eased her through the lobby. She could barely stay on her own feet, her eyes drifting shut while he cradled an arm around her shoulder and helped her shamble to the elevator. He felt the heat of a dozen stares, heard questioning murmurs, but nobody got in their way.

He got her into his suite, got her into bed, and she turned the sheets into a drenched sweat puddle while he paced a groove in the floor. More blisters had broken out along her arms. Her skin was an oven, and her breath had gone shallow.

"Maddie, I don't . . . I don't know how to *fix* this," he said. "Please, help me out here."

"Hey," she rasped, "Lionel."

He leaned close, straining to hear her voice.

"I like you." Her hand weakly lifted, and her finger dragged across the tip of his nose. "Boop."

Her hand fell back to the mattress, limp.

He needed outside help. Somebody with experience, somebody who knew things. He called Regina. The phone rang. And kept ringing.

"Really?" he snapped. "*Now* you're not home? The one time I absolutely need you, you're not picking up the fucking phone?"

The line clicked and played a voice-mail recording. "You have reached Regina Dunkle. I'm unavailable at the moment, but if you leave your contact details—"

He waited for the beep while he paced. "Regina. It's Lionel—listen, call me back *right now*. Maddie's hurt, and she's getting worse. I mean, she's getting worse *fast*. We need help."

He hung up. Waiting wasn't an option. He had no idea when Regina would call back, or if she'd even bother. He didn't how much time Maddie had left.

Memory sparked. He grabbed his wallet, fumbling past folded bills, and tugged out the business card from the art gallery. The herbalist's name stood out, terra-cotta ink type on pale-violet stock, with a phone number beneath.

She picked up on the third ring, answering with a clear, crisp voice. "Wen Xiulang."

"Ms. Wen," Lionel said, "I need your help. I mean, a friend of mine does. It's an emergency."

"And the nature of your problem?" the woman asked.

"She says you know each other, or used to know each other. Her name is Madison—" He paused. It suddenly occurred to Lionel that he had no idea what Maddie's last name was. "Anyway, please don't hang up, but I'm about to say something that's going to sound really crazy, okay?"

No reply. The herbalist listened in quiet expectation.

"Maddie is a witch," Lionel said, "and she sucked up some death energy, and she tried to spit it out again, but some of it got . . . stuck inside of her, I think? And it's killing her, and I just started doing magic literally yesterday, and I don't know what to do."

Again, no reply. She held her silence for so long that Lionel checked the connection, thinking she might have hung up on him.

"Give me your location," she said. "I'll be there directly."

Forty

Three crisp knocks sounded at the hotel room's door. Lionel raced over and pulled it open. Half an hour had passed since his desperate phone call, and Maddie hadn't gotten any better. Her eyes had fallen shut, her delirious murmurs fading into silence, and only the slow, shallow rise and fall of her chest offered proof of life.

Wen Xiulang swept right past him without a word, lugging a heavy lacquered case the size of a fisherman's tackle box. When he thought of a Chinese herbalist, Lionel had pictured an ancient, wizened crone; what he got instead was a sharp-eyed woman in her early twenties with a short, side-swept haircut and the moves of a corporate raider, dressed in a raw-silk tunic and designer jeans. She dropped her case on the bedside table and gave it a sharp slap with the side of her hand. The lid popped open, three tiers of trays springing up and outward, ready for action.

The air filled with a musky aroma, the tang of dried roots and mushrooms, as Xiulang studied Maddie with an appraising eye.

"You were right to call me," she said.

"Can you save her?"

She looked at Lionel for the first time. She gave him a disgusted little snort before turning back to Maddie and plucking a pair of latex gloves from her case.

"I saw a coffee stand downstairs," she replied. "Go down, get two cups of water for tea. Hot as they can make it."

Lionel raced for the elevator. Soon he was riding back up with a thick cardboard cup in each fist, feeling the glow of boiling water against his sweaty palms. Back in the room, Xiulang was spreading a mask of paste across Maddie's forehead and cheeks. The salve was smog yellow and smelled like woodsmoke.

". . . hate you so much," Maddie was muttering, her eyes still closed.

"I know," Xiulang told her. She snapped her fingers at Lionel and beckoned for the water. "Good. Now bring me more water from the bathroom. Cold as it gets. Might need you to fetch some ice."

She did. He ran back downstairs on a hunt for a bag of ice. Maddie had fallen silent again when he came back, but her breathing was a little deeper now, a little steadier. Xiulang had one of her arms, turning it to expose her palm and wrist. The herbalist leaned close, frowning and listening intently to something Lionel couldn't hear.

"What can I do now?" he asked her.

Xiulang pointed to the corner of the room. "You can stand there, very still, and say nothing."

Two things he wasn't good at, but he made an effort. He watched as Xiulang took a tiny silver mallet and tapped it up and down the inside of Maddie's arm. Every strike seemed to tell her something. She studied the color of Maddie's skin, then scooped up a beadlet of sweat on her finger and tasted it. She took a mortar and pestle from her case.

"Where do you know her from?" Lionel asked.

She shot him a two-second look that could slice glass, then turned back to her work. She plucked pinches of herbs from the case, little twists of green and brown, and mingled them in the marble pestle.

"First thing I teach my apprentices," she said. "Speak only when spoken to. You learn more that way."

"I mean, she mentioned you have a history together, so I was curious."

Xiulang inhaled and let it out as a long, slow sigh. She closed her eyes, as if silently counting under her breath.

"The second thing I teach them is that a rattan cane, in the right hands, is extremely painful." She pinned him under her gaze. "Should I go get my cane, or are you going to let me work?"

Lionel held up his open hands. "Sorry."

She clicked her tongue and went back to mixing herbs.

He watched, mute, trying to understand. There were poultices and creams, and an incense that smelled like grass after a rainfall. Xiulang held up a tiny brazier, wafting the smoke in Maddie's face while droning a singsong chant in a language Lionel had never heard before. Outside the windows, the sun slipped below the Manhattan skyline and the sky turned russet, then dark.

Maddie woke up at one point, long enough for Xiulang to prop her head up on a couple of pillows and feed her sips of tea. Her eyelids opened, but her vision was droopy, unfocused. The blisters on her skin had begun to fade.

"Lionel," Maddie sighed.

"I'm right here," he said.

"Hate you so much right now."

Xiulang snorted at her and tipped another mouthful of tea between Maddie's cracked lips. Not long after, Maddie fell asleep again, now with a light and contented snore.

"She'll recover," Xiulang said. "She'll be up and moving in a couple of hours. Angrier at you for a little longer. That, I can't cure. She'll get over it."

"Why would she be angry?" She gave him another *Be quiet* glare, and he held his ground. "C'mon. At least tell me that much."

The herbalist held up two fingers. "This is the *second* time I've had to do this for her. First was a very long time ago. She's owed me a debt ever since. Now, she owes me two. Don't let her teach you internal alchemy. Clearly she's still very bad at it."

"How long ago was this?" Lionel asked. "I mean, no offense, but you look like you should be in college."

Xiulang went back to her work, wiping out the pestle and hunting for another batch of herbs in her case. "You don't even know her real name, do you?"

"It's Madison," Lionel said. "She was named after that movie. You know, *Splash*? With Daryl Hannah and Tom Hanks?"

Her lips curled in a mean-humored smirk. "Is she your mermaid, then? Are you going to shed your old life and run away with her, into the sea?"

Lionel hovered over the bedside, watching Madison sleep.

"Still figuring that part out," he said.

"Honest answer. Dumb but honest." She pointed to the door. "Go for a walk now. Come back in one hour. No sooner."

"Why? I mean, I'll stop talking—"

"I have to realign her internal pathways, to make sure the last of the toxins are out of her system and her good energy returns quickly. That involves words and prayers that aren't yours to know about. Go. She'll be fine. The moment I'm done, she'll be up and awake and most likely complaining. That, or out looking for you. Enjoy the peace while it lasts."

Lionel went for a walk.

He considered the bar, thought that a cocktail might even him out, but he didn't want a buzz right now. His thoughts were too jumbled as it was. He was thirsty for clarity. Maybe he'd find solace in the city night air, cooling fast and carrying the tang of gasoline. He left the hotel's walled garden, turned south on Tenth Avenue, and wandered.

He could handle the grief all surging back at once, the pain he thought he'd moved past all those years ago, the memories of the night his mother died. He could handle the rage of standing ten feet away from the man who murdered her, and the bastard getting away. He could handle everything but the guilt.

Maddie was in his bed, hurt, pulled from the edge of death's doorstep, because of him. He was the one who led them into a trap. He was the one who brought them to that apartment building. He couldn't prove it, but he knew, in his gut and in the marrow of his bones, that he was the reason she was here in the first place. The blue-eyed man was right: this was no coincidence. Regina had engineered their reunion somehow, setting him and Lionel on a collision course and throwing Maddie into the mix for good measure.

But Maddie was the only one who'd paid a price for it.

Never again. This was his battle. He'd fight it on his own. Somehow. He called Regina and got her voice mail.

"Maddie's going to be okay," he said, his voice weary. "Call me back. We need to talk."

He had no faith in Regina's answers, but he was going to demand them anyway. The sky had gone dark, and he'd lost track of his turns. He walked in some quiet urban canyon, sparse traffic on the street, too buried in his thoughts to pay attention. Then a jangling sound broke him from his reverie. A pay phone on the corner was ringing.

He stopped in his tracks.

Back home in Chicago, pay phones had largely gone the way of the dodo. In an age when everybody carried phones in their pockets, they'd become superfluous. He assumed New York was the same way. He hadn't thought to notice one way or the other. One thing he was certain he hadn't seen since his arrival, though, was a phone *booth*. And yet, there one stood. A vintage kiosk with scratched-up Plexiglas walls, an accordion door, and an inner light that flickered and buzzed in the dark. A sticker on the phone advertised three-minute calls for a dime.

Lionel approached the booth like the sliding door might be a mouth, ready to slam shut on him. The phone kept trilling. He stepped inside. The bulky black receiver felt cold to the touch as he picked it up and raised it to his ear.

A whistle kissed his ear, so crisp and clear it was like the blue-eyed man was standing right behind him, crooning the opening notes to "Buffalo Gals." Lionel slammed the receiver back on the hook. He jumped back as a shock of adrenaline lanced through his chest.

The phone started ringing again. He took a few deep breaths, steadied himself, and answered it.

"What's the matter?" the man said in his ear. "Don't you like music?"

"Who *are* you?" Lionel asked.

"The man whose pet you just killed. I'm a little miffed about that."

"Get a cat," Lionel said. "Less maintenance."

"You might just be right. I'll take it under consideration. Tell me something, Lionel. That night we crossed paths at the Blackstone. Why were you there, if you weren't looking for me?"

Lionel gripped the receiver a little tighter. "Let's trade answers. I know you were hunting for the Poe manuscript. You tortured Ray Barton for information; he told you Wade Dawson had it, but you waited. You waited until the auction so you could kill everybody who ever laid eyes on the thing. You even hunted for the woman Wade hired to authenticate the handwriting, and I noticed that you trashed her computer on your way out. I figure you're cleaning up your tracks. Making sure there's no proof that the manuscript ever existed."

"I don't hear a question."

"*Why?*" Lionel said. "It's not even a lost manuscript; it's the first draft of a short story that's been in print for over a hundred and fifty years. It's *valuable*, sure, but we're not talking about a Rembrandt or a Picasso here. Why kill all those people?"

"Maybe I just like killin'."

"Maybe you're full of shit. No. You're trying to bury this thing. I want to know why."

A sigh rustled across the line, like a tumbleweed kicking across the desert flats.

"Like I told you before, it was just an errand. We all answer to a higher power, Lionel. And sometimes, to keep that higher power happy—and keep the gravy train rolling—you gotta do some scut work. That's all this was to me. Scut work. I have to confess, I'm not much of a reader myself. And I got my own thing going on."

Lionel's thoughts trailed backward, grabbing stray bits and pieces, weaving them together. The complete absence of death energy after the ballroom massacre. The graveyard with no ghosts. The line connecting a suicidal playwright, her favorite coffeehouse, and the painting from his tarot vision, luring him onward.

"Like that machine hidden in the junction box behind Spence's Coffee?" Lionel asked. "The one sucking up dead people's souls?"

There was a tiny hitch in the blue-eyed man's voice. Almost too slight to catch, but Lionel felt the thrill of a direct hit. For the first time, the man was off-balance.

"Found that one, huh."

That one, Lionel thought. Meaning there was more than one out there.

"You said you looked me up," Lionel said, "so you ought to know that digging up secrets is pretty much what I do for a living. I've been told I'm good at it."

"So you say." He paused. "You know, I've been thinking we oughta have a sit-down. Face-to-face. Lay our cards on the table."

"Where did you have in mind?"

"Somewhere nice and public," he said. "Real peaceful-like. We can talk, if we feel inclined. And after we've said all we want to say to each other, if we feel like going to war . . . well, we can go out back, and we can do that, too."

Lionel knew he shouldn't go. He'd seen what the man was capable of, how he took lives and commanded the dead with equal, careless ease. But as he tried to pull the receiver from his ear, to hang up and walk away, all he could see was his mother's face.

He remembered the last time she'd held him. She'd squeezed him tight as flames licked at the compound walls and the burning forest choked the sky with billowing clouds of black smoke. She'd whispered something in his ear, something important—and the memory danced out from under his fingertips. Gone. Stolen.

All he could remember was her face, and the look in her eyes when she kissed him goodbye.

"Time and place," Lionel said. "I'll be there."

Forty-One

The blue-eyed man gave Lionel an eager, bone-dry chuckle.

"No time like the present. Far as the place, goes . . . no. You gotta earn that. See, I'm still not convinced you're worth my time. Hell, your mama's goddess didn't think you were even worth keeping tabs on, much less staking her claim. She left your ass on the curb with the rest of the trash. But maybe, just maybe, you inherited a little of Sheila's spark. Sheila did have *quite* the spark. You know, till I snuffed it out."

Lionel bit the inside of his cheek until it stung. He refused to take the bait. The man waited a beat, letting it dangle, then kept talking.

"I wanna test your eyes a little. Start walking. If you've got the chops to be a real witch, you'll find me."

"Start walking in which direction?" Lionel asked.

"Easy," he replied. "The one that leads to me. All the others don't."

The line went dead, and the horn blare of a dial tone filled Lionel's ear. He put the receiver back on the hook.

Lionel stepped out of the phone booth, stood on the street corner, and contemplated the crossroads. Four choices, four roads, nothing standing out in any direction. His gut said left. He turned left and started walking.

At the next intersection, he glanced back the way he came. Seeing an empty corner behind him, bare pavement where the phone booth had just been standing, didn't surprise him in the slightest.

He focused on his senses. The hard pavement under his tired feet, the cool night wind brushing fingers against his skin. The sounds of city life surrounded him: rumbling wheels, engines, the far-off and fading wail of a police siren. The crash of metal on stone. Up ahead, dogs were barking. The dogs felt like a good sign, though he didn't understand why, so he stayed the course.

Lionel walked, and wandered, and felt his thoughts slipping outside the walls of his skull. He felt the city like it was a living thing; the people, the towers, the arteries of traffic and trains, all part of one vibrant and breathing organism. He sensed it, and he thought the city sensed him in return. It wasn't friendly, wasn't hostile. It just *was*. It regarded him with a vast and distant eye, curious but not invested in his plight. There were too many humans living in its body to care too much about any single one of them. The city was so old, and humans died so fast.

Which way should I go? he asked.

Left at the next corner, New York replied.

Maybe it was all in his head. Or maybe this was just what a witch's intuition felt like. He turned left and offered up a silent prayer of thanks. The city had already swiveled its gaze away, forgetting him.

One block up, a green chalk arrow, scribbled in a child's unsteady hand, had been sketched on the sidewalk under his feet. The arrow pointed right. He followed it. By now he had no idea where he was. He knew he could take out his phone, check an electronic map, and let GPS answer the question, but the thought of it made him flinch on a gut level. This was no place for maps. Even the street signs slid off his vision, white block letters blurred under a gauzy smear and swapping places until they were alphabet-soup gibberish. He stood under a lonely lamppost, its bulb shattered and dark, at the intersection of Vinea and Astaroth. A shuddering breeze pushed him to make a left turn. He took the wind's advice.

Lionel's ears perked up at a new sound, luring him close. Drumming, faint and fast and rhythmic, flowed up from the pavement under his feet. Along a street of shuttered storefronts—window displays of dust and dead black flies, every door barred and boarded over—his path ended at an open doorway and a narrow staircase with a dirty red runner over wood stained to the color of crude oil. He heard the music thumping down below. The notes were harsh, violent, industrial. Along one black wall someone had spray-painted cherry-red words in big, jagged letters.

FOLLOW ME DOWN.

Lionel wasn't sure if it was the name of the club, or a message just for him. Either way, this was the place.

At the bottom of the steps, a bouncer in a muscle shirt and cheap plastic sunglasses hauled open a steel-plated door. The full force of the music hit Lionel head-on. His heart pounded in time with the thumping bass, and his bones rattled like they wanted to dance.

"Is there a cover?" he shouted over the din.

The bouncer, his eyes concealed behind smoky lenses, gave him a blank look.

"Not tonight," he said, and jerked a beefy thumb toward the open door. "You comin' in or not?"

Lionel went inside, swallowed by the music. He didn't even hear the door clanging shut at his back. Strobes washed his vision in flashing white and scarlet, ambulance lights, turning the crowded club into the scene of an accident. Bodies writhed in the glow—dancing, fighting, bounding against each other like pinballs of flesh and bone. In the space between flickers of light, when the dance floor was drenched in shadow, their outline resembled one amorphous mass. Like a single creature made of a hundred fused arms and heads, flailing madly to the beat.

He made his way to the bar, where steady and pale lights along a dusty shelf offered a shroud of respite from the strobes. The bartender was a string bean in a ragged T-shirt. His eyes were sallow, with the sunken-eyed stare of a professional heroin junkie, and his jaw was too long and narrow for his face. He ambled over like his job was an unwelcome obligation and he resented Lionel for making him do it.

"I'm looking for somebody," Lionel called over the music.

The bartender waved a dirty rag around, taking in the scene. "Everybody's looking for somebody."

Lionel pointed two fingers at his own face. "Man with blue eyes. *Real* blue. Think he's expecting me."

"Oh, yeah. Him." The bartender made a sour face and pointed. A staircase curled around the rim of the club, each step lit by a bar of purple light, up to a balcony overlooking the dance floor. "He's up there with Dergwyn."

Lionel wasn't sure if that was a name or a thing, or if the music had swallowed part of his answer. "Who?" he shouted.

"Dergwyn." The bartender shook his head. "You aren't supposed to be here. You know that, right?"

Lionel had to shrug. "Somebody thinks I am."

"Your funeral."

He walked away and found something to do on the other end of the bar. Lionel climbed the steps. They were sticky under his shoes, caked with spilled beer. The stairway opened up onto a rounded balcony, just big enough for a single table, the color of a pearl, and a scattering of plush white leather chairs. Above the speakers, the space had been designed to cut the music to a low roar, just softened enough to hear yourself think over the noise.

The blue-eyed man sat at the table. He had a glass of bourbon at his left hand, his Stetson hat at his right. He wasn't alone. There was a woman with him, and she swiveled her chair around to give Lionel a feral smile.

Feral. That was the only word that fit. She looked like a Wall Street stockbroker on the wrong end of a nuclear war. Chic and savage, wearing a cream-colored Chanel blazer with popped stitches at one shoulder, bell-bottomed slacks with shredded hems, and a floppy silk bow tie that hung at a lopsided angle. Twin smudges of dirt smeared her cheeks like dark blush, too artful to be an accident, and rusty streaks ran through her chopped and ragged blonde mane. A bracelet dangled from one wrist: a bracelet of teeth, human teeth, drilled and strung on a delicate silver chain. Most of the teeth still had rusty smears of blood caking the roots. She sipped from a water-spotted glass of red wine.

"Well, well," said the blue-eyed man. "Look what the alligator dragged in. I gotta be honest, I figured you wouldn't find me."

Lionel spread his open hands. He stood at the top of the staircase, square between his mother's killer and the only way out. "Here I am."

"Here you are." He lifted his glass of bourbon in salute and tossed back a swallow. "So much for my quiet evening. Sorry, I don't mean to be rude; Lionel, this is Princess Dergwyn. Dergwyn, this is that boy I was telling you about. He's a little raw because I murdered his mama a while back."

"So?" Dergwyn's voice was harsh, chopping her words on the edge of an ax blade. "Same thing happened to me. Don't hear me crying about it."

"*You* killed your mother, as I recall."

Dergwyn's eyes widened with pleasure, and she showed him her teeth. Her canines were a little too long. A little too sharp.

"Princess of where?" Lionel asked.

"Here." She squinted at him, still grinning. Her voice took on a harsh singsong cadence. "Don't know where you are. Don't know who you face. Little. Lost. Lamb."

The blue-eyed man shook his head, almost regretful or just doing a good job of faking it.

"I told you this wasn't your world, Lionel. See, you're suffering from a regrettable lack of education. If you'd been trained right, like a real witch, you never would've done what you just did."

"Track you down?" Lionel asked.

He contemplated Lionel over his glass. Now he had a mischievous glint in his eyes, and the slow smile of a poker player laying down a royal flush.

"Track me down to the heart of a ghoul nest," he said.

The music shifted, speakers rumbling under the balcony. The new tune was faster, harder, the beat driving with hurricane force as synthesizers played a mad and high-pitched riff.

"News flash, son," said the blue-eyed man. "You and I are the only human beings in this room. And I'm the only one with an invitation."

Lionel felt the walls closing in around him. The music took on a physical force, the beats wrapping him in bands of iron. Dergwyn's hungry stare rooted him where he stood.

"You set me up," Lionel said.

"Nope," he replied, "you set yourself up. You know anything about the tarot, Lionel?"

"Only a little bit. But I learn fast."

"First card in the major arcana's called the Fool. Now, the Fool is not a fool, not like we use the word. He's not stupid—he's *new*. Empty of experience, taking a fresh start and setting out on a journey. All the same, there's a crumbling cliff at his feet. He might be going on to great things, or he might just be going down." The blue-eyed man pointed at him. "That's you. You're the Fool."

Lionel still felt squeezed, suffocated by the trap, but he took a deep breath and steeled himself. He put his reporter hat on and shoved his emotions down into a steel-lidded box. Survival meant keeping the man talking, and learning everything he could. Any scrap of knowledge could be the one that saved his life.

"I . . . won't take that as an insult, I guess."

"Good. You're listening. Second card up, that's the Magician. A man of magic, strong in his powers. He knows things, and he can make things happen. A lot of people think that it's the same man on both cards. Sometimes he's drawn that way—depends on the deck. You follow?"

"The Fool becomes the Magician," Lionel said.

"At the end of his journey." He contemplated his bourbon. "*If* he doesn't fall off the cliff first. With you, I figured it could go either way. I still don't know how or why you crossed my path after all these years, and to be honest, it bothers me. It bothers me a *lot*. I figured maybe you've got your mama's spark, after all. That something buried deep down inside, some reserve of power you don't even know you have, pointed you my way. And if you've got her spark, that's a problem that needs fixing. I can't tolerate anybody tripping me up right now, least of all some hot-blooded buck out for revenge. I'm on a real tight timetable. So, I made a decision."

He tossed back the last of his drink. Then he slapped the empty glass down on the pearl-sheen table and looked Lionel in the eye.

"I'd give you a test, one you couldn't pass unless you had a real gift for magic. If you failed, and I figured you would, it'd be proof you weren't a threat and I could forget all about you. I'm not a kind man by any definition of the word, but I don't go out of my way to pull the wings off flies. Not when I've got better things to do."

"And if I passed?" Lionel asked.

"Well, then, that'd mean you might actually pose a threat to me someday." The blue-eyed man nodded to his companion. "So if you passed—which you did with flying colors by finding this place, con-gratulations—I figured I'd feed you to Princess Dergwyn. Her and her hundred closest friends. They're all downstairs, hungry and waiting for you."

Forty-Two

The rattling beat of the dance music took on a jungle cadence. Fast, flowing, hard, the shadows pulsing in time with the bass. Lionel's heart pounded along with it, a hundred beats a minute and speeding up. He thought he'd trapped the blue-eyed man between him and the stairs. Now he knew the truth: he was the one trapped, between the stairs and the only way out of the club, and a small army standing in between.

Lionel had walked into a lions' den, and the lions knew he was here.

"He's all yours," the blue-eyed man said to Dergwyn. "Do me a favor and make it snappy. I still got things to do tonight."

Her eyes flashed, a faint hint of anger. "Maybe I'm not hungry yet."

"When are you not hungry? C'mon, I'm tossing you a juicy steak here—"

She slapped her palms on the table. Her necklace of teeth rattled on her wrist.

"I am not," she seethed, "your *animal.*"

He chuckled and shook his head, giving a condescending roll of his eyes. "Whoa, hey. This is what I get for trying to be nice? Princess, sweetheart, you know I respect you."

"Do you?"

"I'd respect you a lot more if you'd just do what I tell you once in a while. Don't be difficult. You're too pretty to be difficult."

Dergwyn swiveled her chair. She studied Lionel, looking him up and down, and rubbed a finger across her lips. She carried a wolfish cunning in her eyes. Something sly and unpredictable.

"I want to play a game."

The blue-eyed man sighed and pushed his seat back.

"That's my cue to leave. Your games get a little rough for my tastes."

He clambered up onto the balcony railing, casual, as if it were a perfectly normal thing to do. He stood upon the railing with perfect balance, put his hat on, and stretched his arms wide.

"Lionel." He glanced back over his shoulder. "This was never personal. Not until you made it personal. I hope you know that."

Dergwyn was closer to Lionel now. The pink tip of a tongue ran across the ridges of her teeth. She smelled like musk perfume and fresh-tilled dirt. He swallowed a surge of anxiety, fighting past it.

"This isn't over," Lionel told him.

"You have no idea how right you are. You had a good run, kid. Did your best. You failed, but you tried, and I respect that. Anyway, you're about to learn an important truth. There's two kinds of people in this town: the living and the dead. The living, they can do as they please. Free will and all that jazz. But the dead . . ."

The blue-eyed man turned away, balanced like a bird on the railing's edge. He looked down over the mass of seething bodies on the dance floor below.

"The dead belong to me."

He pitched forward and made a swan dive.

Lionel's paralysis broke, and he ran to the railing's edge. There was no sign of him in the pit of strobe lights and sweat, just a horde of faceless shadows grinding to the jackhammer beat. He turned. Dergwyn was right beside him. Grinning now, showing her teeth.

"You don't have to do this," Lionel said.

"Eh," she replied. Her grin faded, and she gave an irritated little shrug, glancing off to one side. "We have a pact."

Lionel thought fast, hunting for an angle. He'd caught her annoyance earlier, when the blue-eyed man had tried to push her into action. Maybe he could use it.

"So, what, you do his dirty work?" he asked. "I thought you were some kind of princess."

Her nose twitched. "I ate anyone who ever said I wasn't a princess. That means I am one."

"Kind of looks like he treats you like a lapdog."

"You're talking yourself right onto my dinner plate," she snapped. She forced a humorless smile. "Keep going. I like the foreplay."

"Did you wonder *why* he insisted on you killing me, when he was standing right here? You've seen what he can do, right? I'll tell you why. Because he's scared."

Dergwyn squinted at him.

"*Something* is happening here," Lionel told her. "My path and his, crossing again after all these years, here and now? Everything falling into place just right? Someone is pulling all of our strings. It's out of his control, and I'm gathering that he doesn't *like* it when things are out of his control. He gets nervous. I'm right, aren't I?"

She nodded, very slowly.

"He is . . . *careful.*" She spat the word like it was rancid on her tongue. "But he is strong."

"He's scared. He knows there's something going on under the surface, something he can't see. And that's why he wanted you to kill me instead of doing it himself. So that if there's some kind of trap in play, something that might hurt him, you'd take the hit instead."

She reached out. Her sharp little nails trailed along Lionel's chest, just hard enough to leave a sting.

"And are you a trap?" she asked, looking him in the eye.

He was pretty sure he wasn't, but he sold the bluff as hard as he could. His life was hanging in the balance. He held her gaze and lifted his chin a little.

"Do you really want to find out the hard way?"

His hopes fell as she let out a raspy snicker.

"Know what I think?" she asked. "You're no magician. Not yet. Still the fool. Still the pawn, not the player. But . . ."

Her voice trailed off as she deliberated. She thumped her nails against his chest and pulled her hand away.

"*But.* Maybe the one playing you would smile on us, if we let you go. But if I let you go, that's trouble for me and mine."

"If you're worried about your boss," Lionel said, "then help me to stop him."

"And if you fail and fall, and you *will* fail and fall, my pack will suffer for our treason. No. Hmm." She snapped her fingers. "I said I wanted to play a game. He didn't say I couldn't."

Lionel didn't like the sound of that. "What did you have in mind?"

Dergwyn moved closer, pressing against him, intimate as a lover. She took hold of his shirt collar and gave it a tug as their noses brushed.

"We let fate decide."

The music reached a crescendo, winding higher, higher, the crowd below erupting in a throaty roar as it peaked like a roller coaster just before the first plunge. The sound froze. Then the bass dropped. The beat lunged forward, a synthesizer torrent surging downward at tornado speed, and Lionel felt his pounding heart plummet with it.

"The music stays on," Dergwyn told him. "The lights go off. If you make it from here to the front door on your own, without getting caught . . . I'll let you go. My pack won't chase you past the foot of the stairs."

"What happens if I get caught?"

"Then we're having fool for dinner tonight." Her tongue flicked across her lips. "Want to play?"

"Do I have a choice?" Lionel asked.

"Sure. Bare your throat to me and I'll rip it out, here and now. Quicker death than the one waiting downstairs. They'll take their time.

Eat you slow. Humans taste better when they're alive and screaming. Fear chemicals marinate the meat."

Her hand idly trailed sharp nails along his collarbone.

"Are you afraid of pain?" she asked him.

Lionel looked inside himself. He was afraid of a lot of things. Being eaten alive by monsters wasn't even at the top of the list. He was afraid of dying without seeing things put right, without making his mother's killer pay for what he'd done. He was afraid of dying without understanding, without exploring more of this strange new world he'd been thrust into.

He was afraid of dying without seeing Maddie one more time. And if he had a chance to hold her in his arms again, to see her smile, to hear her laugh, then he had to try.

"Let's play," he said.

Dergwyn clapped her hands in delight. She stepped to the railing, leaned over, and shouted to the dancing throng below. It sounded like a command, but it wasn't in English—it wasn't even words, as far as Lionel understood them. More like a braying jackal howl, too harsh and discordant to come from a human throat. She let out two short, sharp barks, and a chorus of eager yips and howls rose from the dance floor in response.

She pointed to the lights. They died, quick as snuffing out a candle, and plunged the club into darkness. Nothing remained but the music, loud enough to drown out the world. Dergwyn's irises glittered like twin opals in the shadows as she looked to Lionel.

"*Run,*" she hissed.

He took the stairs two at a time, loping down as fast as he dared. Unless the pack thought he'd take a dive from the balcony like the blue-eyed man, they'd have to expect him at the foot of the staircase. Getting clear was his top priority. Fear wove a net of barbed wire around his thoughts, and he struggled to think his way out, picturing the layout of the club. Cutting across the dance floor was the shortest route between the stairs and the door. It was also a sucker bet. If he got turned around, lost in the shuffle, or just bumped into somebody on the way, they'd mob him from all sides.

The outer wall, then. He could keep his right hand on the wall, feel his way past the bar and around the outskirts of the floor, and it'd take him straight to the exit. He hit the foot of the stairs and almost tripped over his own feet, expecting another drop where there wasn't any. He caught himself and sprinted with his head ducked low. He was under the speakers now, the music so loud he felt the beat more than heard it, every rhythmic thump an atom bomb rattling his bones.

The bar offered twenty feet of good cover. He ducked behind it, scrambling, almost daring to hope that he might pull this off. Then a blur hit him from behind. The bartender. The thing that used to be the bartender. Lionel hit the corrugated rubber mat on the floor, rolled, and stared up into the creature's contorted face. His eyes were chips of glittering opal, his jaw distended like a snake's. It hung open so far that the corners of his mouth were torn and bloody raw, flashing two rows of jagged teeth. The bartender's tongue was a thin ribbon of black, leathery sinew that whipped from side to side as he lunged in for the kill.

Forty-Three

Lionel hadn't been in a fight since high school, but he still remembered how to throw a punch. His fist cracked against the bartender's jaw and slammed the side of his head against the bar. Lionel scrambled back, buying a second of breathing room, and clambered to his feet. He reached for the unlit shelves to his left, to the ghosts of dusty bottles. His hand squeezed around a glass neck as the bartender charged. He barreled at Lionel with his hands hooked into claws, his fingernails long and rotten.

Lionel brought the bottle down on his head as hard as he could. It exploded, glass shards and tequila spraying like a supernova in the dark. The bartender didn't go down. He shoved Lionel back against the bar, wood digging into his spine. His claws closed around Lionel's throat, dug in deep enough to tear the skin, and squeezed. Lionel had two things left: desperation, and the jagged end of a broken bottle in his fist.

Hot blood sprayed across Lionel's face as he drove the broken glass into the side of the bartender's neck, punching through flesh and muscle, then ripped it free. The body landed at his feet in a twitching heap. Lionel didn't have time to come to grips with what he'd done. He ran, racing to the end of the rubber mat until he hit the far wall with his shoulder. Then he scrambled over the top of the bar. He rolled on the sticky wood, came down on the other side, and the small of his back cracked against the edge of a barstool. The electric jolt of pain up his spine stole what little breath he had left.

He had to keep going. The exit was a hundred, maybe a hundred and twenty, feet ahead of him. Shadows were darting, diving, scampering through the dark, lighting the shadows with glimmering opal eyes. Hunting for him. He stumbled, almost falling, his momentum giving him one last burst of speed—then a leathery hand clamped around his wrist. It yanked him backward, off his feet, and he landed hard on the edge of the dance floor.

Another hand grabbed his other wrist. They hauled him across the floor, to the heart of the club. Howls of victory split the air on gusts of rancid breath. Lionel kicked, flailing, still trying to fight, and the press of bodies held his legs to the ground. They were dogpiling him now, climbing onto his stomach and his chest, nearly cracking his ribs as the last breath squeezed from his lungs. He couldn't move. Rough hands tore his shirt open.

Then the first mouth closed over his skin, just above his left nipple, and bit deep. The music and the braying howls drowned out Lionel's scream as his flesh tore. Another set of jaws clamped down on his left forearm. He felt warm spittle and the pressure of stone-hard teeth on bone, and four sets of hands were fighting for his belt, his zipper, trying to get his pants off, and he realized he was going to die here. He was going to die in a frenzied pile of bodies, chewed and pulled to pieces, and there was nothing he could do about it.

All he could think about, past his fear, past the searing pain, was Maddie. He'd fucked up. He'd let her down. He'd gotten the impression—seeing her in the bathroom after they'd made love, the hidden face of her depression and self-destruction—that pretty much everyone in her life had let her down. He wanted to be the one man who didn't. And he couldn't even get that right.

I'm sorry, he said to the darkness.

And the darkness replied.

He squeezed his eyes shut as the shadows exploded in white-hot flame. It was like a hundred torches ignited at once, flooding the club with diamond-hard lights.

No. One light. Maddie's light. She stood at the edge of the dance floor with her arm held high, clutching a long, antique skeleton key in her hand and pointing it to the heavens. The key burned brighter than a star, and a cascade of sparks showered and danced at her feet.

"By Hekate Phosphoros," Maddie roared, "by the oaths that bind you to earth and tomb, by the covenants of the dead, and by my command: *scatter or burn!*"

The creatures shrieked, throwing their hands over their contorted faces, hiding their eyes from the light as they scampered and ran in all directions. Lionel saw them loping for cover on all fours, fighting each other to squirm into crawl spaces, some of them clambering up the walls to escape. Roaches, fleeing from the light. Soon he was alone, lying disheveled and bleeding on the dance floor.

The key faded to a soft, luminous red glow, like a coal in a fireplace. The last few sparks petered out on Maddie's shoes as she approached him. She held out her open hand.

"Let's go home," she told him.

⌇

She knew the way back. Maddie led Lionel through sleeping streets, winding their way in silence. At the hotel, she went in first. She waved him through the door once the coast was clear. He caught a glimpse of himself in the glass: torn clothes, his face spattered in blood, his eyes glassy. He looked like he'd either survived a massacre or committed one. The lobby was empty, save for a late-night doorman who greeted them with wide eyes.

"Are you okay? Sir? Do you need an ambulance?"

"He's fine." Maddie passed him a couple of folded bills. "You don't even remember seeing us."

Maddie took Lionel up to the room, got him undressed, and sat him on the edge of the tub while she ran warm water. He tried to process things, sorting a hundred questions into some semblance of coherent order before he could give them voice, while she held a gauze pad to a brown plastic bottle.

"This is Bactine," she told him, "and it's going to hurt. A lot."

She pressed the pad to the ragged wound on his chest. She wasn't lying. He hissed through gritted teeth as the antiseptic sizzled like cooking oil against his skin.

"We're going to have to watch these bites," she said. "You do *not* want to know what those things put in their mouths."

"Yeah, speaking of?"

"Ghouls," Maddie replied, as offhandedly as if she were discussing the weather. "Bottom-feeders. They're . . . sort of parasites, I guess? They eat carrion, mostly. Dead humans. Live ones if they can, but mostly they scavenge for corpses. So they live where humans live. *Under* where humans live."

Lionel told her what he had seen, what he had learned. He wished he had more to offer.

"No, this is good," she said. "Now we know there's more than one soul collector out there. Don't know what he's *doing* with them, but we know what to look for."

"We also know he's got a boss, somebody he answers to. Everything he did for the Poe manuscript—stealing it, covering the trail—it wasn't for his own benefit. So . . . how'd you do that thing? With the key."

Maddie's gaze went distant. She looked to the window, as if she could see beyond the drawn shade, and shook her head.

"That was a mistake."

"You saved my life."

"Lionel . . . I'm in a lot of trouble here."

He reached out and took her hands in his. Squeezing gently as he looked her in the eyes.

"Then let me help," he said. "I'm not leaving, okay? I'm not walking away, no matter how tough it gets. We're in this together."

He watched her fight with herself, a war raging behind her stormy eyes. Eventually she beat herself down enough for one side to wave a white flag. Then she spoke.

"Hekate. Do you know that name?"

He did, but only vaguely. Something from mythology, something from Shakespeare, fragments of forgotten trivia.

"She's a goddess, right?"

"No," Maddie said. "She's a Titan. The Titans were here *before* the gods. Before anything in the universe. And they're all dead now, except for her. She's the queen of magic. The mother of witches. And she was my teacher."

Lionel's eyebrows lifted. "Damn. You did say you learned from the best."

"I did. And . . ."

She pulled her hands away from his, turned her back on him, and paced to the bathroom window. She gave herself a sidelong look in the mirror.

"God, it's so long ago, I almost wonder how much I really remember and how much I invented after the fact. We do that, you know? Remember things the way we want, not how they really happened. Anyway. I was married once."

"Bad divorce?"

"He wounded me. Betrayed me. Slept around behind my back. I wanted to hurt him. I wanted to hurt him more than I wanted anything in the world. More than breathing. So I made a very, very bad mistake."

She turned to face Lionel. Pinpricks of blood glistened in the corners of her eyes.

"I prayed to my mother," she said, "for the power to claim my rightful vengeance. And she gave it to me."

"Maddie? What did you do?"

"Something unforgivable. When I came to my senses and realized . . ." She squeezed her eyes shut. "I was furious. I was furious at Hekate for granting my prayers. Furious at myself for what I'd done. I had to leave. I couldn't face her, or my sisters. I had to go out into the world and find some semblance of . . . I don't know. Penance? Forgiveness? Eventually I learned there wasn't any to be found. The only thing out there was me. The one thing I couldn't run away from."

"Hey." Lionel stood up. He touched her arm. She flinched away from him. "Hey, whatever you did, *nothing* is unforgivable—"

"I have been running for a very long time, Lionel." She eyed him, uncertain. "You do know that, right? You know I'm older than I look. You have to have figured it out by now."

He knew. He had known for a while now. He'd been shoving the evidence into the back of his mental closet, blinding himself so he wouldn't have to consider the implications, but it was time to lay all the cards on the table.

"When I was pulling you out of the tunnel, after the alligator," he said, "you told me it takes a hundred years to learn how to do what you did. You were delirious, and I wanted to chalk it up to that, but then I met your buddy Xiulang—"

"Not my buddy."

"—and she just about came out and spilled the beans. And on that note, if she's in her early twenties, I'll eat my socks. Then I got to thinking. About Melpomene."

Maddie tilted her head. "What about her?"

"You said that every Muse claims to be the 'first of her sisters,' except for one—what's her name?"

"Polyhymnia."

"Right. And Melpomene said she's changed since the industrial revolution, not in a good way. I didn't pick up on it right then, seeing as I was a little freaked out and disoriented, but later I realized what was bugging me about that. You didn't know about Polyhymnia changing. And there's only one way that could be."

He held her gaze and dug for the courage to voice the truth.

"Because," he said, "the last time you spoke to her was *before* the industrial revolution. You're at least two hundred years old."

She gave him a slow, sad smile. The ruby tears glimmered in the corners of her eyes.

"More like three thousand," she said.

"Years."

"Years," she echoed. "I was born in Greece, decades before the Trojan War. I did tell you the truth about coming from a town called Athens."

"But not about your name."

"No. Obviously, it's not Madison. I just . . . well, I really liked *Splash*, so I've been using it for a while now. And technically it is. I mean, that's the name on my driver's license, just not—"

"Maddie," Lionel said, "you don't have to tell me anything you don't want to tell me."

She nodded, swallowed, and looked to the mirror. She met his eyes there, in the glass.

"Medea," she said. "My name is Medea."

Forty-Four

Maddie dabbed at Lionel's cheek with a damp, warm washcloth, clearing away spatters of dried blood. His skin shone through, bit by bit, as the cloth turned russet red. She had splashed some water on her face and washed her budding tears down the sink. Her sharp cheeks had a glow now, like alabaster, as she gently steered the subject.

"Funny thing is," she told him, "becoming immortal isn't nearly as hard as it sounds. Some gods will just *give* it to you. Y'know, as a reward or a punishment. Mostly a punishment."

Three thousand years. He was still trying to wrap his head around it.

"You've seen . . ." He peered at her, as if trying to glimpse the truth beneath the face she wore. "Everything. You've seen everything."

"Not *everything*. Though I did see the Beatles play at Shea Stadium back in '65."

"Good concert?"

She winced at the memory. "Sucked. The whole crowd screamed from start to finish, couldn't hear a thing, and they ended the show after half an hour. But still, saw it. Let's see . . . I was at the Chicago World's Fair in '93—1893, I mean. Marched with Madge Breckinridge in Kentucky in . . . 1918, I want to say. Around then."

"Who?" Lionel asked.

"Seriously? Breckinridge? The suffragette? I was *big* into the suffragette thing. You can probably understand why. I mean, make a Venn diagram, label one circle 'human history' and the other 'times when it really sucked to be a woman,' and those circles mostly overlap."

She paused, distant for a moment, and tapped the side of her head.

"Live long enough, and this is what you end up with. Trivia. Bits and pieces of standout moments in a long river of nothing much. And the older you get, the less relevant any of it becomes. The best musical performance I ever saw was in the early 1300s—couldn't even tell you the year now. A Frenchman named Courtemanche. Made a vielle sound like an angel weeping. Never been equaled, before or since."

Lionel shook his head. "Never heard of him."

"Exactly. Nobody has. He lived and died in obscurity, and now he only exists in a little smudge of my memory. Y'know, I see the way you're looking at me now. Like I should be this grand witness to history, some . . . repository of ancient wisdom." She lifted a hand, shrugged, and let it fall. "I'm just me. I can tell you what I do know. Best time and place in history to be alive? Right here, right now."

She leaned over the rim of the tub and pulled the lever. Water splashed into the basin. She pushed the lever and cut off the flow.

"Look at that. Hot, clean water, as much as you want, whenever you want. You have no idea how amazing that is. I promise, you don't even know. Also, there isn't shit all over the street."

"You mean," he said, "literal—"

"Literal shit. For most of human civilization. I swear, if you could get in a time machine and go back to, I don't know, Victorian England? You would be begging to come home the second you got a good whiff of that place. Indoor plumbing and personal hygiene are amazing innovations."

Lionel tilted his head, studying her. "So, you're immortal. Does that mean *nothing* can kill you?"

"If only. No. I'm still flesh and blood, same as you. I just don't age, and I mostly don't get sick. Like, not *sick* sick. Immortality didn't do a damn thing for my hay fever. For that, I take Claritin. And thank you again, modern science."

He could feel her edging around the subject, the silent elephant in the room. Animated and bright-eyed again as long as she wasn't talking about one specific part of her past. The part she was still running away from.

"Tell me about Hekate," he said.

Maddie didn't answer right away. She tilted her head back. The lights over the bathroom mirror caught in her eyes, tiny round orbs like white-hot moons. She curled her arms around herself, hugging tight.

"She is the mother of darkness, the goddess of the crossroads, the queen of the night." Maddie's shoulder gave a little shiver, almost sensual, as she spoke. "Key bearer. Light bringer. When she feels inclined, she sends her faithful gifts. Whispers, secrets, nightmares, dreams."

"I'm . . . not sure why I'd want a goddess who sent me nightmares."

She gave him a little lopsided smile, her eyes wistful.

"Nightmares can tell you what you're ignoring while you're awake. The problems you need to fix. She isn't always easy to serve, but . . ." She frowned, hunting for an analogy. "Have you ever had a mentor who pushed you to excel? Really pushed you, not strictness for the sake of strictness, but because she wanted you to be the very best you could be?"

Lionel caught a fragment of warm memory. He hadn't thought of her in years. "My journalism professor at Northwestern. She rode me harder than anyone in her class; I thought she just didn't like me. Then one day, she took me aside and told me why. She said I was one of her only students with real career potential. 'Lionel,' she told me, 'you're graduating my course as a real journalist, or you're not graduating at all.'"

"You get it," Maddie said.

"I swear, the day I turned in a project and got an actual smile and a 'good job' out of her, I felt like the champion of the world."

"You definitely get it. My lady has her moments. She can be capricious, when she feels inclined. She has her bouts of dark humor. She taunts, she teases." Maddie hugged herself a little tighter. The light orbs glimmered in her eyes like moonlight on water. "And she loves. So fiercely, so sweetly."

"So why did you leave?"

The glimmer faded. Her head bowed, the reflection slipping from her eyes, and her arms slowly fell to her sides as her shoulders slumped.

"After . . . the things I did, the way I misused the power she gave me, I couldn't face her again. So I ran. I ignored her call, and I ran. You have to understand, I swore myself to her. I promised her my life. My soul. You don't break a deal with Hekate. Of all the forces in the universe, she's the last you *ever* want to betray. So that just made it worse."

Her gaze trailed across the bathroom window, the closed drape. She wore her anxiety in the faint creases of her brow.

"My sisters, her other daughters, pursued me for years. Decades. Centuries. You don't know how exhausting it was. Then I crossed paths with Regina Dunkle. You have to understand, she's . . . old."

"Considering you're celebrating your three thousandth birthday—"

"*Older.* I mean, born in a cave, first shaman of her tribe. That old. She told me she was a vizier to a pharaoh, once, and I believe her. Anyway, she had left Hekate, too; I still don't know why—she won't discuss it—but she found the secret to making herself invisible."

Their phone calls, Regina's threats—it all made sense now. "She won't teach you the trick, but she'll share it. So you're safe from Hekate as long as Regina wants you to be."

"That's right," she said. "And in return, I do . . . well, whatever she tells me to. And here we are."

"Maddie, this isn't right. Regina treats you like a slave."

She clenched her teeth. "I *am* her slave."

"She said you can walk away whenever you want."

Maddie's glare almost pushed Lionel back a step. He felt her eyes bore into him like a pair of heat lamps.

"And what's my alternative, huh? Tell me, please, I'd love to hear your amazing insight. Where am I going to go?" She threw her hands in the air. "This is *her city*, Lionel. As much as a goddess 'lives' anywhere, New York *belongs* to Hekate. She likes it here. If I leave Regina, she'll find me in a heartbeat. I'm already on a ticking clock. That key I used tonight, to pull you out of the ghoul nest? Hekate gave it to me. It was my initiation present. There's no damn chance she didn't sense me firing it up, which means it's only a matter of time before she sends her coven into the streets or comes hunting me herself."

Her hands fell. Her anger faded, spent. She slumped back against the bathroom wall and let her eyes fall shut.

"I'm stuck," she said. "I've got nowhere to go."

"What's the worst that can happen?" Lionel asked. "I mean, if she did find you, what would she do to you? Kill you?"

Maddie opened one eye. She stared at him.

"You don't get it."

"Then help me to understand."

"I broke every vow I ever made. Trampled on my responsibilities, my oaths. I'm a failure. A disgrace. I'm not running to escape being punished. I'm not afraid that she would hurt me."

She closed her eyes again.

"I'm afraid that she would forgive me. Because I'm not worthy of her love. I'm not worthy of anyone's love."

Lionel moved close. He reached out and took her hands. This time, she didn't flinch away.

"That's not true," he said.

She let him pull her close, folding his arms around her. She rested her head against his shoulder. They stayed that way for a while, quiet, swaying from side to side, slow-dancing to the sound of cars on the street outside the window.

"If you leave," she said, "I'll understand."

He ran his fingers through her curls.

"I'm still here," he said.

He was still there in the morning as the first rays of dawn glowed soft against the bedroom shades. She was still there, too. They embraced, curled against each other, stretched like cats under the warm and tangled sheets. She pushed herself up and took him by the hand. He followed her into the bathroom as he rubbed the sleep from his eyes.

The warm spray of the shower pounded life back into their muscles as they embraced, wreathed in a billow of steam. Lionel leaned in and kissed her, long and slow.

"See?" she told him. "Best time to be alive."

"Y'know," he said, "I've been accused of chasing *younger* women. You broke my track record."

"Mmm, sure, but with age comes experience." She winked at him. "I know tricks."

"I think you showed me some of those the other night."

She reached for a washcloth and held it under the warm spray, soaking it through.

"Oh, just wait. Case in point, here's something that was very popular back in the proverbial day, but I guarantee you've never read about it in a history book."

A little shiver rippled along his skin as she reached around his shoulders, the washcloth slowly trailing down his spine. She whispered something in his ear.

"Was . . . was that Greek?" he said. "I have no idea what you just said."

"There's no direct English translation. Let me show you instead."

She showed him. Later, after they'd cleaned up and found their clothes, he was still a little wobbly on his feet.

"I've been thinking," he said. "Not that I'm doing a great job at the moment."

Maddie perched on the edge of the rumpled bedspread and pulled on a pair of socks. She paused, pantomimed licking her finger, and drew a tick mark in the air. "Victory," she stage-whispered.

"Do you think Dergwyn will admit her pack didn't actually manage to kill me last night?"

"Hard to say. Ghouls aren't exactly known for their trustworthiness. Comes from being born opportunists. They'll break a deal at the drop of a hat, if there's something in it for them. Which is why anyone with any sense doesn't make deals with them. I wonder why *he* did."

"You said they live underground, right?" Lionel buttoned up his shirt and checked his hair in the hallway mirror. "We know that's how he gets around, too. Which doesn't make sense; I've seen him up close. He's a monster, but he doesn't *look* like one. All he'd have to do is put on a pair of sunglasses, and he could travel aboveground like anybody else. Nobody would give him a second glance."

Maddie cast a baleful glance at the floorboards.

"It's not him. He's hiding something down there."

"We've got a lot of ground to cover, and not much time," Lionel said. "Especially if blue eyes finds out I survived last night. He knows who I am. Probably knows everything about me by now. You're not going to like this, but . . . I think we need to bring in some outside help."

Forty-Five

The news cycle never stopped rolling. Brianna navigated the bustling newsroom floor with a cup of coffee in one hand, half a bagel tucked in a napkin in the other, and her phone pressed to her ear. She'd been trying to get to her office for twenty minutes now, and every five feet marked another plea for her attention.

"The graphics are good," she said to a designer, leaning over his chair and eyeing his monitor. Then she turned her attention back to her phone call. "No, the *graphics*. The *optics* are bad. I'm talking to my— No, listen, Morty, Lionel is our ace reporter, okay? The studio needs to be standing behind him right now, weird as that may—"

She paused. Karen was standing by her office door. The admin bounced on her heels, waving frantically. Brianna jogged past the last few desks like a runner crossing the finish line at a marathon.

"Take one of these from me," she said.

Karen grabbed both the coffee and the bagel, navigating them over to Brianna's desk.

"Wrong choice," she sighed. "You were supposed to take the phone with the lawyer on it."

Karen pointed at her desk phone. "Call from Lionel," she whispered. "He says it's urgent."

"No, I'm sure he's— Hey, Morty, have to go, got a call on my other line."

She hung up her cell and dropped into her chair. It rocked, groaning on a loose spring.

"I hate my life."

"You got another call from the police an hour ago," Karen said. "I took a message."

"Yeah, and Legal is on my ass about it. They want to know why Lionel hasn't gone in for an interview yet, and why I'm 'hiding' him. I don't even know where he *is*."

Karen wriggled her hands at the desk phone. Brianna snatched up the receiver and punched the hold button.

"Asshole."

"Hey," Lionel said, "is this a bad time?"

"Oh, no, it's peachy. CPD hasn't put out a warrant for your arrest. Yet. Except the longer this drags on, the more it looks like you didn't leave the state so much as *flee* the state. Considering they've got a dead reporter, no suspects, and you were the last person to see him alive, you *really* need to deal with this. Where are you calling from? I can barely hear you. Please say the airport. Please say the airport and that you're on the next flight back to Chicago."

"I need your help, Bri."

Brianna squinted at the phone. "What is this? You never call me Bri."

"I'm in trouble. Serious trouble. I mean, bigger than the Chicago thing. And I'm on a story. You know . . . we never really talked about my past. Not in detail. But you know I'm an orphan, right?"

"Sure," she said, not following.

"He's here, Brianna. The man who killed my mother is in New York. That's why I can't leave yet."

She put the receiver to her chest and looked at Karen.

"Give me a little privacy, okay?"

Karen shut the door on the way out. Brianna squared herself in her chair, pulled over her keyboard in case she needed to make notes, and put the receiver back to her ear.

"Talk to me, Lionel."

"I can't explain everything over the phone. Some of it . . . You have to see it to believe it, okay? I need you to come to New York."

"I can't just drop everything and—"

"Please," Lionel said. "I wouldn't ask if I wasn't desperate. It's an hour-and-a-half flight, okay? You'll be back at your desk by tomorrow afternoon, I promise."

She took a slow, deep breath. Steadying herself. The man was amazing and infuriating by turns. They'd loved each other, then they'd hated each other, and when the dust of their relationship settled, they'd ended up something like best friends. She knew her answer before it reached her lips.

"I'm on my way."

"Okay, write this down," Lionel said. "Fly in to JFK, and take the AirTrain to the Jamaica stop. From there, you want the E train to Court Square; then transfer to the number-seven line. That'll bring you right to Grand Central Terminal. We'll be waiting for you there."

She frowned, rattling keys as she took his instructions down. "Who's 'we'? And why don't I just grab a taxi from JFK and save a lot of trouble?"

"Because a cab will run you at least sixty bucks, and I doubt the newsroom's going to reimburse you. Also, with afternoon traffic, the train's probably faster."

⟋⟍

Brianna's voice echoed over a tinny receiver. More of a crude walkie-talkie, dangling from an exposed box of cables by a half-stripped wire.

"Yeah, okay, fine. I'll let you know when I'm close." She sighed again. "You better not be jerking me around, Lionel."

A gnarled hand clutched the receiver. The creature squatted on the dank tunnel stone with bare feet, his nails yellowed and broken. A filthy T-shirt and sweats held up by a belt of scavenged rope draped his ragged form.

"This means the world to me," the ghoul said with Lionel's voice.

"We're gonna have a talk when I get there," Brianna said. "A *serious* talk."

She hung up on him. The ghoul dropped the receiver and looked back over his shoulder, distended jaw dangling slack. His eyes, glittering opal in the dark, begged for approval.

Dergwyn stood behind him. A tattered parasol with broken ribs dangled over her shoulder, and she twirled it like a graveyard fashionista. She barked at him, a string of growling yips. He broke into a maniacal grin, yipped back, and loped off into the darkness on all fours. Distant howls rang off the maintenance-tunnel walls. Traffic rumbled on the street above their heads, oblivious.

She looked to the blue-eyed man. "Happy now?"

"I'd be happier if you'd done your job right in the first place."

She frowned and turned on him. "You didn't tell me he had a *friend.*"

"The friend in question was a wild card. Didn't know what she was capable of." He shrugged. "Now I know."

"Do you know how I became princess?"

"Your daddy was the king?"

She poked her fingernail against his chest. "No. The title isn't passed down. Any ghoul can become pack leader. All you have to do is fight for it. All you have to do is kill, and eat, anyone else who wants it. And keep killing. And keep eating. If a member of my pack challenges me, anytime, anyplace, I *put them down.*"

He rolled his eyes. "Sounds exhausting."

"I stay well fed." She leaned closer, fixing him with her gemstone glare, and lowered her voice. "If my pack suspected me of being a coward, they would tear me to pieces. And they'd be right to. A coward cannot lead."

"It feels like you're taking a roundabout approach to accusing me of something, Princess. Maybe you should come right out and say what you mean."

His hand shot out and clamped around her throat, suddenly squeezing like a steel vise.

"Or better yet," he said, "you can keep your bitchy little mouth *shut* and remember who's in charge here. I'm not down here with your permission, Dergwyn. You're down here with mine."

"You're hurting me," she rasped.

"I'm aware of that."

He gave her a shove and let go, sending her sprawling to the tunnel floor. She landed on her parasol and snapped it.

"My work is almost done," he told her. "Stay the course, stay in line, and I *might* let you keep your crown and your pack when I'm finished."

A quarter mile away, in Lower Manhattan, Maddie walked the streets alone. They'd decided to split their efforts and try to save time: Lionel would go back to Lana Taylor's apartment, hoping to see if any clues had been left behind, while Maddie secured the extra help they needed.

She still wasn't happy about it.

She followed the crowded sidewalk along Grand Street, where Little Italy faded and Manhattan's Chinatown began. There were no borders marking the demarcation line, no official CHINATOWN STARTS HERE signs, just a slow shift as the awnings turned bright red and gold. She turned onto a side street, traffic crawling along a two-lane road only wide enough for one car and a half, and walked in the shadow of lime-green fire escapes and Mandarin signs. Off the tourist trail, half of them didn't bother with an English translation at all.

She pushed through a faded doorway the color of olives, into a dimly lit shop, and took a deep breath. The air smelled like chamomile and fresh parsley. Glass jars lined the tight walls, labeled with Chinese characters in felt marker on ragged strips of tape. Inside were dried leaves, fuzzy clumps of herbs, small piles of amber-colored shards. Wen Xiulang looked up from her counter at the back of the shop. A thin plume of smoke, drifting up from the lacquered curve of an incense stand, slid along her chin and framed her cheek in the gloom.

"Look who's all bright-eyed and bushy-tailed," she said. "That's odd, though—your hands are empty."

Maddie flicked the lock on the shop door and turned the sign to read CLOSED. "Why's that odd?"

"I was just thinking, seeing as I saved your life—twice now—you might have brought me a thank-you present."

"Here's your present." She took a deep breath and squeezed her arms against her sides. "I need your help."

"My first thought is to jump in the air, clap my hands, and squeal like I was a child again," Xiulang said. "My second is to get my phone out and ask you to repeat yourself while I get a good recording for posterity."

"I appreciate your restraint."

"But," she said, "for you to come here . . . it's bad, isn't it?"

Maddie nodded. "It's pretty bad."

"I take no pleasure in your pain," Xiulang said, "only your severe discomfort. Lines must be drawn."

"You are decorous, as always."

Maddie approached the counter. She held up the tiny disk, with its windows of blue light, tiny human shadows floating past in the maelstrom. Xiulang's eyes widened as Maddie set it down between them.

"There are more of them, somewhere in the city. I'm hoping that if we figure out the where, we'll figure out the why."

The herbalist dived under her counter. She came up wearing a head-set of metal and glass, buckling leather straps behind her head to fix it in place. It resembled a vision-testing machine at an optometrist's office, with rows of thick, owlish lenses over her eyes. She flicked tiny metal levers at the sides of her face and slid the lenses of colored glass up and down while she studied the disk.

"Fascinating," she murmured. "A disgusting abomination, but fascinating. It's like . . . a battery."

"A battery powered by human souls." Maddie nudged the disk with the tip of her fingernail. "Can we get them out?"

"Not safely. Not yet. Need to know more."

Xiulang flicked her lenses again. She looked up at Maddie, one eye sheathed under an oval of red glass, one eye in green.

"I'm thinking we should employ a water compass."

Maddie snapped her fingers. "With a sympathetic sample."

"And the Knot of Three Branches for cross-astral cancellation!" Xiulang chirped, growing animated now, as Maddie mirrored her excitement.

"Like in Prague!"

Xiulang slapped the side of her headset. The last row of lenses flicked upward, baring her eyes. She hesitated, her rare smile frozen on her lips.

"I missed you," she said.

Maddie's gaze dropped to the counter between them.

"I missed you, too." She waved a hand, taking in the shop, the city. "It's just . . . hard, you know?"

"Only as hard as you make it. Come. Let's go on a field trip. We only have about two hundred years of gossip to catch up on."

While Xiulang rummaged in her drawers, picking out bits and pieces—a lacquered wooden dish, an iron needle, thin strips of parchment—Maddie checked her phone. Lionel was calling.

"Hey," he said, "I've got some good news. Blue eyes didn't have time to finish searching Lana Taylor's apartment when we walked in on him. He trashed her computer, but she kept backups. And made copies."

"She made a copy of the Poe manuscript?"

"Oh, yeah," Lionel said. "I'm looking right at it."

Forty-Six

Maybe it was his close encounter last night—the bite wound on his chest still ached, buried under a fresh layer of gauze—but Lionel felt like a ghoul himself as he returned to Lana Taylor's apartment. No one had reported the woman missing; no one had come to check up on her. Her corpse still lay where the blue-eyed man had killed her. Her shriveled, prune-faced corpse hadn't attracted a single buzzing fly—like whatever he'd done to her, draining her life away, had left her meat too toxic to lay eggs in. Her open eyes, winter white and glassy, seemed to follow Lionel as he prowled across her living room.

He poked through shelves, opened book covers to see if anything fell out, searching for a clue. He mostly found old, crumpled receipts and expired coupons. Her tiny office was a disaster; her killer had smashed her computer, crumpling the plastic shell like he'd gone after it with a baseball bat. A computer-forensics expert might be able to get something out of the wreckage, but that was miles away from his skill set. Lionel bent low to check a cubbyhole. Nothing but a clutter of hardbacks, college-level dissertations on the art of handwriting analysis, half of them with Lana's name on the spine.

He paused. A little black lump stood out in the corner of his vision.

It was a USB drive. A strip of Scotch tape held the thumb-size shell to the underbelly of Lana's desk. He peeled the tape away and pocketed the stick.

He didn't like leaving Lana's body behind. It felt wrong, disrespect-ful. On the other hand, he'd been picked up by the NYPD for finding a murder victim while trespassing once already this week. Twice, and not even the best lawyer in town would be able to keep him out of a holding cell. So he left, swift and quiet. Catching her killer would be the best thing he could do for her.

He made his way back to 24 Connect, the round-the-clock PC café he'd used when he first came to town. Fourteen bucks bought him an hour of access time; two dollars more and they gave him a lukewarm can of Cherry Coke. He grabbed a computer in the back corner of the room and slotted the USB stick.

Lana was thorough. She backed up everything from her income-tax papers—going back twelve years, no less—to a few thousand university emails. A folder marked FREELANCE looked promising, until Lionel found another sixty subfolders nestled underneath. He sorted the files by date. The most recent folder, modified just yesterday, was labeled WADE DAWSON—EAP ANALYSIS.

Inside were a handful of image files—maybe a dozen in all—orga-nized in numerical order. He opened the first one. A photograph of a yellowed and brittle page filled the screen, with elegant handwriting in neat, careful lines.

The Strange Inquest of Ernest Valdemar, the underlined title read. *By Edgar A. Poe.*

"All right," Lionel murmured to the screen. "Let's find out what why people are killing to get their hands on this thing."

He opened a web browser and went shopping. Three clicks later he'd purchased an e-book copy of *The Complete Works of Edgar Allan Poe*. He kept it open so he could read the two stories, the handwritten draft and the final version, side by side. The title had changed to *The Facts in the Case of M. Valdemar* on the way to publication, but beyond that, the first paragraphs were almost identical beyond a changed word here and there. Poe's whirling, crisp pen laid out the same basic story about how his good friend, the eponymous Valdemar, was fading from a terminal illness. At Poe's suggestion, Valdemar agreed to an experiment: he would be placed in a "mesmeric sleep" before his final heartbeat, to learn if the arts of hypnosis could overcome death itself.

A pair of doctors, named only by their initials, clustered around the dying man's bedside as Poe made his mesmeric passes and induced the trance. Lionel could understand why people had taken the story as a genuine account: it was written in a blunt, if gruesome, style, recounting Valdemar's slow collapse. The ichor beneath his eyes, the rattle of his rotten lungs, the putrid odor of a dying man's final breaths. His condition froze, somewhere on the threshold of life and death, suspended in place by a hypnotic cocoon. And as Poe asked him to speak, Ernest Valdemar cried out from his deathbed.

"For God's sake!" the published account read, *"put me to sleep or— or, quick! —waken me! —quick! —I say to you that I am dead!"*

This was where the story changed.

The version that horrified Poe's readers in 1845, and that had been in print ever since, ended in a storm of gore. The author released his helpless friend—over Valdemar's desperate, frenzied chant of *"Dead! Dead!"*—and as the trance broke, he looked on in horror while the man's body crumbled to pieces. In the space of a minute, Ernest Valdemar putrefied and decayed, leaving nothing behind but bedsheets stained with liquefied rot.

Lionel thought back to his first meeting with Regina Dunkle, about her eagerness to read the original ending of the story. And the letter she'd shown him, the warning from Poe's friend: *"For the love of G-d, man, at least change that ending. Some stories shouldn't be told."*

"And you ended up going with the one where the guy literally melts," Lionel muttered to the screen. He opened the final photograph on the USB stick.

"I see a cold and Stygian shore!" the mesmerized Valdemar cried. Poe's handwriting was strained here, cramped, as though he was writing

faster and faster. *"I ride upon black water. I must row —quick! —row! —quick! The waters are deep, and churning, and I am not alone. There are men chained and drowning beneath me. They turn their faces up toward my boat, straining with hands that cannot touch the surface!"*

I made an endeavor to compose my patient. His arm had lost all heat, all semblance of life, feeling like whale-fat under my fingertips as I pressed the mesmeric passes. Dr. F— proposed we wake him. I gathered my resolve but M. Valdemar's tongue gave a loathsome twitch and squeezed between his drawn lips. He spoke again in that hideous cat-screech voice:

"There are laughing gods upon the shore! They are reveling upon the shore! They are thirsting upon the shore! Fauns and satyrs dance in the high white mist, and I have seen what they dine upon! My boat moves closer! —closer!"

My hands moved in the mesmeric passes. I kneaded his cold, limp arm to impress the necessary signs and patterns. Dr. F— implored me now to wake him and I sped my exertions. I had to free my patient before he reached that terrible shore. But then M. Valdemar spoke once more, not a cry, not a screech, but the cold and steady voice of a man thirty years his junior.

"Do not wake me. I must reach the shore."

Mr. L— shoved past his colleague, his face a frozen mask of terror, and rained savage blows across the sleeping man's face. "Wake him! Wake him!" he exhorted. He shook M. Valdemar's shoulders, gripping his soiled bedclothes in both fists, as I struggled to break the mesmeric trance.

My friend's eyes opened. He sat up upon the mattress as if guided by invisible hands. He rose the same way, his movements spare and lifeless, his limbs those of a puppet dangling from invisible strings.

Dr. F— and Mr. L— watched in astonishment. As did I, knowing my experiment had been a success! We had proved the power of mesmerism and triumphed over the sin of death. My friend had returned to us alive and well. And M. Valdemar turned to me as if he could pluck my thoughts from the air.

"Arrogant fool," he said. "I am DEAD.*"*

M. Valdemar walked from the room, alone, and Mr. L— fell into a faint.

Lionel stared at the screen. The café had gone silent around him.

He checked the folder, looking to see if there was a page he'd missed. Some coda, a final piece of the puzzle. He didn't know what he'd been expecting. Some grand revelation, maybe. A clue leading to a buried fortune. Something worth killing for.

He was adrift. No closer to an answer than he'd been since he landed. There was *something* here; people had been tortured and murdered over these pages, and it had happened for a reason. He just couldn't find it. He felt like he was holding a treasure map, but he couldn't tell where the *X* had been marked. The mountains and valleys on the page, the peaks and loops of Poe's pen, didn't match any land he knew.

"I'm looking right at it," he said, talking to Maddie on his phone.

"And?"

"And I'm not sure." He squinted at the photograph. "Maybe the valuable thing isn't the actual story. Maybe it's something hidden on the paper itself."

"Like, written in invisible ink?"

"Sure," Lionel said. "Spies were using lemon juice to write invisible messages back during the Revolutionary War. People knew that trick long before the 1800s. That's what I learned in the Boy Scouts, anyway."

"You were a Boy Scout?"

"Briefly," he said.

"Could also be something on the backs of the pages," Maddie mused, "something Lana didn't scan. Do me a favor and send copies to my phone? I want to give it a read. I might recognize something you don't. Besides, it should keep Regina happy for a while. Meet me at Xiulang's shop?"

When Lionel arrived, the door to the herbalist's shop was closed and locked tight, no lights burning inside. He knocked, then he waited. He stood under the tiny green awning, doing his best to stay out of the flow of traffic. People choked the sidewalk in both directions, an endless hustle, the blood in the city's veins. Horns blared as a delivery truck muscled its way down the too-tight street. A little farther up, a red-faced man was in a shouting match with his taxi driver; they were hurling Mandarin at each other like daggers.

The city was a great and lumbering beast, armored in granite and chrome. Unstoppable, titanic. It wore the scars of past battles, but its muscles and bone always knit back stronger. All the same, now Lionel saw the dangers lurking under the surface. He'd seen an army of ghosts unleashed in a ballroom. He'd witnessed a monster in the tunnels beneath the city streets, and a nightclub infested by cannibals. This entire city was suspended on a web of nightmares, fragile and brittle as glass. Anyone could step the wrong way at any moment, break the strand under their feet, and plummet into the hungry dark.

After all, he had. He'd just been lucky enough to survive.

Now that he knew the truth, waiting around gave him time to ask the inevitable question: *What now?* His instincts told him to blow the lid open. Take everything he'd seen and learned, and tell the world.

Sure, he thought, *and they'll find a nice cell with padded walls to put me in.* It was ironic; he'd spent his entire career debunking quacks and frauds, exposing claims of the supernatural. Now he'd seen the real thing, and he'd be run out of town on a rail if he tried going public. *I could put an actual ghost on live television, and they'd say I did it with CGI. People believe what they want. Always have, always will.*

He could hear Brianna's voice in his head, that constant refrain: "Your job is to *report* the story, not to *be* the story."

Usually, she was right. But he wasn't entirely sure that was his job anymore. In the last few days, he'd seen and experienced things that he couldn't have imagined. These people thronging the sidewalk, working through another ordinary day, had no idea what kind of danger they were in. But he did.

Now he had to figure out what to do about it.

He glanced left. Maddie and Xiulang were coming up the sidewalk, and they didn't look happy. The herbalist clutched a lacquered wooden tray in her cupped hand. In the tray, a twist of paper inked with swirling symbols floated on a tiny layer of water, bobbing as they walked.

"Everything okay?" he asked.

Xiulang passed the tray to Maddie and fished out a ring of keys, unlocking the door. She waved them both inside and locked it behind them.

"Not remotely," she said.

Forty-Seven

Blue light rippled behind the windows of the steel disk and cast a cold sapphire glow across the darkened shop. Maddie laid down the disk on the herbalist's counter. On the other side, Xiulang set down its identical twin.

"There are more of them," Maddie said to Lionel. "We found this one a block away, inside another disguised junction box."

"Outside a *hospice*," Xiulang hissed. "He's planting them at sites of misery and loss. Like dream catchers, for the souls of the dead."

"Dead catchers," Maddie said.

"It gets worse," Xiulang added.

"Oh," Lionel said, "of course it does. Please go on."

Maddie's fingernail traced the contour of one of the disks. "Xiulang noticed this. See these grooves here?"

Lionel leaned in. He hadn't spotted it before: a needle-thin track on the outer face of the disk. Maddie flipped it over. On the reverse side, it sported a raised ridge.

"They're designed to snap together," she said. "The ridges are engraved, laser cut, with almost microscopic seals. Designed for . . . conductivity, basically."

Lionel's eyebrows tightened. He got down low, eye level with the disk, trying to make them out.

"And you'd want to do that why, exactly?"

"Because these aren't just for storage." Xiulang took a dead catcher in each hand, holding them an inch apart. "Build enough critical mass, enough soul energy in one place, it activates their intended purpose."

She united the steel disks with a metallic *snap*.

Lionel felt the change before he saw it. As the tiny shop bathed in blue light, a tremor passed through his stomach. It shivered down through his bladder, down to the soles of his feet.

"What was—"

Maddie held up a finger. "Wait for it. We found this out the hard way, in the alley where we tracked down the second disk."

A stagnant odor blotted out the clean, chamomile-scented air. Festering and foul, it smelled like something had crawled into the air vent and died. Roadkill festering on a hot summer day. Lionel cupped his hand over his nose and mouth.

The world changed at the corners of his vision. Something else, creeping in around the edges. He caught faint glimpses, translucent and superimposed upon the world he knew. Rusted metal, webs, jagged splinters of a human rib cage jutting from rotten soil. When he turned to look directly at the images, they vanished before his eyes could focus on them, only to come creeping back into his peripheral sight.

Something moved above his head. Something leathery and vast—

Xiulang yanked the dead catchers apart. Their sapphire light sputtered, flickering, and the phantasms vanished. A moment later the stench had gone with it. Lionel took a deep breath, drinking in the clean, tea-scented air, and blinked.

"Okay," he said, "I'm the newbie here, so help me out. What the hell just happened?"

"We thought these were batteries," Maddie said. "That's only half of it."

"It's a *doorway*," Xiulang said. "What you just saw, that was only a crack. Of course, things can still pass through a cracked door."

"A door to where?" Lionel asked. "What the hell *was* that?"

Maddie drummed her nails on the table. She took one of the dead catchers and slid the other toward Lionel.

"Let's keep these safely apart, for the moment. And to answer your question, we have no idea. Not anywhere good. The spell is fueled by the souls inside. Get enough of these things together, connected in one place at one time, well . . . you saw what two of them did."

"Link enough together," Xiulang said, "the door opens. All the way. Maybe not cleanly. Or in a way that could ever be closed again. We could be looking at a complete breach between worlds."

"And that would be . . . bad," Lionel said.

"Well, let's see," Maggie replied. "Beyond whatever lives over *there* coming over *here*—and I kinda doubt it's a world of magical love and friendship—we don't even know if the air on the other side is breathable by human beings."

"Imagine an earth like ours," Xiulang added, "but with an atmosphere made of chlorine gas. Now imagine tearing open a permanent hole to that world. In the middle of New York City."

Lionel had reached for the dead catcher closest to him. His fingertips grazed the cold steel face as Xiulang spoke. He yanked his hand away like he'd touched a hot stove.

"Jesus," Lionel breathed. "He could kill . . . *everybody*."

"He," the herbalist echoed. "What do we know about this man?"

"He's a necromancer," Maddie said, ticking off facts on her fingertips. "He enslaves and empowers the dead to fight for him. Uses a brooch of some kind—either it's a channel for his power or a relic in its own right. He's got a deal going with the city's ghoul pack, which is weird, because otherwise he seems smart, and he gets around under the city streets."

"And he killed my mother," Lionel said.

Xiulang pursed her lips. She wagged a finger at Lionel, working through her thoughts.

"That," she said, deliberating, "is no coincidence."

"Regina set this up," Maddie said. "She must have known about blue eyes, and more about Lionel's past than she let on. She's also stopped answering her phone. If we could find out why she arranged all this—"

Xiulang shook her head. "No. You're taking the wrong focus. The why we really want is at the root of the story. Lionel, *why* did he murder your mother? Who were they to one another?"

"I don't know. I don't even remember the entire night she died, and I was there. She said something to me, and then out on the road, someone picked me up, but . . ." He grimaced and pressed his knuckles to his forehead. "Something happened to me that night. But it's just *gone*. All I know is, when we confronted him, the blue-eyed man said he killed my mother in self-defense. That if he didn't do it to her, she would have done it to him."

"And what do you know about her?"

He lifted his open hands. They fell limp to his sides.

"I remember her smile. I know she loved me. I was five years old. That was all I needed to know." He glanced over Xiulang's shoulder, eyes going distant as he thought back. "Knowing what I know now, I think she was a witch. Her name was Sheila Paget. I think, anyway. When I got older, I tried tracing her back to . . . well, anywhere, and hit nothing but dead ends. No paper trail, and as far as the cops were concerned, she was a ghost. No family but me, no ID, no fingerprints on record, nothing. She appeared out of nowhere, at that commune in Michigan, just in time to die there."

"Someone must know her," Xiulang said.

"Yeah. The guy we're chasing, and he's not going to help."

Lionel paused. Another possibility occurred to him. He raced for reasons not to think about it.

Maddie caught the look on his face. "What?"

"I know . . . one person who might have something. The one person who's spent more time digging into my past than anyone."

"Who?" she asked.

"Bo Henley," Lionel said. "The man who wrote the magazine article about me. The one that ruined my life."

Maddie touched his shoulder. Her fingertip traced the curve of his neck.

"Do you know where to find him?" she asked.

⁓

He knew. He'd known for years. Lionel had looked up Bo Henley a decade ago, planning to drop in on the man and confront him. He'd canceled his plane ticket at the last minute. Then a few years later, after a binge of cheap bourbon and self-pity, Lionel came a hairbreadth from doing it all over again. It had happened like that, off and on. Most of the time he didn't think about Bo Henley at all.

When he did, usually after one too many drinks, Lionel wanted to know where he was. How he was living. If he was sleeping at night. By all accounts, he was sleeping better than Lionel, anyway. Bo had retired from the journalism game in 2008. He'd cashed in his chips for a suburban bungalow in Hoboken.

Lionel hailed a cab. He and Maddie swayed in the back seat as the old yellow clunker sailed through the Holland Tunnel and emerged into the sprawl of New Jersey under a greasy afternoon sky. The radio was tuned to a news-and-sports station, and the announcer slid effortlessly from baseball scores to the latest on a string of feared abductions—at least twenty bankers, stockbrokers, and Manhattan socialites turning up missing on the same night.

Bo's place was midway down a sleepy patch of matchbook houses, and you could see the Hudson River if you looked between his neighbors and squinted hard. The air had a salty, metallic tang, like river water mingling with distant smokestacks. Lionel tightened his hands on his knees. He'd been hungry for this confrontation for twenty years, and putting it off for just as long. He probably would have stayed that

331

course, waiting for the inevitable back-page obituary telling him about how Bo had died from some preventable disease, surrounded by family and loved ones. Then he could pretend he'd taken the high ground.

"You all right?" Maddie asked him.

He shifted in his seat, elbow propped on the rough plastic armrest of the passenger-side door, feeling the dead catcher pressing against his hip. They'd kept the two disks, Maddie taking one and Lionel taking the other. Maddie assured him they were safe so long as they didn't connect them again like they had back at Wen Xiulang's shop. He grudgingly took her word for it.

"I've pictured this going down a hundred ways," he said. "Mostly just walking up and punching the guy out. But that's . . . that's not real life, you know? That's just the kind of revenge movie that plays out in a person's head. I'm not the noble, wronged hero, and he's not an evil monster. I think that's what always kept me away in the end. The only reason I had to show up on the man's doorstep was to hurt him."

"And you don't really want to hurt him."

He had to smile at that.

"I wish I was that virtuous," he said. "The truth is, I just didn't care enough to make the effort. The wound's just about healed over. That's what I would have said, anyway, before that kid showed up at my office and tried to rip it open for me. Then Regina called me and, well . . . here we are."

"Here we are."

"It's not so bad," he said.

He reached over and rested his hand on hers.

"Met you. I'd say that makes it all worthwhile."

They got out of the cab at the edge of Bo Henley's lawn. The grass was fighting the good fight against drought and the summer heat, scraggly and yellow in spots but managing to cling on. The drone of a lawn mower competed with birdsong. They were approaching the front porch when the mower rounded the side of the house.

The years hadn't been Bo's friend. He wore a polo golf shirt stretched over a beer belly, his hair a rounded tuft ringing the back of his head.

Lionel imagined he started every morning drinking black coffee from a *World's Greatest Grandpa* mug. Judging from the spiderweb of blood-shot veins along the bulb of his nose, he might splash in a little whiskey, too. Just for the taste. He saw Lionel and Maddie and killed the mower. The motor wound down, grinding into silence.

"Bo Henley," Lionel said. More of a statement than a question.

Bo gave them a hesitant smile, uncertain, and pointed to the sten-ciled sign beside his front door. **No Solicitors.**

"Might save you some time," he said. "That includes JWs and Mormons, for the record. Selling is selling. God or magazine subscrip-tions, I ain't buying."

"I'm Lionel Page. Paget, when you knew me."

Bo had been ambling toward them. Now he stopped in his tracks. He looked Lionel up and down and rubbed his knuckles across his lips.

"This is a long time overdue," Bo said. "I was you, I would have come around and kicked my ass years ago."

Lionel shrugged. "When I wanted to, I didn't have the money or the means to track you down. When I had the money and the means, I mostly didn't want to anymore."

"Mostly."

"Mostly," Lionel said. "We need to talk. I need your help."

"Me? What can I do?"

"We found the man who did it."

It. He didn't need to specify. Bo's lips parted. His tongue tapped his uneven teeth.

"*The* man. Singular."

Lionel nodded.

"Damn it all," he said. "I was right. They said I was crazy, and all these years I was right."

Bo gestured to his front door.

"Think we'd better take this inside."

Forty-Eight

Lionel had *almost* been right. Bo took his coffee in a *World's Greatest Dad* mug. The grandkids—at least eight of them, from the pictures crowding every inch on the mantel—weren't around. Neither was the woman, Bo Henley's age, in most of the shots, the two of them smiling and clinging together like newlyweds.

Bo wore a gold band in the photographs. His hands were bare now, and his kitchen table had a single vinyl place mat.

He poured fresh and mismatched mugs for Lionel and Maddie, one white porcelain, one brick red and stamped with the logo of a long-bankrupt trucking company, and they sat down around the table. Bo was the first to talk. He cupped his hands around his mug like he needed to warm them up.

"I suppose it doesn't mean anything—what's done is done—but I never meant you any harm."

"You did plenty, though."

"I did." Bo nodded. He squeezed his coffee cup and looked Lionel in the eye. "I did. And I'm sorry."

Lionel fought a short and dirty war in his stomach. He wanted to unload on the man, to let out twenty years of frustration, to walk him through every scrap of humiliation and ache.

But there wasn't any point.

He was right. What was done was done, a long time ago. Twisting the knife wouldn't change a damn thing. It wouldn't make him feel any better; it would just make Bo feel worse. Lionel sagged in his chair and let a little of the past go. Not all of it. Just a little.

"You stuck to the facts," he said, "which is more than the tabloids did."

"Seen you, you know. On TV. My satellite dish gets the Chicago stations, so I can watch baseball." He put his hand to one side of his mouth and gave Maddie a conspiratorial look. "Don't tell my neighbors, but once a Sox fan, always a Sox fan."

"I got a firsthand taste of the power of the media when I was a kid," Lionel said. "I wanted to make up for other people's mistakes. Turn the spotlight where it belonged. Maybe do some good out there."

Bo's chapped lips curled in a tiny, wan smile. "Like one of those superhero movies, isn't it?"

"How do you figure?"

"Isn't that how those stories all go? The villain creates the hero, or the other way around, and everything comes full circle? I wrote that magazine article about you, and years later, you're a reporter yourself. If journalism was a superpower, I'd say we have a franchise here."

Lionel thought about that. Full circle.

"One man created the person who I am today," Lionel said. "And it wasn't you."

"No. Guess that's the truth of it."

"What did you mean out there?" Lionel nodded to the window, to the patch of lawn out front and the abandoned mower. "That all these years you were right?"

Bo rested his mug on his knee. He spoke slowly, weighing his words.

"You gotta understand, the story that I wrote is *not* the story that ran. See, I cut my teeth on the crime blotter at the *Trib*. I never wanted to go glossy, writing puff pieces. It just . . . kinda happened, the way lives and careers do. One day you've got dreams of being the next Truman

Capote, next thing you know, you're following Beyoncé at Fashion Week. My editor wanted me to do the Emerald Ranch retrospective—and tell the world your story—as a human-interest piece. Light on the blood and guts, just enough to make readers' mouths water."

"The Real Boy Who Lived," Maddie said.

Bo winced. "Yeah. In retrospect, I'm not proud of that, but at the time it made for a killer headline. Anyway, I got sucked in. Deep. Scoured every public record and bribed my way into a peek at the private ones, trying to reconstruct the night of the crime. Not even what the article was supposed to be about, but I just . . . I couldn't let it go. And everything I saw pointed to one conclusion: the cult-versus-cult story was a pile of crap. Those murders—fourteen women and a half dozen kids—were committed by one man, acting alone."

"Why wasn't that in your article?" Lionel asked.

"It was, in the first draft. My editor cut it. He thought I was acting like a crackpot. Suppose I was, at the time, but I knew I was right."

Bo set his coffee mug on the table and pushed his chair back.

"Come with me. Want to show you something."

Down a stubby hallway, Bo reached up and tugged a length of dangling rope. An access hatch groaned open, attic steps squealing as they touched down on the carpet. He led the way upstairs. The old wooden steps sagged under Lionel's feet.

A bare, dangling bulb clicked on, flooding the attic with pale-white light. Cardboard boxes lined every nook and cranny. They stacked up to the sharply arched rafters, some of them old and yellowed, some dressed in coats of dust and dead flies. Stark black lettering in permanent marker gave each box a name. Some were dated; others bore initials or cryptic strings of letters and digits. Bo led Lionel and Maddie to one particular box, perched waist-high on a jumble of crates at the far end of the attic. There was less dust on this one, like he came back to it every so often. This box was labeled LIONEL PAGET.

"Every story I ever broke." Bo waved a hand at the clutter. "Every note, every scrap of research. When I die, it'll probably all get tossed in the trash. This one's you."

He pulled back the cardboard lid and set it aside. Inside was a clutter of photographs, faded police reports, typed statements on strawberry-colored triplicate. Bo plucked a pocket-size spiral notebook from the top and flipped through page after page of old, almost-illegible ink.

"My notes," he explained. "You could get these spirals at the 7-Eleven, three for two bucks. It was my ritual: every new story got a new notebook. When I filed my piece, the notebook went into the box."

Lionel could feel him hedging, losing himself in nostalgia. Maddie could, too. She put a hand on her hip and frowned.

"If I wanted to learn about journalism techniques," she told him, "I'd ask Lionel. You said you knew a name."

Bo bit his bottom lip.

"A cop who worked the scene, one of the first responders . . . he had a thing for taking souvenirs."

"You mean evidence," Lionel said. "He stole evidence."

"Nothing crucial, nothing that'd swing a case one way or another. He was a magpie, that's all." Bo rummaged in the box. He looked toward Lionel but couldn't quite meet his eyes. "I found him when I was doing the article about you, and he sold me something. The thing he took from the ranch that night. I should have contacted you a long time ago. I should have given this to you. I just . . ."

"You didn't want to face me," Lionel said.

"That's about right. I'm not going to make any excuses for it. Don't have any. I'm just glad . . . well, I'm glad you're here now. This belongs to you."

He offered Lionel his find. It was a teakwood box, eight inches wide and three deep, with a tiny pewter clasp and delicate hinges. Like a simple jewelry box, or something for keepsakes.

"It belonged to your mother," Bo said.

Pressure surged in Lionel's heart. He didn't have anything of his mother's. He never had. Nothing but broken memories of the night she died. And all this time, her last treasure had been gathering dust in some washed-up reporter's attic. All these years.

"You goddamned *coward.*" Lionel's voice cracked, crumbling at the edges. Clutching the box was the only thing keeping his hands from balling into fists. "You *thief.* You fucking—"

"Lionel."

Maddie's hand was firm on his wrist, her eyes soft.

"This is more important," she said with a nod to the box. "This is your inheritance. Open it."

He took a slow, deep breath to steady himself. Then he flipped the clasp and pulled up the lid.

Inside was a handwritten note, a photograph, and a key.

Forty-Nine

The key inside the keepsake box was an antique. A skeleton key forged in old brass, about six inches long, with its handle an elaborate and scalloped fleur-de-lis design. Lionel held it up, catching light along the cold metal, and looked to Maddie. The blue-eyed man's words came back to him, clear as a bell. *She also had the hand of a goddess on her shoulder.*

"It's like yours," Lionel whispered.

"I didn't know," she said. "I swear to you, I had no idea. I parted ways with—with *her*—a very long time ago. I stopped keeping tabs on her servants once I started working for Regina."

The photograph was an old Polaroid from an instant camera, the image framed in a rectangle of glossy white plastic. From the fashion and the puffy hair, Lionel figured it was taken sometime in the late '80s. A gathering of people, maybe twelve in all, mostly women, gathered in ragged, tight rows for a group shot. He recognized his mother in the front row. She was beaming, her skin glowing, with her hands resting on her pregnant belly.

The blue-eyed man stood just behind her left shoulder.

He hadn't aged a day since. Lionel would have been mystified, but that was before he met Maddie. After all he'd seen since he'd landed in New York, a man who didn't age was low on the list of things that could still shock him. It was strange how quickly the impossible could seem as natural as breathing.

"Look," he said, touching his finger to the photograph. He didn't recognize any of the other faces, but an elderly woman down in front wore a familiar jeweled brooch on her sharp-shouldered blazer.

"Same one from the Blackstone ballroom," Maddie murmured. "He has it now."

Lionel turned the picture over. A neat, feminine hand had written, *Sisters of New Amsterdam/Festival of Olympia '86*. He wondered if it was his mother's handwriting. He ran a fingertip over the ink, aching for some kind of connection. Some kind of reunion.

He set the photograph beside the key, and unfurled the note.

Sheila, it read, *a little keepsake from happier times, to keep you warm on your travels. I wish I had good news to go with it. I've confirmed what happened when the order to scatter came down. J— came back from his exile just long enough to betray us. The miserable worm murdered M—, literally stabbed her in the back, and stole the Lapis Manalis. He tracked down K— in Ontario last week and threw her off a bridge. B— fled to Houston, and she's gone dark. I think he found her, too. J— thinks that if he can silence us all, it will save him from our queen's wrath.*

Maddie fingered an invisible brooch on her chest and murmured in Lionel's ear. "*Lapis Manalis*. Means 'stone of the manes' in Latin. It was a term for a ritual stone, sort of a . . . capstone on the gate to Hades. Land of the dead."

J— will pay for what he's done, the letter continued. *I'm organizing a war party. We will hunt him, and we will destroy him. The lady commands it. As for you, stay on the road, keep moving, be swift and silent. Our distant cousins in Michigan have a safe harbor for you, if you can make it that far. I'm keeping you on the sidelines, just in case something goes wrong. If you don't hear from me again, you know your duty.*

That said, I wouldn't worry. We will be bloody, bold, and resolute in this matter, as in all things. My love to little Lionel. Once this is all over, and we can come together as a family again, we'll see to his proper dedication before our queen. He's curious, precocious, bright-eyed . . . She's going to love him as she loves you.

There was no signature on the letter. Only a sinking, sick feeling in Lionel's stomach as he recalled the blue-eyed man's mockery. *Son, you been kicked to the curb. Your mama's goddess straight up* abandoned *your sorry ass.*

He had to put the letter back in the box before his tightening hand crumpled the brittle page.

"Did you read this?" he asked Bo.

"That's not any language I've ever seen before," he said. "Took it to a linguist up at Seton Hall, but he couldn't make heads or tails of it."

Lionel blinked. He took another look at the letter. It was perfectly legible English. Maddie gave him a tiny head shake.

"You need the right kind of eyes to read it," she told him. "Like your mother's, like mine. Like yours now, too."

"Look," Bo said, "I can't make up for keeping this from you—"

"No." Lionel stared into the box. At the glint of light upon his mother's brass key, the one Hekate had given her. "You can't."

"But I meant what I said. I have a name."

Bo pointed to the Polaroid. His short-chopped nail tapped the face of the blue-eyed man.

"That's him," Bo said. "I can't prove it, I was never able to prove it, but that's the man who killed your mother."

Now Lionel locked eyes with him.

"What do you know?"

Bo rummaged through the box. "I had seen his face somewhere. Not with my own eyes, I mean, but there was a photo from the crime scene—here. Right here."

The black-and-white photo must have been taken the night of the massacre. Thick police tape roped off the dirt road outside the ranch property line, and a row of fire trucks and ambulances stood shadowed in the background. A cluster of locals—neighbors in all directions,

Craig Schaefer

probably drawn by the fire's glow from miles away—stood in an anxious knot behind the tape.

Anxious and worried, except for the blue-eyed man, who looked positively serene.

"Who is he?" Lionel asked.

"His name is James V. Sloane," Bo told him. "Went by Jimmy. He was a traveling salesman from New York City, on the road hawking mechanical typewriters. The police picked him up for questioning, but he was squeaky clean. So they decided, anyway. His story was, he was passing by on the road to his next stop when he saw the fire, and pulled in to check it out with the rest of the rubberneckers."

"You don't agree," Maddie said. It wasn't a question.

Bo shook his head. "Sloane was staying at a motel in New Buffalo, about five miles away from the scene. I tracked down the guy who had been working as the desk clerk that night and fed him twenty-dollar bills until his memory came back. He said Sloane checked out at seven o'clock, three hours before he was spotted in this crowd photo. It took him three hours to drive five miles? No. He was there. He *did* it."

Lionel looked from the box in his hands to the crowd shot. "I don't understand. This Polaroid from the '80s puts Jimmy Sloane with my mom. Between that, the timing, and photographing him at the crime scene, why the hell wasn't he arrested? I've seen people *convicted* on less evidence than this."

"It was a cluster from the start. High-profile case, departments fighting for jurisdiction, not sharing information with each other. Didn't help that the local sheriff had it in for the ladies of the Emerald Ranch. Their presence in his fine county offended his good churchly values. He was the one who pushed the 'satanic cult war' narrative from the first minute of this mess, and once a narrative gets hold on an investigation, plus media hype . . . Well, I don't have to tell you what happens. You've seen it."

Lionel's shoulders sagged. "Tunnel vision."

342

"Tunnel vision. By the time anyone latched onto the bright idea of digging deeper into Jimmy Sloane's story, he was in the wind. Traveling salesmen tend to do that. And small-town police departments don't have the resources to launch a national manhunt on a hunch." Bo paused. "Ten years after the massacre, I had time on my hands, plus my editor's expense account. So I tried tracking him down myself."

"What did you find?" Maddie asked.

"Not much, and finding it was like hunting for a needle in a field of haystacks. Sloane popped up here and there, around the country— again, like traveling salesmen do—but I couldn't identify any of the other people in that Polaroid except for Sheila Paget. As for Sloane, he'd show up in a newspaper photo, now and then, somewhere near a burning building or a car crash. Never anything to connect him to what happened, and he was always long gone by the time anyone looked his way. A few years after the massacre, Sloane got hired by a company out in New York. It was . . . hold on."

He paged through his spiral notebook. Lionel waited, his mouth dry and stomach clenched.

"Corbin." Bo tapped his scrawled handwriting. "Corbin Investment Partners."

It took Lionel a second to remember where he'd heard the name. One look into Maddie's eyes and he realized she was thinking the same thing.

Chandra Nagarkar, the playwright. Corbin bought up a chunk of Midtown real estate, planning to develop something big, and she was protesting their plans for that old theater.

The police said it was a suicide. Melpomene said it was murder. Chandra had cried out to her Muse for help the night she died. Then her soul went missing.

And she had seen the dead catcher in the alley behind her favorite coffee shop. Right before she "killed herself," she might have gone hunting for more of them.

"Not a coincidence," Maddie said in a low voice. Lionel nodded.

"After that, he disappeared," Bo said, "or Corbin made him disappear, protecting their own. Either way, the man's been in the wind for over twenty years. And that's the end of the story. I'm sorry. It's all I've got for you."

The three of them walked down the attic steps, silent all the way to the front door. Lionel clutched his mother's keepsake box, closed and clasped again, tight against his chest. It was the closest he could get to her.

"Lionel, listen," Bo said as he opened the door, "I'm not going to ask you to forgive me—"

"Good. Because I don't."

They stood like that, both men silent, eyeing each other. Lionel felt Bo's ache for some kind of closure. Some kind of resolution. Maybe he needed it, too.

"You won't see me again," Lionel told him. It was the best he could offer. He walked outside, into the summer sunlight.

He stood out on the edge of Bo's lawn, looking up the sleepy street with his face turned toward the sun. He closed his eyes and let the dry heat bake against his cheeks and breathed in the dirty, salty air. Maddie stood at his shoulder.

"It's good," she said. "We're making progress. And hey, want to hear something cool?"

"Sure."

"Well, between the note and the name of your mother's coven— New Amsterdam being the original name for New York City—we've figured out where you came from." She lightly punched his arm. "You're a native New Yorker, and you didn't even know it."

"Great," he said.

"Hey."

She moved closer, close enough that the faint, musky scent of her perfume muffled the salt tang on the breeze.

"What's wrong? Talk to me."

He didn't turn to face her. He couldn't. Opening his mother's keepsake box had ignited a bomb under his rib cage. He felt his bones creak-
ing as he struggled to hold the pressure inside.

"Sloane. He wasn't lying. My mother really did walk with a goddess. A real, actual goddess."

"She did," Maddie said. "That's something to be proud of."

He turned, now, and he couldn't hide the wet glint in his eyes.

"Why? I'm not." He shook his head. "I'm apparently not something
to be proud of."

"What do you mean?"

"He wasn't lying about the other part, either. Where was she,
Maddie? Where was Hekate? That son of a bitch killed my mother, he
massacred those innocent people—where *was* she?"

"The gods . . ." Maddie looked to the sky, the clouds like faint
scraps of gossamer. "They're not omniscient, Lionel. They're not omnip-
otent. They can only do so much, and frankly, they don't always *choose*
to help. Hekate, in particular, is very big on letting us stand or fall on
our own two feet. She'll tip the scales in her daughters' favor, sure, but
swooping down from the heavens to save the day isn't her thing. That's
the deal we make going in. Your mother would have known that. When
you play for big stakes . . . sometimes you lose."

"What about *me*?"

She shook her head. "What do you mean? You survived."

"On my own two feet," he echoed, the words bitter on his tongue.
"Because Sloane wasn't lying. Hekate abandoned me. She threw me
out like yesterday's newspaper, and I have spent my life, my entire *life*,
railing against the idea that magic might be real. That there might be
something, anything, outside what I could see and touch and measure."

"You weren't really trying to disprove magic," Maddie said, understanding. "You were looking for it."

He thumped his fist against his chest. "I knew. I knew, deep down
inside. I knew something was missing. Some part of my life that should

have been there, but it wasn't, because it was torn out of me the night my mother died. Obviously I'm not . . . I'm not good enough for Hekate. I was five years old, and I failed a test I didn't even know I was taking. *Why aren't I good enough for her?* What did I do *wrong?*"

The pressure behind his ribs surged up into his throat. He bit down on his knuckles to keep the tears at bay, grief riding on a tempest of loss and humiliation. Maddie put her arms around him, pulled him close, pressed fingers against his hair until he rested his head on her shoulder.

"Sometimes we don't get answers," she told him, her voice soft as she stared at the clouds. "That's magic, too. But I'll tell you this: good enough has nothing to do with it. She has her ways and means, her comings and goings, and she veils her footsteps. Whatever her reason, it wasn't because you weren't good enough."

"Then how do you know?" he asked, his voice broken.

"Because I have spent a very, very long time lost inside my own head," she told him. "Like a rat running in a maze of memories. I built the maze. Forgot to build a way out. No, that's not right—I walled myself up inside on purpose. I didn't think I deserved to leave."

He lifted his head so he could look at her.

"You are the first person I've met in so many years," she told him, "*so* many years, to pull me out of that maze. I have habits, you know. I have really . . . bad habits. I told you. I'm going to hurt you. One day you're probably going to wake up and I won't be there—"

"I don't care," he said.

"I know." The corners of her eyes crinkled as she broke into a desperate smile. "I know. I gave you every chance to leave, every warning, and you're still here."

He squeezed her hand. "I'm still here."

"And that's how I know. So don't ever tell me you're not good enough. Don't ever tell yourself that." Maddie nodded to the road. "Shall we? We've got a name now."

Lionel wiped the heel of his hand across his eye. He nodded and took out his phone.

"Yeah. Two names. Jimmy Sloane, and Corbin. For the first time, we're actually a step ahead."

"Feels kinda nice, doesn't it?"

"Feels good. I'll call us a Lyft." He glanced at the screen. "Huh. Message from Brianna. Must have been while we were in Bo's attic. One sec, lemme check this."

Lionel held the phone to his ear as he listened to the voice mail. The color drained from his cheeks.

"Oh," he said. "Oh, no."

Fifty

Lionel put his phone on speaker and started the message over so Maddie could listen in. Brianna's irritated voice gusted over the line.

"Have I mentioned you're an asshole lately? Because yeah. 'The train's probably faster'? Are you high? If I'd just taken a cab from JFK, I'd have been there twenty minutes ago. And at this point, I don't even care about the money."

"She's *here*?" Maddie asked. "Did you call her?"

Lionel shook his head. His hand squeezed the phone tight enough to turn his knuckles white.

"Anyway, I'm slowly untangling the bowl of spaghetti soup that passes for a subway system in this city, and I'm about to transfer to the number-seven line. Which *hopefully* gets me to Grand Central sometime before I'm eligible for retirement. You'd better be there, preferably with an apology and a nice bottle of wine. Actually, forget the apology, just bring two bottles."

He called her back. She wasn't picking up.

"She's on the train," Maddie told him. "No reception in the tunnels."

"It's him, Maddie. Sloane. He knows who I am. Dergwyn must have told him I survived last night, so he's trying to draw me out."

His fingers hammered the screen, hunting for the fastest, closest ride back into the city.

"And it's working."

Since the hour he first landed, and his jarring moment when he thought—just for a heartbeat—that he was living in a movie, Lionel had been enthralled by New York. The skyline, the mythic echoes, the sights he'd seen in a thousand shows and films coming to life all around him. If Grand Central Terminal was going to be the end of the line— one way or another—he figured he couldn't have picked a better place for the showdown. He and Maddie squeezed through the glass doors at the Forty-Second Street entrance, wading through molasses-thick crowds.

A tall man with mahogany skin stood just inside the doorway, smacking a Bible bound in ivory leather against his open palm. "*Jesus is coming*," he called out with every thud of leather against skin. "*Jesus is coming.*"

His monotone chant followed them to Vanderbilt Hall, where the roar of the crowds washed it away. The towering, vaulted ceilings absorbed a thousand voices and scattered them, turning them to human static like a modern-day Tower of Babel. Commuters were coming and going, long-haul travelers lugging overstuffed suitcases, people winding around clots of tourists as they snapped photos and lit the gallery with flashes of white light. Lionel searched every face, searching for any sign of Brianna—or Jimmy Sloane.

"Maddie," he said. The words tiptoed out, like they were afraid of being heard. "What he did at the Blackstone, when he unleashed that pack of ghosts. If he did that *here*—"

Maddie's eyes were as hard as flint as she scanned the throng of people all around them. She walked faster.

"He'd be insane to. We keep magic hidden for a reason. There'd be retribution if he pulled a stunt like that. Retribution like you wouldn't believe."

"When has Sloane ever cared about retribution? He stabbed an entire coven in the back, and from the sound of that letter, Hekate herself wants his ass dead. He tortured and killed a guy with Russian Mafia connections, he knocked off a roomful of some of the richest and best-connected people in New York—his entire life has been dancing around, thumbing his nose at power and daring the entire world to come and take a shot at him."

"Challenge accepted," Maddie grumbled.

They emerged into the main concourse, the belly of a vast stone whale. Crowds thronged the wide-open floor, an expanse of marble surrounding a rounded information kiosk at the dead center of the room. Above, the arch of the ceiling was an aquamarine sky with golden constellations etched upon its depths. Maddie veered left, heading for the ticket booths and a rolling display of arrivals and departures over the arched teller windows.

"We know his endgame," Lionel said. "No idea what the Poe manuscript has to do with any of this, but he's hidden those . . . those dead catchers all over town. Get enough in one place, build enough power, and he tears a hole to another world."

"A permanent hole." Maddie frowned up at the arrival board. "And whatever's over there can come over here."

"Which isn't going to be good for anybody. What if it's going down today? What if he's got all the juice he needs and Grand Central is ground zero? He sets it off, gets what he wants, *and* takes us out at the same time?"

"I don't think so," she said. "No need to even bother luring us in, if he was ready to make his final move. No, he's got something more personal— *Shit.*"

"What?"

Maddie edged her way to an open window and put on a plastic smile for the teller.

"Hi," she said, "I noticed the number seven is delayed. Do you know if it's still sitting at the Court Square station? My mother is coming to meet me here, and I just want to make sure she's all right."

The teller's apologetic look was almost as fake as Maddie's smile. It was more of a "Please don't shoot the messenger" face.

"I'm sorry, it's actually . . . Well, it's on the way. We've had a power outage, and the train is stalled in the tunnel, but you don't need to worry, they're working on it as fast as they can—"

Maddie didn't wait for the rest. She billowed across the polished marble span like a gathering storm. Lionel scrambled to keep up with her. He knew exactly what she was thinking.

"They live underground and they eat people. Maddie, these ghouls—would they attack a train?"

She held up a finger. "Once. Back in Boston, in the '20s. The pack that did it isn't around anymore. The ghouls who survived got a lot smarter and a lot pickier about their targets."

"But would *this* pack do it? Would Dergwyn, if Sloane told her to?"

"Not betting against it."

She stopped, turned, and grabbed Lionel by the arm.

"Get out of here," she told him. "Go back to the hotel and call Regina. Give her a full update—"

"I'm not leaving you."

"*Lionel.* You aren't ready for this. You aren't ready to face him, let alone Dergwyn and her pack."

He stood his ground. "I'm a witch now. My eyes are wide-open."

"A witch with one spell. One spell that you've got a fifty-fifty success rate on, and that's being generous. And while it's great at clearing out death energy, it doesn't do shit against flesh and blood."

"Then I'll improvise," he said. "Maddie, this isn't just about Brianna now. Every single person on that train is in danger. We are the *only* people who can stand between them and whatever's coming for them. I'm here, I can help, and they need us. That's all the reason I need to stay."

She turned and kept walking.

"Come on, then," she said. "Let's do this."

Craig Schaefer

A wide span of concrete platform stretched between trenches lined with track, like a pier over a dry riverbed. Ahead, both sets of tracks vanished into darkened tunnel mouths. A pair of cops in uniform, wearing the gold-and-black patches of the Transit Police, stood on the platform's edge and talked to a harried-looking maintenance worker.

"Tunnel on the right," Maddie murmured. "Jump down, hug the wall, stay *off* the tracks. Third rail's electrified, and it'll kill you faster than the ghouls will."

"What are you doing?"

She nodded at the men on the platform's lip. "Keeping you from getting tackled and arrested. I'll be right behind you."

The worker was on his walkie-talkie, listening to a squawk of garbled chatter. "—telling you, backups are dead. Everything's fried, from the lights to the AC, and we're sitting here with our thumbs up our—"

"Copy," said the maintenance worker. "Just sit tight. We've got crews on the way, and if worse comes to worse, we'll do an evacuation on foot."

Lionel took a deep breath. Then he jogged to the end of the platform, sat on the lip, and dropped down into the trench. He instantly heard shouts at his back.

"Hey!" one of the transit cops bellowed, "get back here! You're gonna get yourself killed!"

Hopefully not, Lionel thought. *We'll see how it goes.*

He broke into a run and sprinted into the tunnel mouth. The darkness swallowed him whole.

The transit cops and their buddy were distracted for one crucial second. That was all the time Maddie needed to rush up from behind, snake a chunky black automatic from one officer's gun belt, and jam it in their faces. They backpedaled, hands up, the other cop making a slow reach for his pistol.

"Don't," she said. His hand froze somewhere around his belly.

"Hey, lady," the maintenance worker said, "whatever your beef is, you don't gotta do this—"

"Listen carefully," Maddie told them. "There's a clearly emotionally disturbed woman on this platform with a stolen service weapon. Go, call it in, and request backup. Tell them to send in the Apprehension Tactical Team."

They stared at her, faces pale, feet rooted to the concrete. Maddie rolled her eyes.

"Oh, for the love of—" She pointed the muzzle skyward, squeezed the trigger, and blasted two holes in the ceiling. Concrete dust rained down as the shots echoed like cannon fire. "Crazy woman with a gun! *Go*, already!"

There weren't many civilians on the platform, but that started the stampede. The cops ran right along with them. Maddie waited a second, making sure the platform had cleared out. Then she hopped into the trench and followed in Lionel's wake.

The light on Lionel's phone strobed across the silent, darkened nose of the number-seven train. It sat in the tunnel about three hundred yards from escape. Stone dead, a sailboat on a windless, glassy sea. He scrambled past the cab, breathless from his run, and up to the first set of side doors. A conductor had forced open the doors, wedging a collapsed stroller between them, to let a little air into the lightless train. The tunnel was sweltering, like a coffin buried under desert sands, and it could only be worse inside the train. Sweat plastered Lionel's shirt to his skin, and he brushed away a dripping bead as it tickled its way down his cheek.

"Hey," the conductor said, hitting Lionel with the beam of her flashlight, "what are you doing out there?"

He could see passengers moving around behind the woman, restless and angry. Lionel got close, pitched his voice low, and kept his gaze steady. Donning a mantle of authority he didn't have and hoping she didn't challenge it. It was a trick he'd used a thousand times as a reporter to go places he wasn't supposed to be, but lives had never hung in the balance before.

"Listen to me. You need to get these people off the train and up to the platform, *now*. Can you do that?"

"Yeah, I *can*," she said, "but we're supposed to wait for the go-ahead. We don't evacuate on foot if the train's fixable. The liability involved—"

"It's not fixable. I can't go into details, but this wasn't a random failure. We've had a credible threat. Do you understand me?"

Credible threat. After September 11, everyone knew what those words meant. Especially in Manhattan. The conductor glanced back over her shoulder.

"On it," she said. "I'll notify the train operator. Can you help?"

"That's what I'm here for."

She passed him a pry bar. It was long, thin, heavier than it looked, stout steel with PROPERTY OF MTA stamped along one side in chipped yellow paint.

"We'll get the evac under way," she told him. "Go two cars down, crack the doors, and start getting people off. Tell them to walk this way, single file. More doors we have open, the faster we can clear the train and get everybody home safe."

"On it."

Lionel raced along the train. He came to the doors, wriggled the thin, bent end of the pry bar, and shoved his chest against it. The doors fought him every inch of the way, but they slowly began to budge. He called out for a hand and got at least six. Passengers inside squirmed their fingers through the crack on the other side, hauling the gap wider.

"We need everybody to evacuate," he called out. "Train's not going anywhere, so the conductor's going to walk you to the platform. I need somebody in the back to run down to the next car and tell everybody to line up. If we work together, we can get everybody out of here in no time."

If there was one thing New Yorkers knew how to do, it was work together when they had to. In five minutes, passengers had run the length of the train, notifying cars all the way to the back and forming lines to the two open exits. A couple of weary-looking commuters, a man in a rumpled suit and a woman in sweat-soaked flannel, came up to hold the doors wide without even being asked. That freed up Lionel to sprint down another couple of cars and get to work on forcing a third exit open.

All the while, no sign of Brianna. Or Jimmy Sloane. As Lionel leaned into his pry bar, throwing his weight against the steel, he looked to the pitch darkness in the wake of the stalled metal beast.

"I know you're out there," he murmured. "What are you waiting for?"

Fifty-One

The exodus from the train was like a swarm of digital fireflies. As the train conductor took the lead, swinging a Maglite like she was directing an aircraft to the terminal, the passengers held up their phones to light the way. A sea of hovering squares glowed white and bobbed in the shadows. Maddie moved upstream, against the flow, shouldering her way through the crowd. She kept her stolen gun low, close to her hip.

She couldn't see Lionel up ahead. She heard his voice, though, ringing out above the din of voices.

"Brianna!" he shouted. "That isn't me!"

$\rightleftharpoons$

Lionel was manning the third open door, taking an elderly woman's hand and easing her down onto the tunnel floor, when he heard his own voice echo off the dank stone walls.

"Brianna, over here! I need your help. I'm stuck."

He squinted into the dark and saw a lone shadow moving in the wrong direction. Away from the last car of the train, away from the fading light of the evacuation. *Brianna*.

He passed off door duties to the next passenger out—not pausing long enough to give him a chance to argue—and ran after her. She was about fifty feet ahead of him—and just ahead of her, at the edge of a sharp bend in the tunnel, stood a figure buried under a ragged, dirty shroud.

"Brianna!" Lionel shouted. "That isn't me!"

She turned on her heel, torn between two voices, two men, as the figure under the shroud broke into a burbling laugh.

"Briaaanna," it said in a gravelly singsong voice, "that isn't meee."

He threw the hood of his shroud aside, baring glittering opal eyes and a distended, jackal-like jaw, as he launched himself at her.

He wasn't alone. Another ghoul burst from the shadows, leaping, filthy claws hooked and going for Lionel's eyes. He grabbed the pry bar and swung for the fences. The steel bar slammed into the ghoul's skull, and Lionel heard the sickly crunch of bone as a spray of hot blood spattered his sweat-drenched face. The creature crumpled to the concrete at his feet. Then another hit Lionel from behind like a freight train, slamming into him and wrapping gangly, too-long arms around his chest. The creature stank of dried piss and graveyard dirt. Lionel squirmed, kicking backward as the ghoul lifted him off his feet and squeezed the air from his lungs.

He felt himself going up, over—and then the stone floor was rushing up to meet him as the ghoul slammed him to the concrete. Lionel landed on his forearm and gritted his teeth as a muscle in his shoulder tore. The burst of white-hot pain kept him moving, gave him the energy to roll out of the way as the ghoul's crusty boot came stomping down where his face had been a second ago. Lionel took the pry bar with his good hand and shoved himself up to his knees. The steel whistled through the stagnant air and shattered the ghoul's kneecap like it was made of glass. He clambered to his feet as the monster fell, took his steel in both hands, and raised it high above his head. Then he brought the bar down in one brutal, sweeping arc with all the strength he had left.

The creature in the shroud had Brianna by the wrists, trying to wrestle her toward the tracks. She shot out a foot and drove the heel of her running shoe straight between his legs. He doubled over, groaning, and she twisted her right arm free. Her hand dipped into her messenger bag. He was rallying, scrambling to grab her again, when she stuck a can of pepper spray in his face and let it rip. The ghoul's ear-piercing scream of pain was almost as loud as the sudden gunshot just behind Lionel's back.

Maddie was here, and she had her own company. All he could see was shadows dancing, flying, bounding off the tunnel walls in the darkness. She squeezed the trigger. The gun boomed, and a flash of muzzle flare captured the moment in a freeze-frame flicker: a bullet plowing through a ghoul's forehead as his head snapped back, painting the rails red, another leaping through the air at her back with claws out. One heartbeat of darkness. Then another flare and another thundercrack of the gun. Maddie low, one leg bent and the other stretched long like a gymnast, a bullet punching through the jaw of the leaping ghoul and out through the crown of its skull. Two more were rushing her from the far side of the train. Two more flashes and their corpses were tumbling, rolling on the concrete and leaving smears in their wake, carried by momentum.

Brianna's attacker clawed at his own eyes, still screaming. His heel caught on the edge of the track. He tumbled backward and landed with his spine on the third rail. The creature kicked and his fists slammed the ground as the current baked him alive, until his body finally fell limp and motionless. The tunnel air filled with the stench of scorched and spoiled pork. Silence fell, the last reverberation of the last gunshot rippling into the distance.

Brianna took a halting step away from the rails. She looked at the dead body on the tracks, his opal eyes still open, jaw hanging loose and flashing rows of jagged teeth. Then she looked at Lionel. Then at the body again.

"I'm going to need a minute," she said.

"Can't give you one," Lionel said. "There's more where these came from. A *lot* more."

"The kid's right, you know."

Lionel's stomach clenched as Jimmy Sloane's voice, weathered, faintly mocking as usual, echoed off the tunnel walls. He strolled around the bend, casual and slow, with his hands in his pockets and the Lapis Manalis—the brooch he'd stolen, the one Lionel's mother and her coven mates had died over—glittering on the lapel of his jacket. A cold blue glow lit the tunnel at his back, casting his companions in silhouette. Dergwyn strolled at his side and one pace behind, the ghoul princess looking like she'd rather be anywhere but here. And behind her, her pack. Two dozen figures, maybe more, shadows shambling and crawling in the dark as they bellied up to the dinner table. An electric tension hung in the air. It felt like the horde was yearning to attack, starving for it, and only Sloane's will held them back.

Lionel squeezed the bloody pry bar in his hand and winced as a fresh lance of pain shot up his injured shoulder. He glanced to Maddie, standing at his side, and lowered his voice to a whisper.

"How many bullets do you have left?"

"One," she murmured back.

"Can you do that . . . that thing you did at the club? With your key, and the light? They really hated that."

"The key," she said, "which is sitting on the edge of your bathroom sink, back at the hotel. Trying to *avoid* my former employer, remember? I didn't see myself taking that kind of a risk twice."

He fumbled in his hip pocket. On the drive over, he'd emptied out the keepsake box, pocketing the folded letter, the Polaroid, and his mother's antique key. The box was just a box; he'd left it on the back seat. He tugged out the key and offered it to her.

"What about this one?"

"It's . . . they're *personalized*, Lionel. I can't use that one any more than your mother would have been able to use mine."

He looked down at his hand. He strained to see it—to *see* it—with the new eyes he'd been given. To find some wellspring of power, some hand-me-down from his mother that he could use to save the day.

All he saw was dark, hammered brass, cool against his clammy palm. If there was any magic left, it was hiding from him. Which didn't mean there wasn't any to be found.

"Maybe I can," he told her.

"Lionel, *no*—"

Her hand grabbed at his sleeve, then slipped free as he strode forward. He planted himself in front of Maddie and Brianna, drawing an invisible line across the tunnel floor. He brandished the key and held it high.

"I know who my mother was now," he said to Jimmy Sloane. "And I know what you did."

The ghouls at the front of the pack cringed, some clawing the air, others hiding their eyes before the shadow of the key. Dergwyn folded her arms tight across the dirt-stained folds of her designer blazer and pursed her lips, looking more irritated by the second.

Sloane just smiled, cool and easy.

"Well," he said, "we've got all the fixings of a good time here, don't we? Drama! Revenge! The son rising to avenge his mother! Very nice, very Greek. I can only think of one thing that'd make this even better, don't you? Lionel, are you sure you *can* strike me down? After all . . . I'm your father."

Silence fell across the tunnel, on both sides of the line. Then Sloane burst into giddy laughter.

"Holy *shit*," he said, slapping Dergwyn on the back. "Did you—did you see the look on his face? Did you *see* that?"

"I saw it," she said, her voice flat as she glared at him.

"Sorry, sorry." It took him a second to get over his fit of giggles. "Nah, I'm lying, I just . . . wouldn't it be great if I *was*, though? Man, wouldn't that be perfect?"

Lionel's arm, holding the key aloft like a beacon, began to waver. Sagging under the weight of Sloane's careless mockery.

"In case you're curious," Sloane said, "your daddy was a one-night stand, some long-haul trucker on the road between nowhere and nowhere. Sheila wanted a daughter. A husband, not so much. And you can give your arm a rest. The key is a cute bluff, but you're forgetting something."

"Do tell."

Sloane's eyes bored into him as the man's lips curled into a smug, cruel smile.

"Hekate doesn't give a shit about you. She ain't coming, and that key isn't gonna open anything but your tombstone." He looked to Maddie. "And you? I know who you are now. She *definitely* doesn't give a shit about *you*. You two got nothing but the magic you brought down here with you, and it's not enough to beat me, let alone me and my good pals here. You know I'm right."

He turned to Brianna. He gave her a slightly awkward shrug.

"You," Sloane said, "are collateral damage, and I suppose I owe you an apology for that. You were bait. I needed someone to draw the kid and his girl out, to finish things proper, and, well . . . you're it. Nothing personal—it's just a sad fact that bait exists to get hung on a hook and eaten."

Brianna squared her footing. She braced her canister of pepper spray like a medieval knight with a sword in her hand, getting ready for a battle.

"Will someone," she said through gritted teeth, "please tell me what the hell is going on here?"

"I'll let your ex do the honors," Sloane said. "You figured it out by now, right?"

Lionel held his gaze. "The dead catchers. You're planting them all over the city. Stealing people's souls when they die."

"Fifty-five thousand," Sloane replied. "That's the number of people who die in New York City every single year. Four thousand five hundred and eighty-three a month. We've been skimming off the top for *years*. So far, no divine power's come around to check the books. It's almost like the universe doesn't care. Little depressing, when you think about it."

"'We,'" Lionel echoed. "You and Corbin Investment Partners."

"Huh. Now that—that's farther than I expected you'd get. Good one, kid. You earned your junior detective badge."

Maddie stepped up beside Lionel. Her fingertips brushed his shoulder, lending her strength to his arm as the key remained sullen and silent in his hand.

"You're trying to tear open a hole between worlds," Maddie said. "What do you get out of it? What's waiting on the other side?"

The cold blue glow at Sloane's back grew stronger, congealing, as he reached into his breast pocket. Once he slid it out again, he twirled his seemingly empty hand and flourished it like a stage magician. Three slender dead catchers sat nestled between his fingers. Trickles of sapphire mist leaked from the steel disks, pooling on the tunnel floor around his polished leather spats.

"I could tell you, but I'll do better than that," he said. "I'll show you."

Fifty-Two

Two of the dead catchers clicked together in Sloane's hands, connecting with a metallic *snap* that echoed off the subway tunnel walls. Just as it had back at Wen Xiulang's shop, the world began to change at the edges of Lionel's vision. Bits of tunnel brick fell away, exposing impossible tunnels, openings that hadn't been there a moment earlier. He thought he spotted something scurry at his feet, something with a glistening, fat, vomit-yellow shell and too many legs, but it vanished when he looked down. Now something was crawling along the tunnel just above his head, something that smelled like rancid milk on a hot day.

"This is just a taster," Sloane said. "It isn't a proper doorway, just a little . . . temporary overlap, if you will. These prototypes can only do so much, no matter how many you hook up together. It's like plugging too many appliances into a single outlet: eventually you're gonna blow a fuse."

Maddie shot a glance down at her phone. She slid it back into her jeans pocket and leaned close to Lionel.

"No matter what happens, we need to buy about five more minutes."

"Why?" He gave her a sidelong look. "What happens in five minutes?"

"Just keep him talking."

"See, you shouldn't feel bad," Sloane told Lionel. "Getting abandoned after your mom died, that's probably the best thing that could have happened to you. Me, I went all in with Hekate. Swore myself to her service, to one of her covens, and what did I get in return? A big fat goose egg. Everyone told me, you want the *real* power, the kind of magic that can change the world, that's where you go. Lies."

Maddie's eyes narrowed, hard as flint. "That's the last reason to go to her. You don't do it for the power. She isn't some kind of slot machine, where you can plug in tokens of devotion until prizes pop out."

Sloane looked at her like she'd sprouted a second head.

"That's just stupid. Why would you pledge yourself to a goddess for any reason *but* the prizes?"

"If you ever really knew her," Maddie said, "if you'd met her even once, you wouldn't have to ask."

"Well, I went looking for alternatives. And I found one. A force stronger than her. Bigger than this planet. Louder than an A-bomb blast at ground zero. He reached out to me, across the veil of worlds. He told me that if I opened the way for him, if I gave him a sacrifice worthy of a king, he'd give me . . . *everything*."

The connected dead catchers in his hand throbbed, pulsing, their icy light spreading along the tunnel as the distortion grew at the corners of Lionel's vision. There were skittering, crawling things infesting the brickwork—what was left of it—as more tunnels fell open, archways shaped like puzzle pieces where solid walls had stood a second before.

Now, when he turned his vision, not all the changes vanished from sight. The effect was getting stronger. The other side closer now. Dergwyn stood closer to Sloane. Her gaze darted from side to side as her pack, huddled tight behind her, grew restless.

"Easy," he told her. "They won't hurt anyone with me. They know me. And they know who I'm gonna be. No more Jimmy V. Sloane, coven *bitch*, door-to-door *typewriter salesman*. No. I'm finally going to get the respect I deserve. And when the dust settles, anyone left standing will know my name."

He raised the joined disks to his face and basked in the sapphire glow. His other hand cradled the third dead catcher, turning it in his fingertips.

"They'll call me the Prince of Lament."

Lionel held his sweat-plastered arm higher, squeezing his mother's key in a death grip as his thoughts cried out . . . somewhere. Below the tunnel walls, below the city streets, reaching deeper and deeper.

Hekate. I don't . . . I don't know how to pray. It's not a thing I've ever done, for any god by any name. But right now, prayers are all I have left. If there are special words I'm supposed to say, I don't know them. If there's some kind of ritual I should be doing, I don't know that, either.

All I know is that my mom was special to you. I don't care that you didn't want me. That's fine. But she was special to you, and Sloane took her away from both of us. So, please. Help us. Help Maddie and Brianna. Fuck, forget me. Just save them. Please. For my mom, for her memory. Just save them.

Silence. The key sat dead in his hand.

Lionel's arm slowly fell to his side. His shoulders sagged.

"And there's the moment of realization," Sloan said, almost oddly gentle now. "It's over. The cavalry isn't coming. No last-minute reprieves. That's it, kid. All that despair—drink it in. Hurts a lot less if you accept it. That's the human condition, when all is said and done. Like the man wrote: 'Mortal fate is hard. Best get used to it.'"

He snapped the third disk into place. The blue lights flared and cast glittering motes across the brickwork. A stench of rot flooded the tunnel, so strong that Lionel felt like he'd stuck his nose in a road-killed carcass after two days in a hot sun. Behind him, Brianna cupped her hand to her mouth, gagging.

Keep him talking, Lionel thought. Maddie had something in the works. Maybe the cavalry *was* coming. Just had to keep him talking. A spark of hope ignited in his heart, and he fanned it into a tiny, desperate flame.

"That quote," he said. "That was on Chandra Nagarkar's tombstone. You killed her, didn't you?"

"Guilty," Sloane replied. "Wasn't personal. I liked her play. But she got a little too nosy for her own good."

"Sure," Lionel replied. "She discovered one of the dead catchers near her favorite coffee place. Meanwhile, she was on the committee trying to stop Corbin Investment Partners from rehabbing that block in Midtown. She must have found some evidence, put two and two together. There's one thing I'm missing, though. We know what you think you're going to get out of this. What does *Corbin* get? They won't be developing any real estate once your buddy on the other side comes through."

"Well, that's the thing. I heard the call, I had my mission, and I had the skills to get it done. Only one critical part was missing." Sloane rubbed his thumb against his fingertips. "You think it's easy to build fifty-odd prototype soul batteries, each one with precision occult microelectronics, not to mention an engine capable of harnessing all that collected power? Just the casings alone needed a custom machine shop, skilled labor, twenty-odd years of field tests. We're talking serious cash here. I needed a patron with deep pockets, and I found one."

"But still, why would they . . ." Lionel's voice trailed off. His sinking feeling turned into a rock-in-the-stomach plummet as he pieced it together. "They don't know, do they? Corbin has no idea what your real plan is."

Sloane broke into a toothy alligator grin.

"I've always had a talent for necromancy. My little acquisition from my former coven"—his fingers traced the brooch on his lapel—"only expanded my repertoire. I did a few party tricks, enough to convince my backer that we're going to an entirely different corner of the universe. A much friendlier one. By the time anybody knows any better, it'll be too late to stop me."

"We know better," Maddie said.

"And if I thought there was any chance of you leaving this tunnel alive, I'd be a mite more circumspect. But here we are."

He brandished the cylinder, the three conjoined dead catchers, in one hand like a stubby magic wand. He extended the palm of his other hand as the cold and the rot pressed in all around them, stealing Lionel's breath. From the tunnel ceiling, a spider the size of a fist descended on a strand of scarlet. It plopped down into Sloane's palm, fat and black, its chitin glistening.

Lionel looked up. The tunnel roof was a curtain of spiders.

There were thousands of them, chittering and squirming and scrambling over one another. Some were starting to descend over their heads, gliding down slowly on red lines, their mandibles clacking.

"Maddie . . . ," he said, squeezing out the word on his final breath.

"It's been about five minutes," she said, and raised her stolen pistol.

Sloane blinked at her. "Really? A gun? Do you really think a bullet is going to stop me?"

"Not *you*, no."

She swiveled her aim, squinting down the barrel, and fired her last shot.

The bullet slammed into the dead catchers, sparking as the cylinder blew out of Sloane's hand. It trailed a spray of sapphire mist like heart blood as it tumbled through the air. The cylinder clattered to the tunnel floor, dented and dead, the last of its light guttering out.

A rush of hot air ripped the spiders away, the puzzle-piece doors, the rotten stench. The reality of the city flooded in with a vengeance and took back its stolen ground. As Sloane glared at Maddie, wearing his fury on his face, Lionel heard another sound: faint, echoing bootsteps coming up from behind. Distant but fast.

"You think that accomplished anything?" Sloane slashed his hand through the air, waving at Dergwyn and her pack. "I was just being creative. We can still do this the quick and dirty way. Princess, rally your boys and take these three out. I'm done here."

"No." Dergwyn's opal eyes glittered. She squinted into the dark, back toward the stalled train, past Lionel's shoulder. "No, no, no."

She backpedaled, barking orders to her pack. They scampered and broke formation as they faded up the tunnel. Sloane turned on the ball of his foot. "What are you *doing*?"

"We *live* here," she hissed at him. She broke into a loping run and followed her pack into retreat. The bootsteps were louder now, carried on the crackle of walkie-talkies. Maglite beams broke and scattered the shadows.

Maddie smiled, dropped her empty gun, and got down on her knees on the tunnel floor.

"Lionel, Brianna, you should follow my lead." She laced her fingers behind her neck, serene. "Sloane, you can do what you want. I mean, you might not be afraid of *a* bullet . . ."

"Get on the ground," bellowed a woman's voice through a bullhorn. *"Drop your weapons and get on the ground."*

Lionel fell to his knees. He winced as he tried to raise his hands, and his injured shoulder screamed in protest. Maddie gave him a cheerful smile.

"Remember your very first lesson? Like I said, being a witch is all about knowing things. Sometimes it's the right way to parlay with a demigoddess. Sometimes it's about the symbolism of the tarot, or the right herbs to poison or heal."

Lionel squeezed his eyes shut, suddenly blind as a white-hot beam of light hit him square in the face. Rough hands wrestled his arms behind him and shoved him onto his belly. A knee dug into the small of his back, pinning him like a bug as cuffs snapped tight around his wrists.

"And sometimes," Maddie said, "what you *really* need to know is how fast the NYPD's Apprehension Tactical Team can respond to an active-shooter report."

Fifty-Three

Lionel had been here before. Well, not here, but a room just like it. Dirty eggshell-white walls, a stainless-steel table, two chairs, one door, and a one-way mirror smudged with desperate fingerprints. Lionel sat under the hot overhead light with his wrists shackled to the table.

"Let's go over this," Detective Mathers said, "one more time."

"Don't know what you're expecting me to say differently."

"The truth would be nice," she told him.

"Already gave it to you," he lied.

Mathers shoved her chair back and stood up. She paced the room like a lioness in her den.

"You show up in New York on a job your own employers can't substantiate and get caught at the scene of a murder. The murder of a low-level flunky for the Russian mob, no less."

"I wasn't *caught*," Lionel said. "I was the one who called it in."

"Subsequently I've learned that you left Chicago on the very same day another man was murdered. You were the last person to see him alive, and the CPD very much wants a word with you about it."

"I can account for my whereabouts that entire afternoon," he said. "I just . . . haven't yet."

The cops, looking like armored black beetles under their riot gear, had marched Lionel through the evacuated station and shoved him into the back of a squad car, alone. Brianna and Maddie got their own separate rides. He hadn't seen them since. Sloane had decided—as usual—that caution was the better part of valor and made himself scarce just before the police flooded in.

"And now," Mathers told him, "you appeared at the scene of a stalled train, claiming to be a Homeland Security agent—"

His chains rattled as he poked the table for emphasis. "I never said that. I never said those specific words."

"—but you *did* tell the train conductor that you had information on a credible threat and ordered the evacuation of the number-seven line."

"That . . . that may have been a thing I said. But I had a good reason."

"Right. Yet another mysterious unnamed source. See, here's the problem, Mr. Journalist—you fucked up. You brought terrorism into the mix. That's federal. And when the feds get here, they aren't going to give a damn about your 'journalistic integrity' or your 'unnamed sources.' They've got all kinds of ways to get around that."

She put both palms on the table and leaned in. Lionel fell under her shadow as she loomed over him.

"You know what they're going to do to you?" she said. "They're going to shove a hundred-foot steel rig straight up your ass and drill for oil."

Lionel tried to swallow the bone-hard lump in his throat. She wasn't lying. He'd gone far beyond anything he could explain at this point. He'd committed crimes today, serious ones, and nobody was going to care that his motives were good. Not when the only true explanation involved an immortal magician and a pack of cannibalistic ghouls under the city, trying to steal people's souls.

It was looking more and more like he had only one choice left: to decide whether his new home was going to be in a prison cell or in a psych ward. He fought through his rising fear and struggled for some scrap of bravado.

"Detective Mathers," he said, "that . . . is the worst metaphor I've ever heard. You should stop using them. Unless you're being literal, in which case . . . ow?"

She slammed her fists against the table hard enough to make him jump in his chair. She went back to pacing and pointed a furious finger at him.

"The only reason you're here and not on your way to Club Fed is because we *know* what this is about."

"You . . . do?" He half hoped she was right, but he doubted it.

"You're covering for her."

"Just to be clear, which her are we talking about?"

"Your psycho pal, Madison Hannah," she said. "You know, the one who assaulted a transit officer, stole his service weapon, and opened fire on a crowded platform?"

"Oh."

Mathers's rage softened, blunted as she took a deep breath and let it out. She came back to the table, conciliatory now, her voice softer. He knew it was an act, but he still wanted to buy it. The detective was good at her job.

"I get it," she said, dropping back into her chair. "I really do. Your friend was having a . . . a bad day, let's call it. We all have bad days, right? She snapped. You wanted to cover for her, to make a distraction and get her out of there, and you panicked. So you pulled your train-evacuation routine because that's the only thing you could think of."

He held his silence, following her along the trail of a bad theory.

"You didn't want anyone to get hurt. And really, Lionel, nobody did. But as it stands, you're both looking at serious prison time. It doesn't have to be that way."

"No?" he asked.

"No. Just tell the truth. You saw her steal the gun, you saw her open fire *at* the police officers—thank God she missed—and she pushed you into ordering everyone off that train. It was all her."

Mathers set a yellow legal pad on the steel table. She laid a ballpoint pen down on top of it. Then she slid it over to him.

"All you have to do is write that down and sign your name to it. You do that, and you can go home. Today. Not saying there won't be charges, but honestly, they'll probably chalk it up to a couple of misdemeanors with time served." She gestured to the only exit. "You can walk right out that door."

"And what happens to Maddie?"

"Madison is going to prison for a very long time. There's no getting around that. One way or another, she's done."

"Really?" Lionel asked. "Because it sounds like you're really invested in getting me to betray her. If you had an airtight case, why do you need me to rat her out?"

"We just want the truth."

"But that isn't the truth," he said.

Her geniality frosted over. Mathers rose, crossed to the other side of the room, and looked up to the surveillance camera in the corner.

Then she pulled the plug. The camera's red light faded to black.

"Lionel," she said, "you're going to write that confession. You're going to write it exactly the way I tell you to, word for word. Then you're going to sign it."

His mounting anxiety turned to a cold sheen of ice caking along his spine.

"What is this?" he said.

"You're going to sign it, and then you're going to leave. You're going to leave this room, leave New York, and you are never, *ever* going to come back to this city again. You are going to forget all about Madison Hannah, and you're going to forget about everything you might or might not have seen or heard since you arrived."

Detective Mathers came back to the table. She leaned over him again. This time, something slipped from the neck of her prim ivory blouse.

A tiny antique key on a silver chain.

"Oops," she said, her voice flat. "Goodness. How did that get there?"

She held his gaze and pointedly tucked the key back into hiding.

Now the ice along Lionel's spine spread to his arms, his legs, freezing him to his chair. A winter storm raged in his stomach.

"Why are you doing this?" he whispered.

"Nobody walks away from our queen," Mathers said. "Nobody. Maddie broke her oaths. There's a bill for treason, and sooner or later, no matter how far you run, no matter how long, it always comes due. My sisters and I have been hunting her down for a long, long time, Lionel. And you walked her right into our arms. So thank you for that. Let us reward you by sending you home."

"Maddie isn't the one you should be angry at. Jimmy Sloane—"

"Is being dealt with. It's none of your business, and it isn't your fight."

She picked up the pen, shoved it into his manacled hand, and closed his fingers around it.

"Write the confession," she said.

"No."

"Lionel, it's real easy, okay? You can either write what I tell you, and walk out that door a free man, or you can spend the next twenty years—minimum—in a prison cell. And if you think we can't get at you inside, you'd better think again." Her eyes narrowed to iron slits, like gun ports, as her voice dropped to a graveyard whisper. "You will spend the rest of your life in an endless living hell, suffering every indignity you can imagine—and a number you can't—every single hour of every single day. And then, on the very last day of your sentence, you'll be stabbed to death in a prison riot one hour before your release. You will *never* breathe free air again."

She stood back and gestured at the pad.

"It's her or you. Doesn't get any simpler than that. Make the smart choice."

Lionel looked down at the blank yellow pad. He rapped the pen against the paper.

Then he began to write.

He finished, swiveled the pad around, and slid it across the table. Detective Mathers glanced down and read his confession.

I won't betray her.

Also, go fuck yourself.

Sincerely, Lionel Page.

Mathers's hands curled into fists.

"Okay," she said, stepping around the table and moving in on him. "If you really want it the hard way, we can—"

The interrogation-room door swung open. Mathers froze as another woman stormed inside. Dressed in a vintage pantsuit, she was short and wiry, her steel-gray hair pinned in a bun with chopsticks. She glared at Mathers over the rims of her bifocals.

"Lionel, don't say one more word. Detective Mathers, are you interrogating my client without his lawyer present?"

"He didn't ask for one."

"I don't even have—" Lionel started to say. The newcomer slapped down a business card on the table, right next to his shackled hand. He picked it up.

AGNES ASHCROFT, it read, ATTORNEY-AT-LAW. Beneath her phone number, cramped handwriting in scarlet ink added, *I work for Regina Dunkle. Now SHUT UP.*

He decided to follow her advice. The detective actually took a halting step back under Agnes's ferocious advance, the lioness outmatched in her own den.

"That surveillance camera," Agnes said, "is unplugged. Care to explain why?"

"I . . . I hadn't noticed," Mathers said.

"There are a lot of things you apparently *hadn't noticed.* A word? Outside?"

They left him alone with his thoughts, sealed in the musty room with his hands still shackled to the table. He folded them and left them there.

Regina was trying to get him out. *Great.* But that didn't help Maddie. Well, it might, but only if Regina really wanted to. And given the way she treated her, Lionel didn't want to gamble on it. And here he was, sitting in the heart of the tempest, and he couldn't do a damn thing.

The frustration, the helplessness, was the worst part. He felt like an ant in a world of gods and monsters, watching them tear everything apart, and he couldn't do anything to stop it. All he wanted was to carve out a little bubble in the middle of all the chaos. Their very own eye in the storm. Someplace Maddie could breathe easy, and rest her head, and stop running.

As it was, he'd be lucky if they both survived long enough to see another sunrise.

The door swung open. Detective Mathers looked like someone had run over her dog. She unceremoniously unlocked Lionel's shackles. Not a word, and she didn't look him in the eye.

"You aren't being charged," Agnes told him. "Let's go."

Dumbfounded, he followed her into the cinder-block hallway. "Wait, why *not?*"

"Because after speaking to the powers that be, and enumerating the specific, exact laws you violated on your little adventure, I also enumerated all the ways I—and Ms. Dunkle—can make it very painful for them to pursue prosecution. Simply put, you aren't worth it."

"But what about"—he dropped his voice to a whisper as a pair of uniformed officers walked by in the other direction—"what about the *bodies*? The dead ghouls?"

"Mr. Page," she said with an indulgent sigh, "do you really believe that in this day and age, a clan of cannibalistic human offshoots could live beneath a major metropolis without being detected by city officials?"

"Wait. They . . . they *know?*"

"The people who need to know, know. They know enough to leave such things where they fall, and not mention it in the official reports. By now, those corpses have been ferried away nicely and tidily by their kin." She gave him a wry glance. "Ghouls don't waste meat. And they aren't sentimental."

"What about Maddie and Brianna? You've got to get them out of here. I'm not leaving without them."

The lawyer breezed through the precinct lobby. Lionel followed her through the doors, out onto concrete steps and the harsh, hot light of the late afternoon. The sun was simmering its way down like an egg in a cast-iron skillet, orange and watery around the edges.

"Your employer was released an hour after she was brought in. Innocent bystander, got confused and went the wrong way during the evacuation. Done and done. As for Madison . . ."

She gestured across the parking lot. At the end of a row of cars, near the sidewalk's edge, Brianna and Maddie were deep in a conversation. Maddie seemed to sense him before she saw him. She turned her head, and her eyes lit up like a kid on Christmas morning.

He ran, and she ran, and they met each other halfway and ended up tangled in each other's arms. Squeezing awkwardly, trying for a kiss and missing each other's mouths, and he broke out laughing into her chin while her lips crushed against his forehead. They tried again. This time, they got it right.

Maddie broke their embrace but stayed close, her fingertips clinging to his arms.

"We've got work to do," she said.

Fifty-Four

Standing behind Lionel, the lawyer cleared her throat.

"Not to belabor the point," Agnes said, "but you certainly do. And considering your former sisters are now aware of your presence in the city . . ."

"Right." Maddie grabbed Lionel's hand. "Come on, we've got to get off the street."

Brianna wasn't far away. She had a new look in her eyes that Lionel had never seen before. Something off-kilter. Haunted. He wondered what they'd been talking about.

"Ms. Dunkle wants you to report in as soon as Sloane is dealt with," Agnes said. "Madison, she'll have new identity papers ready for you. I'm afraid Madison Hannah is going to skip her court appearance, forfeit her bond, and spend the rest of her life as a hunted fugitive."

"Not the first identity I've had to burn," Maddie said. "Not by a long shot. Still. Sucks. I liked that one. My driver's-license picture was *really* good for once."

Lionel looked to Brianna. "Hey. You okay?"

It took her a second to find the words.

"After what I saw today? After what your friend's been telling me for the last hour or so?" Brianna looked at him like he was a stranger. "No, Lionel. I am not okay."

"You should go. Get to the airport, take the next flight out—"

"Did you?"

He stared at her.

"When you found out the truth," she said. "Did you? No. So neither am I. See, this ex-typewriter-salesman douchebag just made one fatal mistake."

"He . . . messed with your ex-boyfriend?"

Brianna snorted at him. She looked to Maddie. "You believe this guy? No. He messed with *me*. Which means, by extension, he messed with the Channel Seven News team."

"A team I'm also on," Lionel pointed out.

"Look, I can't do the . . . things you can," Brianna told Maddie, "but if you need some dirt dug up, I've got professionals on speed dial."

"We'll take all the help we can get," Maddie said.

Maddie wanted to put some distance between them and the precinct, and no one could argue with her. They ended up in Long Beach, a stretch of road and bright sand south of Queens where a spear-shaped peninsula curved along the water. Maddie knew a diner there. It was a long, narrow box of a place where the booths were divided by sheets of decorated glass and rainbow-colored puff balls dangled from the ceiling. The hostess sat them in the back, near a wall of autographed photos capturing local celebrities and minor-league athletes. The laminated menus bore '80s-style neon triangles and loud, cursive fonts, and Lionel wasn't sure if it was a deliberately retro theme or the diner's original look. They'd arrived between rushes and had most of the place to themselves.

"Try the milkshakes—they're amazing," Maddie said. "I'm glad this place is still here. Got me through the most epic hangover years ago."

Lionel eyed the menu. "What am I allowed to eat?"

"Rule of thumb: Waffles are vegetarian. Chicken and waffles are not."

"Wait." Brianna was midway through setting up her laptop, pulling it from her bulky messenger bag. "Vegetarian? Lionel Page. Going vegetarian."

He gave her a sheepish shrug. "Trying new things."

"Uh-*huh*." She buried her face in the menu and muttered, "My ace reporter's been replaced by a pod person. I'm having a turkey burger, and you can sit there and like it."

They were finally out of danger, maybe just long enough to take one deep breath before plunging back in. Lionel could work with that. He leaned back in his booth, the plush seat molding itself around his aching shoulder, and used the moment's peace to formulate a plan of attack.

"Corbin Investment Partners," he said. "They know everything. Where the dead catchers are, where we can find Sloane. He's conning them, but they still know enough to help us bring him down."

Deep in thought, Maddie contemplated the wall of photographs. "Probably not the entire company. Whoever is at the top, though—whoever signs the checks and authorizes payments—that's the one we want. But we have to be careful. Just because Sloane is taking advantage of his patron doesn't make his patron a good guy. I mean, whoever he is, he financed the construction of the dead catchers. He *knows* what they do."

Brianna was rattling away on her keyboard. Lionel was on the opposite side of the table so he couldn't see her screen, but he heard the multiple muffled telltale *bwoops* of a Skype session in action. Eventually, after the waitress came around to take their orders, she spoke up.

"I got word to the Technical Twins. Karen's on board, too." She paused, looking to Maddie. "Our support team at the newsroom, and my aide-de-camp, who brooks no foolishness. Anyway, they're on board and digging in. Obviously I didn't tell them everything, just enough that they know what to look for. Namely, anything and everything about Corbin."

"That name," Lionel said. "It's bugging me."

The waitress came by with a platter, laying out a trio of milkshakes in tall, fluted glasses. Maddie's looked like a rainbow had exploded in an ice-cream factory.

"Corbin?" Maddie asked. "It's old French. Means 'raven.' Maybe the Poe connection is what's standing out? 'Quoth the raven, nevermore'?"

"Maybe, but . . ." He shook his head and reached for a straw. "No. That's not it. It'll come to me."

Between the three of them, and the news team digging for data gold back in Chicago, it was easy to put together the broad strokes. Corbin Investment Partners was a ghost; it had sprung up in the wake of the Great Depression, taking advantage of a turbulent time and coming out a rare winner. When World War II rolled around, it quadrupled its fortunes by speculating on munitions and war material. Since then it had just been there, an ever-present and ever-silent fixture in the New York business scene. The founder himself had vanished into the mists of history, not even leaving a name behind. Just a son.

"The son of Corbin's founder took over in the 1930s," Maddie said. "The entire board of directors is locked down tighter than Fort Knox. It's a private firm, so they don't have to release any notes or financials. Anyway, this guy's got to be ancient by now."

"He is." Brianna frowned at her screen. "One source says he's ninety-two years old; one says ninety-six. And a recluse, which is why he's not on anybody's social pages. Apparently he suffers from hyperesthesia."

"Which is?" Lionel asked.

"Abnormally sharp senses. Sounds are painfully loud, light hurts his eyes. According to the only puff piece Karen was able to find about him, all his clothes have to be custom-tailored from silk—with the seams on the outside—because anything else feels like a cheese grater on his skin. Lousy way to live, rich or not."

Lionel was following a tangent. He couldn't let go of that name. He knew he'd read it before, something from a book, when he was young, and it wasn't about ravens. Then he found it on his phone's web browser. He just wasn't sure what it meant.

> Corbin is an alternate name in some sources for Corbenic, in the Arthurian literary tradition. Corbin/ Corbenic is, per Thomas Malory's *Le Morte d'Arthur*, the home of the Holy Grail . . .

"That was from a few years back, too," Brianna said. "Fisher hasn't granted an interview in ages—"

"Wait." Lionel locked eyes with her. "What's his name?"

"Fisher. Rex Fisher."

He sagged back in his seat.

"No," he said. "It isn't. It's a fake name. He's sending a message. It's a cry for help. He's been crying for help since the '30s."

Maddie sipped her milkshake. "What do you mean?"

"Corbin. Home, per Arthurian myth, of the Holy Grail and the Fisher King. Fisher. *Rex* means 'King.' Fisher. King."

"You," Brianna said, "are sounding very conspiracy-nuttish right now. Wanna clarify?"

He set his phone on the table.

"Okay, look. The Arthurian myths are a mess. They evolved over time. There's like, ten different versions of each story, and half of them contradict each other. But here's the gist of this one: The Fisher King is horribly wounded, crippled. He's sitting in Corbin Castle, waiting for a knight to come and heal him."

"Heal him how?" Brianna asked.

"With magic." Lionel tapped his phone. "He needs someone to heal him with magic. So, in the story, Sir Perceval shows up, and he's supposed to ask the Fisher King a special question, and if he gets it right, he'll be healed."

"Does he?" Maddie asked.

"Nah, he screws it up, and the ending, well, that depends on which version you're reading. It doesn't matter. The point is, Rex Fisher is Sloane's patron. That's the con. He thinks Sloane can heal whatever's wrong with him."

"The hyperesthesia," Brianna said.

No. He was missing something. Lionel stepped back through the timeline, walking through the clues since he'd first landed in New York. And farther back, since he'd first stepped into Regina Dunkle's mansion, saying goodbye to the world he knew.

The final piece clicked into place.

"He doesn't have hyperesthesia. That's a lie, too. We need to talk to Rex Fisher in person. Tonight."

"He still financed building the dead catchers," Maddie said. "He's still dangerous. Maybe not dangerous like Sloane is, but we can't just walk into his office."

"Sure we can," he told her. "Because I know what his injury is. And I know exactly what he wants."

⌇

Brianna's team tracked down Fisher, hunting his ghost through three layers of corporate shells. Officially, Corbin Investment Partners didn't even have a physical presence in the city. Unofficially and under a different name, they occupied a converted office building on the edge of the Hudson, down near the Meatpacking District. Brianna gave them an address. Then, while Maddie took care of the bill, she met Lionel outside on the sidewalk.

"I hate doing this," he told her.

"Lemme save you a second or two. This is the part where you tell me I can't come, it's too dangerous. Then I say, 'Oh, *hell* no, you didn't just tell me it's too dangerous.' Then you dig deep and tell me that it's probably a suicide mission and you probably aren't going to make it back, and I say that's exactly why I should come, and . . . am I on the right track? Tell me if I'm close."

"You're cheating," he said. "We've had so many arguments, it's hard to surprise you."

"Yeah. True. True."

She glanced away. They watched the sluggish traffic inch along the beachfront boulevard while the last rays of the sun sizzled and died on the cold blue water.

"Tell me one thing," she said.

"Shoot."

Now she met his eyes.

"You ever coming back?"

"Assuming I live through this?"

"Yeah," she said. "Assuming."

"I'd like to think so."

"But you don't know."

He had to think about that.

"I'm going through some . . . changes right now," he said. "Hey. I'm not going to disappear on you. I don't know if I'm coming back to the station. I don't even know if I'm coming back to Chicago. But . . . I'll come back to you. We're still friends. Nothing ever changes that."

She punched his arm, featherlight. "Asshole. You did the thing I told you not to do. A hundred damn times, I told you not to."

"Yeah? What's that?"

Brianna smiled. The streetlamp came on with a humming flicker, white light glistening wet in her eyes.

"You became the story," she said.

He pulled her close, holding her tight, because that was the only way he could keep himself together.

"You take care," he whispered in her ear.

That was all either of them had to say. He let her go. She flagged down a taxi. He watched her leave.

"Gonna be okay?" Maddie asked. He wasn't sure how long she'd been standing there.

"Yeah." He nodded. "So. Shall we?"

Maddie raised her open palms and let them fall, a shrug and a fatalistic smile.

"This will all be over by sunrise, one way or another," she said. "Hey, did I tell you the most fun part of being a witch?"

"No. What's that?" he asked.

"Making trouble. C'mon, let's go."

Fifty-Five

The Corbin Investment Partners building didn't have a name. No signage, nothing to indicate who rented the place or why. It was a mollusk on the Hudson River shore: half the building in brick, three stories, stout, while the left side ended in a twisted framework of glass and steel that curved like a snail's shell. Old-world economy colliding head-on with modern art. The lobby was on the snail-shell end, and a taxi dropped Lionel and Maddie off at the closed double doors. The lights were all doused. The great glass panes looked in on a silent span of marble floor and an empty security desk.

"It's seven," Maddie said. "They're either closed up for the night or they're never actually open to visitors. I'd give it even odds."

"Fisher is in there. He is, or someone who can tell us where we can find him. We've got to get inside."

Lionel scouted around for a side door while Maddie contemplated the two decorative trees, young saplings in ceramic pots flanking the front walk. He glanced over his shoulder.

"Maybe if we go around back—"

One of the trees went flying. The front door shattered on impact, a cascade of glass raining down as the pot exploded on the lobby floor and painted the imported marble in a spray of soil and fallen leaves.

"Or," Lionel said, "that's also an option."

She stepped carefully over the doorframe, watching for the jagged edges, and Lionel followed. No sign of an alarm. Not an audible one, anyway, but he figured there was a good chance the cops were already on their way. He imagined himself stuck in an interrogation room with Detective Mathers—again—and his already-pounding heartbeat kicked up to a new tempo.

"If your theory is right," Maddie told him, "we don't need to worry about breaking in. If you're wrong, we're screwed anyway."

"I feel like you're putting a lot on my shoulders right now."

"Hey, I *agree* with your theory." She pointed to an elevator on the far side of the abandoned lobby. "Stairs. Let's try the top floor and work our way down. Big shots like to be on the top floor."

They were ten feet away when the elevator door chimed and rumbled open. There was suddenly a whole bunch of angry faces and a whole bunch of matte-black steel barrels pointed in their direction; Lionel counted seven guns, but it was hard to be sure when the muzzles were all waving in his face over shouts for him to get on his knees. He held up his open hands and stood his ground. Maddie did the same.

"We're here to see Rex Fisher," he said.

The shouting faded into silence. Six pairs of eyes looked to lucky number seven, a man in a tight crew-neck shirt and cargo pants with a buzz cut that made his head look like a bullet. He swaggered up with authority. Then he pointed to the broken glass behind them.

"That isn't how you make an appointment."

"We're in a hurry," Lionel said.

"Cops are on their way. When you get out of jail, try calling Mr. Fisher's secretary during office hours."

"He's been waiting for us."

"I doubt that."

"Call him," Lionel said. "Tell him that Sir Perceval is here."

The guard stepped back. The confidence in his eyes guttered like a candle in a sharp breeze, flickering but clinging to life.

"Watch these two," he told the others. Then he stepped into the corner of the lobby. He hunched into his phone, talking in a whisper.

He came back a couple of minutes later and jerked his thumb toward the elevator door.

"Okay. The man says okay."

They didn't take the elevator up. They went down, two stories below the city streets, to a floor marked B-2. The elevator door made a grinding sound as it opened onto a long and narrow corridor paneled in rich mahogany. A pale-blue runner lined a polished parquet floor all the way from the elevator to a single closed door at the hallway's opposite end. Along the way, a pair of electric sconces fashioned like brass candlesticks struggled to provide illumination. The tiny, flickering bulbs offered more shadows than light.

"Down the hall and through the door," the man with the buzz cut told them. Lionel and Maddie stepped off the elevator. He didn't. The door slid shut at their backs.

They walked. Lionel wanted to say something, but disturbing the silence felt heretical somehow. The corridor had the musty, dry air of a library. Or a mausoleum. The door on the other side opened with a whisper of freshly oiled hinges.

An empty puddle of light shone down upon the jigsaw parquet. Just one spotlight, pointed downward at the heart of the room, the rest shrouded in darkness.

Lionel and Maddie stood on one side of the light. From the opposite side, a man's voice rasped out. It was a wet, phlegmatic sound, like his throat was caked with graveyard soil.

"Sir Perceval. Have you come to ask the question? The question that will heal me, and end my sorrows?"

"I'm sorry," Lionel said. "No. I don't have that power. I don't have a question. Only a name. Your name."

He took a step forward, up to the edge of the light.

"Your name is Ernest Valdemar."

Across the spotlight a shadow shambled, inch by painful inch. Gangly limbs unfurled like a half-dead fly mired in glue, struggling to tear itself from a spiderweb. The man ambled slow to the other side of the light, his features cast in ashen gray.

He wore a suit that would have been stylish once, patched and frayed now, and too big for his tiny shoulders, like he'd shriveled up inside it. Too-long trouser cuffs dragged along the floor, and the jacket sleeves swallowed his thin hands. He had skin of dried leather and eyes like blurry watercolor paint. A ring of raw, red flesh circled his throat like a necklace, an ancient rope burn from a noose that had failed at its task. He contemplated Lionel and Maddie, his nearly hairless eyebrows clenched, and spoke.

"How did you find me?"

"The piece that didn't fit," Lionel said. "We found the dead catchers, worked out Jimmy Sloane's plan, and found out he had financial backing from Corbin Investment Partners. But Sloane had another job to do, one that didn't seem to have any connection at first. Laying hands on that manuscript."

"A lost first draft by Edgar Allan Poe," Maddie said. "At first we thought he wanted it for the money. But why go to all that trouble when he had Corbin footing his bills? Then it became clear: he wasn't trying to sell the manuscript—he was trying to make it vanish from the face of the earth. But he missed a copy, and we gave it a read. The only difference between the original story and the one that was published in 1845 was the ending. The ending where you survive. When Sloane bragged about his skills as a necromancer, that was the last piece we needed to put it all together."

Lionel wasn't sure what he had expected. After all the death that had brought him and Maddie to this room, this moment, face-to-face with the architect of so much pain, he'd imagined Valdemar as some kind of archvillain. A cackling mastermind, maybe, or a sinister, confident puppet master. Not this broken-down old man whose rheumy eyes struggled to focus on them. Lionel wanted to hate him. The best he could muster was pity as he made his accusation.

"You can't die," Lionel said. "When Poe published that story as a true account, it wasn't a hoax. Every word of it was true except for the ending he changed, just before it went to press. You can't die. And you *want* to."

Maddie spread her hands. "The dead catchers, the machine you're building . . . that's what this is all about. Sloane was on the run; after he stole the Lapis Manalis and murdered his old coven mates, every servant of Hekate in America wanted him dead. He needed safe harbor, and you were exactly the kind of sucker he was looking for: rich, reclusive, and desperate. He showed you some spirit-conjuring tricks and told you he was a master of necromancy. You believed him. Just like you believed him when he told you he knew a way to tear open a door between worlds."

"A door to the afterlife," Lionel said.

Valdemar gave a weak nod. His jaw twitched as his spindly neck made faint popping sounds.

"Mr. Poe's miraculous cure for death, I fear, pulled me back from the River Styx. But it did nothing to alleviate the symptoms of my condition. One of my lungs is ossified. The other, rotten, and adhered to my ribs so that I feel the bones crackling, the wet flesh tearing, with every breath I take. I have a tumor in my belly. It weighs as much as an infant. Sometimes I think I can feel it kick."

He took a long, wet breath.

"I have been in agony, every waking moment, since October the twelfth of 1845. And I do not sleep. I have tried to end myself, of course I have. Poison, asphyxiation, slitting my wrists in a warm bath." His trembling fingers brushed the rope burn at his throat. "I never heal entirely, and each attempt layered fresh torments upon the ones I'd already collected. I went to a mortuary, once. I stood at the door of the crematory oven, planning to crawl inside and submit to the flames.

And do you know what stayed my hand? The most terrible thought occurred to me."

Valdemar shambled closer. Under the stark spotlight, glistening off his sparse black hair and snow-white whiskers, they saw the full ruin of his body. The man was a corpse, choked with bile and phlegm where healthy blood and air should have been. A cage of mottled skin and brittle bone. Something in his moist eyes made Lionel think of a fly slamming itself against a window, over and over again, desperately trying to escape.

."What if I burned?" he rasped. "What if I burned until there was nothing left of me but ashes . . . *and I could still think and feel?*"

"So you turned to Sloane," Maddie said.

"So I did. Building a fortune is child's play when you have time enough. I was already a man of some modest means before my . . . condition, and a talent for speculation—plus a convenient war or two—gave me the resources to do as I pleased. Eventually I had to let Corbin's founder 'die' and pass the company to his son. I really should have done it more than once. Rex Fisher is becoming improbably old. That said, I've gotten adept at evading the gaze of the media and, well, faking your death, posing as your own child, and passing your assets to yourself is a lot harder than it sounds. Really, you can't imagine the paperwork."

"Actually, I can," Maddie said.

"I plumbed the mysteries of the occult," Valdemar said, "but I've no real talent for it. Then I met James Sloane. He showed me his genius, and he shared his plan: to open a doorway to that far shore, the respite I was dragged from in what *should* have been my moment of death, all those years ago. I'll simply . . . walk through. And rest. Finally. Sweet, blessed rest."

"Sloane lied to you," Lionel told him.

"No. No, I don't believe that. He has no motive to lie. He's the designated heir in Rex Fisher's will. Once he fulfills his end of the bargain, he'll inherit my entire fortune. We're so close to a breakthrough. Don't you see? That's why I had him retrieve that manuscript, once I heard rumors of its existence. The published story is one thing; I *know* what that contains. I didn't know what Edgar had written in his first draft, how many details he'd recounted, or if anything he'd penned could lead to my doorstep. I couldn't take any chances. Couldn't risk anyone following my trail and ruining what we've labored so long to build here."

"He's after more than money," Maddie said. "And as far as the story goes . . . really? You had all those people killed, all that bloodshed, because the draft *might* say something dangerous? You didn't even *know*?"

He waved a twitching hand. "How could I know? I've never read it. I just knew it existed, that's all. But you're making far too much of this. No one was *killed*."

"There are thirty or so dead bodies in a Lincoln Square high-rise who would disagree with you," Lionel said. "Not to mention Lana Taylor, the handwriting expert who Sloane murdered just to clean up your trail."

"I . . . no. No, you're both mistaken. My orders to James were very particular. He was to purchase the manuscript, bring it to me, and we'd assess our plan from there. I know that he has a . . . checkered past, I suppose, but he understands my principles. I would never order him to hurt anyone."

"You have dead catchers hidden all over this city, sucking up stray souls so you can use them like batteries," Maddie said. "If that's not hurting people, what the hell would you call it?"

"A momentary inconvenience, in the grand scope of things. James assures me of that. The captive souls won't be harmed in the slightest. Their collective energy will open the door, and once I pass through, they'll be freed."

His voice had taken on a wheedling, pleading tone. Lionel's sense of pity curdled in the pit of his stomach like milk going rancid, turning into disgust.

"You know better," Lionel said. "A 'checkered past'? You know Sloane is a killer. You know what he's done."

"Not the gross details, but—"

"Because you didn't *want to*. You sit down here in your little bunker, hiding from the world, while a man with blood on his hands goes out and does your dirty work. And you have the gall, the unbelievable fucking *gall*, to pretend he's suddenly going to play nice because you dangled some cash over his head."

He brandished the Polaroid from his mother's keepsake box as he strode into the circle of light. He shoved it into Valdemar's face.

"Look at it. That's my mother, in the front row. Sloane murdered her in cold blood. All those smiling people with her? Them too."

"That—that was a long time ago," Valdemar stammered. "People change—"

"He hasn't. Sloane's been leaving bodies all over this city, and the only reason you don't know is because you don't *want* to know. You've been keeping your hands over your ears and your eyes squeezed shut because you know exactly what kind of monster you made a deal with. You shook hands with the devil, and you've been lying to yourself ever since. And, please. The trapped souls are just going to fly free once the door is open? Those people—innocent human beings, just like you were, once—are *batteries*, Valdemar. Know what happens when you put batteries in a machine? They get *sucked dry*."

"And the punch line is," Maddie said, "you're not even going to get what you want. Sloane is using you. He's trying to open a door between worlds, but it's not anywhere you want to go."

The room fell silent. And one last spark of hope, small and delicate and warm, shattered behind Ernest Valdemar's eyes. His gaze fell to the floor like he could see it there, a porcelain teacup in a hundred pieces, broken beyond repair. Broken after he'd been carrying it for so long.

"I'm sorry," he whispered.

The last of his lies lay scattered at his feet. His shoulders sagged, and his spine slouched, like they'd been propping him up this whole time.

"I didn't want to hurt anyone. I didn't. But Sloane said all the right things, and made all the right promises and . . . I just want the pain to stop." He closed his eyes, trembling. "I'm so tired, and I just want it to *stop*."

Lionel reached out to him. He rested his hand on Valdemar's shoulder. His frail, thin bones felt like balsa wood, like they might snap in a stiff wind.

"It's time to do the right thing," Lionel said. "It's time to end this. This machine you're building—take us there."

Fifty-Six

There was one more subbasement under the building. The elevator ride took twice as long.

"How deep is this thing?" Maddie asked.

Valdemar stared up at the panel of lights above the door. "Not deep. Tall. The Liminal Engine is . . . Well, it's one of a kind, and miniaturization was not a design priority."

Lionel glanced at him. "Liminal?"

"In-between. That's what *liminal* means. States of matter and energy, places, times. To enter a sphere of liminality is to be suspended between possibilities. Which is exactly what my engine is designed to do; it will engineer a point of transition between worlds, where both and neither coexist in the same space, allowing transition from one to the other."

The elevator rumbled to a stop. The doors opened with a chime.

This level had been built for utility. Workmen's lights in plastic orange cages dangled along a thick power cord, shining on concrete floors and bare drywall. Valdemar led them to a pair of double doors and keyed in a three-digit code on a wall pad. The doors swung open with a pneumatic hiss.

Beyond, more dangling bulbs cast hard white light across a cold and lonely vault. The bare ceiling was twenty feet high. The floor was a hundred feet across, just as deep and just as bare.

"No," Valdemar said.

He hobbled in, head darting, bobbing. He turned, and his face was contorted in horror.

"No, no, it's . . . This is wrong, this is entirely wrong. Where is it?" He stood in the heart of the empty vault and threw up his arms. "Where is my machine?"

"When was the last time you came down here?" Maddie asked him.

"Months, months ago. James told me there was no need, he had everything under control. But . . . you don't understand, it couldn't just be taken—"

"Piece by piece, it could," Lionel said. "If a thief, for example, had a pack of ghouls working for him, and free rein under the city streets. Now we know why Sloane joined forces with Dergwyn."

Behind them, the double doors swung open wide. Valdemar's pack of security guards filed in and formed a firing line.

"To tell you the truth," Sloane said, sauntering in behind them, "once I relocated the engine, I wasn't ever coming back here. This is kind of a last-minute change of plans."

Valdemar's hand shook like a leaf as he pointed. "Detain this man."

The guards drew their guns, but every muzzle pointed squarely at him. Sloane let out a weary sigh.

"Sorry, they work for me now. I made 'em a better offer. With your money, ironically enough, but you were the one who gave me signing authority over your bank account." He looked to Lionel and Maddie. "Anyway, I figured you two would piece together the rest of the story and end up here soon enough. I don't like leaving loose ends behind."

Lionel took an angry step forward. Seven pistols swung to point his way, steel clicking as nervous hands thumbed back their hammers. He stopped in his tracks.

"You don't go anywhere without people to hide behind, do you?" Lionel asked him.

"Not if I can help it. I've worked too hard, too long, to take unnecessary risks. I'm a cautious man."

"You're a coward."

Sloane's confident smile faded as his lips went tight.

"I'm too cautious to be baited by cheap taunts, kid. Save it for the schoolyard."

One of the security guards stepped behind the firing line. He stood close to Sloane, lugging something in an oversize duffel bag. Sloane reached inside, nodded at whatever he saw there, and beckoned to Valdemar.

"I have to tell you, this is kind of fortuitous. Really, Ernest, I was just going to take your money and run, but seeing as I'm here . . . maybe I can help you after all."

"You . . . you can?" Valdemar's washed-out eyes widened.

"I owe it to you, don't I? C'mere."

"He's lying," Maddie said. "Don't do it."

Valdemar hobbled toward the firing line. Maddie lunged, reaching for him. One of the guards pulled his trigger. The pistol went off with a peal of thunder, and the slug chewed a canyon in the concrete at Maddie's feet. She jumped back, and Lionel got between her and the guns, trying to shield her with his body.

Valdemar crossed the vault like he was approaching the gates of heaven. He'd found one last glimmer of hope, and he clung to it with all the strength left in his twisted bones.

"Let's see if we can't send you to your final reward," Sloane told him with a beatific smile.

Then his hand whipped free from the duffel, and the stark light shone on the blade of his machete. Valdemar had just enough time to realize, to see the razor-edged steel high in his betrayer's grip, before it whistled through the air.

Ernest Valdemar's head hit the concrete and bounced, rolling like a misshapen basketball. His body crashed to the floor a second later.

Yellowed, bubbling pus leaked from the ragged stump of his neck, mixed with a trickle of dust-flecked raspberry blood.

"Let's see," Sloane said. He handed off the machete and crouched down to grab Valdemar's severed head by the hair. He held it up, face-to-face.

Valdemar's agonized eyes swiveled and rolled in their sockets. His mouth gaped, cracked lips squirming, trying to speak as air whistled through his neck.

"Nope," Sloane said, "you're still alive. Huh. Well, can't say I didn't try. At least my curiosity's been satisfied, so we can all agree that something good came out of this. Now, as for you two . . ."

Lionel gauged the distance. Ten feet between them and the firing line. No cover, nowhere to hide. If they stayed where they were, they were dead. If they charged, they were dead. Panic surged in his chest, an electric hand clenching around his heart.

"Sir?" one of the guards asked. He looked from Sloane to the sights of his pistol, waiting for the order.

"No."

Sloane edged toward the door, Valdemar's head dangling at his side. Lionel caught the flicker of uncertainty in his eyes, that same cowardice that had stayed his hand once before. He still didn't entirely trust that this wasn't some sort of elaborate trap, a doom that would spring from Lionel's spilled blood. He put on a sneer and cast his decision as bravado. "No, after the trouble you two caused me, all the headaches . . . you get something special."

He took one last look around the empty vault, then turned his back and strode to the double doors.

"Seal them in."

Lionel made a move. Another bullet cracked into the floor, kicking concrete dust into the air and forcing him back. Maddie's arms folded around him, tight.

"Don't," she whispered. He was at war with his own body. Every muscle screamed at him to *do* something as the guards made a slow retreat in Sloane's wake. At the same time, he knew that as long as they were breathing, they had hope. Getting himself shot wouldn't help either of them.

The last guard left. The doors slammed shut, leaving them alone with Valdemar's headless body. Lionel broke from Maddie's arms and charged across the vault. He hit the door with his bad shoulder and bounced off, groaning, as the steel held fast. He jammed against the handles. They barely jiggled in his hand, wedged tight.

He heard something from the other side. A gaseous hiss, then a gout of focused flame. He felt the air change, growing hot, and smelled the sharp, acrid tang of melting metal. His heart pounded like a kettledrum as he threw himself against the doors again.

"They're welding us in. Maddie, they're welding us in!"

The vault had no air vents. No other exits. It was a box of stone. Lionel felt the walls closing in, the room shrinking, growing coffin tight—

—and then she had him again. Turning him around, pulling him close and holding him.

Someone killed the power. The overheads died, plunging the vault into darkness.

"Hey," Maddie said. "It's okay."

~

They sat side by side on the cold stone floor. He wasn't sure for how long. They just leaned on one another, skin to skin, feeling each other's slow and careful breaths.

He wanted to see her. He reached into his pocket. Not for his phone—that was the first thing they'd tried, only to find they were too far underground to get a signal. All the same, he wanted to conserve the battery. Just in case.

Instead, he took out the dead catcher he'd been carrying since they left Wen Xiulang's shop. Cold sapphire light misted from the tiny windows, casting their faces in its midnight glow.

"Maddie," he asked, "what happens when we die?"

She snuggled against him and leaned her head against his shoulder.

"Complicated question. Lots of answers. Depends on who you are, what you've done, who you know."

"Like a goddess."

"Like a goddess. Your mother, for instance . . . Hekate probably came for her. Took her home."

"To *her* home. So . . . when our air runs out . . . I'm not even going to see her again, am I? I mean, when people talk about going to heaven or wherever, the one thing they dream about is seeing their family again. And it's not going to happen." He paused. "So what about you and me?"

Her hand slid around his. She gave it a squeeze.

"Hold on tight and stay close," she told him. "Whatever happens, just try to stay close."

They just breathed for a while. The air had a stale taste to it.

"It's funny," Lionel said.

"What is?"

"I was just thinking, the night I landed in New York, and everything was so . . . unreal. All I saw was the echoes of a hundred movies, TV shows . . ."

"Stories," Maddie said.

"I remember thinking, huh, maybe I'll have a meet-cute with some manic pixie dream girl, and, you know, she'll shake up my stodgy perspective and teach me how to appreciate life."

She burst out laughing, leaned into him, and punched his arm. He laughed, too. He couldn't help it. It seemed like a good use of the air they had left. He curled his hand around her shoulder and held her close.

"That trope is *so* sexist," she said.

"I know, I just . . . I like romantic comedies, okay? Don't tell anyone. You'll ruin my reputation."

"Your secret is safe with me." She eyed him. "So. How'd that wish work out for you?"

"Well . . . met a real woman instead. She turned out to be pretty amazing."

"Even the not-so-perfect parts?"

He kissed her forehead. "*Especially* the not-so-perfect parts."

They fell into a comfortable silence.

"You know what bothers me?" Lionel said. "I'm never going to solve the mystery."

"Which one?"

"That night. My lost memories. Whatever it was that my mother said to me before she died, what happened to me out on that road, between running from the fire and being rescued. I know, it sounds petty—it's not like we don't have bigger problems. Stuck in here while Sloane tears a hole in the universe."

Maddie sighed. "And probably destroying the world, all because he's an entitled jerk with self-esteem issues. Not a great way for humanity to go. That said, I can't pretend to be all that surprised. I've been around for three thousand years, Lionel. I've seen a *lot* of Jimmy Sloanes. One of 'em was going to get lucky eventually."

"Whatever this thing is on the other side? The one he's been in contact with? I hope it eats him first."

"Probably will. From what little we saw of the other side, I'm thinking it's not exactly a bastion of puppies and hugs."

The other side. Lionel sat up straight, so fast Maddie almost jumped. "What?" she said.

"Maddie. The other dead catcher from Wen Xiulang's shop. Do you still have it?"

Her hand snaked into her jeans pocket. "Yeah, why?"

"Remember the subway tunnel? The longer Sloane's catchers stayed hooked up, the more it changed around us."

"Yeah. Like the hundreds of giant spiders. Kind of hard to forget."

"The *walls*," he said. "The walls changed, in spots where our worlds overlapped. There were points where the subway tunnels just weren't there anymore."

In the glow of the dead catcher, her eyes locked onto his.

"Wait a second. You want to snap these together and *deliberately* cause a dimensional rift."

Lionel pointed to the welded doors.

"All we need is one gap," he said. "One wrinkle between worlds where the open air on *that* side overlaps the solid door on *this* side. We run through, we disconnect the disks, reality goes back to normal."

"And what if the spot on the other side isn't open air? Or what if it's, you know, filled with something that's going to eat us?"

Lionel had to smile.

"It's worth a shot," he said.

She held up her disk, right next to his. Their hands touched.

"Worth a shot," she said. "Let's do this."

Fifty-Seven

Their dead catchers snapped together. A metallic hum split the silence.

"Get ready," Lionel said.

They rose from the concrete, facing the welded doors, as the world twisted at the edges of their vision. Chaos leaked in around the corners. Chaos and rot. The concrete, cast in the sapphire glow of the dead catchers, became mottled and streaked with rust. Shapes skittered and writhed around their feet, poking the air with twitching tendrils as they sensed the overlap between worlds. Something loped along the ceiling high above their heads, something made of wet tongues and teeth.

"Whatever happens," Maddie said, "stay close to me."

The effect grew stronger. Lionel slapped at his cheek as something—moist, soft, hungry—brushed against his skin. A flood of tiny chitinous shells washed over Valdemar's headless body, and the air filled with crunching, suckling sounds.

This would be the world, once Sloane powered up his engine. First New York, then spreading outward in all directions, a contagion infesting the entire globe. Lionel wondered how long it would take. Years? Weeks? Hours? Maybe scattered pockets of humanity could survive, for a little while.

And then, assuming the creature pulling his strings didn't stab him in the back, this would be Jimmy Sloane's reward. The crown prince of a dead planet.

Something big was coming.

They heard it in the darkness, the end of the vault too far for the dead catcher's glow to reach. Something heavy, elephantine, dragging its way toward them with legs that *squelched* with every step. Lionel pictured a rotted blue whale, vast and beached and its maw open wide—

The vault shifted out of focus. Dead ahead, a ragged chunk of door and part of the wall faded away as the world on the other side asserted its dominion over steel and stone.

"Now!" Maddie shouted. They lunged through the gap, side by side.

They burst through, into the hallway beyond, and yanked the dead catchers apart. The blue light sputtered, sparked, and died. Air roared in Lionel's ears as their reality flooded back in and the other side sucked away with a distant, bellowing groan.

Just for a second, he'd looked back. Back over his shoulder and into the darkness of the vault, an instant before the welded door slammed back into existence. Just for a heartbeat, he'd seen a glimpse of the thing that had been coming for them.

"Lionel?" Maddie said.

He realized he was staring. At nothing now, just the sealed and mundane doors, while his brain sparked like a misfiring car battery. He was looking for his voice and couldn't find it.

"What did you see?" she asked him.

He took a slow, deep breath and turned to face her.

"We have to stop him."

The elevator still had power. It crawled upward at a snail's pace, and Lionel wondered how much time they had left.

"We know he moved the engine," Maddie mused. "We know he probably used Dergwyn and her pack to do the heavy lifting, which means it's somewhere under the city. Even if we assume it's still in Manhattan, that's something like twenty-two square miles to search."

"It has to be someplace with some legroom. You saw the vault: he's going to need a place with high ceilings, which rules out your average sewer tunnel."

"A place under his total control," Maddie said. "Not anywhere some city employee or urban explorer can just wander in on. Sloane is over-cautious to a fault. So presumably a piece of property he owns."

The elevator chimed. The door rumbled open, and they crossed the empty, silent lobby with matching strides.

"Or a place Corbin owns," Lionel said. "Remember, he said Valdemar pretty much gave him a blank check. If we can get a rundown of their real estate holdings, then narrow them down by size and access to the underground . . ."

He trailed off. Then he dug into his back pocket.

"I know where it is."

He still had the flyer he'd been given at Calvary Cemetery, the one from Chandra Nagarkar's old professor. The murdered playwright's final cause. He unfurled the lime-green stock to reveal the faded headline:

Save Our City's Heritage! A Meeting of the Committee
to Preserve the Parthenon Theater.

~

The Parthenon Theater had lived up to its name, once, with soaring Ionic columns and an overhanging granite arch, a monument to beaux arts architecture: the best of France and ancient Greece together, merging with filigrees and baroque detail. Cherubs and goddesses danced in the stonework above the high, arched windows.

Today those windows were covered in plywood, and heavy boards shrouded every exit. It sat cold and silent and sealed tight, a temple to a forgotten deity on a dark and lonely street. A light rain was coming down, cold and tinged with the scent of salt, kicking up a mist on the streets just ahead of a summer storm. Lionel and Maddie stood on the sidewalk across the street from the theater. Lionel welcomed the droplets on his upturned face; freed from the vault, every breath of fresh air felt like a blessing.

"He's in there," Maddie said. "It's perfect. Corbin owns it, it's completely sealed at the street level, and it's plenty big enough to hide whatever he wants inside."

"So how do we get in?" Lionel asked. "First we've got to find a way to reach it underground, then get past . . . oh, six or seven guys with guns, plus Dergwyn and whoever she brought with her."

"Maybe not. They abandoned Sloane in the subway. Which is pretty typical; like I told you before, ghouls never keep their word if they see an advantage in breaking it. If we're lucky, Sloane finally figured that out and cut his ties. The engine's been relocated, so they've done the job he really needed them for."

"Which leaves the gunmen."

Lionel paused. He looked to Maddie.

"So . . . ghouls are opportunists."

"Comes with the territory. They're scavengers. Bottom-feeders."

"So if they *can* get something by sticking to a deal, they'll keep their word, right?"

She shrugged. "Sure. Why?"

"Maybe his loss is our gain. Hey, remember what you were telling me back at the Blackstone? About how witches make all kinds of deals with all kinds of creatures? It's part of our job description, right?"

Maddie slowly arched one eyebrow. "I'm not sure I like where you're going with this."

"You're still my teacher." He curled his arm around hers. "How about you show me the basics tonight?"

They made their way back across Manhattan. Lionel was lost by their fourth turn on the rain-washed streets, but Maddie knew the way.

All the way back to the black stairway running down, and the spray paint on the wall reading **FOLLOW ME DOWN**.

The bouncer at the bottom of the steps held up a beefy hand. "Private party tonight. No admittance."

Lionel turned to Maddie. She shook her head at him.

"Don't look at me," she said. "You take the lead. Do it just like I taught you on the way over."

He took a deep breath and faced the bouncer, trying to recall all the steps and phrases Maddie had given him to memorize.

"Our regards to Princess Dergwyn, first and most fierce of her pack. Despoiler of graveyards, bringer of bounty for her people, quick and fearless and strong. We have arrived under the Accord of Persephone and trust that no harm will come to ours, or to yours, until our business is done here."

Lionel lifted his left hand, drawing an intricate, sinuous curve in the air as his other hand crooked at an angle. The sign complete, he lowered his arms to his sides.

"We are witches," he told the bouncer, "and we are here to parley."

The bouncer's eyes were invisible behind his bulky plastic sunglasses, but his face went tight.

"Wait here," he said, and vanished behind the steel door.

Maddie leaned close and murmured, "Good job. Keep your left hand about half an inch lower, but you got the gesture perfect. Also it's 'until our business here is done,' but these days most people aren't going to ding you over something that petty. Oh, and one other thing? Just remember that you can invoke the right accords all night long, but whoever you're dealing with has to *want* to uphold them."

"Meaning they might eat us anyway," Lionel murmured back.

"Hey, this was your idea."

The bartender came back a minute later. This time, he held the door open. Music washed out from the darkened club. Not the driving, bone-jarring dance music of last time, but a subdued, almost subliminal sound. A steady *thump-thump-thump* like an underwater heartbeat, occasionally dressed up by faint and staccato flourishes of a synthesizer.

"You're lucky," the bouncer told them. "Dergwyn just got back with the raiding party. Everybody's in a good mood tonight."

He gestured to the open doorway.

"Welcome."

Fifty-Eight

Point lights tinted cherry red and molten gold swirled across the night-club. The beams wheeled, turning as they slid, scattering shadows and painting the gathered faces—opal eyes, distended jaws, elongated limbs, and jagged teeth—in a whirlwind of color.

Body bags littered the dance floor.

The stench of coppery blood and raw, putrefying meat choked the humid air. Dergwyn's pack huddled in clumps around the stolen bounty, tugging down zippers, digging their heads into the black vinyl bags, howling out over the thumping beat as they dug into their midnight meals. Lionel swallowed hard and kept his eyes dead ahead, trying not to watch.

The princess herself stood upon the bar. She walked from end to end like a runway model, her snowy-white raw silk Dolce & Gabbana tunic spattered in dirt and blood. A crowd of admirers called up to her, braying like hyenas, and she wore a mad grin on her face as she barked back at them. Something long and limp went flying, an offer of tribute hurled up to her, and Dergwyn snatched it out of the air. Lionel's stomach clenched as she turned and gave him a good look at her prize.

It was a human arm, roughly chopped at the elbow. Dergwyn held it by the wrist, raised it to her lips, and locked eyes with Lionel as she took a slow, deep bite.

She was still chewing when she leaped down from the bar. "Unexpected," she said with her mouth full, looking Lionel and Maddie up and down. "Come to share the feast? Or be the feast?"

"We came to bargain," Lionel told her.

He felt eyes on the back of his neck and caught shapes pressing in from both sides. They were surrounded. Dergwyn swallowed her bite, then let out a little yip of a laugh.

"We scavenge off the bones of your world. Everything that is ours now was yours before you wasted it and threw it away. So what do ghouls have that two humans could want?"

"Muscle," Lionel said. "We know Jimmy Sloane is holed up inside the Parthenon Theater, and the only way in is underground. We want to bargain for safe escort and protection."

"Jimmy, Jimmy. We are *not* on good terms with Jimmy right now. Antagonizing him would be . . . bad. Bad for me, bad for my pack."

"What you're saying is, you'd all be better off if Sloane was dead." Lionel held her gaze. "That'd be good for us, too. Help us make it happen."

She looked him over. Her brows knitted as she took another bite of flesh. A trickle of blood, like juice from a rare-cooked roast, dribbled down her pale chin.

"And if you fail, we suffer reprisal. No. Better to stand aside and let you and him fight it out. Whoever loses, we win."

"That's not true," Lionel said. "You're not seeing the big picture."

She turned her head and let out a string of fast, guttural barks. The crowd around them burst into braying laughter. Dergwyn wore a cruel, lopsided smile as she looked back to Lionel.

"My pack thinks you're funny. I think you're funny, too."

Maddie leaned close and whispered into Lionel's ear. "*Careful.* If she thinks you're challenging her in front of her people—if you're questioning her ability as a leader—she *has* to kill you. It's how they establish their pecking order."

Lionel considered his next words very carefully.

"You just said it yourself: you live off the bones of our world. Our civilization. Our bodies. Ghouls and humanity are linked. Isn't that right?"

Dergwyn's smile faded as she nodded at him. "That's right."

"You saw what happened in the subway tunnel. You got a glimpse of the other side, same as we did. When Jimmy opens that door all the way, humanity as we know it is over. Maybe not tomorrow, maybe not next week, but eventually the world as you know it is *gone*. And then what?" Lionel spread his hands. "When the last human is gone, Princess . . . what's for dinner?"

Her eyes glittered like a sheen of fresh winter snow. She fell silent for a moment.

"Can you kill him?" she asked.

Lionel looked to Maddie. She looked back at him and nodded, once. Their hands clasped tight.

"Get us past his guards and into that theater," Lionel said. "We'll do the rest."

Dergwyn stepped back, held the gnawed arm above her head like a club, and let out a hoarse, strangled yowl at the top of her lungs.

"War party!" the ghoul princess roared. *"We ride!"*

—

"Don't ask questions," echoed a voice from the far end of the tunnel.

The stenciled block letters on the wall read MAINTENANCE ACCESS 93/A. Just another endless stretch of beige tunnel down in the guts of the city. The glow of a battery-powered lamp marked a makeshift guard post and pushed back the shadows. Not far enough. Lionel and Maddie crouched low in the darkness, beyond the perimeter, surrounded by Dergwyn's hunting pack. Canine teeth gnashed the air as rivulets of hungry drool spattered the concrete.

"Closer," Dergwyn rasped, and the pack advanced on the clicking claws of their feet. "Closer."

"I'm just saying," argued another voice. "The guy's head was *still moving.*"

The first guard sighed. "Buddy, seriously. I've been on this job for five years. Know how I've lasted that long? I don't ask questions. Jimmy says, 'Guard this tunnel,' I guard that tunnel. Jimmy says, 'Dig up this grave,' I dig up that grave. Jimmy says, 'Shoot this guy,' I shoot that guy. Life is a lot easier when you're not curious."

"Closer," Dergwyn breathed. Her opal eyes shimmered at the edge of the electric light.

"Did you hear something?" one of the guards asked.

Dergwyn howled. The pack surged as one, a tide of loping, running bodies and bared teeth with the speed of a piranha swarm. They raced on all fours along the tunnel floor, some clinging to the walls, baring iron nails and eager teeth.

One of Jimmy's guards fired wild, blind, squeezing the trigger and watching bodies drop in the muzzle flash. Then he fell under a tide of ghouls. He shrieked as a dozen wet mouths tore into his skin and peeled away ragged strips of flesh. The other man's nerve broke. He dropped his pistol and ran, arms flailing, desperate to get away.

He made it five steps before they dragged him down. The blood-spattered shell of his walkie-talkie shattered on the cement floor.

Lionel and Maddie walked through the carnage. The hunters were crouched all around them, feasting, savoring their victory. Dergwyn pointed to an access ladder and bowed with a mocking flourish.

"We go no farther," she told them. "*Your* prey waits above."

⌐

The Parthenon Theater and the Liminal Engine were both one-of-a-kind creations. The Parthenon had been built for beauty. From its towering proscenium arch, still framed by drawn curtains of red velvet, to the scalloped seashell design of the overhanging balconies, every detail came together to create an art deco masterpiece. Now the theater's nine hundred seats sat empty, a blanket of dust upon the gilded railings and the broad center aisle, and only one man stood in the footlights.

Jimmy Sloane gazed upon his masterwork and smiled with pride. He'd left Valdemar's head on the edge of the stage, perched so he could watch. Everyone needed an audience once in a while.

The Liminal Engine, relocated to the stage, hadn't been built with looks in mind. It was a Rube Goldberg behemoth, a jumble of mismatched parts and jury-rigged contraptions. A fat-bellied boiler clanked and banged as steam backed up and hammered the machine's metal guts. Wheels spun and a leather bellows wheezed, billowing clouds of white-hot vapor. At the heart of the device, ninety-nine dead catchers were strung on vertical rods like the glowing beads in an abacus, waiting for rows of pistons to force them together.

It was enough. He'd scoured the city and harvested the dead catchers from junction boxes and telephone poles, hospital generators and graveyard caretakers' shacks. Every last device, brought together at last, and stuffed with enough power to blow a hole in the fabric of the universe. He had wanted to be absolutely certain, to hold off until every last catcher was full to bursting, but given the events of the last few days . . . for once in his life, rushing in felt like a smarter play than watching and waiting. It was time.

Time to get everything—the power, the respect, the adulation—he'd always been denied. Time to get his rightful due.

~

Lionel and Maddie picked their way through backstage warrens choked with dust and cobwebs, vintage dressing-room furniture buried under painters' tarps, and followed the sounds of the machine. The groaning, wheezing, steam-hammer banging of the Liminal Engine drew them around one last bend, and out onto the stage.

"Why?" Sloane asked them.

"Why, what?" Maddie said. "Why aren't we dead?"

"That too, but mostly . . ." He raised his hands and let them fall to his sides. "Why can't you just let me have this?"

"You can't be serious," Lionel said.

"You." Sloane jabbed his finger at him, stabbing the air. "You, of all people, should be on my side. Your mother's goddess threw you out like a piece of trash. You've never had a place in this world. And you've always known it. I'm right, aren't I? You've always felt like something was missing. Like you didn't belong. And you. Witch girl. Blessed with immortality, and you've spent most of your life on the run. What's the point? You're both trying to protect this world, and I gotta ask: What's this world ever done for *you*? Maybe it's time for a change."

Lionel gestured to the machine. And to the long control lever that was too close to Sloane's hand for comfort.

"You turn this thing on, a lot of innocent people are going to get hurt."

"Who's innocent?" Sloane asked. "What's innocent? It's a word. An empty, stupid word. Nobody's good, kid. Nobody's good, nobody's pure, this entire planet is a shit pile, and to be frank, it could benefit from some new management. There's no right or wrong. All that matters in life is what you can get for yourself."

He turned to the machine, his face bathed in the glow of the dead catchers.

"I'm here to get mine," he said. "I'm here to get what I earned."

"You never *earned* a damn thing." Maddie took a step toward him. "You just expected a participation award for showing up. Hekate didn't shower you with blessings, so you betrayed her. Your coven didn't put you in charge the day after your initiation, so you murdered them. You're not exceptional, Sloane. You're not special. You're just another entitled asshole. I've seen lots of guys like you over the years, and you know what they all have in common?"

His lips tightened into a bloodless line. "Do tell."

"History *forgot* them. Just like it's going to forget you."

"You've *never* met anyone like me." He pointed to the brooch on his lapel. "I've taken on anyone who ever crossed me, and I won. You want to talk about being forgotten? The Sisters of New Amsterdam treated me like a goddamn errand boy. They're dead and buried; I'm still standing."

The doors at the front of the theater opened wide.

Lionel almost didn't recognize the new arrival at first; then he remembered: the woman from the art gallery, with her strand upon strand of necklaces, her dark wrists dripping with bangles. She walked in from the vestibule, past an entrance that should have been sealed, as if she were the first audience member to arrive for an evening performance.

"Coven *members* come and go," she said, her voice carrying across the gallery as she took a seat by the aisle, "but a true coven is a sacred bond. It's an idea, and a calling. You don't have the weapons to destroy something that powerful. You never did."

"What is this?" Slone muttered. He looked to Lionel and Maddie. "She with you?"

Maddie shook her head. "Unh-uh."

She was only the first arrival. More women came, filing down the aisles, taking their scattered seats in the first few rows. Some Lionel didn't know; others he did. There was Helen, Chandra Nagarkar's former professor, who had given them the Parthenon Theater flyer at her fallen student's grave. Wen Xiulang wasn't far behind her, offering Maddie a sardonic smile as she took a chair up front. There was the check-in clerk at their hotel. On the other side of the aisle, the hostess at the diner in Chelsea, the one who sat Lionel next to Maddie the night he arrived in New York. Lionel's eyebrows lifted at the sight of Detective Mathers and Agnes, Regina's lawyer, taking their seats side by side.

"Why are you *together*?" Lionel asked them. "What's going on here?"

"You haven't figured it out, my young lion?" called a voice from the back of the theater.

The final arrival. Regina Dunkle, striding imperiously down the aisle.

"It's a play. *My* play. It took me over thirty years to write, all for an exclusive one-time-only engagement. And now we come to our final act. I think we should bow to the classics, here. How about a good old-fashioned deus ex machina?"

Her German accent faded away as she spoke. So did her face. Regina's features ran like melted wax, reshaping themselves as she walked with smoother, more powerful strides. Her silver hair rippled, growing longer, flowing into a raven-black wave of curls, and her bone-colored housecoat shimmered as it turned bloodred. The gathered women rose from their seats, lifting their hands in praise as the coat became a vintage dress with a flowing train. An antique key dangled at Regina's throat.

Not Regina, anymore. The pale woman smiled up at Lionel, cool and hungry, as a single word rose to the theater rafters on a dozen whispered voices.

Hekate.

Fifty-Nine

Hekate tilted her head, her dark eyes gazing up at Maddie.

"Medea, my beloved daughter. Did you really think you could escape me?"

Maddie stared at her in horror. She took a staggering step away from the edge of the stage. Lionel put his hand on the small of her back, reminding her she wasn't alone. She grabbed for his hand, fumbling, and squeezed it tight.

"*Why?*" Maddie whispered.

"When you had your bout of madness, when you bloodied your hands and fled your home, you were . . . very cruel to yourself, my dear."

"I deserved it."

"I would say that's for me to decide. But you were determined to punish yourself, determined to suffer for your sins. So I invented your tormentor."

"Regina Dunkle," Lionel said.

The goddess nodded to him. "That's right. I wasn't going to let someone *else* punish my daughter. My hope was that she'd tire of the abuse, decide she'd done her penance, and return to me. I was mistaken. A light had gone out of her. She fell into a rut of self-abuse and despair. The treatment simply wasn't working. I decided she was spending too much time alone, and it was reinforcing her behavior, so . . . I played matchmaker."

Craig Schaefer

"*That's* why you hired Lionel?" Maddie asked. "For . . . for me?"

"For you." Hekate's pomegranate lips curled in a cold smile. "Don't tell anyone, but sometimes I enjoy a bit of romance. I already had a purpose for both of you, and the timing lined up nicely. I thought he might shake up your perspective. Teach you how to appreciate life again."

"Wait," Lionel said. "You mean *I* was the manic pixie dream girl?"

Hekate arched one eyebrow at him. "I . . . would call you her motivation, but . . . certainly. If you like."

Lionel looked to the front row of the theater, where Detective Mathers was sitting.

"Wait. What about you, then? You tried to make me betray her, send her to prison . . ." His voice trailed off as he figured it out. "You were testing me, weren't you?"

Mathers cracked a rare grin. "I put you up against the wall, and you didn't break. We had to make sure you were worthy of her."

"And to make sure you were worthy of us," the lawyer added. "There's a place for you here, Lionel, with our coven. If you're ready. When you're ready."

"Medea," Hekate said, "you have subjected yourself to more pain than a dozen mortal lives could endure. You have done more penance than any mortal court could demand. It's time to stop. Your sentence is up. It is time for you to come home. You and Lionel both."

A crimson tear welled at the corner of Maddie's eye. She gave the faintest nod and whispered, *"Yes."*

The goddess swung her gaze to Sloane. He stood like a deer in the headlights, one hand frozen midway to the Liminal Engine's lever.

"And then, there's you. You and the unfortunate M. Valdemar, two problems in need of solving. I had to find you first. Draw you out of hiding. And what better device than a 'lost manuscript,' one Ernest would desperately want and send you to retrieve? It was fascinating, watching you all chase it down. But did any of you wonder how it all began? Did you speculate how the late and unlamented Raymond

418

Barton—a pornographer and a petty criminal—ended up with the treasure in the first place?"

"It was you," Lionel said. "You gave it to him."

"After I created it. There never was any 'lost manuscript.' It was a forgery from the start. Bait, custom-created to start our little play on the right foot."

Hekate sauntered to the foot of the stage, the train of her scarlet dress trailing in her wake. She gently picked up Valdemar's severed head and cradled it in her hands as his mouth strained to speak.

"Shh," she said. "You've been badly done by, Ernest. The victim of a cosmic fluke, a one-in-a-billion mistake. I can't erase the suffering you've endured, but I can grant you this much."

She leaned in and kissed him upon the lips.

"Sleep now," she whispered.

Valdemar's eyes rolled back as his flesh decayed in her hands, sloughing off like the petals of a dead rose, baring yellowed and brittle bone. A chunk of his skull caved in, then the rest, collapsing and crumbling away in the space of a breath.

Nothing remained of Ernest Valdemar but a bit of powdered bone. Hekate dusted her hands off and turned back to Sloane.

"I see only one person here who truly deserves to be punished. But there are traditions to be upheld. Customs to honor." Her hand slowly swept across the stage, gesturing to Lionel. "You slew his mother. By right, your blood is his to shed. And so I engineered all of this, my little drama, to bring you face-to-face. Here and now. Tonight."

"You're lying," Sloane stammered. He inched closer to the engine's control panel. "You're a lying *bitch*. You never gave a shit about this kid."

As her smile grew, her lips parted. Showing a little teeth. "Didn't I? Lionel, the night you lost your mother—the night this man took her from you—she told you something very important. You remember, don't you?"

Lionel furrowed his brow, struggling to think. The echoes of that night, his mother's words, his lost minutes out on the road, were like smooth gaps in the grooves of his memories. "I . . . I can't. I've *tried*."

"Let it come."

"This is a joke. This is—" Sloane shook his head. He let out a nervous, high-pitched giggle. "It's a joke. What's the point? The kid's barely a witch. Does he even *know* any magic? I could tear him apart without breaking a sweat."

"I enjoy surprises," Hekate replied. "Don't you? And I might just have one left. In the meantime . . . *Medea*."

Maddie stood sharp. Her eyes, still dotted with the drying remnants of tiny scarlet tears, blazed with new and ferocious life.

"My queen," she said.

Hekate beamed at her. "I have been waiting *so* long to hear you say those words again. My sweet daughter . . . if he activates that disgusting machine, I will be very, very cross. Do make sure it doesn't happen?"

Maddie flexed her wrist. Her silver bracelet chain fell free and dropped into her fingertips. It crackled, giving off electric sparks, as it began to twirl.

"With pleasure, my queen."

"You don't understand," Sloane stammered. "None of you understand. I'm not the bad guy here, okay? All I wanted was my fair share. If you'd just *given* it to me—"

"Shut up," Lionel snapped.

Something inside him, some dark and buried rage, boiled over at long last. He strode across the stage.

"*Shut. The fuck. Up.* You have done nothing but hurt people, kill people, leave a trail of human wreckage everywhere you've ever been. And it's never your fault, is it? Nothing is ever your fault." Lionel squared off in front of him, five feet of polished stage and the beam of a footlight between the two men. "No one's coming to bail you out this time. Your guards are dead, Dergwyn's on our side, Valdemar is gone. And you've got nowhere left to run."

Sloane's face contorted into a mad grimace as his world slid out from under him. He pointed a trembling finger at Hekate.

"She's setting you up, kid. She's setting you up to die. Can't you see that? It's just one of her sick games. You aren't even a real witch, and I've got two hundred years of magic under my belt. You *can't* beat me."

Lionel unbuttoned the cuffs of his shirt. He folded one back, rolling it up, as he stared into Sloane's eyes.

"She thinks I can," he said. "You know, it's funny. Until a few days ago, I didn't believe in gods. Now, standing here, I'm realizing two important truths."

"Which are?"

Lionel rolled up his other sleeve.

"Number one," he said, "sometimes you have to have a little faith in a higher power. And number two . . . you have an *amazingly* punchable face."

Lionel lunged. His foot stomped down on the stage as he threw his weight into a right hook. His fist slammed into Sloane's mouth, splitting his lip, knocking a tooth loose as he staggered back. Panic in his eyes, Sloane lunged for the control lever. Maddie snapped her bracelet like a whip. A lance of blue-white fire streaked across the stage and slashed across the back of his hand before he could reach it, leaving a jagged line of charred skin in its wake.

Sloane wiped the blood from his lip, smearing it across his face, as his eyes darted between them. "Think I'm out of allies, huh? You forgot a few."

His hand slapped across his stolen brooch. The Lapis Manalis flared, gemstones blossoming with buried light, and the dead came to serve him.

Specters burst through the walls, rained down from the ceiling, their gaping jaws wide as they thrust out long, misshapen claws. The coven, scattered across the first rows of the theater, leaped into action. Some, like Maddie, spun lengths of chain and wove shields of desert-mirage air, sending the phantoms veering off in all directions. One of the women—the clerk from the hotel—spat a venomous chant and met one of the ghosts with open hands. She clapped her palms together with a peal of thunder, and the creature burst like a ruptured cloud.

One of the phantasms whirled in the air, shrieked, and hurtled itself at Lionel.

He didn't think. He didn't try. In the heat of the moment, with death streaking toward him, Maddie's lessons came back to him as naturally as breathing. He hooked his fingers and called upon the *voces mysticae*.

"Akhas. Dromenei." He thrust out his hands and *felt* the magic. It rose up inside him, surging up his spine in a line of midnight fire. *"Keh!"*

The power burst from his hands and seared through the air, striking the phantom dead-on. The creature exploded into a billowing gray mist.

He had two seconds to savor his victory. Then a length of black iron chain, as thick as his fist, lashed through the air and plowed into his stomach. Lionel collapsed to his knees on the stage and struggled to get his breath back.

"This is what you wanted, huh?" Sloane roared. "Is this what you wanted?"

His body glowed, rippling with a sickly gray aura as he closed in on Lionel. A greasy sheen coated his skin. The air at his back was a black, smoking mirror. A window to someplace else, someplace dark and cold. Two thick lengths of iron chain stretched from the void like metallic tentacles, hovering over Sloane's shoulders, snapping at the air.

The heel of his shoe snapped out and slammed into Lionel's chin. Lionel fell to the stage, rolling out of the way as both chains thundered down. They cracked against the polished wood, splintering it, carving out jagged rents.

Sloane stalked him, relentless, as the coven fought off his swirling horde of apparitions. Lionel ducked under one of the whipping chains. It crashed against the boiler of the Liminal Engine and ruptured the metal, sending a gout of white-hot steam blasting into the air.

"Is this what you wanted?" Sloane screamed. The other chain slashed through the air and caught Lionel across the chest. He felt ribs crack, something inside him turning wet and cold as he fell to the stage again. Sloane stood over him, grabbed him by the shirt collar, and hauled him up. His knuckles rained down, opening a cut on Lionel's eyebrow and blinding him with blood, his next punch shattering his nose.

Sloane was still shouting, but Lionel couldn't hear it. Everything had gone gray and red and distant, the world washing away on a tidal wave of pain. He was thinking about his mother. How he was failing her, how he was failing all of them. He fell, his mind letting go as Sloane beat the life out of him, and tumbled free into a vast, empty abyss.

And then he remembered.

He remembered everything.

Sixty

He was five years old.

The ranch was burning. People were screaming, running. He watched a mustang, its mane on fire, thrash its head and bellow as it galloped into the woods like a living torch.

His mother swept him up in her arms. She brushed the unruly curls from his forehead, kissed him, and whispered into his ear.

"Listen to me," she said.

This was where the memory always ended. But she was still there.

"Mom," he said, in his thirty-two-year-old voice. He was here. She was here, too, alive, and—

"No," she told him, wearing her sadness in her eyes. "If you're seeing this, I'm gone. I'm sorry, Lionel."

She licked the tip of her finger and traced something on his forehead. A sigil, tingling in her fingertip's wake. Sealing the memory.

"I was the only member of the sisterhood with a child," she told him. "When my sisters began to die, and we suspected what was happening . . . well, they sent me away."

"To keep us safe," he said.

"No." She shook her head with a sad, resigned smile. "They wrote me a letter, to remind me of my duty. You see, if the rest of the coven combined can't stop Sloane, we need a fail-safe. I can't beat him, not on my own. I'm not the fail-safe."

She touched his heart.

"You are."

She pulled him close, squeezing him tight. Outside, timbers groaned and shattered as the burning barn collapsed.

"You're going to have to set things right. You'll have to learn to be strong. And someday, when you're grown, you'll face him. But not now. And not soon."

She faced him again, holding his tiny arms in her hands.

"And I'm sorry, I am *so* sorry, baby, but that means you've got to do it on your own. If Sloane thinks you're still alive, he'll come hunting for you, and he'll kill you before you can pose a threat to him. So . . . you know those little rituals we do together? Those prayers and songs I taught you?"

"To our queen," Lionel heard his voice say.

She licked her fingertip again. She traced a second sigil, this one on his left cheek.

"You can't remember it. Any of it. You can't have any magic in your life." She paused, and her eyes began to glisten. "You can't have *her* in your life. Nothing that might draw him to you, or put you in danger before you're ready to face it. You're going to spend so many years thinking you're all alone, and I'm so sorry for that. But one day . . . one day, when the time is right, you'll remember this moment. And you'll remember the most important thing of all."

His mother kissed him on the cheek.

"I love you," she whispered. "I always have, and I always will. And you have *never*, not for one moment of your life, been alone."

He was running. Running through an icy downpour, grass and mud clinging to his feet, the ranch burning at his back and turning the starry night to the colors of a molten dusk. Lionel charged out into the road. Headlights flashed in his eyes, tires squealing and—the car stopped. The engine made faint ticking sounds as it idled. Lionel walked around it.

It was a limousine. A Rolls-Royce, vintage and silver. The back door swung open.

"Hello, Lionel," Hekate said. "Get in."

He sat across from her, his child's body sinking into the plush black leather seats. She closed the door, and the limousine began to roll. She studied him with a sly smile on her face.

"This is what happened," he said. "That night. The memory I lost, between running from the ranch and showing up at the neighbor's farmhouse. It was you."

She winked. "It'll be our little secret."

She picked up a thin box from the seat beside her and held it out to him. It held tiny candies, nestled in crinkled black paper.

"Would you like a toffee?" she asked. "They're very good."

He eyed the box like it was a coiled serpent.

"What if I say no?"

She plucked a toffee from the box, shrugged, and popped it into her mouth.

"Then you don't get any candy," she said. "There's no coercion here, Lionel. Freedom is a witch's creed, and you, whether you like it or not, are a witch born and bred. Refuse me if you will. Refuse me three times, if you like, and spit upon my shadow. But . . . you don't want to."

He reached out with his small hand, picked up a piece of candy, and put it between his lips. He was drenched from the rain and trembling. Beads of water dripped from his pajamas and soaked the leather seat. The toffee, rich and buttery, melted on his tongue.

"Now here's a fun thing to contemplate. Are you a thirty-two-year-old man recovering a suppressed memory . . . or are you a five-year-old boy who just had an extended premonition of his future?" Her feline smile grew. "Don't think about it too hard. You'll fry a circuit."

"I'm dying," Lionel said. "Sloane. He's killing me."

"That's one possible ending."

"Why don't you *stop* him?"

Hekate eased back on the seat, her scarlet dress shifting as she crossed one leg over the other.

"Lionel, if we directly intervened every time one of our children needed help, how would you ever learn to be free? I'd much rather give you the tools to earn your own victory."

"How?" he asked.

"Well, Medea's appointed herself your teacher, but I doubt she'd mind if I stepped in as a substitute. What if I gave you a lesson in witchcraft?" She paused. "Come to think of it, seeing as this is a memory—one we buried deep in your unconscious mind to keep Sloane from catching my scent on you—I guess I *did*, didn't I? Or I do. Time is a funny thing."

Lionel thought back to the tarot vision, his visit with the high priestess. *"I'll tell you a secret,"* she had whispered in his ear. *"You've already been initiated."*

"Is there a price?"

"Everything has a price. Knowledge is its own price. It means you don't get to be ignorant anymore. So many people positively covet ignorance. My children have to be more creative in their quest for bliss. In your case, all I require is a simple token. I would like you to acknowledge what you already know to be true."

He shook his head. "What's that?"

The dim light in the back of the limousine changed. It shifted from moonlight bone to a rich and cold azure blue as Hekate's eyes turned black. Starlight glimmered in their inky depths, all the vastness of space. She grew in size, in presence, filling the air with the scent of roses and driving out anything but her and thoughts of her. Lionel's breath froze in his throat. Maddie's praise for her goddess—*Queen of Magic, Mother of Witches*—reverberated in his ears. Hekate was the night, and fire, and glory.

She was a Titan, bigger than the world. And he had her undivided attention.

"Regina was a mask," she said, "but I spoke the truth: I am an old-fashioned lady, and I believe in doing things properly."

She leaned close, looming over him as she and her shadow filled the back of the limousine.

"Bend your knee, Lionel. *Give* yourself to me. Speak the words so that you know, as I already do, who you belong to."

And Lionel Paget, not the child, but the man who was dying on a stage in an abandoned theater a thousand miles away, sank to both knees on the floor of the limousine. He bowed his head.

"My queen," he whispered.

She trailed a finger along his jaw, smiling in quiet triumph.

"Very good," she said. "Now let's see to your lesson. I'm a strict teacher, so do pay attention."

"But . . . how?" he asked. "I mean, I remember how this night ended. I was only gone for a few minutes before I showed up at my neighbor's house. We have to be close now; how can you teach me anything that fast?"

Hekate snapped her fingers.

The limo had stopped. One of the side windows hissed down, and Lionel peered out into the dark.

The storm was frozen. Raindrops hung in the air, motionless.

"I think I can steal a little time just for us," she said. "So let's begin. Oh, and remember, my young lion: there will be a test at the end, and your final grade is the only one that matters."

The world lurched back into screaming, dizzy focus. Lionel felt like his face was smeared with hot syrup. His blood painted Sloane's knuckles as the man rained down punch after brutal punch. His ribs were fractured; something in his stomach was twisted up and wrong. All around him, Maddie and the coven waged war against Sloane's horde of mad spirits.

Sloane suddenly stopped. He shook Lionel's collar, frowning.

"Why . . . why are you *smiling*?"

"I'm ready for my final exam," Lionel croaked.

"What?"

Then Lionel's hands shot up and grabbed hold of the iron chains thrashing over Sloane's shoulders. Words of the *voces mysticae*, words unspoken for a thousand years, rolled off his tongue. Ice surged like wildfire from Lionel's hands, streaking along the chains, and they shattered like glass. Sloane screamed in pain as the inky-black portal behind him ruptured and collapsed. He staggered back. Lionel pursued him, his bruised legs fueled with a surge of fresh strength. Sloane hissed an incantation. Black vines like whips of leather sprouted from the fingers of his left hand, cutting the air with razor-sharp petals. They lashed out at Lionel—and he spun his hand, chanting under his breath. The vines snapped against a wall of congealed air and burst. They rained down in a cloud of scorched ashes.

"How?" Sloane panted, still backpedaling across the stage. "You don't—you don't know how to *do* that!"

"You took my mother from me." Lionel closed in on him, relentless. "You took the family I should have grown up with. You took my goddess. You took years of my life. My *purpose*."

Sloane's shoulders bumped against the battered hull of the Liminal Engine. There was nowhere left to go. Lionel slid his left foot to one side, squaring his stance on wobbly legs, bracing himself.

"Right here, right now," Lionel told him, "I'm taking it all back."

Sloane's nerve broke. He screamed and threw himself at Lionel in a desperate, last-ditch attack, his face contorted in mad rage. Lionel held his ground. One last spell rose to his lips, and he threw the fading remnants of his strength into a final punch.

His knuckles smashed into the Lapis Manalis as the last syllable of the incantation sparked and fired.

The brooch imploded.

The copper setting ruptured like the ground in an earthquake as the gems shattered inward. The relic's energy, unleashed, followed the course of the blow: straight through Sloane's heart, pulping muscle and flesh, splintering his spine as it exploded from his back. He hit the thrumming boiler of his failed machine and slowly slid to the stage, leaving a slug trail of glistening blood on the polished steel.

The last of the spirits faded into mist. The last broken gem on the brooch glimmered and died. Jimmy Sloane died with it.

Lionel stood over the corpse of his mother's killer. He wobbled, panting for breath—and then the stage soared up to meet him as the wind whistled in his ears, and the world went black.

—

Lionel didn't remember much after the fight. He remembered hands lifting him, so many hands, so gentle, carrying him on his back up the theater aisle. He remembered a hospital, a gurney.

"What name are we—"

"We're not," another woman said. "Just in case."

A nurse nodded knowingly. A tiny key glinted on a chain around her neck as she filled out a clipboard.

There was a room—small, private, dark. People came and went.

"You're an asshole," Brianna told him. She stood in the doorway. He tried to laugh. It hurt.

"We gotta stop meeting like this," he said.

"Don't know if you're aware, but you got a couple of amazons guarding your room. Your new girlfriend had to talk me in. I thought the trouble was over?"

He tried to remember. Someone—Maddie?—had explained this to him, then a second time when he'd stopped abusing the morphine drip. Mostly.

"It's over," he said. "Sloane . . . he was out there, on the loose, for a long time. Just want to make sure he didn't have any friends we don't know about. But . . . yeah. It's over."

"So you can come back. You can come back to your old life now."

The question settled on his aching chest like a lead weight.

"I don't know. Brianna, I . . . I've seen things. *Done* things—"

"And I haven't? Jesus, Lionel, I was in that subway tunnel. You think I don't see the world differently now? Doesn't mean you can't come home again. You've still got your condo in Chicago, you've still got your job at the station—for now, anyway. I told 'em you were in a car accident. You're on leave while you recuperate."

"Thanks for that," he said.

"Yeah. It's unpaid leave. I'm not a miracle worker."

"I notice they didn't send flowers this time."

"They don't know where to send them. You're beyond off the grid right now."

She stood at his bedside and put her hand on his arm.

"You don't have to stay that way," she told him.

He started to drift off again. He must have said something garbled, because she just patted his arm and leaned in close.

"Call me when you get out," she whispered, and kissed him on the cheek. "Sweet dreams, you big jerk."

The next couple of days melted into another blur. He only remembered one thing before he was judged well enough to walk and the hospital cast him back out into the world. He woke from a chemical haze, eyes swimming into smudgy focus.

Hekate sat in a chair in the corner of his room. She'd been watching him sleep. She smiled, content, and twirled her fingertips. A warm, blissful torrent surged up from the back of his mind, curled soft hands around his consciousness, and dragged him back down into slumber.

Well done, he heard her say. *Well done, young lion.*

Epilogue

Lionel and Maddie ran away to the sea.

They needed some time away from everything but each other. So they went to Montauk, at the tip of the Long Island peninsula, and rented a houseboat. Day by day Lionel's strength came back, the last of his bruises faded, and his adventure slowly melted into memories. They'd walk and ride bicycles along the shore. Maddie taught him things. Not magic—they didn't talk much about magic; the time didn't seem right—but she gave him a thorough grounding in the basics of vegetarian cooking.

He hated to admit it, but he was starting to like the food.

At dusk, when the setting sun glimmered against the waters of Fort Pond Bay and mosquitoes buzzed through the hazy air, they sat out on the deck and drank wine. They'd go inside, make love, and collapse exhausted in each other's arms.

Sometimes Maddie still had that haunted look. Once he found her in the bathroom, her straight razor out but unbloodied. She let him take it from her and ease her back to bed. She'd found a new purpose since her reunion with her goddess, a strength and a fire in her soul that he'd never seen before, but he understood. Old wounds still run deep. Old ghosts are the hardest to banish. She'd carried hers behind her eyes, roaming the palace of her thoughts, for a long, long time. He couldn't drive them away, so he'd stand guard at her gates, steadfast, for as long as she needed him to. Forever, if she needed him to.

Then, one morning, Lionel woke up alone.

It had been hard to wake up. He remembered trying, but it felt like something was pressing him to the bed, keeping him anchored under the waters of sleep. When he finally managed to open his eyes, he was alone in a mess of tangled bedsheets. He got up, groaned, stretched, and rubbed at his eyes.

"Maddie?" he called out. He listened for the sound of the shower. Nothing, just the lapping of gentle waves against the hull of the boat.

He searched for her. Then he searched for a note, anything, while he racked his brain. Had she said she was going shopping? Were they already out of groceries? Were—

He froze. She'd left one thing behind, lying out on the narrow counter of the kitchen nook.

A crumpled black candy wrapper. He picked it up, put it to his nose, and sniffed.

Toffee.

He didn't know how to pray, but he knew how to use a phone, and he still had Regina Dunkle's number. He listened to it ring.

"Pick up," he said. "Goddammit, *pick up*."

The line clicked. Hekate's voice washed across the line, so close he thought he could feel her breath on his ear.

"Don't take my name in vain, Lionel."

"Where is she? You were here. You kept me from waking up—"

"*She* kept you from waking up. I very much wanted your involvement in the discussion, but she begged me to leave you out of it. I had an errand that needed running. A task requiring her talents. And yours, I hoped. But again, she insisted."

"She just . . . left? And she didn't even tell me? Why?"

The goddess sighed, a featherlight gust of breath.

"Two reasons, I think. One, it's a personal matter, one she feels a bit raw about. The task in question involves her ex-husband. He's home from the war."

"What war?"

"*All* the wars," she said. "There's a considerable amount of danger involved. She wanted to keep you safe. Also . . . I think she's holding your options open for you. You're still taking calls from Chicago, aren't you?"

"Well, yeah—" Lionel started to say.

"Meaning you haven't closed the door. You're still thinking about your old life, your old job, your colleagues, the camera and lights . . ."

"What about it?"

"Lionel . . . you needed time to rest, but that time is over. Now you have to decide. You can return to your old life, or you can embrace your new one. But you can't have both. If you want to pursue Medea, I'll lead you to her, but I require your absolute commitment. You will have to serve me as she does. There will be pain, sometimes. There will be danger, always. You will face risks you have never dreamed of."

"For eternity," he said.

"If you earn that burden. For now, let's just call it a career commitment."

"Everything has a price, right?" Lionel leaned against the counter. "And if I want to be with Maddie . . . that's the price."

"This is the life she chose, Lionel. She serves me willingly. If you want to go where she goes and stand at her side, you have to do the same. And say goodbye to your old world, once and for all."

—

A cool morning breeze ruffled Lionel's hair as he walked down the dock. It carried the taste of salt and some distant, half-remembered fragrance. He buttoned a fresh shirt as he walked. He had a duffel bag slung over his shoulder and a pair of cheap sunglasses shrouding his eyes. The world was waking up, shutters opening, tourists coming out to soak up the summer sun.

He stood at the end of the pier, where a strip of pavement formed a three-way crossroads, and made his choice. Then he called a taxi. In the end, standing between two worlds, it wasn't hard to decide.

He chose magic.

He chose Maddie.

And he never looked back.

Afterword

No book is written alone; I give my love and gratitude to the women who shared the keys to success with me and helped deliver this story into your hands. Special thanks to Andrea Hurst, my developmental editor; Sara Brady, my copyeditor; Jill Kramer, my proofreader; and Adrienne Procaccini at 47North Publishing. Thanks to Susannah Jones for her invaluable aid in exploring New York City, and to her and her fellow artists in the Sycamore Theatre Company for their continuing inspiration.

Thanks also to my assistant, Morgan Faid; to the folks at the Empire Diner and Tenth Avenue Cookshop; and to the always-amazing staff at the High Line Hotel. And thank *you* for taking this journey with me.

If you'd like release notifications when my books come out, I have a newsletter over at http://www.craigschaeferbooks.com/mailing-list/. If you'd like to reach out, you can find me on Facebook at http://www.facebook.com/CraigSchaeferBooks, on Twitter at @craig_schaefer, or just drop me an email at craig@craigschaeferbooks.com.

About the Author

Photo © 2014 Karen Forsythe

Craig Schaefer's books have taken readers across a modern America mired in occult mysteries, from the seamy criminal underworld of the Daniel Faust series to the supernatural espionage and intrigue of the Harmony Black series and the apocalyptic parallel worlds of the Wisdom's Grave trilogy. He currently lives in North Carolina, where he can be found haunting museums, libraries, abandoned crossroads, and other places where dark-fantasy authors tend to congregate. To learn more about the author, visit www.craigschaeferbooks.com.